Daughter of the River

Irene Northan was born on Tyneside, NE England and raised in Devon. Phyllida, published in 1976, was the first of 20 fiction titles and 1 non-fiction title written before her death in June 1993. Irene was a founding member of Brixham Writers' Circle, a member of the Romantic Novelists' Association, Librarian of Brixham Museum, and Reader for the South West Arts.

Irene
NORTHAN
Daughter of the River

CANELO

First published in the United Kingdom in 1993 by Headline Book Publishing

This edition published in the United Kingdom in 2021 by

Canelo
Unit 9, 5th Floor
Cargo Works, 1-2 Hatfields
London, SE1 9PG
United Kingdom

Copyright © Irene Northan 1993

The moral right of Irene Northan to be identified as the creator of this work has been asserted in accordance with the Copyright, Designs and Patents Act, 1988.

A CIP catalogue record for this book is available from the British Library.

Print ISBN 978 1 80032 495 4
Ebook ISBN 978 1 78863 323 9

This book is a work of fiction. Names, characters, businesses, organizations, places and events are either the product of the author's imagination or are used fictitiously. Any resemblance to actual persons, living or dead, events or locales is entirely coincidental.

Look for more great books at www.canelo.co

Printed and bound in Great Britain by Clays Ltd, Elcograf S.p.A.

1

To Andrea and Faye

Chapter One

1869

It was a bright Devon spring Sunday when the Bradworthys brought their latest baby to Stoke Gabriel church for the first time. From her seat in the pew behind them Maddy watched as the child's mother, Janie, beamed with pride at her son and pulled her fine new paisley shawl more comfortably about her shoulders.

A pretty penny that bit of frippery must have cost, decided Maddy. No doubt 'tis her reward for having given Rob a boy at last, after disappointing him with three girls.

Then she felt ashamed. You'm turning into a jealous old maid, Maddy Shillabeer, that's what you'm doing, she scolded herself. Thinking such things, and in church, too! Rob were always a generous soul. Why shouldn't he buy Janie something pretty after her lying-in?

Steadfastly she tried to turn her concentration back to the service, but for once the intoning of the Reverend Bowden, imploring divine protection for 'our blessed Queen Victoria and the royal family', could not hold her attention. Her eyes kept straying back to the sleeping infant, and the sight of him brought back a dull ache of loss such as she had not experienced in a long time. The new babe might so easily have been hers, along with his three chubby, flaxen-haired sisters, for Rob Bradworthy had been her love long before he had looked at Janie.

But that was before Maddy's mother had died. After that everything had changed. It had also been a long time ago. Maddy was now resigned to the fact that it was her lot in life to look after her father and her brothers. Only occasionally, such as on the sudden appearance of the newest Bradworthy, was she caught unawares and thought of the sort of life she might have enjoyed if circumstances had been different.

She looked along the pew at the five men who now dominated her life: Father, Bart, Lew, Charlie and young Davie. Her brothers looked sullen and mutinous, as they did every Sunday.

Regular attendance at church was one of the few things that their father insisted upon. He had a superstitious fear that if the regular Sunday observance was not maintained then God might punish them by stopping the salmon from running, or, worse still, cause the great silver fish to avoid the Shillabeer net and cast themselves into someone else's.

The church band, led by Henry Beer on his fiddle, struck up with the final hymn, 'Rock of Ages', and the congregation did its best to join in. The trouble was that old Henry was self-taught and had very individual ideas on timing. Despite the vicar's determined baritone trying to keep to a more accepted rhythm, Henry led his small band of musicians in the way he meant them to go.

The discord woke the Bradworthy's new baby. Convinced it was feeding time, he announced his hunger at the top of powerful new lungs, all but drowning out the vicar's final words. Thus the service came to a noisy end. Normally, after the departure of the vicar and choir, everyone waited for the squire and his family to leave the church first. On this occasion, however, the squire halted beside the Bradworthy pew.

'Janie,' he roared genially above the cries of the infant. 'Never let it be said that I stood in the way of such a promising young trencherman. Off you go and feed the poor child.' And he stood aside while, flushed and laughing, the Bradworthy family collected up the children and hurried out.

The incident brought smiles to the faces of most of the congregation. It also brought chaos, for the customary order of filing out of church was quite disrupted. Hemmed in the pew by the crush, Maddy cast a look behind her. Of her father and brothers there was no sign. They would already be on their way to either the Church House Inn or the Victoria and Albert – whichever hostelry could provide them with the swiftest pints of rough cider.

Eventually she squeezed her way out into the aisle, and found herself jammed shoulder to shoulder with Calland Whitcomb and his mother. They did not speak. Although they were kinsfolk, the Shillabeers and the Whitcombs had not spoken to one another, except in dire necessity, for over sixty years. There was not room for them to move forward together, so Maddy stood back to let Mrs Whitcomb go first. The stuck-up Whitcombs were never going to be able to accuse her of having no manners. Mrs Whitcomb acknowledged her action with a slight inclination of the head and a glare of disapproval.

Maddy waited her turn and would have continued waiting until Cal Whitcomb had passed, but he was evidently eager to prove that a Whitcomb could be as polite as a Shillabeer. He came to a halt, then gave a bow to indicate that she could precede him. Trust him to do something as fancy as bowing. Unlike his mother, he did not seem to find the situation irritating. Maddy was certain there was a glint of amusement in his eyes as he stood there, obliging her to step in front of him.

He found her funny, did he? No doubt he was looking down his nose at the shabbiness of her cape and dress and at the unadorned state of her Sunday bonnet. The way he was dressed was certainly high and mighty enough – the carefully brushed suit, the pure white shirt with its perfectly starched collar, and boots that were reckoned to be the most highly polished in Stoke Gabriel. Even the squire was not so well turned out, yet Cal Whitcomb was just an ordinaiy farmer, nothing more.

Certain she was being mocked by one and criticised by the other, Maddy was forced to leave the church sandwiched between the Whitcombs, mother and son.

As she did so she became aware of a pleasant scent of cedar wood overlaid with some sharper fragrance such as lemon or verbena. Cal Whitcomb was wearing cologne! The sheer pretension of it almost made her laugh aloud. She could not wait to tell her brothers; they would never get over it. Then she changed her mind and decided not to mention it. There was enough trouble between the Shillabeers and the Whitcombs without stirring up more. Besides, she did not object to the scent of decent cologne on a man; it was a good deal more agreeable than anything she would encounter at home.

Once outside the church, there was no stopping to gossip or pass the time of day for Maddy. The dinner was waiting among the hot ashes of the hearth, and the vegetables were still to be cooked. The menfolk would expect their meal to be ready and waiting for them when they got in. Walking briskly, her cloak swirling about her slim figure, she hurried homewards. Making her way past cottages of cob and stone, and apple orchards already misted with the pink of opening buds, she turned into a lane away from the village.

When she was beyond the observation of critical eyes she threw propriety to the wind and began to run. It was not at all the thing for a staid old maid of twenty-five to do, especially on a Sunday, but she revelled in the freedom. It was the one occasion when she was unhampered by shopping or other burdens. In her downward flight she did not notice the banks thick with primroses and violets, it was too exhilarating gathering speed on the steep path, her boots slithering, her skirts flying – until she came to a skidding halt against the wall of her cottage. Her bonnet was awry and her fair hair, wildly unruly at the best of times, stuck out about her head like a wayward bird's nest, but she did not care.

'One of these days you'm going to miss and finish up in the river,' remarked a voice. Annie Fleet, her neighbour, and wife of the local ferryboat man, was regarding her with amusement.

'If I do, you'll be there to fish me out,' panted Maddy, grinning.

'Not if the tide be out I won't. If you falls in that mud 'tis there you'm staying, as far as I'm concerned.'

'A fine friend you'm turning out to be.' Maddy noticed the empty bucket in Annie's hand. 'You weren't going to get water by yourself, were you?' she said reprovingly. 'Why didn't you give me a shout afore I went to church?'

'You'm enough to do, maid, without taking on my fetching and carrying.'

'One of the boys could've done it.'

'Oh yes?' Annie Fleet's tone told exactly what she thought of that idea.

'Yer, give me the pail.' Maddy took the bucket from the other woman's gnarled grasp and hurried past the three cottages which nestled on the river foreshore to the spring beyond.

Slowly and painfully Annie followed her for a step or two. Barely ten years older than Maddy, she had been struck by rheumatism cruelly young, making her joints distorted, her movements painfully slow. Maddy had deposited the water pail in the Fleets' kitchen and was on the path to her own home before Annie had reached the cottage end.

'Let's have a cup of tea, shall us?' Maddy suggested, already untying her Sunday bonnet as she stepped over the threshold. 'I can drink mine whilst I gets on with the dinner.'

Steadfastly Annie followed her into the Shillabeer home and sank thankfully into a chair beside the scrubbed deal table. 'Did you see the new folks who've taken the White House?' she demanded. 'I hear they'm powerful grand.'

'I meant to, but there was such a crush I couldn't get a good look,' said Maddy. She did not like to say that her attention had been so absorbed by the Bradworthy baby that she had forgotten to be curious about the newcomers. Strangers were such a rarity in the village she would have been admitting just how much memories of the past had affected her.

'Oh, you idn't no good!' protested Annie, good-humouredly despite her disappointment, for she was always hungry for news of the outside world. 'I was hoping you'd tell me what they were wearing, the mother and daughter. They'm got some outlandish name. Fitz-something... Fitzherbert, that be it! They'm a handsome family according to our Kitty. Her saw the daughter riding out along the Waddeton road, and her looked a proper picture, Kitty says. A green velvet riding habit she had on, with proper black frogging on the jacket just like the soldiers has. According to our Kitty the wench must have been sewed into it, it fitted that perfect.'

'I don't know what you'm asking me about the news for,' Maddy grinned. 'You knows more of what be going on than I do.'

'That's only because our Kitty had time off yesterday and dropped by for half an hour.' Annie's sister was in service with the squire's family and an invaluable source of gossip. Annie's appetite for news was insatiable. 'Come on,' she pleaded. 'Didn't naught of interest happen at church?'

'Janie and Rob Bradworthy brought their new baby,' Maddy said, and went on to tell of the resulting chaos.

'Idn't that typical of the squire?' chuckled Annie. 'He'm a proper caution. I bet Janie were ready to sink through the floor.'

'Never mind Janie, what about me, having to leave church squashed atween Mary Whitcomb and her precious son?' protested Maddy.

'There's plenty of maids in the village as would've been pleased to change places. A fine figure of a man be Cal Whitcomb, and handsome.'

'Handsome? With that red hair?'

'Tidn't red, 'tis auburn.'

'Makes no difference – auburn be just a fancy name. To me he'm got red hair and always will have until he turns grey or goes bald.' The idea of a bald Cal Whitcomb pleased her. ''Twould serve him right, to lose all his hair. What price his high and mighty airs then?'

'You Shillabeers and Whitcombs! Always on at one another!' protested Annie. 'He won't go bald. He'm the image of his pa, and Old Man Whitcomb always had a lovely head of hair.'

'I know,' agreed Maddy. 'But 'twas a nice thought while it lasted.'

And the pair of them collapsed with laughter.

The sound of voices and footsteps coming down the lane cut through their hilarity.

'This must be your lot arriving home,' said Annie, rising slowly to her feet. 'I'd best be off and let you feed them. My William'll be wanting his dinner too.'

She reached the door just as Jack Shillabeer approached, his sons following.

'Hullo, Annie,' he said with a cheerfulness that owed much to the scrumpy he had just consumed. 'Been visiting our Maddy, eh? My, it must be grand to be a woman and have time for all these cups of tea.'

'Jack, boy, I won't give the proper answer to that,' replied Annie tartly. 'Not on a Sunday!'

Hearing the exchange Maddy grinned to herself. Not one to be put down was Annie, for all her disabilities. Then the cottage suddenly seemed overfull of male bodies, as it always did when the family came home, and her thoughts flew to the dinner and getting everyone fed.

'No Bart?' she remarked.

'He'll be along presently. He'm with his mates,' said Jack.

Her heart sank as she dished up her absent brother's dinner and set it to keep warm on the hearth. Bart would be doing some hard drinking. The others had had their Sunday cider as usual, but generally they knew when to stop. Bart did not.

Jack and the others had finished their meal and were lazing by the fire, their belts slackened off, before there was any sign of Bart. Hearing the heavy clump of his boots coming down the path Maddy had his dinner on the table by the time he came in through the door. He slung his hat at the oak settle, missed, and sat down clumsily at the table. His face was flushed and his eyes over-bright, causing Maddy's heart to sink further. With Bart in this state her hopes of a peaceful Sunday departed.

'What do you call this mess?' he demanded belligerently as she removed the covering plate from his food.

'When I dished un up first I called un a decent dinner,' retorted Maddy.

'I idn't eating that muck. Cook me something decent!'

'I cooked you something decent once, I idn't doing it twice!' Maddy faced up to her troublesome brother. 'It be that or bread and cheese. Take your pick.'

'Bread and cheese? What sort of a dinner be that for a Sunday? Idn't I entitled to one decent meal a week?'

'The dinner was here and you wadn't. That's the long and short of it,' snapped Maddy.

'I be having a real dinner and you'm going to cook it, else you'm going to be sorry!' In his rage Bart had leapt to his feet. 'I'll show you what I thinks of this bloody rubbish!' He made to seize the plate to hurl it against the wall, but having spent the last hour on the trivet above the glowing wood ash it was still very hot. With a curse he dropped it back on the table, blowing on scorched fingers.

Maddy looked over to her father, willing him to intervene, but it was a vain hope. He was engrossed in lighting his pipe and did not seem aware of the disruptive behaviour of his eldest son.

'If you don't want that dinner, I'll eat un.' It was Lew who spoke up. Next in age after Bart, he was the tallest of the family and always hungry.

His request had the required effect. Bart dropped back into his chair and began eating. He might not want his dinner but he was not going to let anyone else have it.

Over his head, Lew winked at Maddy. The most good-natured of the lot, it was a pity he was so often under the influence of Bart. Fiercely loyal as she was to all her brothers, she had to admit that there were times when she and Bart did not get on.

It troubled Maddy that she had not been a better influence on her eldest brother. She and Bart were too close in age, that was the problem. With only a year between them, he had scorned to take notice of what she said. Looking back she felt she could have handled matters differently. If only she had used persuasive words and laughter from the beginning, as their mother had done, instead of anger and confrontation. But at fourteen she had been numbed by grief at her mother's death and bewildered by the heavy responsibility suddenly thrust upon her. Her father had seemed impervious to her problems, bowed down by his own sorrow. As time progressed he had made no move to lessen Maddy's burden.

'You'm doing fine, maid,' had been his only comment. 'You'm doing just fine.'

Maddy had not believed him then, and she did not believe him now.

Bart's plate was scraped clean and he pushed it aside, anticipating the immediate appearance of the next course.

'What'd Cal Whitcomb to say to you?' he demanded, his mouth full of suet pudding and plum jam.

'Cal Whitcomb?' Jack Shillabeer's head went up at the sound of the name. 'Who's been talking to the likes of he?'

'Our Maddy came out of church with him and his ma this morning, bold as brass.'

'Did you, maid?' Jack regarded her suspiciously. 'What did he say?'

'He just asked me up to Oakwood to take tea with him and his mother,' replied Maddy. 'Then afterwards he said us could go walking down round Byter Mill Copse and do a bit of courting.'

'He never did!' Young Davie leapt to his feet, his face scarlet with indignation. 'The cheek of him! I'll go up to Oakwood this minute and thrash the hide off him. I don't care if he do be bigger than me, he idn't insulting my sister!'

He would have rushed off, too, if Charlie had not restrained him by the seat of his pants.

'I were only joking,' said Maddy, immediately regretting her attempt at humour. She should have known that Davie, so young and gullible, would believe her. 'And before you dashes off to thump his head because he don't consider me worth taking courting, you'd best knows as I wouldn't have gone even if he'd asked me.'

'I think not indeed.' Jack gave an indignant snort. 'There'd not have been much left of he after us had finished with him, not if he dared suggest such a thing.'

A murmur of assent went round the table.

'He'm selling his cider,' said Charlie, breaking the silence which followed.

The others looked at him in surprise. Charlie was not much of a one for conversation.

'Who? Cal Whitcomb?' asked Jack. 'What be newsworthy about that? Lots of folk sell their spare cider.'

'This idn't spare. He'm making it special to sell. Even got fancy labels with oak leaves round them and "Oakwood Farm Cider" in the middle.'

'If that idn't exactly like Skinflint Whitcomb!' exclaimed Jack. 'Do anything to make money, he will! 'Tis a wonder he't got his ma tramping round the countryside with a barrel on her back selling the cider by the tankard to anyone her meets.'

'Give him time, Father. He idn't so quick-thinking as you,' said Lew, and everyone laughed. All except Bart. Still half drunk, he glowered at his empty pudding plate.

'That's our land he'm making his money on,' he said. 'Every penny piece that Whitcomb puts in his pocket should be ours by rights. They Whitcombs be naught but common thieves, and if the law were halfway just it'd be prison or the poor house they'd be in, not prancing about the place having fancy labels printed for their rotten cider.'

For a second time a murmur of assent went round the table, this time with a strong undertone of resentment. This was one subject upon which the Shillabeers were in complete agreement.

'Think what Oakwood would be if us had un,' said Bart dreamily. 'A showplace, that's what it'd be with us all working together.'

While Maddy shared his opinion of the Whitcombs and their misappropriation of her family's birthright, the idea of her brothers working in unison was not so easy to accept. They were bad enough fishing for salmon together. She had lost count of the times when one or other had stormed off after a quarrel.

'Us don't really know much about farming, do us?' she pointed out.

'Us could learn! Us idn't stupid!' snapped Bart. 'Besides, if us'd been brought up to farming it'd have come as natural as shooting a net for salmon do now.'

Maddy had to admit he had a point.

'And when us sold our cider,' said Davie, still clinging tenaciously to the dream of farming at Oakwood, 'us'd have fancier labels than old Cal Whitcomb. Ours'd have gold on them. And I'd be in charge.'

'What, you in charge of making the cider?' said Lew in mock derision. 'You'd drink the profits, you would.'

Davie pretended to protest, but his face went red with pride. He equated the ability to down copious amounts of cider with manhood, and above all else Davie, at fifteen, wanted to be considered a man.

'Whitcomb habn't been selling his spare apples for a year or two,' muttered Bart. 'I should've guessed he were up to something.' He gave a snort. 'Mind, us'd have thought of the idea ages ago if us had been in his shoes. Us'd have had a rare old cider business going by now.'

'Where'd us have got the extra apples from?' asked Maddy. 'Oakwood habn't much in the way of orchards. Cal Whitcomb's got his father's trees down to Church Farm. They never was part of Shillabeer land.'

'Then us'd have bought in, like other folks do,' retorted Bart irritably. 'Or else us could've married you off to some old fool with more land than sense. Exchanging a useless wench for some decent orchards seems like a good bargain to me, though I doubt us'd have got anyone daft enough to wed you.'

Maddy drew in her breath to make an angry retort, but she did not get the chance.

'If only Great-grandfather Shillabeer hadn't gone soft in the head in his old age!' broke in Lew. 'He should've left the farm to our grandad, he was the eldest.'

'Your grandad's brother, Matt, took advantage, that's what he did,' Jack said. 'While your grandad were away on his travels he persuaded the old man to leave everything to him. It's just the sort of mean underhanded thing that side of the family'd do. Look at Cal Whitcomb! He'm Matt's grandson and as slippery a character as you'd find on a day's march. As soon as he inherited the farm what did he do? Dismiss most of the men because he were too mean to pay their wages.'

Silently Maddy rose and, unnoticed by the others, began to clear away the dishes. She shared her family's indignation at the unfairness of their treatment, but she had heard it all before, and she did not see how repeating the details yet again would change anything.

Her chores finished, Maddy left the menfolk to their favourite pastime – going over how they had been cheated. If there was one thing the Shillabeers were good at it was bearing a grudge. At least they were not fighting among themselves, which was a common occurrence on a boring Sunday.

She took the steep path back to the village and made for the churchyard. She rarely missed these weekly visits to her mothers grave. They were a haven of calm in her busy life. On this occasion, however, her tranquillity was shattered. The plants she had so carefully tended the previous week were crushed, the neatly dug soil disturbed. Unmistakable signs of iron-shod hooves were imprinted in the earth.

A horse had got into the churchyard and stamped all over the grave. At the sight of it Maddy gave a cry of distress.

Hasty footsteps sounded behind her and the vicar's voice demanded, 'What's wrong, Maddy? I heard you call out.' Then he, too, saw the damage. It was not Lizzie Shillabeer's grave alone: right across the churchyard there was a trail of destruction. The Reverend Bowden clicked his tongue angrily. 'Really, this is too bad! People should make more effort to keep their livestock secure. I shall mention this at Evensong most strongly.' He looked down at Maddy with concern. 'I know you set great store by keeping your mother's grave beautiful. I hope the damage is not too severe.'

'Naught I can't replace, I suppose, thank you, Mr Bowden. I be sorry I cried out. It just upset me to see such destruction.'

'Rest assured, when I find the culprit I will say a few well-chosen words to them on the irresponsibility of people who let their animals stray.'

At this Maddy could not help smiling. He was quite a firebrand, was the vicar. Someone was going to get a scorched ear when he caught up with them. Still muttering to himself he wandered off in the direction of the vicarage.

Maddy turned her attention back to the grave. There was too much damage to be rectified that afternoon. She would have to come back later with fresh plants and do the job properly. She set off back to the cottage at Duncannon to get tea for the menfolk before Evensong. Sunday might be a day of rest for some folk, she observed wryly, but as far as she was concerned it was not much different from other days.

–

Once it was light next morning the five Shillabeer men launched their boat and took themselves off to the fishing. The tide was dropping, leaving expanses of glistening mud on either shore of the River Dart. Still bleary-eyed, Jack and his sons had set out early, determined to get to the prime positions first, for they knew that there would be plenty of others hard behind them.

The village of Stoke Gabriel was famous for the quality of its Dart-caught salmon, but it was the tiny hamlet of Duncannon, hard on the river's edge, that had the advantage. Already Joe Crowther, who lived in the third cottage at Duncannon, would be astir, for he, too, held a net licence. But he had to wait for the rest of his crew to come over from the village. Jack Shillabeer was proud of the fact that, in his four sons, he had provided himself with a full complement.

'There idn't many with that sort of foresight,' was his usual boast.

'Just give us a few years and then us'll see who's got the last laugh,' was Joe Crowther's cheery reply, for the Crowthers' young brood was numerous and fast increasing.

For the moment, though, the Shillabeers had supremacy and they meant to make the most of it.

As always, Maddy paused in her work to watch them make the first cast of the day. Born and bred in the riverside cottage, it was something she had seen frequently enough, yet it never lost its magic. Often, especially on a perfect spring morning such as this, she wished she could have accompanied her menfolk in their stealthy pursuit of the great silver fish; but that would have been unheard of, despite the fact that she could handle a boat as well as any of her brothers, and was strong enough to haul in the catch with the rest of them. Salmon fishing was exclusively men's work. For a woman to join in would have earned her the stern disapproval of the entire village; Maddy had to be content with watching from the garden.

Slowly and steadily Jack was rowing the boat in an arc, with Davie carefully paying out the long length of net over the stern as they went. With one end firmly secured on shore, it hung in the water, buoyed up by cork floats on top and weighted with lead at the bottom, hopefully making an impenetrable wall for any luckless salmon encircled within its mesh. But the salmon were swift and agile, and could escape from the tightening circle if anything alarmed them, which was why Jack's movements were stealthy as he rowed back to the shore, and why the others hauled in the net with steady, unhurried movements.

It never failed to amaze Maddy that her brothers, normally so volatile and argumentative, could be so restrained the instant they actually began hauling in the catch.

The curve of the net had been gradually growing smaller as the boys pulled it in, till now it was only a few feet across. The water within its bounds seethed with silver bodies. Maddy continued watching while her brothers stunned the fish and laid them in a basket on shore. Later, when cleaned and properly packed, they would be sent upriver to Totnes to the fishmonger there who acted as agent for the big London market at Billingsgate. Maddy had counted six salmon, a respectable first catch of the day.

Already Jack was stowing the net meticulously back in the boat for the next casting. The river had fallen a little more. Bart had stuck twigs in the mud at the water's edge to check how much the tide was dropping. He untied the net, and they moved further downstream, to begin the whole patient process again. But Maddy could not watch any longer, she had her own work to do.

She had more than enough to keep her occupied. As soon as she had risen that morning she had set the copper to heat, and now it was ready to take the mountain of washing that was her lot every Monday. As she was pegging out her second batch of clothes the sound of boots crunching on the pebbles of the foreshore caught her attention.

A stout stone wall protected the cottage and garden from high tides, for the River Dart was tidal way beyond Duncannon, up as far as Totnes. Looking over, she found herself staring down at a stranger. It was early in the year for 'foreigners'. They usually arrived in the summer – rich folk who had nothing better to do than admire the scenery. This young man was not like the usual seasonal visitor. He was not so well-dressed, for one thing, but when he smiled Maddy forgot about the shabbiness of his coat and the scuffed state of his boots. All she saw was that he had the bluest eyes she had ever seen on a man, and those eyes seemed to sparkle as they lit upon her. Maddy, who normally cared nothing for her appearance, was suddenly conscious of her faded calico dress and coarse sacking apron.

The newcomer wore a black slouch hat ornamented by a single peacock's feather. He took it off with a mighty flourish, exotic plume and all, exposing dark waving hair worn longer than was customary among the village men.

'Good morning,' he said. 'You've a fine day for drying your washing.'

He was from up-country by the way he spoke. Much more crisp and swift than the normal Devon burr, and quite gentlemanly. He sounded almost like the squire. More incredible to Maddy was his remark about the washing. Her lot would not have known a good drying day from a downpour. For drying salmon nets, yes, but for clothes…

'Good morning,' she replied. 'Yes, there be a decent breeze today. You'm off one of the boats?'

'No, I've been following the river. I'm trying to get to Stoke Gabriel. By my reckoning I can't be far off.'

'No, you'm yer.'

'This is Stoke Gabriel?' He looked at the three cottages with something like dismay.

'Well, as good as.' Maddy laughed at his expression. 'This be Duncannon, we'm in the parish. The village proper be just downriver, past the old quarry and round the point into the creek.'

'Can I get there along the foreshore?'

Maddy looked at the cracked state of his boots.

'I wouldn't recommend un,' she said. 'Best go overland. That be the path, behind the house.'

'It looks steep.'

'You'm welcome to come in and rest yourself for a while afore you tackles un, if you wish.'

'How kind of you.' Gratefully he strode up the narrow slipway between the cottages and came into the garden, but he would not enter the house. 'My boots are far too muddy,' he said, depositing his two bundles on the path. ''Til do fine here, on the wall.'

Such consideration impressed Maddy.

A rich savoury smell was coming from the kitchen, and the stranger sniffed appreciatively. Maddy grinned. She could take a hint.

'You'm welcome to a drop of broth,' she said. 'There idn't no dumplings, though. I habn't made they yet.'

'The broth alone will be delightful.'

Will be delightful… She considered the words as she went indoors. She had never heard anyone speak like that – leastways, not to her. Quickly she filled a bowl with broth and added a hefty slice of bread. Scalding as it was, he devoured the broth and the bread with the concentration of a man who had not eaten for some time. Yet Maddy noticed that despite his evident hunger, he ate neatly and without noise. A well-spoken man with tidy manners. Again, she was impressed.

He finished eating and set aside the bowl. 'That was food for the angels, and no mistake,' he said, beaming at her.

Maddy felt that both the compliment and the smile were a bit excessive for such a simple meal, but she liked them just the same.

'I suppose you'm passing through,' she said.

'Not at all – well, I hope not. It will depend upon circumstances. If I can find a job.'

'You'm looking for work? What can you do?'

'Anything that needs doing.'

'You idn't fussy, that's always a help. Tidn't a good time of year – too early for harvesting or the apple gathering.' She pondered for a moment. 'The Church House Inn may still need a potman, since young Alfred joined the army.'

'That sounds an excellent possibility. Is the remuneration good?'

Remuneration! He was certainly one for fancy words.

'Why do you think young Alfred took the Queen's shilling?' she replied, and they both laughed.

The young man rose to leave with evident reluctance. 'I must be on my way, I suppose,' he said, 'before someone else snatches the post of potman from under my nose. I never expected my arrival at Stoke Gabriel to be so filled with agreeable people. May I know your name, you who have shown such kindness to a stranger?'

'Madeleine Shillabeer,' said Maddy, somewhat flustered by his unaccustomed compliments.

'Madeleine. I might have known you would be called something elegant... Madeleine.' He repeated the name softly.

Maddy did not know why she had told him her full baptismal name – to sound all fancy like he did, she supposed.

'Lor', don't go calling me that,' she said, increasingly embarrassed. 'Folk wouldn't know who you was on about. I be known as Maddy, plain and simple.'

'Miss Maddy it shall be then, but definitely not plain and certainly not simple. I am Patrick Howard. At your service, ma'am.' He gave her a bow.

When Cal Whitcomb had made such a gesture she had found it pretentious, but the stranger made it look natural.

'I fear I have no money to pay for the excellent food you have given me,' he went on.

'I don't want paying for a bit of broth and the end of the loaf,' she protested. 'You'm welcome to un.'

'In that case, will you permit me to show my gratitude in the only way I can?'

Mystified, Maddy watched as he opened the smaller of his bundles, a canvas sack.

'A fiddle!' she exclaimed with delight, as he took out the instrument. 'You play the fiddle!'

'It is my one small talent. Do you like music?'

'Above all things, only I don't get the chance to hear much.'

'Then this shall be for you, with my thanks for making my arrival at Stoke Gabriel so memorable.'

He tuned the strings for a few seconds, then he was away.

He was good. Even Maddy, whose knowledge of music was rudimentary, recognised his skill. She had never heard a violin sing so sweetly, nor the notes fly from the strings with such consummate ease. He played an old country dance that she knew well; then a sweet melody she had never heard before; finally he finished with the liveliest of jigs, setting Maddy's toes tapping and the blood coursing through her veins. By the time he stopped her eyes were bright and her cheeks flushed with pleasure.

Slipping the fiddle back in its bag, he shouldered his pack and began to move towards the lane.

'I hope I have the opportunity of playing for you again,' he said. 'Oh, and Miss Maddy—'

'Yes?'

'Do you know you are the only person I've ever met who has aquamarine eyes?' With this he smiled his bright smile and strode away.

Aquamarine eyes! Maddy did not know what aquamarine was, but by the way Patrick Howard had said the word it sounded beautiful. That could not be right. Someone telling her she had beautiful eyes. She must have misunderstood.

'Well, did you ever hear the like,' said Elsie Crowther.

'That man be a charmer and no mistake,' added Annie.

It was too much to expect that the arrival of Patrick Howard would have passed unnoticed by the occupants of the other cottages. But Maddy had been so fascinated by the newcomer that she had scarcely been aware of Annie and a whole brood of Crowthers pressing against the garden wall, listening to the music and the conversation as well.

'The lads of the village be going to have to watch out,' chuckled Elsie. 'They'm got some competition with the maids now.'

'And a few husbands'll have to look to their laurels as well, if I be any judge,' agreed Annie. 'Though maybe we'm wrong. Maybe that young fellow's eyes have already lit on the one he fancies.'

'And who would that be?' asked Maddy.

'Why, you, you daft ha'p'orth! He were flirting with you enough, goodness knows!'

'You'm the daft ha'p'orth,' retorted Maddy good-humouredly. 'He were just being polite. But I'll give you he were something fancy in his manner. He'm made me all hot and bothered. I idn't used to such things.' And she put her hands to cheeks that were burning.

'Be as hot and bothered as you please,' grinned Annie. 'That were flirting talk or I never heard none.'

'Get off with you!' Maddy pretended to threaten them with the copper-stick. 'How's a body supposed to get her work done with you lot jawing away?'

Cheerfully the others returned to their own homes, excited by such an unusual morning.

Maddy, too, was affected by the events of the day. Any interruption in her humdrum life was bound to be welcome, but the arrival of Patrick Howard... He was like no one she had ever met before, as far removed from the village lads as the stars in the sky. Could Annie have been right? Had he been flirting with her?

Now don't go getting mazed ideas like that, not at your time of life, she admonished. Why should the likes of he show any interest in you? No other man has these last eleven years. You idn't naught special and you knows un. He'm just got a flowery way of being polite.

But the idea, once planted in her brain, refused to be dislodged, and despite herself she began to look forward to her next trip into the village. Such a visit promised to be uncommonly interesting if Patrick Howard had found work and she met up with him again – if he remembered her.

Chapter Two

'What's this us hears about you having a man in the place?' demanded Bart. 'Young Joey Crowther were full of you dancing and jigging and everything in an uproar.'

'Then young Joey's imagination be as big as his mouth. For goodness' sake stop milling around and sit down! There be little enough room as it is without you great lumps filling up space.' While she was talking, Maddy had been serving up platefuls of broth and dumplings from the black pot on the fire.

'Us wants to know what's been going on,' retorted Bart, but he sat down just the same. 'You'm telling us there wadn't no man?'

'I be telling you there wadn't naught to make a fuss about.'

'Then why'm you being so secret?'

Maddy gave a sigh and put aside the ladle. 'I idn't being secret, I be tiying to set out the dinner. I gave a bowl of broth to a fellow as looked as though he needed it. Surely there idn't no harm in that? He didn't even come in the house. He sat on the wall to eat.'

'That idn't no reason for you to give food us've worked for to any vagabond as passes,' insisted Bart.

'Don't worry, there be plenty left.' Unbidden, Maddy replenished his empty dish. 'And before you objects further and begrudges a few spoonfuls of broth, it were made with vegetables I grew, barley I gleaned from up Farmer Churchward's, and stock bones I bought with my egg money. You'm getting your share, that's all that concerns you.'

'Where be he from, this fellow?' asked Lew.

'He didn't say. From up-country somewhere, by his voice; and my, did he talk something grand.' Maddy smiled at the memory. 'Called pay "remuneration" and things like that.'

'What be he doing yer, then?'

'Looking for work, he said. I suggested he tried the Church House, in case they habn't got a replacement for Alfred.'

'Then there wadn't no music or dancing?' Davie sounded quite disappointed.

'There wadn't no dancing, that was for sure,' laughed Maddy. 'What breath have I left for cutting capers on a wash-day morning? There were music, though.' She grew serious. 'It were a pity you wadn't here to hear it, the lot of you. It would've pleasured your ears like nothing you've heard in many a long day.'

'A damned mountebank! I might've knowd it!' said Bart with satisfaction. 'Us bain't having trash like that round yer, be us, Father?'

'He don't sound the sort as you should be taking up with, maid,' said Jack.

'You'm making a lot out of one bowl of broth,' Maddy replied. 'I don't think you'm got aught to worry about. I idn't likely to be taking up with anyone, mountebank or no, not now.'

Maddy did not expect anyone to contradict her, which was just as well, because no one did.

–

The winter had been exceptionally mild and the clement weather had continued into spring, tempting Maddy to work in the garden. Her efforts kept the family in fresh vegetables throughout the year and she was always pleased when she could make an early start.

'You'm going to be well ahead of yourself this year,' remarked Annie, looking at the lines of sowings, neatly marked with twigs.

'The ground's been easy to work, that always helps.' Maddy straightened up and leaned on her hoe.

'I don't suppose you'm had time to go up to your mother's grave and set that to rights?'

'Not yet. It be nagging at me, I don't like to think of un all bare, especially at this time of year.'

'That were a vexing thing to have happened. Folk shouldn't have animals if they idn't going to look after them proper.'

'I doubt us'll ever find out who it were,' said Maddy. 'That horse'll be back grazing in its field by now and no one the wiser.'

'No doubt you'm right. When you do go up the churchyard, us've got some fine young pansies coming on nicely, that you'm welcome to. They'm in the border by the washhouse.'

'That be real generous.' Maddy beamed at her friend. 'I've got alyssum and snapdragons. Along with your pansies they'll make a brave show.'

'You just help yourself to what you'm wanting.' Annie's eyes suddenly twinkled. 'And while you'm in the village no doubt you can keep your eyes open for your sweetheart.'

'And which sweetheart would that be?' asked Maddy innocently. 'Having that many, how'm I supposed to know which one you'm on about?'

'The newest one, that's who. The one who talks fancy and plays the fiddle.'

'Oh, him. Yes, I remembers him, just about.'

'Get along with you,' chortled Annie. 'It'd take a female with a very weak mind to forget that young man. If you wants to hang on to him you'd best get to the village sharpish. He'm causing quite a stir among the maidens, from what I hears. Tis a pity he can't see you now, with your petticoats hitched up. You'm showing a very shapely bit of leg.'

'Only to you,' grinned Maddy. 'My legs is well enough. They reaches the ground, which suits me fine. That young fellow did find work, then?'

'Yes, didn't you know? He'm potman at the Church House Inn. By all accounts Harry Ford wadn't too pleased with him at first. Not being used to the trade he wadn't swift enough serving nor clearing to suit Master Ford, but you know what he'm like. Anyway, during a quiet spell, your friend got out his fiddle and played a tune or two to himself. That did un! Him and his fiddle, they'm been drawing folk to the Church House like wasps to a honeypot ever since.'

'I be glad he found somewhere,' said Maddy. Then she looked at Annie curiously. 'But how do you know these things when I don't?'

'My William told me. He went up the Church House for a drop of cider last evening and heard your Patrick a-fiddling. Very impressed he were.'

Maddy's father and brothers had been up to the Church House the previous night, too, but they had never said a word. And why should they? she asked herself. Yidn't as though Patrick Howard be anything to me.

In the few days since the excitement of his unexpected arrival, her common sense had reasserted itself. Of course he had not been showing a special interest in her! It had been foolish of her even to imagine it.

Go on like this and you'll end up one of they old maids that imagines a man's dying of love for them just because he'm said 'Good day', she thought wryly.

Thankfully the good weather held, and next afternoon Maddy set off up the path, a basket of young plants on her arm. As she went, she planned how she was going to set them out on her mother's grave to give the best effect. So great was her concentration that she passed the short cut to the churchyard and was at the corner by the Church House Inn before she realised her mistake. Not that it made much difference, it added only a few minutes to her journey.

'Miss Maddy! Miss Maddy!'

She was halfway along the cobbled path to the ancient lych gate when the sound of someone calling her name made her spin round. Hurrying after her was Patrick Howard.

'I am glad I caught you!' he exclaimed, slithering to a halt on the smooth cobbles. He was smiling. How could she have forgotten the power of that smile? It gave her a warm, glowing feeling inside.

'Mr Howard,' she said. 'You'm managed to get work, then?'

'Yes, thanks to you. When I caught sight of you going past I had to rush out to say how grateful I am to you. Without your help I would never have got this situation.'

'I be glad you'm satisfied,' she said.

'Indeed I am. Not two minutes in the village and already I am head potman.'

'I thought Harry Ford only had one potman?'

'He has.' Patrick Howard spoke in a conspiratorial whisper. 'But please don't tell anyone else, it would lessen my prestige considerably. And you have to admit I have a most impressive livery.' He indicated the voluminous apron that was tied about his waist. 'Don't you think the beer stains add a certain distinction?'

Maddy was not certain about the meanings of some of his words, but she could appreciate his joking.

'Very stylish,' she agreed gravely. 'Shouldn't wonder if the fashion don't catch on.' Then she could not keep her face straight any longer. 'I'm soon going to be as mazed as you at this rate,' she chuckled.

'Mazed?' He looked puzzled.

'Crazy. Silly. Daft,' she supplied. 'Habn't you never heard the word before?'

'No. I'm glad I've learned it now, though… Mazed.' He savoured the word on his tongue. 'It gives a picture of folk whirling about in complete confusion. I like it. From now on I shall use mazed whenever possible.'

''Tis plain you idn't from these parts,' said Maddy, still smiling at his nonsense.

'Ah now, Miss Maddy, there you are in error. I must inform you that I was born here, in this very village.'

'What, in Stoke Gabriel?' She was astonished. 'But I can't recall seeing you before, nor hearing of no Howards round about neither.'

'I doubt if you would.' His smile widened, showing very white teeth. 'My family's stay was fleeting. As I understand it, I made my appearance in this world earlier than anticipated, which necessitated my family stopping off from their travels at Stoke Gabriel. I had been born and gone to pastures new doubtless before you had drawn your first breath. We Howards are a nomadic lot.'

Maddy wondered if he meant they were gypsies, but then decided against such an idea. Not with those blue eyes and that light skin; although his hair was dark it was not the blue-black of a Romany.

'What brought you back?' she asked.

'Curiosity. I've always wanted to know about my place of birth, and as I found myself wandering westward one day I decided to press on until I reached here. And very glad I am that I did.'

'The place don't disappoint you, then?'

'No, certainly not – nor the people.' The emphasis he put upon these last words brought a flush to her cheeks.

'I hear you'm drawing in the crowds with your fiddle,' she said, hastily covering her embarrassment.

'I'm not sure that Stoke Gabriel can run to much in the way of crowds,' he smiled. 'However, we're doing quite nicely. I only play for half an hour or so during the evening. Any longer and the novelty would soon wear off.'

Maddy thought that the novelty of Patrick Howard would take quite a bit of wearing off, even without his music.

From within the Church House someone was calling his name.

'There,' he said. 'I'm in demand again.'

'You'd best go, before that demand wears off too.'

'Don't worry, Miss Maddy, I'm indispensable. You know, I owe you an apology.'

'You do? What for?'

'For calling you Miss Maddy. It is most impolite and forward of me, but I have to confess that I can't manage your surname.'

'What, Shillabeer? Tis ordinary enough.'

'Not to me. To me it's something else completely new. Madeleine Shillabeer.' He repeated the two words thoughtfully. 'Such an individual name. How nice to be called something distinctive. Howards are ten a penny, but Shillabeers...'

Maddy was surprised. Never in her life had anything about her been considered out of the ordinary. She had always thought Maddy Shillabeer to be a very common title, yet this extraordinary young man thought it was individual and distinctive.

The voice from the inn was becoming louder and more insistent. 'Perhaps I had better go and see what's wanted,' he said. 'It must be farewell for now, I'm afraid. Not for long, though. I hope we meet again soon.' He turned away with evident reluctance.

Maddy was so shaken by his sincerity that she could only reply, 'No doubt us will.'

'Then *au revoir*, for the present.' Seeing her puzzled expression he said, 'That's French for until we see each other again. Oh, and I was right about one thing, Miss Maddy Shillabeer, your eyes are aquamarine.'

In a daze Maddy continued towards the churchyard, his departing footsteps ringing in her ears. How was it he had defined the word mazed? Whirling about in confusion? That was exactly how she felt: Patrick Howard had sought out her company, he had laughed and joked with her, paid her compliments, even spoken French to her. Not since the days of Rob Bradworthy had any man paid her such attention. And not just *any* man, but Patrick Howard, a fascinating being from beyond the tight confines of the village, someone quite outside her experience.

Maddy's feet led her automatically through the lych gate into the churchyard. Absorbed by her thoughts, she was standing beside her mother's simple headstone almost before she knew it. Thankfully she sank down onto her knees.

Taking a deep breath to calm herself, she closed her eyes, letting the peace and quiet of the churchyard wash over her. She had the place to herself and, as the tranquillity soaked into her, bit by bit something of her normal serenity was restored.

Well, you'm certainly got yourself in a state over naught there, didn't you? she told herself reprovingly. There idn't no call for you having a fit of the vapours just because a decent-looking fellow has a bit of a jaw with you. Any fool can see Patrick Howard be the sort of man who can't help flirting with a female, whatever her age. Tis his nature, that's obvious. With all the trim maids about the place, he idn't going to seek you out special, don't be mazed enough to think he be.

She felt much better after she had given herself the scolding. For a moment the regular tenor of her life had been shaken; she had allowed herself a brief glimpse of dreams that were an impossibility.

She stayed on her knees, enjoying the warm sun. Then she noticed a weed had sprouted in the red earth. She removed it. Then she saw another and another and another. Before long she was weeding briskly, using the hand fork she had brought with her.

The systematic work absorbed her; the pile of immature weeds by her side grew. Soon she had the earth neat and smooth, and was laying out the young seedlings on the soil when a soft whinnying disturbed her. Surprised, she looked about her. Then she heard the jingle of harness and the thud of hooves. From behind her, from the direction of the short cut she had meant to take, came a young woman on horseback. She was riding at increasing speed. There was no mistaking who she was. The green velvet riding habit made recognition immediate. She was one of the new tenants of the White House, Miss Fitzherbert. Not that Maddy cared who she was, it was what she was about to do that brought a gasp of horrified disbelief to her lips.

With deliberation Miss Fitzherbert gathered her mount and directed it towards the first grave. Effortlessly horse and rider cleared the headstone, then the next, then the next. The elegant Miss Fitzherbert was making a steeplechase of the churchyard. Nearing the hedge, the young woman turned her mount, then once more urged it forward ready to jump again. She was heading directly for Lizzie Shillabeer's grave.

Until that moment Maddy had been frozen into immobility. Now she was galvanised into movement.

'No!' she screamed, leaping to her feet and flinging her arms wide to fend off the oncoming pair. 'Don't you dare!'

Her sudden appearance, as much as her shrill cry, startled both horse and rider. She had been half hidden by the headstone and neither of them had been aware of her presence. Her abrupt emergence proved too much for the horse. It reared on its hind legs, deposited its rider on the ground, and ran off.

Maddy strode over to the young woman. She did not ask if she was injured. She did not care.

Miss Fitzherbert proved she was unhurt by sitting up and exclaiming angrily, 'You fool! I could have been killed. What on earth were you about, leaping out of nowhere like that?'

'I were stopping you leaping over my mother's grave, that's what I were doing. Don't you know where you be? Can't you see this be a churchyard?'

'Yes, I know where I be,' Miss Fitzherbert mimicked her Devon accent. 'And of course I can see this is a churchyard. Where else would there be so many graves and headstones?'

'You knew, yet you still went on jumping?' Maddy was aghast at such insensitivity.

'Why shouldn't I?' Miss Fitzherbert rose to her feet somewhat stiffly and brushed away the mud that marred the green velvet.

'Why shouldn't you? Because this be holy ground that belongs to the church, that's why. It should be treated respectful, not as a place to exercise your horse.'

'Oh yes?' Miss Fitzherbert gave an arrogant glance about her. She was as pretty as Annie had described, with her stylish clothes and her sleek honey-coloured hair. Her features were small and regular, but her lower lip protruded, betraying a wilfulness she seemed determined to prove. 'And where does it say anything about not riding here?' she demanded.

'It don't need to say. Everyone knows this be consecrated ground.'

'Sadly I have not had the benefit of your superior education.' Miss Fitzherbert's voice was heavy with sarcasm. 'I know none of these things. Really, all this fuss about a lot of dead people who can't feel anything.'

'Maybe they can't, but us as is left can! And us don't like to see our loved ones trampled on to make sport for someone as should know better.' A thought occurred to Maddy. 'This idn't the first time you'm done this, be un?' she accused. ''Twas you as spoiled the graves the other day. *And* you was at Evensong afterwards when the vicar spoke up most particular. You was lying! You did know 'tis wrong to ride in here.'

'He was talking about some stray animal, as I recall. It was nothing to do with me.'

'Yes it were, and you knows it! Don't make things worse by telling more lies.'

Victoria Fitzherbert gave an arrogant toss of her head and looked haughtily down her small, straight nose.

'I refuse to stand here and be abused by a dirty country drab. If I wish to ride here then I shall. Now fetch my horse, my good woman, and help me mount up again.'

'I idn't fetching no horse and you idn't riding over no more graves, not while I be yer.'

'Don't be insolent. Fetch my horse, I say.' Irritably Miss Fitzherbert began slapping her riding crop against her thigh.

Miss Fitzherbert might be gentry but Maddy had no intention of being intimidated. She was far too angry and distressed. 'I tell you I idn't fetching no horse and you idn't riding in this churchyard again.'

'Then I suppose I must fetch him myself. Stand aside.'

'No.' Maddy faced her, solid and resolute.

The contrast between the two young women could not have been greater, the one smart and elegant despite her fall, the other shabby and slightly dishevelled in her cotton dress and shawl, her hair wildly disordered as usual.

'Stand aside, I say!' ordered Victoria Fitzherbert. When Maddy made no move she took a step to one side, then a step to the other, but her opponent was too quick for her and blocked the way.

'It idn't no use trying to dodge,' Maddy declared. 'You'm going back the way you come, and you'm going on foot.'

'I have never heard such impertinence!' declared Victoria furiously. 'Stand aside, I tell you, or you'll be sorry.'

She raised her riding crop to strike a blow, but again Maddy was too quick for her. She seized the other woman by the wrist. It was no contest. Maddy's grip had been strengthened by a lifetime of toil, she could wield a spade or an oar with the best. Victoria Fitzherbert had never done anything more strenuous than ride a well-schooled horse. With a cry of pain, she let the crop fall to the ground. Maddy kicked it far out of reach before she let go of the young woman.

'Robbins, help me!' cried Victoria, nursing her bruised wrist. 'Where are you when I need you? Can't you see I am being attacked and assaulted? Come and give this woman a thrashing this instant.'

There was a movement where the footpath entered the churchyard, and from beyond the sheltering elderberry bushes emerged a groom. He looked the picture of reluctance and discomfort.

'Come away, Miss Fitzherbert,' he said uneasily. 'Let's be going home. I'll fetch your horse.'

'Is there something wrong with your eyes, man?' snapped Victoria. 'This woman has just assaulted me. She is preventing me from getting by. Do something!'

The groom took a couple of hesitant steps further into the churchyard. 'See here, young woman, just you step back a bit and let your betters be,' he said in a voice that was meant to be authoritative but which failed by a large margin.

'There be plenty who'm my betters,' retorted Maddy, never once taking her eyes off the other woman, 'but there idn't none within spitting distance.'

'Don't stand there bandying words,' declared Victoria, her anger increasing. 'You've got a riding crop. Use it! Get this wretch out of my way!'

The groom looked at the crop in his hand as if he had not noticed it before. 'Miss Fitzherbert...' he began miserably.

'Do something, you fool, if you value your position!' Victoria cried impatiently.

The groom took another reluctant step forward, the crop raised half-heartedly in his grasp.

'That's far enough, friend,' a new voice suddenly rang out across the churchyard. Of all people, it was Cal Whitcomb.

How long he had been standing there observing the scene Maddy did not know; he seemed to have emerged from behind the church like a shadow. He moved forward until he was level with her.

'I wouldn't come any nearer, if I were you,' he went on brusquely, addressing the groom. 'I suggest we let the ladies sort this out themselves. If you were to take a hand I'd be obliged to join in, to even things up.'

The poor groom looked intensely relieved at this unexpected intervention, but Victoria's lower lip became more mutinous.

'Obey your orders, Robbins,' she persisted. 'Take no notice of this country oaf.'

'Madam,' continued Cal Whitcomb, 'country oaf though I doubtless am, I am also head and shoulders bigger than your manservant over there. I assure you I will not let him intervene in your dispute with Miss Shillabeer.' He spoke calmly, patiently, yet there was a determined undertone to his voice. Cal Whitcomb was not a man to be trifled with.

'Come away, please do, Miss Fitzherbert,' implored the groom. 'I'd be no match for this gentleman, anyone can see that. And, besides, you know how much your father disapproves of his servants getting into fights.'

Victoria's mouth lost its customary pout and assumed a grim line. The inequality of a match between Robbins and this interfering newcomer was certainly obvious, and despite her wilful determination she also recognised in Maddy someone who had been brought up in a much harder school. For once in her life she was not going to get her own way.

'Collect my horse, Robbins,' she snapped. 'We're going home.'

'I'll fetch the horse and lead it back to the road,' said Cal Whitcomb in a voice which brooked no argument. 'You can mount more easily there; we don't want any more leaping over gravestones on your way out, do we?'

He strode over to the animal that was now grazing peacefully among the more neglected graves, and led it away, taking care to keep it on the path.

Maddy watched as Victoria Fitzherbert and her groom followed in silence, one sullen, the other relieved. The sound of hoofbeats receding up the hill echoed from beyond the hedge. Then Cal Whitcomb returned.

'They've gone, thank goodness,' he said. 'That's a troublesome young miss if I ever saw one. I don't envy her groom.'

Maddy regarded him, not sure how to reply. She was struck by the enormity of the situation. For a brief moment a Shillabeer and a Whitcomb had been on the same side. Nothing of the sort had happened since the days of the war against Napoleon. She ought to be antagonistic towards Cal Whitcomb, but she was grateful for his intervention. The Fitzherbert female would have no compunction in having her thrashed, and Maddy had not relished the prospect of being beaten with a riding crop like a stray dog. She would have fought back, of course, but she could well imagine the humiliation of the outcome. She was thankful that she had avoided it. Why, oh why, though, did her deliverer have to be Cal Whitcomb?

She ought to thank him, she knew, if she could think of the appropriate words.

'I was lucky you came in the churchyard when you did,' she said at last.

'It was mere chance. I was early for my meeting with the squire and decided to come and visit my family graves. I'd heard about a stray horse doing damage up here. I came to make sure that all was well.'

'And was everything all right?' She still had not thanked him, but the words stuck in her throat.

'Father's grave was untouched. I've not had time to go over to my brother's yet.'

She remembered then: Christopher Whitcomb, the elder son, was not buried in the family plot, for he had died of the cholera some years back. The victims of that epidemic had been laid to rest together under the dread warning, 'These graves must never be opened'.

The tears that overwhelmed her took Maddy completely by surprise. One moment she was perfectly composed, the next she was crumpled against her mother's headstone sobbing as if her heart would break. Her grief had something to do with her recent confrontation with the silly, selfish girl who had thoughtlessly ridden her horse over her mother's remains and, quite illogically, the fact that she could not bring herself to thank Cal Whitcomb.

How long her bout of weeping lasted she had no idea, her sense of time and place had vanished, swept away upon her inexplicable storm of tears. Only as her anguish subsided and someone pressed a large handkerchief into her hand did she realise that Cal Whitcomb was still standing there.

'I don't know what all that were about,' she exclaimed eventually, scrubbing at her eyes with the proffered linen. 'I feel a gurt fool, giving way like that.'

'It's understandable. If some mindless idiot had galloped over my family's graves I'd have been very upset too.'

'You'd not have bawled your eyes out, though, would you?'

'Perhaps not – at least, not in public,' he agreed.

The stiff formality had gone from his voice. In its place Maddy noted a touch of humour, which surprised her. She looked with concern at the crumpled handkerchief she was grasping. It was sodden with her tears.

'I'll wash un and...' She stopped. How on earth was she to return it to him? A Shillabeer could hardly go up to Oakwood Farm and knock on the door. The Dart would flow uphill before that happened!

He understood her problem immediately. 'You'd best keep it,' he said.

'But 'tis good linen!'

'It doesn't matter.' He saw her expression of dismay and. 'Don't look like that. My mother doesn't give me a hiding every time I lose a kerchief these days. I'm too big for that.'

'I suppose you be. You must be as tall as our Lew and I can't reach to clip him about the ears no more, neither.'

'Just as well for your Lew.'

'It didn't happen often. He'm a good sort, be Lew. No trouble really.'

The day was rapidly assuming an air of unreality. What was she doing, standing here discussing one of her brothers with Cal Whitcomb?

The peculiarity of the situation must have struck him too, for he said, 'You know, I should think that today you and I have spoken more than all the other Shillabeers and Whitcombs put together this century. I don't suppose our two sides have exchanged more than a few dozen words over these last fifty or sixty years.'

'Less than that if you cuts out the swearing.'

Unexpectedly they both began to laugh. Maddy had to admit that he was easy to talk to. He was quite the gentleman when he spoke, although he had kept the Devon burr in his voice, but then he had been educated at the grammar school at Totnes and not just at the village school. Although she was reluctant to admit it, she had been quite impressed by the way he had addressed Victoria Fitzherbert. He had tackled her as if he had been her social equal, without a hint of hesitancy or awe. He looked the country gentleman too, in his tailored brown coat, well-fitting breeches, and gleaming leather gaiters. Dressed up to the nines for his visit to Hill House, insisted her inborn animosity; but she owed him some charity.

'You'll be late for your meeting with the squire,' she said, glancing up at the church clock to confirm her words. Then she gasped in alarm. 'That can't be the time!' she exclaimed. 'The menfolk'll be back for their tea and I habn't started putting in Mother's plants yet.'

'I've still a few minutes to spare, I'll help you. You finish setting the plants out where you want them to go and I'll begin putting them in.'

I can't be beholden to him again, I just can't, she told herself, as he crouched down and began planting the alyssum where she had laid it out.

In the absence of another hand fork or trowel he seemed quite content to dig in the soft earth with his fingers. This gave her the opportunity to make some remark worthy for a Shillabeer to deliver to a Whitcomb.

'Bain't you afraid of dirtying your hands, then?' she taunted.

He looked at his fingers, covered in mud. 'I've plenty of time to wash them off under the pump before I go to the squire's,' he said, ignoring her attempted insult. 'Besides, you've prepared the ground well, it isn't any problem to dig like this.'

She was overcome with shame. Her jibe had been unworthy. Hadn't he come to her aid twice in one hour? And, anyway, her remark had been quite unjustified. She had noticed that his hands, beneath their covering of earth, were hard and calloused. The rest of him might resemble a gentleman but his hands betrayed that he was a working farmer.

'This idn't easy!' she exclaimed suddenly, laying aside the snap-dragon she had been about to plant.

'What isn't?' he asked in surprise.

'Well, I should be thanking you, but I can't think of naught to say when by rights I shouldn't be talking to you in the first place.'

'I understand what you mean. At least, I think I do,' he said, the sharp spark of humour returning to his grey eyes. 'It is difficult, I suppose, considering that you and I have both lived here in the village all our lives and this is the first time we have ever spoken to one another.'

'Tis difficult right enough,' agreed Maddy with fervour. 'Father would have the hide off my back if he thought I was just breathing the churchyard air with you, never mind holding a conversation.'

'You aren't alone,' he assured her. 'I've no need to fear a beating from my mother, but I'd have the day I spoke to a Shillabeer served up for dinner, tea, and supper from now until Whitsun without a break. Of the two, I think I'd prefer to have a beating and get it over with.'

She looked at him carefully, not sure whether or not he was joking.

'We'm agreed on one thing then,' she said. 'Us must hope and pray no one finds out about today. Thank goodness 'tis market day up to Totnes, so few folks be about to see us.'

'And I shouldn't think either Miss Fitzherbert or her groom will be keen to spread today's adventure abroad, do you?'

'No, but that don't help my predicament none. I still haven't thanked you.'

'No thanks are needed.'

'Yes they be,' she retorted hotly. 'Us Shillabeers knows our manners, no matter what you Whitcombs think. I wants to thank you all proper and elegant, if you'll only give me a minute to think of the words. 'Twould be easy if you was Henry Beer or someone like that.'

'Then close your eyes and imagine I am old Henry if it will help.'

She was almost caught out, half closing her eyes.

'Oh you!' she exclaimed irritably, opening her eyes wide again. 'Don't you go having me on, just because you'm a Whitcomb and you think you'm superior. I be determined to thank you, so here I goes.' She hesitated, not even certain how to address him. The usual prefixes to the name Whitcomb that were bandied about at home were singularly inappropriate. 'Mr Whitcomb,' she began in her best manner, learned at the village school, 'I be most grateful for the way you come to my aid today. As our families having been daggers drawn since goodness knows when, 'twas most generous of you. You could've walked away and let me get a thrashing from that Fitzherbert creature's groom. And thank you for helping mend Mother's grave and getting in a mess when you'm on your way to the squire's and everything. I were always taught that there wadn't never no good in a Whitcomb, but I knows now that idn't true – don't let Father or the boys know I said that or the fat'll really be in the fire. Oh, stop laughing! I knowd that didn't come out right, but you knows what I meant to say.'

'Yes, I know,' he said, still chuckling. 'And in turn I thank you for the most original and sincere speech that's ever been addressed to me. Under the circumstances, I don't suppose we'll ever get a chance to talk to each other again. But let me assure you I'll never forget meeting you, not until my dying day.' And he began to chuckle again.

'Gurt fool,' said Maddy ungraciously.

Before the day was out rumours of the confrontation between Maddy and Victoria Fitzherbert were spreading about Stoke Gabriel like a grass fire. In the mysterious ways of the village telegraph, no one would admit to being the source, but the story gradually became embellished so that in the most popular version the two women had been rolling about among the gravestones, tearing each other's hair out. The cause of the conflict spread about too, causing an angry outcry. As a result Dick Matthews, the village glazier, was hastily summoned to the White House to replace several windows which had been broken in an outburst of stone-throwing.

For some reason Cal Whitcomb's presence during the fracas in the churchyard was never mentioned; Maddy never discovered why not, and she was too thankful to investigate further. Nevertheless, during the following days she began to feel strangely unsettled.

For years her life had been busy yet uneventful, one day much like another with only the progressing seasons marking any change. Now, in a very short time, so much had happened that was new and disturbing. Normally the arrival of new tenants at the White House would have been enough to absorb her interest – and that of the village – for weeks. Used to a quiet life, she was finding damaged graves and skirmishes with high-born females almost too much to cope with, let alone being beholden to a Whitcomb.

Although she was reluctant to admit it, there was another reason for her unsettled state – Patrick Howard. Under normal circumstances, his arrival, too, would have been enough to set the village by the ears, but among the other dramatic happenings his presence had been overshadowed. Not in Maddy's case, however. She found him disturbing. Not simply because of his undeniable appeal – he was without doubt the most attractive man who had ever crossed her path – it was what his presence was doing to her thoughts. He was beginning to stir in her emotions and aspirations she had thought buried for eleven years. Something about him reminded her that twenty-five was not beyond hope, that she was not the desiccated spinster she had convinced herself she was.

But it did not matter what she dreamed or how many Patrick Howards disturbed her quiet life, her duty was to her father and brothers. They had no one else to look after them, just her. She was bound to them, and that was the cruel truth of it.

Chapter Three

'Oh Victoria! How could you have disgraced us so?' Mrs Fitzherbert wept copiously into a tiny scrap of cambric.

'I've never been spoken to in such a manner!' George Fitzherbert strode back and forth across the floor in short, angry strides. 'And by a tuppeny-ha'penny country parson too!'

To say that the atmosphere in the elegant drawing room at the White House was tense was an understatement. The Reverend Bowden had left barely five minutes before and the room was still charged with the force of his wrath.

His message had been short and sharp and fiery: to desecrate a holy place and ignore the sensibilities of the bereaved was an abomination, not only to the Lord but to the God-fearing people of Stoke Gabriel. Even the meanest pauper in the parish would have shrunk from defiling the graves of the dead in such a way. Miss Fitzherbert had shown herself to be on the path to hellfire and damnation if she did not mend her ways immediately. The Reverend Bowden had not excluded her parents from the scorch of his reproof. They had failed abysmally in their sacred trust, as her father and mother, to guide their daughter onto the path she ought to follow. They had a moral obligation to perform their duties more effectively in future.

'To have a paltry village cleric speak to me in such a way! And it is all your fault, miss!' George Fitzherbert glared at his daughter with animosity. 'What possessed you? Answer me that! What possessed you?'

'I was bored.' In that room Victoria was the only one who appeared calm. She sat upright, apparently serene, the wide silken skirts of her pink crinoline spread about her, as if nothing untoward had happened. Just the tightening of her lips betrayed her reaction to Mr Bowden's castigation.

'Bored? Bored?' cried her father.

'Yes, bored!' she retorted, showing animation for the first time. 'Have you any idea what it's like for me being buried in this deadly dull hole?'

'Well, thanks to your idiotic pranks it is likely to be even more dull,' replied her father.

'The social life of this place can't get any worse!' declared Victoria emphatically.

'It can and it will. It has begun already,' he answered.

'What do you mean, Papa?'

'It has been so pointed I'm astounded it has escaped your notice. The soiree being held at Waddeton Court tomorrow – I don't see our invitations upon the mantelshelf. In fact, I see remarkably few invitations, whereas a week ago there were plenty.'

'You mean we are being ostracised?' His wife was aghast.

'I mean that local society is politely but firmly showing its disapproval of Victoria's behaviour.'

'It will be no loss.' Victoria tossed her head arrogantly.

'I hope you think the same way after being obliged to play solitaire every night for the next three or four months.'

'It won't come to that, surely?' cried Mrs Fitzherbert.

'Maybe not. For some relief Victoria could read aloud to us, an enlightening volume such as *Fordyce's Sermons* perhaps. That would please the wretched vicar.'

'It can't happen! Not for months and months!' cried Mrs Fitzherbert.

'Papa is joking,' said Victoria sourly. 'And I don't see that being ostracised by the people round here would be so terrible; it isn't as though there is a single person with style or wit.'

'What Victoria means is that there are no eligible young men with whom she can flirt,' replied her father.

'Victoria does not flirt,' stated Mrs Fitzherbert. 'How can you say such a thing about your own child, George? I agree, there is a distinct shortage of suitable young men here. Now if we had only gone to Boulogne as most people do in our situation... It isn't too late. I am sure we could find somewhere quite agreeable and you know how I love France...'

'You loathe France,' answered her husband brusquely. 'And I refuse to spend the next few years in some cheap *pension* that stinks of garlic when I can be decently housed here.'

'Few years?' exclaimed Mrs Fitzherbert. 'I thought you said it was for a few months?'

Her husband rolled his eyes heavenwards, as he did frequently when his wife's lack of intelligence tested his tolerance.

'Our being ignored by our present neighbours will no doubt last for a few months,' he explained with exaggerated patience. 'It is the wider problem which will take years. I am referring to our serious lack of funds. We cannot afford to go to Boulogne now. When we originally broached the subject it was you who wished for a simple rural retreat somewhere in the depths of England.'

'You are making out that this is my fault. You always do.' Mrs Fitzherbert began to sob once more. 'I meant somewhere pretty and... and accessible.'

'This place is pretty enough in all conscience,' replied her husband. 'We would be hard pressed to find another such superior house at so low a rent.' He breathed silent thanks to the Admiralty, who had sent the White House's owner to the West Indies on a two-year tour of duty. The absent naval gentleman was not interested in making a profit by letting his home, he was content to have it lived in and the servants kept in permanent employment.

'This place has one overriding asset,' he went on. 'It would take an intrepid debt collector indeed to follow us here. And you are mistaken, my dear. I am not blaming you for our present predicament. The fault lies entirely with Victoria.'

'Simply because I was overcome with boredom?'

'Simply because you were overcome with stupidity. For the sake of a few minutes' diversion you have made us unacceptable to local society.'

'I certainly shook them up, though, didn't I?' said Victoria with satisfaction. 'I am sure they haven't had such a talking point round here since Adam ate the apple.'

'You have, as you say, made us a universal source of gossip.' Her father ceased his pacing and sat down, taking up a newspaper as if he were losing interest in the topic of conversation. 'By choosing the churchyard for your escapade, you have succeeded in muting the entire population against us, from the highest to the lowest. Congratulations, my dear. Few people can have achieved such a major effect with so little effort.' He disappeared behind *The Times*, shaking its pages irritably.

'I still don't understand how this whole story came to be known abroad,' said Mrs Fitzherbert, her brow wrinkled in perplexity. 'Who can have been gossiping? If it were Robbins then he must be dismissed immediately, without a character.'

'There was the village woman, Mama.'

'Ah, yes. The one who jumped out on you in that alarming manner and startled your horse. What a wicked thing to have done. You might have been killed. Yes, I had forgotten her. Who was she?'

'Good heavens, I don't know, Mama! I don't know one of these wretched village women from another. She was shabby and her hair looked as if she had been dragged through a hedge. She was very abusive too, and insolent. But not for long. I soon let her know that I wouldn't tolerate any impudence, and she scurried off as fast as her filthy boots would let her.'

Victoria had been selective in what she had told her parents. Being bested by the village woman and the red-haired man were details she had chosen to forget.

'You did right, my dear.' Mrs Fitzherbert nodded approvingly. 'The lower orders need keeping in their place. It must have been this village woman who spread those wicked stories, I am convinced of it. How unjust that we should have to suffer the aftermath of that creature's spite, when you behaved exactly as you ought.'

'Victoria behaved exactly like a complete fool!' roared Mr Fitzherbert impatiently, flinging down his paper. 'Have you not understood one word of what has been said this evening? She did not behave as she ought. She deliberately galloped about in the graveyard. Even a crass idiot would know better than to do that! Do not pretend that our present situation is some sort of bucolic conspiracy. It is Victoria's fault, plain and simple.'

'I suppose I am to bear the blame for ever,' said Victoria sullenly.

'You will be blamed for as long as is necessary,' said her father. 'And do not make a lip at me, miss. I don't mind that you have caused me to miss a handful of dull tea parties or a few discordant musical evenings. But it will be a long time before I forgive you for causing me to be lectured about my duty by a miserable country parson. Yes, my girl, you will be much older before I forgive you for that!' So saying he got up from his chair and strode out of the room.

'See what you have done? You have upset your papa most frightfully.' Mrs Fitzherbert began to weep into her minuscule handkerchief once more.

Victoria took no notice of her. She picked up her embroidery and began to sew, stabbing the needle viciously through the canvas as if she were impaling the inhabitants of Stoke Gabriel one by one. All the while her pouting lip protruded ominously and her thoughts were mutinous. With each passing minute she hated this place more. There was no society, no amusements, above all, no unattached young men upon whom she could exercise her wiles. Victoria liked doing that, seeing how swiftly she could charm some unsuspecting male into falling at her feet in adoration. But where was the challenge, where the thrill of conquest when there were no suitable men?

Then her thoughts fell upon the red-haired man who had been so brusque with her in the churchyard. She could not recall any male, with the exception of her father and the Reverend Bowden, who had treated her in such a churlish manner. He had been quite oblivious to her pretty face, her elegance, her breeding, but had seemed more intent upon siding with that country drab. She wondered who he was. He had the bearing and dress of a gentleman, yet his voice betrayed his Devon origins. It had been he who had helped her to mount her horse, not by clasping his hands for her to step into but by lifting her bodily – and effortlessly – into the saddle. At the time she had been speechless with fury, but now, thinking back, she realised it had not been a disagreeable experience.

She began to be intrigued. He was not the usual sort of man who crossed her path, yet she felt that he might prove a worthy adversary. It would not be easy, bringing him to kneel humbly at her feet, but what a challenge! Especially after the way he had treated her in the churchyard. Her protruding lip receded, the action of her needle became less violent as she plotted how she could discover the identity of the auburn-haired man, and then how she could ultimately meet, charm, and ensnare him.

–

'They say the vicar spoke up real brave, so that the windows of the White House fair shook,' said Annie with considerable satisfaction. 'You knows what he'm like when he'm proper riled. Told that hoity-toity piece her were due for the hellfire. I bet that set her back a bit.'

'I doubt it.' Maddy wiped the heated flat-iron on a cloth before applying it to her father's shirt. 'From what I saw of that madam, her'd not pay much heed, vicar or no vicar.'

'Her paid heed to you, though. You chased her out of the church-yard.'

'Not exactly. There wadn't no chasing, I keeps telling you. I caught her by surprise and her horse threw her. I reckon that's what rattled her.' Like Victoria, Maddy had been selective in her version of events.

But Annie was not satisfied, she was determined to give her friend more credit. 'That, and the fact that you'd have given her a hefty clout if her hadn't shifted,' she declared loyally. 'What a creature! Her must've been brought up a heathen, that's what I think.'

The story had already been gone over time after time, and Maddy knew it would be many months before Annie tired of repeating it. For herself she would be heartily glad when it faded into village memory. She felt uncomfortable at being considered a heroine, yet she dared not admit that much of the honour belonged to Cal Whitcomb.

'It'll soon be your William's busy time,' she said, in a determined effort to change the subject.

'That it will. The *Newcomin* will soon be steaming up from Dart-mouth to Totnes, starting next week. It'll mean a nice bit of extra work for him, taking folks out to her and fetching them off, instead of rowing back and forth across to the Ashprington side all the time.'

'I always likes to see the *Newcomin* going by with her paddles splashing away. Her makes a nice change from the never-ending stone barges and trading wherries sailing past. Her'll mean there's more folks coming through here for you to watch, too. You'm certain to like that.'

'There'll be a bit more life about the place, that's true, but recently the village have seemed quite lively enough as 'tis.' Annie enjoyed the story of Maddy's confrontation with Miss Fitzherbert, and she was not going to relinquish it easily.

Maddy bit back a sigh and, as she set the iron to heat again, she wondered how she could divert the conversation once more.

She did not need to, a shadow suddenly darkened the kitchen. Looking up she saw a woman standing in the open doorway, a scare-crow of a creature, dressed in a ragged dress and shawl, a cotton sun bonnet hanging by its strings off the back of her unkempt head. There was a dull, confused look in her eyes as she asked, 'Have you seen my childer, Maddy? I been looking everywhere, but they'm hiding, the little devils.'

'Sorry, Biddy, I habn't seen your youngsters today,' said Maddy kindly.

'If that idn't vexing! I bet they'm gone up the old quarry. I tells them time and time again not to but they go on playing there. I'll go along and see if I can find them, and my, will I wallop their backsides when I does.' The words were fierce but the tone was gentle and loving. 'My word, their pa idn't half going to lay into them when he gets back from work. You will send un home if you sees un, won't you?'

'Yes,' said Maddy, but she knew it was an empty promise.

Biddy's children would never go home, just as her husband would never return from work. Her entire family had perished in the cholera epidemic, leaving her the sole, deranged survivor. She had been looking for them ever since.

'Just a minute!' Maddy exclaimed as Biddy began to move from the door. Turning to the dresser, she cut off a hunk of bread and put a piece of cheese in the middle. 'There,' she said, handing it to the other woman. 'Eat this as you go along.'

Biddy took it. 'You'm a good soul, Maddy,' she said, and for a moment her eyes were lit with intelligence, then they clouded over again with their habitual confusion. 'I must find my childer,' she said. 'They'm hiding somewhere…'

She left the garden and set off along the foreshore. Maddy and Annie stood in the doorway and watched her go, splashing through the water, for the high tide had just turned, oblivious of her soaking boots and drenched petticoats. She took a few bites of the bread and cheese then let it fall as if she had forgotten its existence. Not even the raucous quarrelling of black-headed gulls pouncing on the feast caused her to turn round.

'That poor woman.' Maddy heaved a sigh of pity. 'There weren't a more decent, cleanly creature than Biddy afore her family were took, and now look at her. 'Twere a shame her were spared, and that's the truth of it. Still, 'tidn't for us to question such things, I suppose.' She turned back to the ironing. 'The kettle be boiling. Shall us have a cup of tea?'

Annie accepted willingly enough.

'On condition us talks of something bright,' insisted Maddy. 'Nothing about dying nor graveyards nor nothing like that. Tis too nice a day.'

'Very well,' agreed Annie. 'What shall us talk about then? I knows – that sweetheart of youm! He'm a lad as'd brighten any woman's day.'

'You'm determined to give me a sweetheart. I hope he'm the one with the shiny carriage and the silk top hat.'

'He'm the one with the fiddle, the one as doesn't need no carriage nor top hat.'

'What's he'm been up to now?' Maddy asked.

'Naught, far as I knows. Except as Sam Watkins, down to the Victoria and Albert, idn't too pleased the Church House'm getting all the trade. When Patrick be playing the place be that full they'm handing the drink out through the door, and folk be sitting in the lane.'

'Let's hope it keeps fine for them then, else they'll get water in the cider.'

'There's some as says it don't need to rain for that to happen,' chuckled Annie. 'But yer's a nice titbit about your favourite as I've been saving for you: he were born right here in Stoke Gabriel. There, what do you think of that?'

'Naught,' replied Maddy straightfaced.

'Naught?' The expectant beam on Annie's face faded. 'Idn't you surprised?'

'No.'

'Why not?'

'Because I already knowd.'

'Oh you wretch! And you didn't say a word!'

'I wadn't sure it were anyone else's business.' Maddy nearly added that Patrick had told her the facts himself, but she held back. Such an admission would only encourage Annie's romantic fancies.

'Twas touch and go, according to Henry Beer's missus. Her remembers un happening, and now I thinks on I've some recollection of un. Travelling players, or something of the sort, his parents were. They was going in the carrier's cart from Totnes to Brixham, but Patrick's mother must've started with him afore they set out, because her was well on the way by the time they was nearing here. As soon as the carrier realised the situation, he were down into the village that fast they reckon there was sparks coming off his horse's shoes. He wadn't carrying three when they'd only paid for two, that's what he said. Any road, he turned them off at the top of Mill Hill. Fortunately they was close to old Susan White's place, her as used to do the birthing and laying out, and her took them in. Just in time, mind. The boy were born within the hour. Then, bless me, they took off again sudden the very next day. And they never paid Susan her dues.'

'No doubt she can claim them now,' said Maddy.

'Her'd have a job. You knows very well her've been dead a good ten years.'

'Then when I sees Patrick Howard I'll tell him he's to put flowers on her grave or summat.'

'Oh, you'm likely to see him again, then?'

'No more than anyone else, but if I does, I'll tell him.'

To herself Maddy had to admit that she looked forward to meeting Patrick Howard again. In such a small village it was inevitable that she would, and the prospect filled her with a fidgety anticipation. There was something in his manner which made her feel different. Quite what it was she was not sure, some quality he brought with him of having been out in the wide world and seen wondrous things, a quality he seemed able to pass on.

In the event, their next meeting began prosaically enough. Maddy had a flourishing crop of early rhubarb in the garden which was likely to earn a useful penny or two. She filled a basket with it and, along with some fresh eggs from her hens, set off to sell her produce.

The village of Stoke Gabriel was actually sighted away from the River Dart, tucked protectively beside a creek. The creek had long since been dammed and could now boast a watermill at its head and a tidal mill set on the edge of the dam itself. The flat land alongside the creek made an excellent drying ground for the fishermen's nets, and over the years it had become a popular meeting and trading place. That was why Maddy took the steeply sloping lane to go 'down mill' to sell her produce.

She was in luck, she did not have long to wait for purchasers. Jingling the pennies in her pocket she considered what she needed to buy on her way back through the village: tea, matches, an ounce of blue for the washing, and tobacco for her father. So intent was she on the shopping list that she almost missed Patrick. Then she saw him, and a feeling of pleasure went through her.

He was approaching along the creekside from the direction of the watermill, pushing a barrow. He waved, sending the barrow on a path dangerously close to the water's edge. By the time he had it under control again he had reached her.

'There be no prizes for guessing where you'm been,' she greeted him, indicating the dusting of flour on his clothes.

'No, indeed.' He made a half-hearted attempt at brushing himself down. 'Nothing would please Mrs Ford but I must dash off immediately to fetch a sack of flour. That's why it's a double blessing to meet you this morning, Miss Maddy.' He gave her his sudden dazzling smile. 'Not just for the pleasure of seeing you but also because you have given me an excellent excuse to set down this wretched thing.' He gave the barrow a kick and looked at his hands anxiously.

'You'm got splinters?' asked Maddy. 'If so let me see to them for you, they can turn very nasty, else.'

'How kind of you to show such concern,' he smiled. 'But no, it's not splinters which bother me. It's the callouses.'

'Callouses never harmed no one,' smiled Maddy.

'They do if you're a musician,' he replied.

'I hadn't thought of that.' Maddy was struck by the problems that must confront him. 'Of course you must take care of your hands, how stupid of me not to realise un. Surely working as a potman must do them harm?'

'It's not too bad, there are many jobs far worse.' Then he exclaimed suddenly, 'Will you look at that!'

She turned to follow his gaze. 'I can't see naught,' she said. 'Just the hedge…'

'But what a hedge! Did you ever see such blossom? It clings to the bough like curds of cream. And how beautifully it shows against the blue sky. Oh, that I was an artist and could paint such a picture!'

For a moment Maddy still could not comprehend why he should be so excited about a bit of blackthorn. But his enthusiasm infected her and she looked again. It was beautiful, the masses of small white flowers packed tightly on the spiny black branches, the blue sky showing each creamy spike to full advantage.

'Yes, it be a lovely sight,' she agreed. 'A real pleasure to behold. Why habn't I noticed un afore? I must've seen scores of they old bushes and I've only thought as there'll be a good picking of gribbles this year.'

'Gribbles?'

'The fruit. Sloes, some folks call them. They'm like tiny plums and taste terrible bitter, but my, do they make a warming drop of sloe gin for a winter's night.'

'You did notice the blossom, you see, but your thoughts were practical.' As he spoke he resumed pushing the barrow again, and automatically Maddy fell into step beside him.

'I should've noticed how pretty they blossoms were.' Somehow she felt that not having done so indicated she was lacking in some way.

'You're a very busy person, and most conscientious in your duty to your father and your brothers. I've noticed that about you already. But it's not disloyal of you to pause for a moment to enjoy the sight of a bank of primroses, or to listen to the lark sing. Everyone needs beauty in their lives and you are no exception.' He spoke in gentle reproof.

'I does well enough,' she replied, startled and perplexed that he should claim to know her character so well.

'Are you sure you couldn't do better? Wouldn't you like to have some time to yourself?'

'Doing what?'

'I don't know. If you could please yourself, what would you do?'

The idea was breathtaking in its novelty.

'Read!' The reply came out explosively.

'You've never learnt?' he asked curiously.

'When Mother was alive she saw to it that I got some schooling, along with the boys. But I don't get no time, and there idn't much at home to read. There be the Bible, of course, I reads that of a Sunday, and once in a blue moon Father or one of the boys might bring in the *Totnes Times*, but naught else.'

Patrick made no immediate comment because the hill was becoming increasingly steep.

'Yer, let me lend a hand.' Maddy added her weight to his at the barrow and when he protested she retorted, 'Don't be mazed. Tidn't no bother to me. If I had a penny for every load I've helped up here I'd have a different feather in my bonnet each Sunday. Watch out!' she protested, as the barrow made as if to roll back down the hill. 'I don't mind helping you once, but I be blowed if I be pushing this lot twice!'

Eventually, laughing and puffing, they reached the top of the slope.

'This is the parting of the ways, I think,' said Patrick.

'It be indeed. Tis downhill for you now, the going'll be easier. And don't go sitting on the barrow hoping to ride the rest of the way,' she cautioned. 'Else you'm back to Byter Mill afore you knows it.'

'I'll take your advice,' he replied gravely. 'I thank you for it and for your help coming up the hill. It was worth taking such a hard road for the pleasure of your company.'

'You don't half gammon a body,' retorted Maddy.

He pretended to be affronted. 'Would I do that?' he demanded.

'Yes,' she replied promptly.

'Perhaps I would,' he agreed smiling. 'But not you. Never you, Miss Madeleine Shillabeer.'

His words, and the expression in his eyes as he said them, remained with her as she continued on her journey home. As she was about to turn into Duncannon Lane she became aware of someone calling her name. It was Patrick again.

'You must've run at a fair pace to catch up with me,' she said with alarm. 'Is aught amiss?'

Too out of breath to speak, he shook his head. 'Good job – I play the fiddle – and not the flute,' he panted at last.

'You idn't in much of a state to play either at the moment. Bide still a minute.'

'There, I think I'm fully restored.' He straightened up and took a deep breath.

'Thank goodness. What were so urgent you had to half kill yourself for?'

'For this.' From his pocket he took out a book. 'I thought you might like to borrow it.'

'A book? You would loan me a book?' Maddy was completely taken aback.

'Of course. Why shouldn't I?'

'Because... because...' Maddy was at a loss for words. How could she explain that a book was well outside the usual scope of her life. It would not be like borrowing a twist of tea until the Totnes agent paid up for the salmon, or an extra cup or two because folks had called and there were not enough to go round. These were ordinary common things, everyone did them at some time or another. But a book! She had never heard of anyone borrowing a book before.

'You can't think of a reason why not, can you?' said Patrick. He pushed the book into her hand.

'*Great Expectations*' she read hesitantly. 'What if it be full of long words? Tis a long time since I read aught, excepting the Bible. I might not be able to manage anything difficult.'

'Why don't you find out by reading it?' He pressed the book into her hand and began to move away. 'I must go if I don't want some harsh words from Mrs Ford,' he said. Then he stopped and eyed her appreciatively. 'You should wear that colour more often,' he said. 'It matches your eyes. Today they are like the river in the sunlight, warm and sparkling. Quite enchanting.' He hurried off as swiftly as he had come, leaving Maddy gazing after him speechless.

Why does he do that? she wondered, almost irritably. Say summat fair outrageous then dashes off afore a body's got time to think straight.

She looked down at her dress. The material had been bought at Totnes market years ago because it was cheap and looked as if it would wash well. She had never considered the colour. She regarded it now. It had wide stripes in a sort of sea-green shade. Was that what Patrick was making such a fuss about? Was that the sort of colour he saw in her eyes? She had always thought of them as wishy-washy, neither one thing nor another. Perhaps, like the blackthorn blossom, she had simply not looked at them properly.

And there was the book! She held it stiffly in her hand, as if not certain what to do with it. Then, as it always did, her common sense gradually reasserted itself. She would return the book to Patrick as soon as she could. In the meantime, the best thing would be to put it in her pocket, away from prying eyes.

–

The first thing Maddy did when she got home was to dash up to her room and look in the mirror. Usually she only gave herself a quick glance to make sure her hair was securely anchored. Now she looked more carefully. And just as she had regarded the blackthorn blossom anew, so she began to see things in herself she had never noticed before: the blue-green in her dress did intensify the colour of her eyes. How had she never noticed it before? And her eyes were the same colour as the river on a fine day, exactly as Patrick had said they were. She could not recall anyone with eyes the same colour – except her mother. The boys, who shared her wild unruly hair, had grey eyes like Father. Did that make her a freak?

No, it makes you distinctive! She could almost hear Patrick saying it. She was the distinctive Miss Madeleine Shillabeer, with distinctive blue-green eyes. What was the name he had first given them? Aquamarine, that was it. She liked the sound, and equally she began to like the idea of having aquamarine eyes. Then she gave a sigh. Being distinctive was all very well as far as it went, but there was nothing to be done about her mop of hair or her bony face.

'You'm idn't getting to be no beauty, but you'm certainly growing more stupid by the minute, girl,' she informed her reflection cheerfully. For good measure she gave an ugly grimace.

One more thing she had to do before going downstairs, and that was to hide the book under her mattress where it would not be found and cause trouble.

It did not need the book to cause trouble. The moment her father came stamping into the house, followed by all four brothers, she knew something was the matter.

'You'm been seeing a man!' Jack declared.

'What's that supposed to mean?' she asked, although she had a pretty fair idea.

'That fiddling knave at the Church House! You'm taken up with him.'

'I have? Then 'tis news to me, and to him too, I dare say.'

'The pair of you was seen down mill,' retorted Jack.

'So were half the village,' replied Maddy. 'It were busy there today.'

'We'm told you once already to keep away from damned trash like him,' broke in Bart. 'We'm idn't having you bringing no disgrace here.'

'He'm a bad sort, Maddy, anyone can see that,' said Lew.

'He'm a bad sort,' Charlie repeated.

'We'm telling you straight, our Maddy, you idn't to have naught to do with him,' added Davie.

The injustice of it took her breath away. Five pairs of eyes glared at her accusingly, waiting for her to give in to their demands, as she usually did. But she had had enough of being ordered about, especially by those with no authority over her. Her temper flared to breaking point.

'What I does idn't naught to do with you four, so you's can either sit down and shut your mouths or get out!' she snapped. Taken by surprise the brothers sat down.

'Now then!' Maddy faced Jack, her arms akimbo. 'You'm my father and I owes you respect and obedience, I knows that, but I be warning you straight. I've always led a decent life and no one idn't going to say otherwise, not even you.'

'You was seen... talking to that fellow...' said Jack uncertainly, looking to Bart for support.

Deliberately Maddy placed herself squarely between her father and her brother.

47

'And that's it?' she demanded angrily. 'You accuses me of bringing disgrace on the family because I spoke to a man? If that idn't the limit! What'll you do next? Shout "adultery" because I says good morning to William or Joe? You'm mazed, the lot of you!'

'No, we'm just determined you idn't going to disgrace us,' declared Bart.

Maddy swung round on him. 'You idn't afeared of no disgrace,' she said scornfully. 'You'm afeared I might go off with someone and leave you lot to fend for yourselves. You'm scared of losing your slavey, that's what you'm afeared of.'

'And if you did go off, what'd be the result?' demanded Bart. 'You'd just be a slavey in some other place.'

'Then my life'd be the same,' Maddy retorted. 'But, my stars, you lot wouldn't half notice the difference! Just as things'd have been a deal harder if I'd gone off when I were younger and had the chance. Two of you at least'd have been brought over to Totnes workhouse, because Father would never have managed to rear four of you alone.' Charlie and Davie, the youngest, stared uncomfortably down at the table, contemplating the fate that had so nearly been theirs. 'As for you others,' went on Maddy, 'and I be including Father, you'd have known the meaning of cold comfort with a vengeance!'

'Us knows how much us owes you, Maddy, my lover,' said Jack in a conciliatory tone, clearly startled by his daughter's rebellious outburst. 'You'm the woman of the household and us thinks highly of you, don't us, boys?'

'Then show me a bit of respect! I be a person too, you knows. I got my own wants and likings, I don't have to dance to your tune all the time.' Then seeing that they did not know what she was talking about, she said more quietly, 'I be a woman, growd, I idn't stupid, and I idn't flighty. Have the grace to trust me like I was a reasonable person as can have friends and do things without you lot forever disapproving.'

Jack's face cleared. 'If that's what you'm wanting, maid, then 'tis fine by us, eh, lads?' he said. 'You feel free to come and go as you please.'

Now would have been a good moment to fetch out the copy of *Great Expectations* and read it openly in front of them, but Maddy did not. She knew they had not really understood. It would be more prudent to keep the book a secret.

There was a surprise in church the next Sunday. Among the musicians stood Patrick, his fiddle in his hand. He caught her eye and smiled, and she felt a wave of disapproval emanate from her brothers. The improvement to the music during the service was astonishing. Although Patrick literally played second fiddle, it was his instrument that dominated the timing and smoothed out the squeaks and squawks that were characteristic of Henry Beer's playing. He did not play loudly, it was his skill and musicianship that had the other players, Henry excluded, following his lead.

As the congregation left the church everyone was talking about how splendid the singing and playing had been.

'We'm having that new fellow to play at our Rose's wedding,' remarked a stout matron, the miller's wife.

'I thought you'd spoke for old Henry,' said her companion.

'Tweren't naught definite,' the miller's wife replied.

'Poor Henry'm going to be some put out, idn't he?'

'Can't help that,' was the unrepentant reply. 'Our Rose be the only girl, her'm having the best us can manage, and that young fellow be the best fiddler. Henry can like it or lump it.'

Maddy could not help hearing the conversation. Although she felt a twinge of sympathy for Henry Beer who had been the village fiddler since anyone could remember, she was pleased to think that Patrick was getting a chance to earn extra money.

To her surprise he was waiting for her outside the church.

'I've been wondering how you're getting on with *Great Expectations*' he said.

An expression of awe spread across her face. 'Tis a brave story and no mistake. After the first page or so I didn't seem to notice the long words. I be most grateful to you for letting me read un.'

'I'm glad you are enjoying it.' Patrick showed signs of wanting to talk more, but Maddy could not stay.

'I can't linger,' she said reluctantly. 'Else the dinner'll dry up. I thought your playing were grand this morning. It were a real treat.'

'Some day, when we get the chance, I'll play just for you again,' he said. 'Exactly as I did that very first day.'

'I remembers. And my, did I feel foolish!' Maddy smiled at the memory.

'You won't feel foolish next time, will you?'

Maddy shook her head. 'I knows better now.'

'Then farewell until our next meeting.'

Maddy set off for home feeling inordinately happy, an emotion that was not the least bit dimmed by the glowering expressions her brothers had given her as they passed on their way to one or other of the inns. She did not care. She would talk to whomsoever she pleased.

This new-found freedom did not extend to Cal Whitcomb, however. He, too, had been in church, and he passed her on the road, driving his mother in their neat gig. They did not acknowledge one another in the slightest. They had spoken once, and that was tempting providence quite enough for one lifetime!

–

'I hears as your lot's been stirring things up,' Annie informed Maddy one morning during the week.

'What they done now?'

'Causing a rumpus up to the Church House. Took exception to that friend of yourn playing his fiddle and threatened to smash it over his head.'

'They didn't, did they?' Maddy asked in alarm.

'Didn't get no chance. The other folks at the inn was on them like a ton of bricks for spoiling the music. My, the fists and feet was flying, by all accounts. Didn't they say naught when they come home?'

'Not them.' Now she recalled it, they had been a bit sheepish. They had also sported an assortment of bruises among them, but that was nothing out of the ordinary.

'Some say as Sam Watkins, down to the Victoria and Albert, have paid them to start a fight up to the Church House, because he'm losing trade.'

'Not my lot!' Maddy shook her head emphatically. 'They don't need paying to cause trouble, they'm happy to do un for free.' She knew beyond any doubt that her brothers had not caused the fight to aid the rival inn. It was Patrick they had been after.

She heaved a sigh. Nothing had changed. Then she reconsidered. Things were different – she had changed. And she was not prepared to let her brothers' bullying come between her and Patrick. Through no fault of their own they had ruined one love in her life; they could not be allowed to ruin another deliberately...

She took in a deep breath, suddenly conscious of what she had been thinking. She had admitted it; although she scarcely knew him, she was falling in love with Patrick. It was quite an admission.

There was no future in it for her, even if he cared for her – which she doubted. Such a love could not come to anything because she was not free, despite her recent threats to her family. But that did not matter; she would cherish this love while she could and just live for the moment. It would be worth it.

Chapter Four

Davie entered the cottage like a whirlwind. 'What be there to eat?' he demanded, flinging himself on the settle in a tangle of lanky adolescent limbs. 'I be that starved my belly be stuck to my backbone.'

'The day you come in not starved be the day we orders your coffin,' said Maddy. 'Wash your hands and come to table.'

The order to wash hands would have been ignored if Maddy had not enforced her words with a prod from the wooden spoon she was holding.

'Aw, I don't have no need to wash, I habn't been nowhere dirty,' complained Davie, heading for the bowl of water nevertheless.

'You habn't been nowhere clean, neither, by the looks of you,' commented his sister. 'What've you been up to? Us've been waiting supper for you.'

'Down mill, larking about,' said Davie sitting down, his hands marginally cleaner than before. 'Us haven't half had some laughs. Daft Biddy came along looking for her childer, as usual, and for a joke I told her we'd seen them up Byter Mill. My, did her go! Her were like a bullet from – Ow!' he yelled as Maddy delivered him a sharp slap on the cheek. 'What were that for?'

'That were for tormenting a poor soul who'm enough to contend with,' declared Maddy angrily. 'Don't you think her'm suffering enough without you baiting her for your own sport?'

'I weren't the only one,' protested Davie.

'No, but you were the one as told her that lie. I suppose the others put you up to un.' Then seeing his shamefaced look, she spoke more calmly. 'Oh, Davie, when will you ever learn? You'm always letting folk egg you on. If they habn't got the stomach to do something themselves, they gets you to do it.'

'For goodness' sake stop getting on at the boy and let's eat,' complained Bart. 'I don't see what you'm fussing about, anyway.'

'Don't you?' demanded Maddy. 'You don't see naught wrong with teasing an unfortunate woman who'm already suffered so much it have turned her brain? Well, I do! I knows Davie didn't mean to be cruel, he wadn't brought up that way – he just don't think. That's what I were on at him for.'

'A lot of fuss about a daft fool,' Bart muttered. 'Be us going to eat tonight or bain't us?'

There was more Maddy could have said on the subject, but she held her tongue, turning her attention to cutting the bread. Davie's problem was that he always mixed with lads older than himself. He was so eager to be considered his friends' equal that he was ripe for any mischief anyone cared to suggest. All too often he was the one who was caught and punished, but it did not deter him.

Basically he was a good-hearted boy and it hurt Maddy to see him behaving so stupidly. She always felt that a firmer discipline than hers might have made a difference; but if Jack had any qualms about the way his youngest son's character was developing he did nothing about it.

Later that evening, when the others were out of earshot, Davie came up to her and said quietly, 'I wish I hadn't said that to old Biddy. It must've got her hopes up, mustn't it? Her'd have been terrible upset not to find her childer.'

'Now I thinks on it I wonders if you made much difference to the poor soul,' replied Maddy gently. 'Her'm that confused in her head there idn't no telling what affects her and what don't.'

'It would've been better if I hadn't said naught, though, wouldn't it?'

'It would,' Maddy agreed. 'If you'd just think first afore you does these things. You'm idn't stupid, you habn't got that excuse.'

'I don't know why I does them.' Davie shook his head regretfully. 'Afterwards I realises how daft I were. Perhaps I'll grow out of un.'

'Perhaps you will,' said Maddy, suppressing a smile, then, because he looked so woebegone, she gave him a hug. 'Of course you'm going to grow out of un. Starting tomorrow.'

Davie responded to her embrace and gave a quick grin, but he did not look very hopeful.

Lack of belief in himself, that was Davie's trouble. Maddy could sympathise with him. She had felt exactly the same way before she had met Patrick. It was extraordinary how meeting him had made such a difference in her life.

During the last few weeks the unthinkable had happened. She had begun to see Patrick quite regularly. At first it had been accidental, and he would greet her with that radiant smile of his and say, 'Why, Miss Maddy, how do we always come to the same place at the same time? It's quite uncanny.'

Gradually the accidental meetings had become deliberate. They were not walking out together, Maddy was quite firm with herself on that point. They simply met sometimes to talk. And how she loved to hear Patrick talk. There did not seem to be a single subject he was not knowledgeable about and could make fascinating. She was learning new things, seeing with new eyes. Sometimes she felt her brain was like a rusty old clock that, having seized up, was slowly grinding back into working order once more. It was as if her whole world was gradually expanding, and all because of Patrick.

One aspect of her widening world had come to an end. In spite of reading as slowly as she could to prolong the enjoyment, she had eventually finished *Great Expectations*. She handed it back to Patrick with thanks and a great sense of loss.

'It were a grand story, I loved every bit of un,' she said, 'even though I were terrified of un getting spoiled or damaged or something.'

'There was no need to be so worried. It's only a secondhand copy I bought for a few pence.'

'Idn't books terrible expensive, then?'

'Not necessarily. You can often pick up bargains if you don't mind a copy that is rather tattered. Just make sure that the pages are intact.'

A bargain was something that Maddy understood very well. She began to consider the exciting possibility that if she saved a few pennies from her egg money and what she got from the garden produce she might be able to buy herself a book.

While she was savouring this wonderful notion, a gust of wind caught her cotton sunbonnet. Only the string tied about her throat prevented it from blowing away completely. It dangled at the back of her head, leaving her wild hair to blow about in unruly confusion, her hairpins flying out in all directions.

'Oh darn!' she exclaimed irritably. 'I be going to have to go home looking a proper scarecrow.'

Rummaging hopefully through the grass, she retrieved one or two pins and the boxwood comb that was her single ornament. She was about to scoop her hair back from her face, twisting it in an attempt to get it under some sort of control, when Patrick put out a restraining hand.

'Don't,' he said. 'Please don't.'

She looked at him in surprise. The expression on his face was one of frank admiration.

'Magnificent,' he murmured. 'Truly magnificent.'

'What be?' she asked.

'Your hair.'

'My hair? You'm joking.'

He ignored her comment. 'Such a superb colour, like ripe corn in the sun. Do you know what you remind me of, sitting there, your hair blowing free? A mermaid. With your wild locks and your incredible sea-green eyes you might be a mythical creature emerging from the sea to lure some poor sailor to his doom. Tresses like yours should not be brought under control. They should be free as the breeze and the roaring ocean.'

Maddy did not laugh at his mad fancies, she was too fascinated by them. The gentle caressing of his fingers through her hair was beginning to have a mesmeric effect.

'But perhaps I was wrong.' He was looking at her critically, almost impersonally. Then suddenly he lifted two thick strands from her temples, and with a 'Yes, that's it!' swept them softly away from her face, fastening them, she knew not how, behind her head. The rest of her hair still hung down her back and with deft movements he spread it about her shoulders in a wild riot of tight waves.

'Oh yes!' He breathed the words with utter satisfaction. 'You are no longer the mermaid, you are a damsel from an ancient time. With your disordered tresses you might be looking at me out of some medieval tapestry.'

Maddy did not dare to speak. There was a rapt absorption about him as he viewed her rearranged hair that made her reluctant to break the spell. Tentatively she put a hand up to her head to feel what he had done, but he gently stopped her.

'Don't spoil the effect,' he said softly. 'Do you know, in London at this minute there are famous artists who would fight one another for the privilege of painting you exactly as you are.'

Maddy did not know how to reply. She thought she was used to Patrick and his fancy talk, but this was different. There was an intensity about his words which stirred her emotions.

'What, sitting here in a field with my dusty boots?' she asked at last, to break the awkward silence.

'Yes, field, dusty boots and all. And with your hair about you in a glorious golden aura. I can think of a name for such a painting of you at this moment: "The Rustic Damozel". That would be perfect.'

Maddy did not know what an aura was, or a rustic damozel, but it did not matter. Before she could ask for an explanation he leaned forward and kissed her.

For Maddy it was like an explosion of light within her. She had been kissed before, in the far off days when Rob Bradworthy had courted her, but his robust smacks had been nothing like this. In Patrick's kiss there was gentleness and promise of a passion that went far beyond her comprehension.

'There, I would not have dared take such a liberty with the wild sea creature.' Patrick caressed her cheek with his fingers. 'But I fancy my gentle damozel will be more forgiving. You did not mind?'

Past speech, Maddy shook her head.

'Good.' Patrick drew her close and kissed her again. Perhaps she should have resisted, it would have been the proper thing to do, but Maddy could no more have pushed him away than she could have flown with the birds in the sky. She responded, matching warmth with warmth. Only gradually did reality intrude and she eventually broke away.

'Us… us shouldn't have done that,' she said breathlessly.

'You are having regrets?' He looked concerned.

'No.' She shook her head and a slow smile of happiness spread across her face. 'I said us shouldn't have done it. I didn't say naught about being sorry.'

He threw back his head and laughed, his white teeth gleaming in the sun.

'Oh, Maddy, you are so much better than any picture,' he said. 'No painted rural damozel would be blessed with such honesty and humour. But what are you doing?' he finished with a cry of alarm as her hands went up to her hair once more. 'You can't spoil my handiwork.'

'I've got to go home and I can't be seen like this,' she pointed out. 'What'd folks think?'

'I suppose you're right,' he agreed reluctantly. 'Here, let me do it.' He gathered together the hair that was strewn across her shoulders and somehow twisted it into a knot at the nape of her neck. It felt softer than her usual scraped-back style, yet comfortably secure. Patrick nodded at her with approval. 'Not quite as delightful as my wild mermaid or my rural damozel, but those creatures are for my eyes alone. As you are now will do very creditably for other people.'

Maddy did not feel as if she walked home; she floated. She felt quite unlike the dull boring Maddy she had always envisaged herself to be. She was now a woman capable of love and, miraculously, worth loving. When she reached home she was glad that neither Annie nor Elsie Crowther were about. She felt that her new being was too recent and delicate to bear scrutiny just yet.

Gazing in the mirror, she could barely recognise the reflection which stared back. She had never noticed before that her hair was indeed the colour of ripe wheat, she had always been more concerned about its wiriness. With the way Patrick had arranged it, its wildness had somehow been tamed into waves. Riotous waves it was true, but very pleasing ones nevertheless. With the softer style, her cheekbones were no longer gaunt and bony, as she had always thought, but more rounded, and in turn it emphasised the colour of her eyes. The face looking back at her was a long way from the doll-like features so fashionable at the moment; it was striking, unique, a face that was ageless in its beauty.

'You'm certainly something different,' she informed herself. 'I idn't quite sure what, but it be a great improvement on what you was before.'

It was inevitable that those about her would notice the change in her – the outward change, at least. Her brothers' reactions were, 'What you'm done up like a dog's dinner for?' while Annie's gentler comments were, 'My, what a change – but it suits you,' said with a twinkle in her eye.

Maddy was certain that not even the ever-observant Annie could truly perceive the changes that were happening inside her.

'I knows now how a butterfly feels when it gets out of one of they chrysalises,' she told Patrick. ''Tis like being a completely different creature.' Then she felt embarrassed at having expressed such a flight of fancy.

But although Patrick laughed at her, it was with pleasure, not ridicule. 'Are you happy at the change? That's the main thing,' he said.

'Oh yes.' Two words had never been spoken with such sincerity.

'Then we must mark the occasion. I have the ideal gift for you.'

'A gift for me?' Maddy was surprised and pleased.

'Yes, it is something very old.' From his pocket he drew a small wash-leather bag. Inside was a silver ring embossed with a mask of a man with two faces.

'He's not a very handsome chap,' said Patrick. 'But he doesn't need to be because he is a god. The old Romans worshipped him and called him Janus. He gave his name to the month of January. Looking in two directions as he does, the Romans made him their god of beginnings and endings. That is why I am giving him to you, to symbolise the beginning of the new Maddy. May she be happier than the old one, though she could not be more delightful.'

'Thank you.' Maddy's fingers flexed over the gift in a gesture of pleasure. 'I habn't never had naught like this before.'

'Nor are you likely to have, it is really ancient. Older than the church, or the village yew tree, or anything I can think of.'

'Oh...' Maddy was impressed by such antiquity. But when she said fervently, 'I'll treasure this always,' it was because Patrick had given her the ring, not because of its age. 'I'll put un on a ribbon and wear un round my neck,' she said.

'Not on your hand?'

She smiled. 'Some of the new Maddy's problems be the same as the old Maddy's – menfolk as'd want to know the why and wherefore of everything.'

'In that case, you would be wiser to wear it on a ribbon,' said Patrick gravely. 'For my sake as well as yours. I have had one set-to with your brothers. It's not an experience I wish to repeat. Though if they would crown me with my fiddle merely for talking to you, what would they consider to be a suitable punishment for this?' Taking her in his arms he kissed her.

It amazed Maddy how a gesture so gentle could convey so much emotion and arouse in her such a welter of feeling.

'Oh lucky day, when I came to this place,' he whispered. 'When I think how easily I might have missed meeting you. If I had come to the village by some other route, or at another time...'

'Don't,' she pleaded, her hand gently covering his lips. 'Don't think of un, 'tis too terrible.' She shuddered at the horror of it. A world with no Patrick! It would be like a world with no sun. True, in never having known him she would not have realized what she was missing, but that was worse, somehow. Not to know what it was to feel as she felt at this moment; not to know the overwhelming happiness, the joy of loving and being loved. Such an existence would have been bitter and empty indeed. Her one regret was that she could not tell Patrick how she truly felt. He could say things to her that were so beautiful they brought tears to her eyes, but she could not reply in kind. She did not have the words.

One day, she promised herself, one day I'll be able to say everything that be inside me, and then he'll hear about love as he habn't never heard it before. They poets and writers he talks about, they won't be naught to me, because I'll be telling what be real.

That day was some way off, but she had made one step towards it by buying a book; during a trip to Totnes market she had plucked up her courage and gone into a secondhand bookshop. Far from being proud and haughty, the proprietor had been most helpful and for her meagre tuppence had found her a copy of *Jane Eyre*. Battered, dog-eared and with its one surviving cover hanging by a few threads, Maddy carried it home, astounded by her own audacity and conscience-stricken that she had spent hard-earned money so frivolously.

That afternoon she sat down on the bench in the garden and began to read. Within five minutes she decided that she had never laid out two pennies to better effect. Within ten minutes she was so absorbed she did not care what she had paid.

'Gawd help us, maid, be you'm deaf all of a sudden?' Annie's insistent tones penetrated her consciousness.

'Hullo, Annie,' she said, not happy at being disturbed. 'You'm wanting something?'

'That be more like it.' Her friend looked quite relieved. 'I were some worried there for a moment. Three times I spoke and got not one flicker from you. I feared you was having a fit or summat.'

'No, I be just reading,' Maddy said, adding half proudly, half apologetically, 'I bought a book up to Totnes market this morning.'

'You never did!' Annie was astounded. 'What be it about, then?'

'It starts with this young maid from up-country going to school, and poor little soul, your heart bleeds for her...' Maddy noticed the immediate interest in Annie's face. 'Tell you what, you sit yourself down and I'll read aloud, shall I? Start from the beginning?'

'Won't you mind going over the same bit of story again?' Annie asked, but already she had settled herself on the bench.

'No, there was one or two long words as I didn't get first time round. I can't read for long, mind. I wants to clear out the fowl-house this afternoon, afore the menfolk gets back.'

'That'll do me fine.' Annie sat waiting expectantly.

Maddy began to read; and the magic of *Jane Eyre* enfolded the pair of them.

A shrill steam whistle made them both jump.

''Tis never that late!' protested Maddy aghast.

'It must be, the *Newcomin* be just arriving.'

Round the bend in the river came the steamer, her paddles already going into reverse to slow her down, her whistle summoning William to fetch the passengers who wanted to be put ashore at Duncannon.

Maddy and Annie looked at one another shamefacedly, then they burst out laughing.

'A whole afternoon us've wasted,' Annie declared. 'And shall I tell you what? I don't care! That book be proper grand. I don't recall when I've enjoyed aught so much.' And she wiped away the tears that had been streaming down her face for much of the reading.

'Yes, you looks un,' grinned Maddy. 'But I agrees. Once you starts 'tis hard to stop.'

'I never realised what a fine thing reading was. Takes you right out of yourself, don't un?' Annie was suddenly regretful. 'I wishes I had the skill. I can write my name and a few bits of things like that, but naught fancy. You'll be reading more of that book sometime, maybe?'

'Yes, tomorrow if I gets a few minutes. I'll give you a call, shall I?'

'I'd like that, indeed I would,' Annie said, beaming. 'I be desperate to know how poor little Jane gets on.'

'One thing,' Maddy called to Annie as her Mend made her slow way to her own door. 'Tomorrow you'd best bring your alarm clock with you.'

'I will,' promised Annie grinning. 'Us can't keep depending on the *Newcomin* to rouse us, eh?'

Maddy's fowls had never been cleaned out with such speed as they were that afternoon. They squawked and grumbled as she raked out the muck and put down fresh straw, moving them from house to run and back again as she did so. Because of their noise she did not hear anyone approach, and as she turned back to the cottage she was surprised to see the solid figure of Constable Vallance sitting on the bench outside the door.

'I be sorry, Constable, I didn't knowd you was there,' she said.

'That's all right, Maddy. I didn't want to disturb you, seeing as you was busy.'

From past experience she knew that his arrival in full uniform boded ill.

'Is there aught I can do for you?' she asked. 'A drop of cider or a cup of tea?' Despite the fact that his presence was ominous, she knew he was a fair man. It did no harm to treat him with courtesy.

'No, thank you, my dear, not when I'm on duty.' At the word duty Maddy's heart sank. As he continued it sank further. 'Your brothers out fishing, are they?' he asked. 'Then if you'd just give them a message, please. I'd like to have a word with them. Straight after tea'd do.'

'What be they done now?' asked Maddy with resignation.

'Same as usual, by the sounds of it. Had too much scrumpy and gone daft.' He rose to leave. 'Be sure to tell them, won't you? And by after tea I don't mean halfway through the night. I'm not using up constabulary candles on their account.'

He would say no more than that, and Maddy was left fuming with impatience and anxiety until her father and brothers returned.

'Constable Vallance was here,' she informed them.

'What the hell did he want?' asked Jack.

'He says he wants to see the boys straight after tea. What you'm been up to?' she demanded, swinging her attention towards her brothers.

'How should us knows?' said Bart with a shrug. 'Didn't he say more than that?'

'No, just that you'm not to be late.'

'If he can't be bothered to say what 'tis about I reckons us can't be bothered to go.' Bart pulled off his boots and let them fall with an exaggerated thud. 'He wants us then let un damned well come back for us!'

''Tis your business,' said Maddy calmly. She knew that his words were mere bravado. Straight after tea, her brothers would be heading up the track to the village and the police house.

Sure enough they departed as soon as their meal was over.

'You'm idn't going with them?' she asked Jack.

'They'm big enough to get into trouble, they'm big enough to get out of un,' was his phlegmatic reply.

It was late, long past dark, before the four of them returned. Their faces were grim, and Bart's was suffused with anger.

'That Whitcomb!' he exclaimed, throwing himself into the chair nearest the fire. 'That bloody high and mighty Whitcomb! I'll swing for him one of these days, I swear I will.'

'Why, what've happened?' demanded Maddy.

'He'm bringing us afore the magistrates up to Totnes, that's what've happened. And for naught! Absolutely naught!'

'It must've been for something,' Maddy persisted.

'Us was only having a joke,' cried Davie. 'Can't the fellow take a joke?'

In her brief encounter with Cal Whitcomb, one thing that had struck Maddy about him was his sense of humour. Knowing her brothers' taste in jokes, she began to fear the worst.

'What did you do?' she asked.

'Us threw some rubbish over his hedge,' said Davie. 'As us were coming out of the Church House the other night there were this dead cat in the hedge and us reckoned it'd make a nice present for Cal Whitcomb.'

Despite the outcome, the episode managed to bring a grin to her brothers' faces.

'But us decided one mangy cat carcass wadn't much of a gift,' Lew continued the story. 'So us got a couple of sacks from the back of the inn and us had a look round to see what else us could find. Then us went out to Oakwood and slung the lot into the garden.'

'And you'm being brought before the magistrates for that?' Maddy was appalled. It was a stupid prank, and she had no illusions about her brothers' state of sobriety after leaving the Church House, but calling in the constable for such a petty offence seemed extreme.

'Us didn't even leave the sacks,' said Davie indignantly. 'Us put them back where us got them.'

'That be disgraceful!' declared Maddy. 'Father, you'm to go up to Oakwood tomorrow and give Cal Whitcomb some straight talking. He'm to withdraw the case against the boys. You make him, Father.'

'I idn't setting foot on Oakwood land!' protested Jack. 'Not unless us be moving in, bag and baggage.'

'You could talk to him,' she insisted. 'Maybe he did un in the heat of the moment. He'm had time to cool down.' She nearly let slip that she had found him a reasonable man.

'Talk to Cal Whitcomb?' cried Bart, before his father could answer. 'Be you'm off your head, wench?'

'Besides, I think 'tis out of Cal Whitcomb's hands,' put in Lew. Of the four he looked the least indignant and the most troubled. 'Us've each to pay a bond, to make sure us don't go traipsing off afore the hearing.'

'A bond? How much? And who said so?'

'Fifteen shillings each. And 'twere the squire as said it,' said Lew quietly.

'Fifteen shillings each! Three whole pounds! How are we to pay that much?' Maddy was appalled, then gradually other thoughts began to creep into her mind. If they had been brought before the squire, the local Justice of the Peace, then there had to be more to the prank than they had admitted.

Lew saw the expression on her face and spoke up. 'It were dark, you understand, and us couldn't see everything as us was putting in the sacks. Us didn't realise us had picked up some yew with some old hedge trimmings.'

'Did that matter? You just slung un in the garden.' Maddy was bewildered.

'We thought un were part of the garden. As un happened t'were a bit of an orchard for the house, like, and...'

'And?'

'Well, us didn't know in the dark, us couldn't see them, but Cal Whitcomb had three of his best cows in there with their calves.'

'Oh no!' Maddy gave a groan. 'Did they eat the yew? Was they poisoned?'

'One did, and it came close to dying; by all accounts it be fair enough now.'

Maddy let out a long sigh of relief. It was going to be bad enough finding the three pounds bail. If they had had to pay out for a cow into the bargain she did not know how they would have managed. Slowly she went over the events in her mind.

'As I sees it 'twere an accident,' she said. 'Oh, you was daft to get drunk and throw the rubbish, you deserves a clip across the ear for that, the lot of you. But the yew and the cow, that weren't deliberate.'

'You try telling that to Cal Whitcomb,' snapped Bart. 'From what was said tonight he'm had the ear of the squire good and proper. Us idn't going to get no justice, I can tell you that. They farmers and landowners, they stick together. When us gets up to Totnes afore they magistrates they'm going to take one look at us and pronounce us guilty.'

'It won't be as bad as that,' said Maddy. 'You'll be let off with a caution, you'll see.' But in her heart of hearts she feared he might be right.

–

The atmosphere in the cottage was strained in the weeks until the brothers appeared before the magistrates, with nerves frayed and tempers short. Ever since the incident in the churchyard, Maddy had harboured feelings of guilt because of Cal Whitcomb. Although she would never have admitted it, she had found it hard to see him as the ogre her family thought him. However, his persecution of her brothers had changed all that. Now she felt able to regard him with the intense dislike proper in a Shillabeer.

She had never expected to speak to him again, but one day they met head on. Normally they would have passed by each other without even a nod of recognition. On this occasion she stepped into the middle of the lane, causing him to rein in his horse abruptly.

'It's a dangerous habit, jumping out in front of horses,' he said.

He towered above her on his chestnut gelding, immaculate as ever. He might have been a gentleman out hacking instead of a plain farmer doing the rounds of his stock fields. Imposing though he looked, Maddy refused to be intimidated.

'I didn't jump out,' she retorted. 'And if you bain't able to control your horse you'm no business riding about the countryside. I wants a word with you.'

'I think I can guess what about.'

'No doubt you can. You'm sending my brothers afore the magistrate for something that was naught but a stupid prank. I knows they shouldn't have done it,' she said swiftly as he opened his mouth to speak. 'There idn't no one as knows better'n me how daft they can get when they'm had a drop too much scrumpy. But they didn't mean no harm.'

'Your loyalty does you credit.' He spoke coldly. 'I doubt if anyone else in the village regards your brothers as delightful rogues, bent only upon innocent mischief.'

'Well, 'tis true!' she exclaimed, stung by his tone. 'They didn't mean no real harm.'

'I call poisoning a good cow real harm, even if you don't.'

She wished he would get down off his horse. She was at a definite disadvantage, having to look up to him, but she was not going to let that deter her.

'That were an accident. They shouldn't have flung the muck over your hedge, there idn't no excuse for that, but they was only having a bit of fun. It were dark and they didn't know about the yew being in the rubbish, and they had no notion there was cows in your orchard.'

'Oh really, Miss Shillabeer.' He raised his eyes skywards in disbelief. 'Even allowing for your sisterly affection, you can't have been taken in by that story.'

'Be you calling me a liar?' she demanded.

'Certainly not.' His response was instant and genuine.

'Then it be my brothers you don't believe?'

'Now you are getting closer to it.'

She was swept with indignation. 'Who do you think you be, calling the Shillabeers liars? You'm naught but a jumped-up Whitcomb.'

'I'm also the man who sat up through the night with a very sick cow because of those delightful rogues, your brothers. It was a miracle she didn't die, yew is usually fatal. Apart from everything else, how does one explain to a poor dumb creature – in agony that its sufferings were only a bit of fun? Tell me that.'

'The boys didn't intend no creatures to suffer. They'm good-hearted really.'

'For pity's sake stop this stupid defence of your wretched brothers before it turns my stomach!' Unexpectedly he dismounted in a single, swift movement, one hand still holding his horse's reins. 'Perhaps I can get some sense into you now that we are face to face,' he said. 'You may believe those wretches are innocent but no one else does. Since you clearly need convincing let me place the evidence before you, ignoring such minor matters as the fact that your brothers were heard offering drunken threats against me and my property. For a start I find it hard to believe they didn't know the cattle were there – even at night cows are not particularly quiet creatures. Also, for your brothers to pretend

65

they thought the orchard was part of our garden is sheer nonsense. Are they trying to persuade folk that they have never gone past Oakwood, not even to gaze at what they consider should be theirs? And why bother to throw rubbish over a hedge? If they did not intend it to do damage of some sort?'

'They must—'

'Pray let me continue,' he snapped. 'You are quick enough to shout insults at me. Please listen to the truth about your brothers for once. We haven't considered the question of the yew. Have you any idea which is the closest yew tree to my farm?' Maddy shook her head. 'Then let me tell you, for I took the time and trouble to investigate. The nearest is the one in the churchyard, best part of a mile away, and scarcely on a direct route between the Church House and Oakwood.'

'Maybe they went into the churchyard looking for rubbish and picked up some yew accidental like,' Maddy suggested.

'George, the sexton, is most particular not to leave yew lying about on the rubbish heap for fear children or animals might get to it. When he has to get rid of any he either burns it immediately or stores it in a separate sack in his shed until a suitable opportunity. He told me so himself. He also told me something interesting: he had half a sack of yew trimmings in his shed until last week, then someone broke in and stole it.'

'Why should that have aught to do with my brothers?' Maddy demanded indignantly. 'Be you'm saying they sought it out deliberate?'

'Who else was abroad with yew in a sack last week? Has the entire village taken a fancy to wandering about carrying bits of yew tree?'

'Don't take that sneering tone with me,' retorted Maddy, incensed. 'I idn't impressed. And I don't sees why it should have been my brothers. They wadn't no more likely to know there was yew in George's shed than anyone else.'

'They weren't any less likely, either. You can be blind if you wish, but I don't need persuading.'

'You'm got a down on the boys, that's what 'tis. It wouldn't matter if the Archangel Gabriel swore they was innocent, you'd still reckon they'm guilty.'

'Because they are,' retorted Cal. 'Prison's where they'll be if I get my way. They think they're the lords of creation, yet they're nothing but a nuisance to the entire village with their drunkenness and rowdy ways. A week or two in jail would drum some sense into them. I give you fair warning that you can pass on to your precious brothers: I mean to see they get the stiffest sentence possible.'

He swung himself into the saddle and, urging his horse into a swift trot, left Maddy standing in the lane.

For a while she was too furious to move as angry thoughts rushed through her mind. Everything detrimental she had ever heard about him was true – and she could not recall a single person having a good word to say about him; the best she had heard was that he was hard-working.

'An ass can be hard-working. That idn't naught marvellous!' She was so angry that she spoke the words aloud. The sound of her own voice on the empty air brought her to her senses. She had tackled Cal Whitcomb and given him a piece of her mind; she had better things to do than waste any more time on him.

As she went on her way she wondered whether to mention the encounter to the menfolk or not. Upon consideration she decided against it. The atmosphere at home was fraught enough as it was. She had had her say, let that be enough.

–

When her brothers were finally summonsed to go before the magistrates at Totnes she stayed at home. Despite her protestations, Jack stayed too.

'Us be having to spend out for they four to go, that be more than enough,' he had stated doggedly. 'Us bain't be made of money, maid.'

'But how do us knows the verdict?' she protested.

'The boys'll tell us when they get back, of course.'

'But if they don't?' She hardly liked to put her worst fears into words.

'Then they won't come home, and us'll knows that way. Constable Vallance'll tell us the details tomorrow, I dare say. 'Sides, there idn't no magistrate'll send them to prison for flinging rubbish.'

Maddy was not so sure. Her father had not seen Cal Whitcomb's grim expression. Although she had been determined to put the confrontation with Cal from her mind, she had found it impossible. What if he proved as good as his word and had her brothers sent to prison? The humiliation and shame would be terrible, for them and the whole family. There were practical considerations too: how would they manage financially? Her father could not manage the net, and a week or a fortnight without income would be a terrible strain.

That day of waiting seemed interminable. Not even the pages of *Jane Eyre* could take her mind off her impatience or her anxiety. It was with intense relief that she heard her brothers' footsteps approaching the cottage.

'Well?' she demanded. 'What happened?'

'We was fined ten shillings each and bound over to keep the peace,' growled Bart.

Maddy let out a sigh of relief. 'I was affeared it might be prison,' she breathed.

''Tis no thanks to Cal Whitcomb it weren't,' Bart retorted. 'If ever a man were set upon getting us jailed it were him.'

'He nearly managed un too,' said Lew. 'The magistrates hummed and hawed while he went on with some nonsense about someone breaking into the sexton's shed. In the end they decided the evidence wasn't strong enough, but it were touch and go. Us could see it on their faces. As if any of us knowd old George kept yew clippings in his shed.'

'Where's us to find another two pounds on top of aught else? That's what I wants to know,' said Jack.

'Us've got to find un or it'll be prison and no mistake,' replied Bart sourly.

'You'm got your bail money back, though, habn't you?' asked Maddy.

'That be gone already,' Bart retorted. 'Us had to pay costs, and such.'

And no doubt some scrumpy to drown your sorrows, thought Maddy silently. Aloud she said, ''Tis going to be kettle broth for everyone for a spell, unless you catches your supper. There idn't going to be money for aught better.'

'And all because of Cal Whitcomb!' Bart spat. 'He idn't satisfied with taking our birthright, he'm out to persecute us too!'

Maddy nodded her head in agreement. After the incident with Victoria Fitzherbert, she had harboured the flickering hope that perhaps the old feud had run its course and that it was time to let it die. Not any longer. After the vindictive way Cal Whitcomb had gone after her brothers, the feud was as alive and bitter as ever.

Chapter Five

'Tell me, who owns the orchards right in the middle of the village?' asked Victoria. 'Is it Farmer Churchward?'

The housemaid paused in her dusting and bobbed a curtsey. 'Oh no, miss. That be Farmer Whitcomb's land,' she replied.

'Is that so?' Victoria looked vaguely interested. 'There is a jenny donkey in one of them with the dearest little foal. I wonder if Farmer – Farmer Whitcomb, you say? – might sell it to me when it is weaned.'

'He might, miss,' replied the surprised housemaid. Miss Victoria wasn't usually one to be friendly with the servants. Spurred on by her young mistress's unexpected affability she added, 'But the price won't be cheap. They say he drives a hard bargain, does Farmer Whitcomb.'

'Does he indeed? In that case, perhaps I won't bother.' Victoria wandered away, leaving the housemaid to get on with her work. She had not been interested in the foal, that had been a mere subterfuge. What she had been after was information about Cal Whitcomb.

The local gentry were slow in forgiving the Fitzherberts for Victoria's misdemeanour; the mantelpiece at the White House remained remarkably devoid of pasteboard invitations. But while her mother might weep and her father curse, Victoria amused herself with her pursuit of Cal Whitcomb.

She planned her campaign with the precision of a general at war. It was obvious that 'chance' encounters would be the only way she would meet him, and to do that she had to know as much about him as possible. For the first time she was beginning to appreciate the benefit of having local people as servants. Most of them had been hired along with the house, and now they were providing her with a host of invaluable scraps of information.

Thanks to her cunning she knew the extent of the Whitcomb land, and much about the man himself. He was efficient, and kept to a routine as rigidly as was possible in the country.

'Does the rounds of his land every day, does Mr Whitcomb,' the gardener informed her in an accent she could barely comprehend. 'Goes round both his father's land down to Church Farm and his mother's land up to Oakwood near enough every day. There idn't many as still does that. The best muck on the land be the farmer's boot, that's what he believes, begging your pardon, miss.'

Armed with this information, Victoria did not need to take many rides into the countryside to establish when she was most likely to encounter Cal Whitcomb. For a while she contented herself with giving only the frostiest of salutes, which Farmer Whitcomb, in all courtesy, was obliged to acknowledge. The grim lack of enthusiasm with which he bowed in return did not escape her notice.

Little do you know it, Mr Clodhopper Whitcomb, but you will soon change your tune, she vowed.

It was like angling for a fish. At the moment she was no more than trailing the bait in the water by these seemingly accidental meetings – accidental and not too frequent; she did not want to frighten off her quarry too soon. Before long, though, she would begin dangling the bait in earnest, and then the fun would begin, for her at least.

'Victoria, my love, where can you be going, dressed like that?' asked Mrs Fitzherbert, encountering her daughter in the hall one day.

'I am going walking, Mama. Have you any objections?'

'It is your dress, my love. Don't you consider it to be somewhat – somewhat brief?'

'Not at all, Mama. This is the fashionable length for walking dresses this year.'

'In Hyde Park perhaps.' Mrs Fitzherbert looked doubtfully at her daughter's outfit. The two-piece in blue barathea was certainly attractive, and the darker braid trim on the fitted jacket made it very elegant, but it was the shortness of the wide skirt that she had doubts about. 'But isn't it rather... short for the countryside? My love, your ankles are clearly visible.'

'What could be more practical for these messy lanes?' demanded Victoria. 'You know the trouble it is getting this red mud off hems, the colour stains so. Besides, I understand Princess Alexandra wears skirts as short as this for walking.'

'Oh, if Princess Alexandra wears them...' Mrs Fitzherbert gave way, though still sounding uncertain.

'If you have no more to say on the matter, Mama, I'll be on my way.' Victoria did not wait for her mother's further comments, she was already making for the front door, her maidservant in her wake. Although her skirt was less than a crinoline its hooped fullness swayed provocatively.

Her mother watched her go with misgivings. If only Victoria were not so headstrong. Her skirt did look indecently short, but if Princess Alexandra wore skirts above the ankles...

Had Mrs Fitzherbert given the matter more thought she would have realised that there was not much mud about. It was an exceptionally dry year and the lanes and footpaths were not at all muddy – as Victoria well knew. That was why she had chosen to make a circuit of Oakwood Farm on foot for a change, wearing a provocatively short skirt and displaying neatly turned ankles. If she should come face to face with Farmer Whitcomb she was determined to be looking her best.

Her first tour of the lanes surrounding Oakwood was a dismal failure. The sole living creature she passed was an elderly dog taking itself for a leisurely stroll. As she set off round again there was a faint groan of dismay from her maid trailing behind.

Mary was one of the few servants the Fitzherberts had brought with them. She had been afforded this privilege because, as well as being good at her job, she had managed to weather the storms of Victoria's uncertain temper for severed years. In addition, if she had been turned off, the Fitzherberts would have been obliged to pay her back wages, something they regarded as a totally unnecessary expense. At that moment her London-bred feet were finding the stony trackway uncomfortable and tiring.

'Can't we stop for a rest, please, miss?' she begged. 'There's a nice grassy bit there that'd do.'

Victoria's first reaction was to refuse, then second thoughts suggested that to pause might be a good idea. It was quite likely that Farmer Whitcomb would come this way, and if he did, there was a better chance of hearing his approach if she were sitting quietly.

'Very well,' she replied. 'But for goodness' sake keep quiet while we rest. I am in no mood for your idle chatter.'

Mary, who had hardly spoken on the walk, kept her feelings to herself as she helped her mistress to sit as decorously as possible, then she sank down thankfully herself.

In silence they stayed there for five minutes, ten, fifteen… Victoria consulted the small enamelled watch pinned to her bosom. Another few minutes and she would return home.

It was then the regular clip-clop of hooves reached her ears. There was no guarantee that it was Farmer Whitcomb, of course, but she had her fingers crossed. At the same moment the elderly dog appeared from the other end of the lane, sniffing its way contentedly along the hedge.

Victoria rose, pulling the reluctant Mary with her. Impatiently she waited to see who the approaching rider might be. Her hopes were answered. It was Calland Whitcomb, on his chestnut gelding. At the sight of her he slowed his horse to a walk, intending to pass by with nothing more than a bow from the saddle. Victoria, however, had other ideas.

'Mr Whitcomb, if you please, will you be kind enough to help me?' she asked, looking up at him.

Cal brought his horse to a halt. 'Certainly, Miss Fitzherbert, if I can,' he said cautiously.

'It is the dog,' said Victoria. 'It makes me nervous.'

They looked in the direction of the animal which was now having a comfortable scratch. As an example of ferocious beast it was a pretty unlikely specimen.

Cal gave a cough to cover his snort of disbelief and said, 'It's only one of my farm dogs. He's quite harmless.'

'Are you sure?' Victoria was careful not to let any unsightly frown pucker her brow. 'One hears such appalling stories of rabid dogs.'

'I promise you he's not rabid. Simply rather old and somewhat flea-ridden,' Cal assured her.

'Then it is safe to pass him?'

'Quite safe,' replied Cal gravely. 'However, since he bothers you, I will remove him at once.'

'I would be so grateful if you would.' Victoria looked purposefully at his riding crop, but it remained idly in Cal's hand. He had no need of it.

'Home, boy!' he ordered. 'Home!'

The dog's response was obedient if slow. It rose and wagged its tail at the familiar voice, approached Cal's gelding and sniffed round its hooves in greeting, then finding a gap in the hedge dutifully climbed through it and ambled homewards.

'There,' said Cal. 'The danger is over.'

'Thank you, sir.' Victoria's upward gaze grew more limpid. 'I find dogs very frightening. It is silly of me, I suppose, but I've always been so, haven't I, Mary?'

'Yes, miss,' replied Mary with a complete lack of conviction.

'You surprise me, Miss Fitzherbert. I would have thought very little frightened you,' replied Cal dryly. 'However, after such a major fright will you permit me to escort you on your way? Or if you feel faint after your experience I could fetch transport to take you home.'

For a moment Victoria was tempted, then she noted the wry disbelief lurking in Cal Whitcomb's eyes. He was no fool, he recognised the artificiality of the situation. It did not do to push too hard too soon. She decided she had sufficiently exploited the circumstances for the time being.

'No, thank you, sir, you have already been more than kind. Pray do not let me detain you any longer. I'm sure you are frightfully busy.'

'If you are certain I can be of no further assistance? Then I will bid you farewell.' Raising his hat to her he rode away.

Victoria set off for home well satisfied with her day. She had made contact with Cal Whitcomb and had carried out a reasonable conversation with him. From now on he could no longer pass her with just a curt greeting; the rules of common courtesy would not allow it. As far as she was concerned, the enemy had been engaged, an odd way of regarding the start of a flirtation perhaps, but it was exactly how she felt.

—

As the spring days lengthened Maddy's regular trips into the village were always tinged with happy anticipation at the prospect of seeing Patrick. She did not mind that they would exchange no more than a smile and a few words, that was enough to feed her love until they could be together in a more private, secluded place. On this particular occasion she was disappointed to see no sign of him, although she made a quite unnecessary detour past the Church House Inn. By the time she had started her shopping she was conscious of an atmosphere of subdued excitement hanging over the place.

'What's been happening?' she asked Mrs Cutmore who kept the grocery shop.

'Oh lor', 'tis been like a tinker's wedding yer and no mistake,' the shopkeeper replied, evidently relishing the recent drama. 'Yelling at each other, they was; and the language! I tells you I had to make my youngsters stop up their ears for fear of what they'd hear. Fancy, two grown men quarrelling like that. I was certain they'd come to blows, so I sent our Johnny for Constable Vallance. He sorted them out good and proper.'

'But who?' demanded Maddy. 'And what be un all about?'

'Harry Ford and Sam Watkins, that's who,' Mrs Cutmore said. 'And the reason was that incomer, who'm such a friend of youm. You knows as he'm been working up to the Church House? Of course you do! Who better? Well, seemingly Sam Watkins have been trying to persuade him to go down the Victoria and Albert instead. Offered him another half-a-crown a week. My, I wishes someone'd offer me another two and six for doing naught different. Any road, Harry Ford got to hear of un, and you knows what his temper be like. Stormed down towards the Victoria and Albert he did, like a man possessed, but he met Sam coming up the hill. That was how they come to have their set-to out in the street with the world and his wife looking on.'

'And what happened?' asked Maddy, anxious for Patrick's well-being.

'Naught, as far as I knows. Constable Vallance sent the pair of them on their way with hefty fleas in their ears, telling them not to be two such gurt fools.'

'And Patrick?' persisted Maddy.

'Patrick? Oh, the incomer. Last I heard he were still serving up Church House, same as usual. Makes you wonder what be there as is worth giving up an extra half-crown for.' Mrs Cutmore gave her a sly prod in the ribs, then suddenly remembered Maddy's relationship with the young man and looked embarrassed. 'Now then, was that a large block of salt you was wanting, my dear?' she asked hurriedly.

Maddy neither heard her nor noticed her gaffe, she was too concerned for Patrick. As the unwitting cause of trouble, she hoped he would suffer no backlash.

'Beg pardon, Mrs Cutmore?' She became aware of the shopkeeper waiting expectantly.

'A block of salt you asked for. Would that be a large or a small?'

'Large, please.'

Maddy paid for her own purchases along with the few goods she had got for Annie, and set off home. She was constantly on the lookout for any sign of Patrick, but there was none, and a niggling nameless fear worried at her. Then, as she passed the back of the Church House, she heard Mrs Ford's voice call, 'Patrick, boy, be you'm going to shift this barrel today or next Christmas?'

His voice replied cheerily, 'For you, Mrs Ford, I'll do it this instant.'

Immediately Maddy relaxed and began to smile. His reply was typical, full of charm and humour, even when the subject was nothing more remarkable than a barrel. She smiled at her own foolishness too. Why on earth should Patrick leave the village? The two landlords had nearly come to blows because they both wanted his services, not because they wanted to get rid of him. Walking along the lane, her fingers strayed to the shape of the Janus ring Patrick had given her, hidden beneath the calico of her dress. She had bought some ribbon specially to hang it about her neck, blue ribbon, chosen because it was exactly the same colour as Patrick's eyes. She smiled at her choice. A few weeks ago such an idea would never have occurred to her, but a few weeks ago she had not met Patrick and had not experienced the new awakening of her senses.

Listening to him, she had become aware of the thickness of her own accent. Patrick had laughed when she had said she wanted to speak like he did.

'Nothing fancy, just nice and proper,' she had insisted.

'But what will happen to my Rustic Damozel?'

'I don't reckon there'll be that much of a change if rustic be countrified. I can't see me losing my Devon tongue altogether, I idn't sure I wants to, any road, but if I could have the rough edges rubbed off. There's some as talks proper, yet you knows they'm Devon the minute they opens their mouths.' She was thinking of Cal Whitcomb. She could never learn to speak as well as Patrick, he was almost as good as the vicar, but the way Cal Whitcomb spoke, that was a different matter. She was confident she could be as good as he was any day.

'If you're sure that's what you want then I'll help you.' Patrick had been smilingly reluctant. 'But the instant I begin to suspect I'm losing my Rustic Damozel I stop. Is that understood?'

''Tis understood,' affirmed Maddy.

'It is,' corrected Patrick gently. 'It is understood. There, that is your first lesson.'

He was a good teacher, and Maddy, with her quick ear and her sharp intelligence, proved to be such a good pupil that he cried in protest, 'We must stop this. You're progressing too well. I haven't heard a "wadn't" nor an "idn't" nor a "where be to" in ages, and I miss them.'

They did not stop, of course, and Maddy continued to watch her speech. Her family mocked and her friends smiled, not that she cared. Patrick had opened one more horizon for her.

Just because she had been a country bumpkin did not mean she had to remain one. She could change herself. She could be anything she wanted – if she discounted the existence of her father and brothers.

Her family was uncharacteristically silent on the subject of Patrick. They must have known she was seeing him frequently, everyone else in the village seemed to, but fortunately they were too wrapped up in their own affairs to do more than comment, 'You'm been with that damned mountebank again?' They could think of nothing these days except their grudge against Cal Whitcomb. It had been so ever since they were prosecuted, and it occupied their minds to the exclusion of nearly everything else.

They came stamping in for their dinner, mucky boots trailing river mud across the clean floor. Maddy had left her copy of *Jane Eyre* on a chair. Bart remarked, 'You'm a fool, addling your brain with such rubbish,' before sitting down. Not so long ago he would have thrown the book on the fire or at her head, but such was his absorption in his grievances that he just flung it on the settle. Grateful for the lack of interest in her private life, she decided not to grumble about the filthy floor and concentrated on dishing up the meal.

'Cal Whitcomb idn't eating plain boiled pudding for his dinner, you can bet that,' declared Jack.

'No, he'm sure to be cutting gurt slices off a saddle of mutton, or maybe a bit of beef,' agreed Bart. 'He idn't bothered about the poor souls he'm driven to near starvation.'

The large portions of pudding Maddy was putting on their plates hardly constituted 'starvation'; as for the description 'plain', she had managed to flavour it well with home-grown leeks and a bit of bacon. But Bart had a point: life for the Shillabeers was not going to be easy.

The netting season was a short one, lasting from March to August, then her father and brothers would have to take what work they could get. Surprisingly, they were content to leave the financial arrangements to Maddy, not only the household budget but the money they made from the salmon too. It was she who kept a tally of how many fish were sent up to Totnes, she who kept a sharp eye on market prices, and she who controlled the money they received. She dealt with the expenses too – the purchase of the annual fishing licence, of new nets and tar to preserve them, and the materials needed to keep the boat well maintained. All this was Maddy's responsibility.

Spreading an uncertain family income over an entire year involved careful budgeting at the best of times. Paying her brothers' fines was going to make things more difficult than ever, and Maddy considered how to cut her already slender housekeeping even more. Apart from potatoes and bread, fish was going to be the mainstay of their diet. Not salmon. That was far too valuable to put on the family table. No, it would be coarser fish such as pollack or mackerel which sometimes got trapped in the net. If the worst came to the worst she would have to take the boat out herself and hand-line for whatever the river had to offer. As she totted up the figures on a piece of old sugar bag, trying to work out how to feed five hungry men on next to nothing, Maddy joined her brothers and heartily cursed Cal Whitcomb and his harsh ways.

Slow footsteps announced the approach of Annie, and Maddy rose to her feet. It had to be something important for her friend to disturb them during their dinner. One look at Annie's grave face betrayed serious news.

'You habn't heard then?' she said.

'Heard what?' asked Maddy.

'About Biddy. Her'm been drowned. The miller found her by the dam.'

'Poor soul,' said Maddy sadly. 'Perhaps it's for the best. She did naught but suffer while she was living. It was an accident?'

'Who knows? My William rowed Mrs Bond, the miller's wife, across the river not half an hour since – her goes over to see her sister to Dittisham, the one as is bedfast – and her were moaning because her were late. Her said there weren't no telling what happened.'

'Which side of the dam were her found?' demanded Bart. 'The river side or the pool?'

'The river side. That's how her wadn't noticed earlier. Her were caught up underneath one of the boats as is moored there.'

The sigh that went round the table was one of relief. The brothers were not interested in the other details of Biddy's death, just where it had occurred.

'We'm safe for the rest of the year, lads,' said Jack.

'That's what my William says. The river have got its due for this year, the rest of us can bide easy. And perhaps 'tis better it were Biddy than some other poor soul,' said Annie. 'Mind, there'm those as say 'tis naught but nonsense, this notion that the Dart claims a heart every year.'

'Then they be danged idiots,' stated Jack firmly. 'Every year there be someone as goes to the river and don't come back. It have been so way back, afore anyone can remember. One body be what un claims and no more. Now it have got Biddy this year, it'll be content.'

Like the others, Maddy had been conscious of a feeling of relief at the news of the drowning, sad though it was. She, too, believed implicitly in the ancient superstition that the Dart demanded one victim a year. Those who mocked at the notion did not know the river as she did, and they did not have loved ones who wrested their living from its capricious waters. The tricky currents could catch the boats of the unwary and overturn them in an instant, the Dart could suddenly change from a serenely flowing river into a heaving, raging torrent which could defeat even the strongest, most experienced boatman. She had never been able to think of the river as an inanimate thing, it was too unpredictable. To her it was a living creature, by turns gentle, generous, and savage.

Patrick did not scoff when Maddy told him of it.

'And why shouldn't water have a spirit?' he asked. 'It moves, it changes, it has life, it's never still. Yes, why shouldn't your lovely Dart have a spirit, albeit a cruel one at times? It is what the ancient peoples believed, people like our friend Janus, and even further back than him.'

'How is it you knows such stuff?' asked Maddy, lost in admiration at his cleverness.

'Because I like to find out things, I suppose. I'm interested... and at the moment my sole interest is in you!'

He pulled her towards him unexpectedly, causing her to shriek with surprise, but once his lips were on hers there was no chance of shrieks or words. All she wanted was to be there in his arms, savouring his kisses, enjoying his presence.

'You are happy?' he asked softly, when at last their lips parted.

'Oh yes,' she said without hesitation. 'I didn't know it was possible to feel like this. It is as if every day I am... am flying inside.' Then she felt embarrassed, as she always did when she expressed her emotions.

But Patrick was pleased with her description. 'Flying inside! I've never heard it better put. Yes, that's it exactly. Flying like a swallow.'

'Or a skylark,' said Maddy.

'That's even better,' he cried with delight, 'for that is a soaring thing, that's lifted up and up to disappear into the blue heaven.'

Maddy wished she had not suggested the image of the skylark. Any notion of disappearing made her uneasy, especially where Patrick was concerned.

'And are you happy?' she asked, to drive away the faint shadow.

'Extremely.' Patrick fell back on the grass, pulling her with him. 'I came back to Stoke Gabriel out of curiosity, nothing more. I did not expect to find so much. This place is more beautiful than anything I ever expected. I have found work and I have found you. What man could want more?'

Listening to his words with her head against his chest, Maddy felt that she, too, could want nothing more. Her days were golden, with nothing spoiling them. For a while they lay without speaking, content to be in each other's arms.

'I hear you was being fought over the other day,' Maddy remarked eventually.

'I was? Who were the lucky women?'

'It weren't – wasn't women, it was Harry Ford and Sam Watkins.'

'Oh them! They didn't actually come to blows that I heard of, but it's pleasing to be appreciated.'

'Did Sam Watkins really offer you an extra two and six a week to work down the Victoria and Albert?'

'No.' Patrick smiled the mischievous smile which so delighted her. 'He offered me two shillings. It was Harry Ford who offered me half-a-crown to stay put.'

Maddy laughed. 'You'll soon have your own carriage at this rate,' she chuckled.

'There's certainly plenty of work for an able fiddler round here. I've been asked to play at more weddings and celebrations than I can manage.'

'That's because the only fiddler we've had till now was Henry Beer. Poor Henry, he was never too able, and now he's getting on in years we can't hope for improvement. You knows what it's like singing hymns when he's playing. Can you imagine what it's like trying to dance to him?'

'I'd rather not, thank you.' Patrick sat up and gave an exaggerated shudder.

Maddy sat up too. 'Poor soul, I suppose he's noticing the difference these days with folks not wanting him to play any more.'

'You think I should refuse to play at weddings and such in favour of Henry?'

'No,' she said firmly. 'You can't go turning down a chance to make an honest penny. Besides, I don't think folks would be satisfied with Henry any more. You see, until you came most of us hadn't heard decent playing afore. We didn't realise how bad old Henry really was. We know now, though, and there's no going back.'

'I'm sorry if I've spoiled things for Henry, but I must admit I'm glad to be so much in demand. But let us forget Henry for the moment. I have something more important to discuss. Would you kindly give me an opinion upon this trifle?'

He reached for his fiddle. There was nothing out of the ordinary in him having his violin with him for he was seldom without it. He had admitted that he was uncomfortable if it was not within reach, and she understood his possessiveness. Taking it from its canvas bag, he tuned it.

The melody which flowed from his violin made Maddy think of many things, of sadness and of joy, but in some strange way the cadence of its notes reminded her mainly of the beauty in life that she had so recently found. She had never known that music had the power to move her, not until she realised her cheeks were wet with tears. When he finished playing she was reluctant to speak for a moment, lest she broke the spell.

'That were beautiful,' she said at last, forgetting her carefully attained speech in her emotion.

'Then you like it?'

'Indeed I do. I've never heard anything as beautiful, saving the once...' Her voice faded away. He seemed pleased with the tune, it was obviously special to him, and she was suddenly afraid she was being tactless.

'Saving the once?' he prompted.

'That first day when you came and you played for me and I felt proper foolish,' Maddy hurried on uncomfortably. 'You played some-thing like it then, only it wasn't as good.'

He seemed delighted. 'What a memory! What a natural ear for music you possess! You're right, of course. I did play it then, or rather a very raw unfinished version. It had just come to me as I was walking. As I worked on it I knew it was something special, which is why I give it to you, Maddy.'

'Just come to you? You mean you thought up that tune out of your head?' Maddy gazed at him in awe.

'Don't look at me with such amazement,' he laughed. 'Lots of people think up tunes.'

'No, they don't.' Maddy was adamant. 'Leastways, no one I've ever known. I thought such things were for grand folk up in London or maybe Exeter, yet here you be saying you made up a tune as calm as you please. I always knew you were different from the other menfolk round here, more clever and such, but I never realised how clever. Have you thought up other tunes?'

'Yes, I do it quite often, but not like this one. This is my very best, which is why it is for you.'

'For me?' She regarded him blankly. Slowly the nature of his gift began to sink in. 'That beautiful tune is for me?'

'Yes, it is dedicated to you, my Maddy. Every note is for you alone.'

'Oh!' The wonder of it almost took her breath away. 'I've never been given anything like that... anything so special... The tune's for me, you say?' She paused, trying to gather her bemused wits. 'Please, please would you play it once more for me?'

'With pleasure.' Taking up his bow he began to play, and again the beauty of the music took hold of Maddy.

When the last notes faded away she was too convulsed with sobs to speak.

'I'm sorry,' she managed to gulp at last. 'I'm happy, truly I am. I don't know why I'm bawling like a babe, save that I never heard anything so beautiful before...'

'I'll take your tears as a compliment.' Patrick smoothed her damp cheek with gentle fingers. 'Any musician would be gratified to move his listener so.'

'Then you aren't angry because I blubbed at your music? To hear such music is a marvel in itself, but to know that it is for me... Has it a name?'

'Of course I'm not angry, and certainly the piece has a name. It is called "Miss Madeleine's Air".'

'"Miss Madeleine's Air".' She said the words aloud, relishing their rhythm. That sounds grand, too grand for me. 'But if you think it is fitting then I do too,' she added hurriedly at his gently reproving look. 'And just to say thank you doesn't seem enough.' To emphasise her words, she held out her arms to him.

Patrick put aside his fiddle and enfolded her in an embrace. 'Oh Maddy, Maddy, Maddy, what a remarkable creature you are! So sweet, so honest and so sincere.'

He held her close, until she could hear the beating of his heart. Not content to wait for his kisses, she drew his face down to hers. Their lips met with tenderness at first, then with increasing passion. Even in the midst of the mounting emotions which gripped her, Maddy was aware of relief within her. For the first time she felt secure, sure of Patrick's love. Of late she had been almost certain of his feelings, only in her blacker moments did it bother her that he had never spoken his love aloud. Now he did not need to. In his music, and in his gift, he had declared his love for her more clearly than with any words.

Later, as Maddy made her way home, in a cloud of blissful daydreams, she sang the air that Patrick had composed for her. She was not afraid of ever forgetting it. It was enmeshed too firmly in her head and in her heart.

–

At church next Sunday there were stirrings of drama in the air. In the minutes before the entry of the vicar and the choir, a shocked whisper went round the congregation that Henry Beer had left the church band. Details were scarce, and everyone waited in eager anticipation as the band struck up. Sure enough, there was no Henry, and in his absence, as the only remaining violin, Patrick led the small group of musicians. There were only five of them, including him, but they blended superbly – cello and fiddle, flute, clarinet and bassoon. It was not only Maddy's biased opinion that the music was the best heard in the church for a long time. Many other people expressed the same view as they filed out.

'Tis a disgrace! After the years our Henry have gived to this church and what happens? He'm thrown aside like an old rag and for what? For a young flibbertigibbet as haven't been here two minutes.' Mrs Cutmore, who was Henry's sister, was not slow to air her grievances as soon as she was through the church door. 'Forty years come Michaelmas! That's how long he'm played the hymns.'

'That be long enough in all conscience,' called a wag. 'Our ears have suffered long enough.'

But many people sided with Mrs Cutmore and argued that Henry had been shabbily treated. The blame fell squarely on Patrick. Not content with taking over every wedding and celebration, the incomer had now taken Henry's church band from him.

Maddy listened without comment. She was sorry for Henry, though she could not see how Patrick could have been at fault. Eagerly she awaited a chance to hear his version of the story. She did not have to wait long. She had barely started to walk up School Hill before she heard familiar footsteps following, and then Patrick fell into step beside her.

'I suppose you've heard the news,' he said. 'Tongues were still wagging nineteen to the dozen as I came along.'

'It's true then? Henry has left the church band?'

'Only Henry himself can answer that one.'

'What happened? No one in church seemed to know for sure.'

'It was trivial beyond words. I'm aware that many people blame me, but I assure you that displacing Henry was the last thing I intended. He was late for practice on Friday so we started on our own, and as is customary, because I play the violin, I led. We were doing splendidly – we played the anthem particularly well, I recall – when Henry arrived. He was most displeased to find us practising without him, and even less pleased to see me in his place. He was determined to start again from the very beginning, right from the anthem. We pointed out we had already done it. He said, somewhat sourly, that we would do it again properly, and I am afraid things deteriorated from then on.'

'And was Henry thrown out?'

'No, he left of his own accord. Stormed out, in fact, swearing never to play a note in the church again.'

'And you were blamed for that? When it was Henry's bad temper?' Maddy was highly indignant.

'We mustn't be too hard on the poor fellow. I can understand how it might have seemed to him. I feel quite guilty at my part in it.'

'You have nothing to feel guilty about!'

'I have. If I hadn't been there the practice would probably not have gone ahead. The church band is Henry's life, I'd not deprive him of it. In fact, I went to the vicar to see what I should do.'

'If you aren't the kindest, gentlest man, being concerned for a pig-headed old lump like Henry who can't even play in tune. And what did the vicar say?'

'He was in favour of letting things take their own course. If Henry decides to come back, then all well and good – not that he was very hopeful, for Henry can be obstinate apparently. In the meantime he said he would be grateful if I would continue leading the other musicians.'

'I bet he would.' Maddy gave a chuckle. 'He's very fond of music, is the vicar. Every service since he came here he's had to battle with Henry, trying to make the hymns sound right. No wonder he's happy for you to take over.'

Patrick smiled with relief. 'Then you don't think I'm to blame? You've made me feel much more comfortable. Not for the world would I cause trouble, yet I must confess that it does seem to follow me about.'

'That's because you aren't in the usual run of folk. People are always suspicious of them as is – those who are a bit different. I don't know why it should be so, but it is.'

'Perhaps you're right. You're a wise creature, Maddy Shillabeer.'

'If I am then it has rubbed off from you.'

He shook his head. 'No. I know facts. You have wisdom. There's a difference. Of the two I'd rather have wisdom. It can only be gathered through understanding and experience. Fools like me can't get it simply from books like we can get knowledge.' They had reached the top of the steep slope down to Duncannon, the place where they always parted, because it was secluded enough for a farewell kiss – or maybe two. On this occasion Patrick raised Maddy's hand to his lips.

'Goodbye for the present, my sweet, wise Maddy,' he said. 'How I wish I could learn from you.'

The serious note in his voice surprised her. For the first time she detected a lack of confidence in him, and she wondered at it as she made her way home. From what he had told her, he had been a wanderer all his life; perhaps this was less through inclination than because of the trouble which undeniably followed in his wake. And now, because of the fuss over Henry and the church band, did he fear he might be forced to move on once more?

Not if I have the say in the matter, decided Maddy. No one idn't going to make him leave if he don't want to, she vowed, all thoughts of correct grammar forgotten.

She turned her mind to her own future. Two dreams had begun to haunt her. The first was a wonderful impossibility; in it she was not tied to her father and brothers. It was a vision of the years ahead spent with Patrick, an idyll where she loved and cherished him with nothing to mar the perfection of their existence. The second was a nightmare, in which she saw a future completely devoid of him, and a black, bitter prospect it was. One image she dared not foster, the other she dreaded, so to force them both away from her thoughts she began to hum to herself. The tune, of course, was 'Miss Madeleine's Air'.

Nothing was resolved about the church band during the next week. Henry showed no sign of relenting, but sat in his pew with his family, grim faced, never once looking towards the small group of musicians. Maddy was proud to see Patrick continuing to lead the group, and even Henry's most stalwart supporters were forced to admit that the music had improved. Whatever discord there was in the church, thanks to Patrick none of it was musical.

When Annie approached the cottage one mid-week afternoon, Maddy saw at once that she had news to tell.

'What's afoot?' she demanded as her friend reached the door. 'Something is, I can see from your face.'

'I had it from the squire himself,' Annie said importantly. 'He'm just back from Totnes, from Biddy's inquest. William rowed him from off the *Newcomin*.'

'What was the verdict?'

'Accidental death, thank goodness. Squire said that since there wadn't no evidence that the poor soul meant to end her life, it were the only verdict possible.'

'Thank goodness indeed. I always feel sorry for those sad creatures who aren't allowed to lie in the churchyard. As if they haven't suffered enough without being buried outside the churchyard wall. At least Biddy can lie decent – decently,' she corrected herself.

'Yes, she can lie *decently*,' repeated Annie with teasing emphasis. 'You *haven't* never said a truer word. My, at this rate you'm going to have me talking as grand as you.'

'It's the book-reading rubbing off on me,' said Maddy.

'If I believed that I'd believe aught,' replied Annie. 'Mind, I misses the book-reading. I regrets us've got to the end of un.'

'I do too,' admitted Maddy. 'Us – we could leave it a spell then start reading it again, if you like. I'd hoped to have bought another one by now, but thanks to Mr Cal Whitcomb, that idea went out the window. Still, if I get a good price for my strawberries, who knows?'

'A new book'd be grand, but I'd be content to hear about Jane again. I can't listen to un too often. That Patrick have given you some fancy ideas, but getting you reading books is the best by far. 'Tis a pity...' Her voice faded.

'What's a pity?' Maddy looked up from the shirt she was mending. 'I didn't say naught.'

'Yes you did.' Maddy gazed at her enquiringly and was surprised to see her friend looking uncomfortable.

'I'd best be getting back,' Annie said. 'I've a pot on the fire as'll be boiling dry.'

'It can last another minute or two while you tell me what you were going to say before you thought better of it,' Maddy insisted.

Annie gave a sigh. 'I always let my tongue run away with me,' she said regretfully. 'I suppose you may as well hear it from me as anyone else. That sweetheart of youm, Patrick, he'm lost his job.'

'From the Church House? Whatever for?'

Annie looked decidedly uncomfortable. 'How should I know?' she replied.

'Annie Fleet, you should give up lying, you're no good at it.'

'I never were,' her friend agreed. 'May as well be hung for a sheep as a lamb, I suppose, though I'd pay no heed to un, if I were you. There's likely no truth in un and, anyway, you knows what I be like, always getting the wrong end—'

'Annie!' said Maddy threateningly. 'Tell me why Patrick was dismissed from the Church House.'

'According to what I heard, and 'tis probably a pack of lies, Harry Ford accused him of carrying on with his wife.'

'With Lucy Ford? It seems a bit harsh, to turn him off because of that.'

'Is that all you'm got to say? You'm a cool one and no mistake,' said Annie in astonishment. 'Don't you mind your sweetheart being accused of flirting with a married woman?'

'I mind, but I don't take it seriously,' said Maddy after careful consideration. 'I dare say he did flirt with Mrs Ford. She's still a fine-looking woman, and he can't help flirting with any female. It's his nature. I doubt if there was any serious carryings-on. It was probably wishful thinking on Lucy Ford's part.'

'Bain't you the least bit put out? I would be if it were my William involved. Crippled as I be I'd get up there and be giving that Lucy Ford a bit of my mind, aye, and I'd tear out a bit of her hair as like as not, for good measure.'

'It'll turn out to be nothing, you'll see. Poor Patrick, petty troubles like this seem to dog his steps. I suppose it's because he's so often the centre of attention. I expect Harry Ford got jealous of Patrick. After all, he's brought far more trade to the Church House than Harry ever managed on his own. That's probably why he took his spite out on him. I doubt if carrying on with Lucy Ford had much to do with it really.'

'If you say so.' Annie looked far from convinced. 'Now I must go. I really have got a pot on the fire. Its bottom'll be burned out by this time.'

After Annie had gone, Maddy considered the new events in Patrick's career. Confident of his love and in the certainty that she understood him, she honestly did not take this latest tale seriously. No doubt she and Patrick would laugh about it when next they met. Nor was she too worried about him getting another job. Sam Watkins would take him on like a shot at the Victoria and Albert – unless Patrick had gained too much of a reputation as a troublemaker; then no one would take him on. Coming on top of the trouble with Henry Beer, might it not force Patrick to leave Stoke Gabriel altogether? Her black dream, of a world without Patrick, came sweeping over her.

Don't let it happen, she prayed. Don't let it happen. She could not imagine what would become of her if it did.

Chapter Six

'I suppose you know I have a new employer?' Patrick greeted Maddy when next they met.

'I'd heard you'd parted company with your old one,' she replied. 'It wasn't fair, you losing your job like that.'

'You believe I wasn't at fault, even though I haven't told you my side of events?' he asked in astonishment.

'Knowing you, I expect you flirted a bit. It comes as second nature, half the time you don't realise you're doing it. As for any serious carryings-on with Lucy Ford, I'm certain you aren't guilty of that.'

'What can I say?' He spread his hands in a gesture of wonder. 'To have such faith in me... it is more than I deserve.' He suddenly looked quite sheepish. 'If you want the truth, I wasn't sure how to face you today after what happened. I didn't know which would be worse, for you to be in ignorance of the story, which would mean me explaining, or for you to know the details and be angry with me.'

'When have I ever been angry with you?'

'Never, so far, but this is different. Also, I fear you may be right and that I did flirt with Mrs Ford a bit.'

'If I know you, you flirted with her a lot, but that's no reason for me to be angry. That's how you are and I accept it. I don't expect you to be perfect. I love you for your weaknesses as much as for the wonderful things about you, you know I do.'

Patrick did not reply but took her hand and pressed it to his lips, keeping it there as if its presence gave him comfort. The breeze ruffled the soft darkness of his hair, lifting the waving strands away from the tan of his face. The sight of his bent head moved Maddy with a great tenderness. Usually it was his eyes, with their irises of that vivid blue, which stirred her, or else the soft sensitive line of his mouth that was so quick to curve into an engaging smile. But now, with his face averted, as he clutched at her hand, she was conscious of his vulnerability. He seemed to have so much – charm, talent, a handsome face – yet she suspected that until now he had lacked the stability of understanding and real love. Maddy was certain she could give him both unstintingly.

With her free hand, she smoothed his hair, then pulling him against her breast, she rocked him gently, almost as if he were a child. This was no time for wild emotions and hectic passion. This was a time for tranquil love. Below them the river flowed on its sinuous way to the sea. It was nearing high tide, the one time when larger vessels could reach as far as Totnes, and the Dart was busy with traffic and noise, from the puffing and chugging of the steamers to the crack and flap of the canvas sails of the wherries, all carrying goods and passengers up and down stream. From their vantage point in the sloping meadow above, with the tall grasses almost hiding them from view, Maddy and Patrick seemed isolated from such bustle. Above them skylarks rose into the blue sky in torrents of song, almost blotting out the noise rising from the water. They might have been the last people left in the world, and Maddy would not have minded if it had been so.

'Maddy,' Patrick said, his voice low and far from steady, 'I don't deserve you. I'm a feckless sort of fellow. I never have any money, I never stay in one place for long. I'll hurt you, Maddy. I won't mean to, but I'll hurt you.'

She did not believe him. Nothing he did would ever hurt her, she was convinced of it. Knowing his character as she did, his mind, his heart, she was proof against the petty jealousies and misunderstandings that could tear a relationship apart. She was certain her own heart had nothing to fear.

Her earlier worries, that the additional troubles might drive Patrick away from the village, proved unfounded. Sam Watkins had taken him on at the Victoria and Albert.

'But at the old rate,' Patrick informed her wryly. 'With no mention of the extra two shillings he once offered me, and definitely no sign of the additional half-crown I was getting at the Church House.'

'Didn't you protest?' demanded Maddy.

'Indeed I did. He just replied that there was no competition for my services these days, therefore why should he pay me more.'

'But you have a situation, that is the important thing,' said Maddy. You won't be leaving the village, she added to herself with silent relief.

Gradually the scandal of Patrick and Lucy Ford died down, and as the spring merged into the lush green of summer, the days were golden for Maddy. The salmon were running well, and of such a good size the agent was paying one and sixpence or more each for them. At last the cracked Delft jug on the mantelshelf which held the family's reserves for a rainy day began to receive contributions again. The odd surplus coppers at first, then occasionally threepenny bits and even a sixpence or two. Maddy found it satisfying to see it filling up after having been empty for weeks.

And there are yet my strawberries to come, she reminded herself.

Maddy's strawberries were her pride and joy. Their spot in the garden was particularly warm and sheltered, and throughout their growing period she watered and fed them, bedded them in thick straw, and fended off the ravages of slugs, birds, and mildew. Her aim was to have the crop ready early in order to get the best price. The fruit was developing well, but needed more rain. Then, at exactly the right moment, the drought was broken by a series of thunderstorms which swelled the succulent flesh to perfection.

'I can't remember a year when they've been better,' she remarked to Annie. 'I'll pick them first thing tomorrow and take them into Paignton.'

'I don't knows as how you can bear to smell them and not eat a few yourself,' her friend remarked. 'There'd be more in my belly than there'd be in the basket.'

'No there wouldn't, not if you thought of them as shillings and pence,' Maddy replied. 'It's easier to curb your hand and make do with the bruised or misshapen fruit if you think what the rest might buy.'

'And what will it be? A silk gown? Or a parasol with an ivory handle and a long dangly fringe all round?'

'That's a bit hopeful for a strawberry patch,' grinned Maddy. 'It might stretch to another book.'

'You'm idn't serious?' Annie stared at her in delight. 'Oh my, that'd be fine. Provided I be invited to the readings, of course.'

'I think I can put up with you, if you don't get too rowdy,' said Maddy with mock seriousness.

'Dang, that means leaving my jug of scrumpy at home,' Annie answered her in kind, then reverted to her normal tone. 'What be going to get, maid?'

'I don't know yet. I'll ask the bookseller what he recommends.'

'The one in Totnes was very helpful, let's hope I find one as good in Paignton.'

'That be something to look forward to. Book-reading be a grand thing at this time of the year, but think how much better it'll be come winter. And us'll have two books to enjoy. Us won't know ourselves.'

Maddy laughed at Annie's excitement, though she was just as enthusiastic herself. Another stoiy to read was a marvellous prospect.

Dawn came early at that time of year, but Maddy was up betimes, her skirts kirtled up against the morning dew, picking the strawberries. It was a pleasing task there in the riverside garden, with the soft pearly mist gradually fading before the sun's strengthening warmth. In Duncannon Copse, a cuckoo was calling its repetitive cry, and from somewhere across the river an invisible counterpart replied. The green freshness of the morning was soon overlaid by the heavier, riper fragrance of strawberries as she filled the baskets. The succulent red fruit, lying in its protective nest of green leaves, looked very tempting; Maddy was sure she would get a good price.

She had chosen to go to Paignton because, since the coming of the railways, the small seaside town was growing into a popular and fashionable resort. The new hotels that were springing up everywhere were willing to pay a good bit extra for the privilege of being able to put 'fresh locally grown strawberries' on their menus so early in the year. It would be well worth the few miles' walk.

With a fresh white apron over her striped dress, she set out, a full basket on each arm. Her skirts were hitched up again, this time to keep them out of the mud. The recent rains had been welcomed by everyone in that dry year, but they had made conditions sticky underfoot. It was a humid day. Already, in the narrow confines of the lane, Maddy could feel the warm, damp air lying heavy, trapped between the high banked hedges. She did not mind the heat, although perspiration was soon beading her face; it was the moisture she did not like. It made her hair tighten into riotous waves which defied even her newly acquired hairstyle. It annoyed her that she was looking so wild. Going into town she had wanted to appear at her best.

The sound of an approaching horse coming up behind her did not disturb Maddy. She had almost reached the crossroads beyond the village and the road was quite wide enough for a rider to pass her, despite her two baskets. The hoofbeats quickened, causing her to glance over her shoulder. It was as well she did, for Victoria Fitzherbert was bearing down upon her. Maddy knew what was about to happen. Ever since the churchyard incident she had had trouble with that young lady. Victoria had grown adept at riding her horse too close to Maddy whenever they encountered one another. A nudge with the horse's flank in passing, a near kick from an iron-shod hoof – Victoria never missed an opportunity to pay Maddy back for her past humiliation.

Fearful for the strawberries, Maddy swiftly looked about for a refuge. There was no convenient field gate she could dodge into, and no gaps in the high hedges where she could lodge the precious baskets for safety. Hampered as she was, there was little she could do except press herself against the bank, hoping the Fitzherbert female would be content with spattering her with mud. It was a vain hope.

Victoria deliberately slowed her mount, collected him, then with the precision of a dressage rider, deliberately rode him close to her victim. Victoria was riding side-saddle, so it was her booted foot that hit first. The impact was enough to swing Maddy half round, spilling some of the strawberries in the process. Then, in passing, the horse's rump caught her a glancing blow. With her balance already unsteady, the second knock was enough to send Maddy sprawling, and what was left of her fruit poured in a scarlet cascade into the mud.

Victoria pulled her horse to a halt, and for a heart-stopping instant Maddy wondered if she was going to be trampled under those solid feet. Not even Victoria dared to go that far, however. She had another target. With a look of intense satisfaction on her face she urged her horse to pound with his hooves on the spot, crushing the strawberries into the muddy earth. Then without a word, she dug her heels into his flank and rode off round the corner.

Slowly Maddy rose to her knees and looked at the destruction about her. All she could do was to utter little cries of distress, as if she were in pain. The months of careful work had gone for nothing, along with all her hopes. Apart from buying a new book, the money from the strawberries would have nearly filled the Delft jug on the mantelshelf, and a full jug meant security. But everything was lost, victims of a spiteful woman's revenge.

Again Maddy heard horse's hooves approaching from the direction in which Victoria had gone. Was she coming back for a second session? Maddy did not care. She did not bother to move.

It was not Victoria who rounded the bend at a brisk trot, it was Cal Whitcomb.

'My God, what's happened? Are you hurt?' He brought his horse to a slithering halt amidst the crushed fruit, dismounted, and was at Maddy's side in an instant.

If it had been anyone else Maddy might have given way to her shock and distress, but this was Cal Whitcomb. She had broken down in front of him once and she had no intention of doing so again. Slowly she rose to her feet, wiping her mud-caked hands on an apron which was only marginally less dirty.

'I am unhurt, though it is kind of you to enquire,' she said, in her most careful accents.

'You are? But...?' He sniffed the air and looked curiously at the red pulp about his feet. His look of concern melted into a grin. 'Strawberries, by heaven! I thought it was blood!' And he began to laugh.

His laughter nearly overset Maddy and she had to struggle to maintain her composure. A growing anger, at Victoria Fitzherbert and also at him for laughing, succeeded in keeping the tears at bay.

'I'm glad you find it amusing,' she snapped. 'If I'd known it would entertain you this much I'd have made a point of flinging good strawberries into the mud more often and jumping on top of them.'

His laughter died instantly. 'I'm sorry, it was wrong of me to find it funny,' he said. 'It was pure relief. Seeing you on your knees and red everywhere I feared you'd had a serious accident. Squashed strawberries seemed a very minor mishap to some of the possible disasters that were rushing through my mind. What happened?' He looked about in puzzlement at the slush of mingled fruit and mud. 'How did things manage to get in this state?'

'There was an accident,' said Maddy, her mouth grim. 'I fell.'

'It must have been quite a fall...' Cal's voice faded as he looked at the ground. With the toe of his boot he traced the fresh outline of a horseshoe clearly impressed in the mud. It was too small to belong to his gelding. 'Ah,' he said. 'I think I understand.'

'There is nothing to understand,' said Maddy, still keeping her speech as correct as she could. 'If you will excuse me, I had best return home.'

'You're sure you're not hurt?'

'Quite sure, thank you.'

She picked up the baskets, one of which was smashed beyond repair. In the corner of the other a few undamaged strawberries had managed to survive, a couple of handfuls at most. They were all she had to show for her efforts. The sight of them inflamed her fury, and she came close to throwing them on the road with the rest. Then she thought of Annie, waiting hopefully for the new book. She would give them to her as consolation.

'Good day to you,' she said politely to Cal. Despite the circumstances, her behaviour towards Cal Whitcomb would be correct, no matter what she thought of him.

She trudged away, conscious that he was watching her. Presently she heard him mount up. To her surprise he did not pass her, although that was the direction in which he had been heading. Instead he turned his horse round and went back the way he had come.

At every step on the road back to Duncannon, Maddy's anger and humiliation seethed inside her. By the time she reached Annie's cottage her inner turmoil had bubbled up to a point that made speech almost impossible.

'Lor' bless us, maid, what have happened to you?' declared Annie with concern when she entered, caked in mud and strawberry juice.

Maddy could not reply. She pressed her lips tightly together to hold back the tears that were welling inside her. Scooping up the surviving strawberries from the basket, she put them on a convenient plate. 'For your tea,' she managed to gasp out before she fled to the sanctuary of her own home.

–

Cal Whitcomb urged his gelding into a near canter as he returned along the lane. He had already passed Victoria Fitzherbert once that morning, and her greeting had been as demure as you please. He should have guessed she had been up to something by the satisfied look on her face. The cat that had got at the cream had nothing on Miss Fitzherbert's expression.

It did not take him long to catch up with her. He had to admit that she made a charming picture, riding her mount with style and elegance, her trim figure looking cool in a light habit of tan piqué. But he had not caught up with her to admire her appearance.

'Good morning once more, Mr Whitcomb,' she said sweetly. 'I wondered who it could be, approaching at such a rate. Have you forgotten something?'

'No, I simply thought I would accompany you on your ride, if you have no objection.' His voice was affable.

'Of course I have no objection.'

'Then perhaps your groom could hang back so that we may talk?'

'Certainly. Robbins, drop back. We wish to be private.' Cal noticed she could not keep an edge of satisfaction from her voice as she rapped out the command. 'And what shall we talk about on this fine summer day, Mr Whitcomb?' she asked.

'Let us talk about you, Miss Fitzherbert.' Again his voice was light, almost flirtatious.

'Oh, I am a very poor subject.'

'I beg to contradict. I think you are a young lady of quite extraordinary qualities. In fact, I am sure I've never met your like.'

'Come, sir, you are too flattering.'

'I am not flattering you at all. Take your riding, for example. I doubt if there is a young lady within twenty miles who sits a horse as well as you do.'

'It is kind of you to say so, but you are flattering me.'

'No, I am not. You have an extremely well-schooled horse, I notice. You could probably pull him up on the proverbial sixpence and have him mark time on a shilling.'

'That's an exaggeration,' smiled Victoria. 'Though I'll admit he answers to the slightest touch.'

'Then trampling a load of strawberries into the dirt would have been child's play to him.' Cal's voice had not altered, but the smile was wiped from Victoria's face.

'I don't know what you mean,' she said curtly.

'Yes, you do.' The reply was crisp. 'It's a pity to waste the talents of such a highly trained horse on a mean and petty exercise like that. It was highly unwise of you, too. I presume Maddy Shillabeer was your target, rather than her fruit baskets. You took a risk, knocking her into the mud. Conditions are slippery underfoot today, and even the best of horses can make an error in such circumstances. If Miss Shillabeer had been hurt you would have had a deal more to contend with than merely being cut by local society.'

'How dare you speak to me in this way!' snapped Victoria indignantly. 'Stop it at once. I shall call Robbins.'

'By all means call Robbins if you wish. I'll have my say in his presence or not.'

'No you won't!' Victoria, her lip pouting ominously, urged her horse onward.

As the animal began to move, Cal caught hold of the bridle and held him back. 'You aren't getting away that easily,' he said.

'Let go, you wretch! Let go this instant!' Victoria had her riding crop raised ready to strike, but he was too quick for her, parrying the blow with his own.

'You are too ready to use that crop,' he admonished calmly. 'I give you good warning, miss. Strike me with that and I'll put you across my saddle and leather your backside — something which should have been done years ago.'

'Really, sir!' gasped Victoria, outraged. 'You are no gentleman!'

'No, I'm not,' agreed Cal. 'I never pretended I was, so if you are relying upon my chivalrous instincts while you give vent to your savage temper then you will find yourself sadly mistaken. And there's no need to look for your groom,' he added, as she glanced desperately over her shoulder. 'Robbins and I have met before, you recall, and I think he took advantage of your order to fall back to keep as far behind as possible. He's quite out of sight.'

'This is disgraceful!' Victoria had never found herself in such a situation before, and did not know how to cope.

'Yes, it is,' agreed Cal again. 'Nearly as disgraceful as your behaviour. You are more stupid than I realised. Haven't you learned your lesson from the churchyard affair?'

'Are you suggesting the neighbourhood would turn against me for bumping into some country hag?'

'I would scarcely call Miss Shillabeer a hag. Considering she works all the hours God gives and hasn't the benefit of a maid to wait upon her hand and foot, she does very well. But to answer your question, yes, the neighbourhood would turn against you, especially as the bump was deliberate and spiteful. If your horse had caught Miss Shillabeer and injured her, you would have had the force of the law upon you, make no mistake about that. The gentry hereabouts don't like you for what you have already done. Instead of supporting you as one of their own class, they are quite likely to condemn you for hurting one of their people. And as for the village folk, Maddy Shillabeer has a father and four hulking brothers, all with very uncertain tempers. Harm her again and you'll have more to worry about than a few broken windows.'

'Are you threatening me!' Victoria asked in horror.

'Of course not. I am giving you a timely warning. The Shillabeers are no friends of mine, far from it, and I've been on the receiving end of their malevolence enough times to know their viciousness. They're the only people I know with a more spiteful temperament than yours, so take heed.'

'You are being horrid. I think it's most discourteous of you to frighten me like this.' Tears trembled on Victoria's long lashes. 'Let my horse go. I want you to leave me.'

'No you don't,' said Cal briskly. 'You are getting exactly what you wanted – the pleasure of my company. Why else did you come out riding at such an unfashionably early hour today? Why else have you been riding round and round my farm so frequently recently that even my dogs recognise you? I must say my mother appreciates your circuits, she much admires your wardrobe, particularly your hats.'

'Oh!' Tears forgotten, Victoria gave un unladylike snort of anger and turned her back on Cal, declaring as she did so, 'You are... are...'

'No gentleman?' he suggested when she failed to find the right insult. 'Then that is fine, for you are no lady, by temperament or behaviour. Had you been a hound you'd have been drowned long since as not worth keeping, for all your pretty looks. Come, Miss Fitzherbert, don't look outraged,' Cal continued as she gasped, speechless with shock. 'You don't abide by the rules, why should anyone else? As we are nearly back at Oakwood now, I'll release you. I give you leave to ride past the farmhouse in case my mother hasn't seen that particular outfit. It would be a pity to deprive her of her chief pleasure.'

But Victoria did not hear him. The moment he let go of her horse's bridle she spurred her mount and galloped away, followed, at length, by a perplexed Robbins.

Back at the White House, the entire household flinched at Victoria's return.

'I don't know what Farmer Whitcomb said to her, but it weren't naught for her comfort,' reported Robbins below stairs afterwards.

'A man to call a spade a spade and no nonsense be Farmer Whitcomb,' stated the cook. 'Whatever it was he said to that young madam, you can bet she deserved it. Knocking a body over in such a way, and all that good fruit going to waste.'

Robbins, an unhappy witness of Maddy's humiliation, had not been slow in repeating the story. The loss of the prime fruit had shocked the cook almost as much as her young mistress's vindictiveness, but she was also perplexed. 'It were Maddy Shillabeer as took the tumble, you say? You're quite certain?'

'Of course it were Maddy Shillabeer. I recognised her easily enough, passing not a yard from her,' said Robbins decidedly.

The cook beat her batter with fierce concentration as she tried to work it out. She was one of the permanent staff who had been hired along with the house. She shook her head. 'He wouldn't have crossed the road to help a Shillabeer, not after everything that's passed between those two families over the years. It must've been something else as Farmer Whitcomb jawed Miss Victoria about,' she decided.

'Whatever it was, I wish he hadn't bothered,' said Mary gloomily above the angry clanging of the bell from her mistress's room. 'It's us who'll suffer for it.'

In her fury Victoria lashed out at the servants unmercifully, wishing it were Cal Whitcomb who was suffering her barbed tongue and her sharp blows. The rudeness of the man! The audacity! To speak to her in such a way! How dare he? Their conversation, such as it had been, rang through her head time after time. It smote her not with remorse or shame, but with anger against the world in general and Calland Whitcomb in particular. In the absence of either target, it was her family and servants who suffered from her temper in the days that followed, exactly as Mary had predicted.

'You seem out of sorts lately, my love,' remarked her mother after one of Victoria's more vituperative outbursts. 'I'm convinced this warm weather is making you liverish. Perhaps you were wrong to give up your early-morning rides. I notice you no longer go on them. Maybe taking exercise when it was cool was beneficial.'

'No it wasn't,' retorted Victoria rudely. 'It was boring. I've gone down every muddy lane hereabouts until I'm sick of them all.'

'Then perhaps we should call in the doctor to give you a tonic.'

'There's nothing wrong with my health, how many times must I say it?' snapped Victoria. 'It's living here, in this wretched place.'

'Then maybe a change of air?' suggested Mrs Fitzherbert hopefully. 'It would do you good, that and a change of scene. Perhaps a stay by the sea?'

'You are by the sea, madam, or as good as,' retorted her husband. 'We are only three or four miles off. How much closer do you want to be? If the girl needs sea air that much then order the carriage and take her to Paignton. She can wander up and down along the esplanade in her finery, that should satisfy her.'

'What good is going to Paignton for an afternoon when we know no one there?' protested Victoria. 'That's no solution.'

'Nor is hiring a house for the summer at Sidmouth or Bournemouth, which is what the pair of you are angling for,' snapped Mr Fitzherbert. 'When will you both get it into your stupid heads that we are here to stay until our circumstances improve?'

'You would sacrifice your daughter's health because a few miserable tradesmen are dunning us?' Mrs Fitzherbert cried.

'It's more than a few, it's a damned lot! And there's nothing wrong with Victoria's health. She is simply an ill-tempered young madam, and always has been, as I remember, since the day of her birth. Having only one child, I would not have thought it too much to expect my daughter to be at least amiable, but no. I have been saddled with a female who promises to be such an out and out virago that no man would be fool enough to take her off my hands. Was ever a father so unfortunate?'

'You are blaming me again,' wailed Mrs Fitzherbert. 'You always blame me for everything that goes wrong in this family, and it isn't my fault, truly it isn't.'

As his wife burst into familiar tears, Mr Fitzherbert did what he always did in such circumstances, he gave a snort of mingled fury and disgust and stalked from the room.

Victoria was not far behind him. She went to her room and flung herself on a chair by the window, gazing onto the garden with unseeing eyes. She felt restless and irritable and also depressed, which was unusual for her. Boredom was the label she had put upon her malaise, but now she recognised that it was far more than that. No matter how she tried to divert herself or how hard she tried to occupy her mind, her thoughts kept coming back to the same subject – Calland Whitcomb.

The way he had spoken to her still shocked and angered her. During her young life Victoria Fitzherbert had never bothered to curb her tongue, not caring whom she upset or hurt. Now, for the first time, someone had replied in kind. If it had been a woman who had said such things to her Victoria would have parried the insults with scorn, and doubtless won the verbal battle. Having heard such insults from a man's lips had really shaken her. In her experience, men did not answer back to a lady – at least, gentlemen did not. They were bound by the timeless unwritten code of chivalry. But Cal Whitcomb was no gentleman, he had admitted it freely, and somehow to have heard such disrespect uttered in his countrified tones had affected her strangely. She was angry, certainly, but inside her something else stirred. An excitement at having met with something – or someone – quite beyond her experience.

A sudden urgent screaming from the drawing room cut through Victoria's thoughts.

'Victoria! Mr Fitzherbert! Come! Oh, for pity's sake, come quickly!'

There was such a desperate appeal in the cries that Victoria sped down, hard on her father's heels, fearing some terrible catastrophe. They found Mrs Fitzherbert standing in the middle of the drawing-room floor, a look of near delirious delight upon her face and an envelope clutched to her bosom.

'Such news! Such news!' she cried at their entrance. 'We have an invitation to take tea with the squire and his family at Hill House tomorrow.'

'An invitation to tea? You scare us out of our wits for an invitation to a tea party?' Mr Fitzherbert glared at his wife. 'Really, woman, I sometimes wonder how you manage with so few wits. I thought the house was on fire at the very least.'

'But aren't you pleased?' Mrs Fitzherbert asked in puzzlement. 'Don't you realise what it means? We are accepted back in local society again.'

'Of course I realise what it means,' retorted her husband. 'I'm no fool – one in the family is quite enough. But that is no excuse for shrieking like a steam whistle.' He made to leave the room, only to find himself confronted in the doorway by several of the servants who had also come running at Mrs Fitzherbert's scream. 'Have you no work to do?' he roared at them. 'I don't pay you to stand around and gawp at your betters.' The thought that he did not pay them at all never occurred to him as he stamped back to his study.

'Can I write and accept?' cried Mrs Fitzherbert after him.

'You can do what the blazes you like!' was the reply.

'You are pleased, though, aren't you, Victoria?' asked Mrs Fitzherbert. 'You can wear the pink and white poplin. It is very becoming and you haven't worn it since we came here that I recall. You are pleased, aren't you?' she persisted when her daughter made no reply.

'Yes, Mama, I am quite delighted,' answered Victoria in tones that suggested otherwise.

'How strange. It was so tedious being ignored by everyone that I thought you would both be over the moon at receiving this invitation. Well, I am pleased, if no one else is. I shall write an acceptance this very minute and then I shall go upstairs and consider what I shall wear. The lilac I think… or would that seem too much like half mourning? Perhaps it had better be the peach… unless the bolero top would not be quite appropriate for a tea party…?'

Victoria left her mother to her letter-writing and her uncertainty. She had to admit that she, too, had been quite surprised at her reaction to the arrival of this first invitation. For weeks past it had been eagerly anticipated, but now it had come she was strangely indifferent. All she could think of was how she could see Cal Whitcomb. This was the conclusion she had reached during her morning of alternate irritability and deliberations, that she had to meet him again, and this time she would be the one to win the battle of words. She was better prepared now, she would not rely upon gentlemanly conduct or any such nonsense. It would be a battle with no holds barred, find she would be the victor, bringing Cal Whitcomb to his knees before her.

Returning to the privacy of her room once more, she began her plan of campaign.

Next morning, long before the usual fashionable hour for young ladies to go riding, Victoria was booted, spurred, and in the saddle, making towards the lanes which surrounded Oakwood. She met up with Cal Whitcomb on the main road as he was coming from the direction of the village. She was so surprised to encounter him in such an unexpected spot that she demanded, 'Where have you been?'

His eyebrows rose in a way that inferred it was none of her business.

'Good morning, Miss Fitzherbert,' he said politely. 'I trust that you are well?'

His reproof was silent, and she found herself saying, 'Good morning, Mr Whitcomb. Yes, I am well, I thank you, and I beg your pardon for my rudeness. You took me quite by surprise, coming out of the turning from Stoke Hill like that.' She listened to herself with astonishment. She was actually apologising.

'I don't know why you should be surprised. As I understand it, Stoke Hill continues to be the public thoroughfare it's always been.'

'Yes, but you usually do the rounds of Oakwood this early in the morning.'

'My, you have made a thorough study of my habits. I shall have to behave more erratically in future, if only to make your life more interesting.'

'My life is interesting, I thank you,' she answered sharply, furious at having given herself away. This was not at all how she had intended their confrontation to be.

Then he smiled at her, not sardonically but with genuine amusement, and she thought he was not ill-favoured for a clodpoll. He wore his working rig of kerseymere jacket and twill breeches with style. She tried to imagine how he would look in evening dress, attending a soiree at the White House perhaps, and decided that he would not be at all out of place. One could quite take him for a gentleman, and an elegant one at that, until he opened his mouth.

'Since you are interested and obviously think I was up to no good, let me explain that I went to inspect some damage at my lower orchards,' he said. 'Someone has broken down a couple of gates.'

'How dreadful! Who would do a terrible thing like that?' she asked. Although she tried to make her concern seem sincere, it sounded stupidly false.

Cal did not seem to notice. 'I have a good idea who did it,' he said grimly, then he relaxed and smiled again, this time with more than a hint of mockery. 'Having come this far I would hate to deprive you of your customary tour round my fields. Will you please let me escort you?'

Her first reaction was to refuse and pretend she intended to ride straight on. Then she reconsidered. She had taken great pains thinking out how she would behave when she met him and what she would say, yet so far matters had been takenof her hands entirely. Cal Whitcomb had dominated the situation for quite long enough. This would be her chance to get things under her control.

'Thank you, I would like that, if it won't be too much trouble.'

'It's no trouble. I am going in that direction anyway.'

They rode on in silence for a while, then Victoria made her opening gambit, a show of interest in his work.

'How is it that you have portions of land so far apart?' she asked.

'They're two separate farms. Oakwood was my mother's dowry; Church Farm, in the village, was my father's land. They chose to live at Oakwood when they married, and the other farmhouse has been let ever since.'

'I expect your mother was too attached to her old home to leave,' said Victoria in a sentimental voice. 'How fond of her your father must have been, to please her by living at Oakwood.'

'I fancy the reasons were more practical than romantic,' said Cal with amusement. 'We've always kept more stock up at Oakwood than at Church Farm. It was more convenient to reside close to the animals rather than to slog up and down the hill goodness knows how many times to see to feeding and milking. Besides, Oakwood has the better house.'

'Could your family not have employed people to do the work?'

'Certainly, but farm workers have a most annoying habit, they insist upon being paid. Otherwise they wander off and work for someone else.'

Victoria sat very upright in the saddle, uncertain whether he was making a pointed reference to the financial arrangements at the White House. He was just the sort of man who would be so indelicate. But when he changed the subject of conversation entirely, she decided she had been mistaken.

'Tell me,' he said, 'it has been intriguing me these last ten minutes. If we had not met by chance at the road back there, what ploy would you have used to attract my attention this time?'

'You seem confident that I would have wanted to attract your attention,' she retorted.

'Well, wouldn't you? I'm still far from convinced that you found my old dog frightening that time we met in the lanes. However, my guess is that you would have used a variation upon the same theme. Something frightening your horse, perhaps. I daresay you have a spare scarf secreted about your person ready to throw into the hedge, for it to flutter in the breeze. Then, of course, that superbly schooled animal of yours would naturally take fright and refuse to pass the strange object the minute I came upon the scene.'

'You are insufferable,' declared Victoria, tossing her head, and hoping the silk scarf in her pocket remained hidden.

Cal laughed. 'I am, aren't I?' he agreed. 'Shall we begin our survey of my land? Today, as well as my usual checking of the animals, I wish to look at the hayfields. You've not seen them recently, have you? You see, I have noticed your absence. So had my mother, incidentally. She hasn't seen a decent hat in ages.'

'Oh really!' protested Victoria indignantly. 'If you insist upon being rude, I shall call up Robbins and ride on by myself.'

'There's no need for that. You are quite right, I shouldn't tease you, not when you've only just ceased punishing me for the last time I was rude to you. That was why you haven't been riding around Oakwood recently, I presume?'

'I have not been riding in these lanes recently because I wished for a change,' Victoria said with careful dignity. 'I was bored by the scenery.'

This encounter was not going the way she planned. Try as she might, she could not gain control of either the conversation or the situation. Cal Whitcomb seemed to dominate her at every turn. For a simple farmer there was an elusive quality about him she had not anticipated. She was not sure she liked it, for it meant she did not know how she stood with him, and this was a new and unpleasant experience for Miss Victoria Fitzherbert. There were well-bred young men in London who would have been eating out of her hand by now, yet she was still sparring with this rustic, and coming off worse too often for her comfort.

If Cal was aware of her displeasure he gave no sign. 'After your absence, brief though it has been, I think you'll see many changes,' he said. 'The hay in particular. This is the first field I want to look at.'

Remaining on horseback, he leaned over and unhooked the gate, holding it open for her. Together they rode in. If Robbins was anywhere in the vicinity, he remained discreetly out of sight in the lane. Cal dismounted and, with a raised eyebrow by way of enquiry, lifted her out of the saddle too. Now was her chance. They were alone in the secluded field, his hands still about her waist.

'Mr Whitcomb,' she said in a demure voice, her eyes lowered.

She was wasting her time. He let go of her, not seeming to have heard her, striding along the field border looking out across his hay as a sailor might look out to sea. Then he plucked a few strands of grass, rolled them between his finger and thumb and appeared satisfied with the result.

'It's ready for cutting,' he said, walking towards her but with his eyes looking heavenwards instead of at her. 'This weather will hold for a few days, if I'm any judge. We will start cutting tomorrow first thing.'

'How gratifying,' she said in a voice heavy with sarcasm.

He chewed his lip, as if trying to contain a smile. 'Yes, it is,' he said. 'An early start to haymaking is always good news. Who knows, we might manage a second cut this year. Miss Fitzherbert, I think you started to speak to me just now. I'm afraid I was a churlish fellow and scarcely noticed, for my mind was completely on the hay, but now my attention is entirely yours. What was it you wanted to say?'

He was doing it deliberately! Ignoring her! Teasing her! How dare he imply she was less interesting than a field of stupid grass! Victoria was conscious that her lower lip was beginning to protrude sullenly. With difficulty she controlled it. He was not going to defeat her. She would gain the upper hand!

'Mr Whitcomb,' she said, her voice demure once more, her eyes lowered exactly as before, 'I am glad of this opportunity to speak to you alone. I was not being quite honest when I said I found these lanes boring. To tell the truth I was too ashamed to ride this way in case I did indeed meet you again.'

'You were?' Cal's voice was grave.

'Yes. You said some terrible things to me that day – no one has ever spoken to me in such a way before, and I confess I was frightfully angry with you. But gradually, as I calmed down, I began to realise how right you had been. I did behave abominably to that poor woman, didn't I? I don't know what makes me behave so. It's as if there is a wicked imp inside me which gains control at times, and then I do things I'm truly sorry for afterwards. I am, you know. Truly, truly sorry, and it was you who showed me exactly how nasty and unpleasant I'd been. If only I had someone wise and sensible like you to guide me and to teach me...'

'To teach you how to control that wicked imp, I think you said it was?' said Cal, his voice serious. 'But, my dear young lady, you have parents.'

'I have, but I fear I can't turn to them. Mama is the dearest creature, but in all honesty her understanding isn't great. As for Papa, he doesn't like me, and never has.' Victoria produced a handkerchief and applied it to her eyes with a facility learned from her mother. 'He wanted a boy, you see, and he has never forgiven me for being a girl.'

Cal cleared his throat. 'I understand now how you need help in controlling that imp of yours,' he said. 'Though I don't think I have the proper experience to assist. The person you need to speak to is my mother.'

'Oh no!' said Victoria in alarm, her handkerchief falling from dry eyes. 'It's you,' she went on hurriedly, resuming her winsome voice. 'You've already proved to be so wise. This unfortunate woman I sent sprawling in the mud, how do you think I should compensate her? I believe she lives in some cottages by the river. Shall I send Robbins to her with half-a-crown?'

'Not unless he can swim,' said Cal, his face still a picture of seriousness. 'I would bet that her brothers would throw him and the half-crown in the river. Come to think of it, Miss Shillabeer is quite capable of throwing him in herself.'

Victoria's small face was raised, her eyes, large and luminous, looked up at him. 'Then what shall I do?' she asked plaintively.

'This,' said Cal. Grasping her by the waist he pulled her hard against him and kissed her.

It was not a gentle gesture, there was no tenderness in it. As his mouth pressed on hers, taking away her breath, bruising her lips, Victoria was aware of a sense of impeding victory and a growing excitement.

Abruptly he released her. 'There,' he said. 'That was what you were angling for, wasn't it? Why didn't you just ask, instead of going through all that rigmarole? You aren't really sorry one bit about Maddy Shillabeer, are you?'

'No,' admitted Victoria, buoyed up by her triumph. She was on surer ground now. 'I said it because I want you to like me. You aren't at all like the young men I usually meet. Compared to you they seem silly and insipid.'

'Perhaps that's because I am not a young man any more. I'm nearly thirty.'

'That's it. You are mature, not some callow youth. That's what first attracted me to you.'

'I'm certainly not a callow youth,' agreed Cal.

Although he had released her, they remained standing close together. With a small, gloved hand, Victoria brushed away a dandelion seed that had landed on his lapel. The intimate gesture brought them closer.

'You do like me, don't you?' she said in a pleading voice. 'Please say you like me the teeniest little bit.'

'I don't dislike you.'

'Then prove it. Kiss me again. You did say I was to ask,' she added as he looked askance.

'I did.'

His kiss was as relentless and impassive as before. For some reason she found it both exciting and disturbing, quite unlike the other kisses she had received, which had been adoring and humble. There was nothing humble about this man or his kisses.

'There, you enjoyed that,' she said when he released her. 'If you are very good I might let you kiss me again.'

'Might you?' he said, remarkably unimpressed by her offer. 'I won't avail myself of your kindness just now. I have the rest of my fields to check.' Without asking her permission, he lifted her back into the saddle.

She did not mind, she was beginning to find his offhand ways quite amusing. 'Then you will have to wait until our next rendezvous, won't you?' she said coyly, confident that now she had hooked her fish. 'I will meet you in this lane tomorrow.'

For a hooked fish he proved oddly reluctant to be played.

'Not tomorrow,' he said. 'Nor the rest of this week if the weather holds. I've more important things to do. I'll be haymaking.'

Chapter Seven

The summer days brought with them increased activity. The whole countryside was astir and on the move soon after dawn, for the haymaking was beginning. Maddy joined a group which was heading away from the village.

'They say Farmer Bradworthy be paying elevenpence a day this year,' commented one woman.

'Yes, but 'tis a traipse out to Aish,' said another. 'I be happy to be took on by Farmer Churchward for tenpence.'

'What's the betting you only get eightpence up to Oakwood,' commented the first. 'You won't catch Farmer Whitcomb paying out a penny more than he must. And there'll be some poor souls as'll have to take what he gives.'

'He do feed his workers well, mind,' pointed out someone. 'And he pays on the dot, not like some of them.'

'He don't have no excuse for being stingy with the cider, not the amount he'm making,' said a voice.

'He don't need no excuse to be stingy, it do come natural,' pointed out another, to much laughter.

'Where'm you hoping to get took on, maid?' asked Maddy's neighbour cheerfully.

'I think I might try Oakwood, just to see if the cider's any good,' she replied.

Everyone knew the situation between the Shillabeers and the Whitcombs and they all laughed.

In fact, Maddy was making for Rob Bradworthy's farm at Aish, on the outskirts of the parish. The band of folk also hoping to work at Aish went at a fair pace for it would be first there, first taken on. Part way along the route Maddy was forced to stop because of a snapped bootlace. By the time she had completed the fiddly task of rethreading the lace her companions were out of sight. At the sound of approaching horse's hooves she stiffened; recent experience had taught her to be wary of lone riders. She felt quite relieved to see the mounted figure of Cal Whitcomb join the lane from a side track. She expected him to ignore her, or at most nod his head in greeting. To her surprise he pulled up beside her.

'You are going to Farmer Bradworthy's?' he asked.

'Yes.'

'You're late. I've just seen the main body of haymakers going along the lane.'

'I still hope I'll be lucky.' She was certainly not going to admit to him that Rob would probably give her a job because they were once sweethearts.

'Well, if you're not...' Cal Whitcomb's voice faded away. He was not the sort of man to be irresolute, and Maddy regarded him with surprise. He coughed, as if to block out what he had been about to say, then continued, 'If you see any others wanting work, tell them I'm paying tenpence a day and four pints of cider.'

'*And* their dinner?' she asked, astounded by such unaccustomed generosity.

'And their dinner,' he said.

If it had been anyone else she might have been tempted, but the workhouse door would have to be staring her in the face before she worked at Oakwood. 'I'll spread the word abroad,' she said.

With a curt nod he touched his horse with his heels and rode off, leaving Maddy feeling somewhat bemused. Had he almost offered her work? No, more likely she had misunderstood. Or maybe it had been a slip of the tongue on his part. The idea of her working for Cal Whitcomb! It was ludicrous.

The crowd of hopeful workers had already dispersed to the fields when Maddy reached the Bradworthy farmyard gate, but she knew from experience which field Rob would start on. Her route took her past the farmhouse. The kitchen door was open and from inside the baby was crying, while Janie's voice, harassed and irritable, shouted at one of the other children. Janie herself appeared briefly at the door to throw out some slop water. She looked hot and tired already, and she had a long day ahead of her.

For years Maddy had envied her. On that fine summer morning, however, she found to her surprise that she had no wish to change places with Janie. If her girlhood plans had gone smoothly and she had married Rob, no doubt she would have been content, for Rob was a good man, but she would have been the old Maddy, dashing about with her senses dead to everything save her next task. She would never have known the wonderful enlightenment that Patrick had brought to her, nor the overwhelming happiness. At that moment she would not have changed places with Janie Bradworthy for the world.

When he saw her Rob smiled his slow, good-natured smile. 'There you be,' he said. 'I thought you'd deserted me this year.'

'No, I got held up by a broken bootlace.' Maddy smiled back. 'Do you still need one more? Or should I see if Janie wants a hand?' she added, suddenly smitten by an uncomfortable conscience. It was a shame to let the poor woman struggle on, and with four small children.

'Lor', you keep away from that kitchen if you'm any sense!' exclaimed Rob in mock horror. 'There idn't a female relation on either side as habn't turned up this morning. How there be room for them all I don't know and I idn't planning to find out. You do what I be going to do, girl. Get out into the fields and the good fresh air where 'tis peaceful.'

Grinning, Maddy did as she was advised and collected a wide rake. The cutters had already started, skilfully slicing through the tall green grass with long graceful sweeps of their scythes. Maddy joined the lines of other women who followed after, raking the fallen grass into lengthy wind rows that would let the hay dry without losing any of its colour or sweet scent.

It was a long day, but there was much laughing and joking, especially when the levels in the cider jugs – kept cool under the hedge and very welcome to throats dry with dust – began to go down. Listening to the singing which echoed across the field, Maddy thought of Rob and his idea that the fields were peaceful. Not at haymaking they weren't, and never had been.

The haymakers were more quiet and less exuberant on their way home. Nevertheless, despite their fatigue, the chatter and banter that was exchanged continued to be good-humoured and cheery. Maddy felt hot and tired, and the road seemed long to her weary bones – until she saw Patrick.

He was sitting on a stile, obviously looking out for her. When he caught sight of her his face lit up with a grin, and jumping down from his perch he came running towards her. His appearance caused a few jovial comments from the others but Maddy did not care. She was too pleased to see him.

'I thought you would come this way so I decided to meet you,' he greeted her.

'How clever of you to work it out, this being the shortest route,' she teased.

'I wasn't to know that, was I? There might be any number of footpaths I didn't know about.'

'Very well, we're agreed, you are clever.' It was strange how, after only minutes in his company, her weariness had dropped from her. She wished the grubbiness, caused by hours in the fields, could disappear as easily, but Patrick did not seem to notice. 'Aren't you working tonight?' she asked.

'Not for a while. Business was slack – something to do with jugs of cider out in the fields at this time of year. Mr Watkins gave me an hour off. I'll have to make up for it some other time, but I don't care. I'm with you and that's all that matters.' It was all that mattered to Maddy too. Hand in hand they walked, oblivious of the others taking the same road. They turned off into the seclusion of the lane down to Duncannon and only then did Patrick slide his arm about her waist. She appreciated his tact in waiting until they were away from the other haymakers. Such sweet intimate gestures, no matter how innocent, were for when they were alone.

Dusk was falling, but in the dark shadows of the narrow lane myriad sparks of light glowed.

'Glow-worms,' breathed Maddy. 'They come out in the dimpsey.'

'I presume dimpsey is what civilised people call twilight.'

Maddy laughed, then smothered the sound. 'No, it's the civilised people who say dimpsey. And we must speak quietly or the glow-worms will take fright.'

'That would be a pity,' said Patrick softly, 'for they are beautiful. I've never seen so many in one place before. It's as if the stars in the sky had come down to light our way. Or perhaps they are giving me light for this.' Turning her to face him, he took her in his arms and kissed her.

'You really are my Rustic Damozel,' he breathed. 'You taste of sun and smell of the sweet hay. You could not be more perfect.'

It was incredible. Not long ago she had felt dead tired, spent, and grubby, then, because of a single kiss and a few words, she felt truly beautiful. How Patrick could inspire such feelings in her she did not know. She only knew that he did.

Down on the river someone was rowing. They stood there, entwined in each other's arms listening to the splash of the oars as the sound carried on night air heavy with the scent of honeysuckle. One tiny navigation light gleamed in the darkness, as if one of the glow-worms had become waterborne.

It was a night made for lovers. She melted against him, conscious of the growing passion between them. To give herself to him, to let him possess her completely was what she wanted more than anything at that moment. When his fingers began unbuttoning her high-necked cotton dress she made no objection. She revelled in the caressing of his gentle fingers and the soft warmth of his lips as they slid down her throat to the curve of her breasts. Then he held her tightly, his body hard and urgent against her, his breathing heavy.

'Some day...' Patrick whispered. 'Some day... And then what happiness will be ours.'

Never before had his words hinted at a future together. He wanted her, and for the first time she dared to hope for the years ahead.

–

The haymaking provided days of work, laborious, good-humoured, and a useful source of extra income. Maddy was sorry when it was over and the last pitchforkful had been stacked and thatched ready for the winter. Working in the fields brought a welcome change from her everyday activities and she always enjoyed the happy time spent bringing in the hay.

It was a pity the atmosphere at home was not equally agreeable. The salmon-netting season, which had begun with such promise, had tailed away sadly during the summer. Some blamed the lack of rainfall, others the growing influence of the railways, which were bound to disturb the order of things with their dashing about at unnatural speeds, disrupting nature. Whatever the reason, there were fewer of the great silver fish in the river.

In the cheap notebook she kept for the purpose, Maddy added up the tally of salmon caught during the last few weeks. Even allowing for the better price prompted by the scarcity of the fish, it did not make a very impressive total, and she felt a growing sense of unease. The salmon just weren't running, that was the sum of it. The heavy splash as a silver body leapt from the river was a rarity that summer, as was the sharp arrow-shaped wave in the water that normally betrayed a salmon swimming below the surface. If things did not improve it was going to be a hard struggle to get through the winter.

The patience and fortitude that the menfolk showed on the river could not be expected to last once they got home. Then it was that their tempers, never very equable at the best of times, became irritable. Anything to do with the Whitcombs was their first target, but these days they had another, one that had been unaccountably ignored over the last months.

'He'm making a damned fool of you, and no mistake,' declared Jack one day. 'To think a daughter of mine could be so taken in.'

'I don't know about that mountebank making a fool of her, I reckon her'm doing a bloody good job for herself, with her fine ways and her Lady Muck talk,' added Bart waspishly.

'Maybe I'm a fool, maybe not,' she retorted. 'Either way, it's my affair and doesn't concern you lot.'

'Don't concern us?' snapped Bart. 'Not when our sister is shameless, trailing after a rogue as come from goodness knows where? No better than you ought to be, that's what folk be saying, and us idn't going to stand for it, be us, lads?'

The other brothers nodded in silent agreement.

'Who said that about me? Name me one person!' demanded Maddy. There was no reply. 'There wasn't anyone, was there? You're making it up as an excuse to get on at me.'

'I don't need to make anything up,' Bart retorted. 'You'm getting yourself gossiped about, and you ought to be ashamed.'

'Then why didn't you defend me if you're that worried about the family honour?' Maddy demanded. 'When that girl out at the quarry cottages got in the family way I went for anyone who suggested you were the father, though I knew it was more than likely.'

'You don't think you'm the only woman he be trifling with?' asked Bart, changing tack. 'A bigger appetite for females than Barneys bull, that's what he'm got.'

'And I suppose you've got proof of that, too?' said Maddy.

'Don't you care that he'm made up to half the women in the village already?'

'No.'

'Then you ought!' Bart roared. 'Habn't you no bloody pride?'

'Yes, I have, but you don't understand.'

'I understands a piece of rubbish when I sees un, and that's what yon fiddling fellow be, naught but rubbish.' Then suddenly his voice became quiet, almost gentle. 'Maddy, us can see him for what he be. Why can't you? We'm worried for you. Where be all this nonsense going to lead? Have he mentioned marriage or ought to do with the future? Us don't want you hurt, maid, and us can see un coming if you don't watch out.'

Maddy was touched. Bart had not spoken so kindly to her in a long time. She was reminded of how he used to be before their mother died. Then he had been the concerned one of the family, the one who liked to see everybody happy. How strange that she had forgotten.

'I appreciate you bothering about me, truly I do, only you don't know Patrick. If you did you'd not have such a poor opinion of him. He's not perfect, I won't say he is, but I'll be all right. I know my own business best.'

'No you don't!' Bart returned to his customary angry growl. 'You be a danged obstinate wench, but if you'm thinking us'll stand by and see our name dragged in the mud then you'm got another think coming!'

He stamped out of the house, the other three plus Jack inevitably following in his wake. Maddy knew she would not see them again until their cider money ran out.

Having belatedly decided upon Patrick as a target for their belligerence, the Shillabeer men made up for lost time. As the summer progressed, they seldom spoke to Maddy without some derogatory remark about him, backed up by threats of what would happen unless she ceased seeing him. Her disquiet grew and she warned Patrick that her brothers were working themselves up for mischief.

'Go away,' she pleaded with him. 'Leave the village before they turn really nasty.'

'Why should I run?' he protested. 'We've done nothing wrong. If I disappear suddenly because of your brothers' threats, everyone will think the worst, and I refuse to leave you to face such a situation.'

At that moment she knew she loved him enough to give him up.

'That isn't important,' she said. 'You don't know them, when they're drunk they're capable of anything. Get away now.'

But Patrick refused. 'It's not the first time someone's been out for my blood,' he said wryly.

It was Annie who told Maddy how her brothers had started to frequent the Victoria and Albert in order to taunt Patrick, making such a nuisance of themselves that the landlord had finally sent for Constable Vallance.

'They must have been bad for Sam Watkins to turn away thirsts like theirs,' had been Maddy's comment, though she had felt far from joking.

'I can't say how sorry I am,' she said to Patrick when next they met. 'To think that you've been provoked like this because of me.'

'I'm losing no sleep over it, I promise you.' He smoothed back an unruly strand of her hair. 'Besides, you aren't to blame for your family. Let's forget them and think only of us.' Gently he pulled her back into his arms. They were at one of their favourite trysting places at the point where the Stoke Gabriel creek met the river. On a promontory, wooded and secluded, it was nevertheless easily reached from the Mill Dam, the perfect place to snatch a half-hour in each other's company.

'You're right, we'll think only of us and how wonderful it is, being here together.' Maddy nestled closer to him. 'Do you think—'

She got no further, for there was a crashing in the undergrowth and an all too familiar voice cried, 'There he be, lads! Let's get him!'

Maddy sat bolt upright. 'Run!' she screamed.

But Patrick had no choice. Her brothers were upon him before he had risen to his feet.

'You leave him be this instant, you gurt brutes!' she yelled, forgetting her fine accent in her distress as she beat at Bart with clenched fists and flailing boots. But she might have been a fly for the notice he took.

'What'll us do with him?' demanded Lew.

'Sling un in the river,' declared Bart.

Patrick struggled with all his might and Maddy continued to punch and kick at her brothers, but it was useless.

'One, two, three!' Patrick's body was swung in time to the chant, then the four brothers flung him as far as they could. There was a huge splash and he disappeared from view.

'There, that should cool un down a bit,' Bart gloated. Then his expression changed. 'Get you home, maid,' he ordered.

Maddy did not hear him. 'Where be he?' she cried in distraction. 'He be drowned!'

'Serves him right. Come on, lads, let's have a drink to celebrate.' Bart started to move away with the others. Only Lew looked back apprehensively. 'Don't be bloody soft, boy,' his elder brother rebuked him. 'He were asking for un.'

The tide was high, and although the water was scarcely a man's height deep at that point, Maddy knew it was more than she could cope with in long petticoats. Moreover, she could not swim. Evidently neither could Patrick. As she looked desperately for him, he rose to the surface, his mouth open in a soundless cry for help, one arm raised in supplication.

'I'm coming, I'm coming,' she screamed, but how?

A little further on she had noticed a boat moored to a branch. Running to it she hauled at the painter, relieved to see that the oars were there. It was no easy task scrambling down the stony bank and climbing on board. Somehow she managed it, strengthened by sheer desperation. A few expert pulls on the oars and she was near the spot where she had last seen Patrick. Then she caught sight of him, floating face down just below the surface of the water. As she reached him she prayed that he was still alive.

Finding Patrick was one thing, getting him into the rowing boat was a different matter. She knew she could not haul him aboard on her own without capsizing the boat.

'Help!' she kept calling until her voice was so hoarse and weak she was sure no one could hear her.

'I be coming, maid! I be coming!' The answering voice seemed like a miracle. Even more wonderful, she recognised it. It was Lew's! Not daring to move for fear Patrick would slip from her grasp, she saw her brother rowing rapidly towards her. He was alone. It took him no more than a few minutes to reach her. To Maddy it felt like hours before she felt Patrick taken from her as Lew dragged him into his boat.

'I'd best get him on land quick,' he said. 'Can you manage?' Maddy nodded, and taking up the oars, followed behind him. Quite a crowd awaited them when they arrived at the Mill Dam. By the time Maddy reached the shore, Patrick was lying on his stomach and capable hands were pressing on his back, forcing river water from his lungs. To the many enquiries of 'What happened?' Lew replied abruptly, 'Accident.' But Maddy's single question 'Will he live?' was harder to answer. It seemed an age before the water stopped spewing from Patrick's mouth and his eyelids flickered.

'He'm still alive!' someone exclaimed.

They carried Patrick to the Victoria and Albert, up to his tiny room above the stables. Maddy would have followed but the solid shape of Mrs Watkins blocked her way.

'Twouldn't be seemly, you being a maid,' she said firmly.

'Please, can't I stay?' begged Maddy. 'I'll wait outside.'

'I idn't having females hanging about yer, this be a respectable inn,' retorted Mrs Watkins. Then she relented. 'Go into the kitchen and dry off by the fire, you'm near as soaked as he be. Sukie'll make you a cup of tea.'

With that Maddy had to be content. As she sat by the blazing fire in the inn's kitchen, Sukie the maidservant said consolingly, 'He'm in good hands. The missus have forgot more about nursing than most folk ever knowd.'

Maddy smiled at her bleakly, hoping she was right.

It was dark by the time Mrs Watkins came back downstairs. 'Best go home now, maid, he'm sleeping peaceful,' she said.

'Can't I see him, just for a minute?' Maddy begged.

'Not till the morning then, if he'm fit, you can peek in on him. I idn't changing my mind, there idn't no point in you pleading.'

Maddy had no option but to obey, although as she walked away from the inn she felt that she should be the one sitting up with Patrick that night. It was her right. She loved him.

As she neared home, her thoughts turned to her brothers and a terrible fury swept through her. They had gone too far this time and she meant to punish them for it. By the time she reached the cottage she was too angry to speak. Her mouth in a tight, grim line, she stormed in, marching through the kitchen and up the steep stairs without a word or a look towards her father and brothers who sat in sheepish silence. Tying a change of clothes and her precious *Jane Eyre* into a shawl, she returned downstairs and made for the door. Bart got there before her.

'Where'm you going?' he demanded.

She did not argue. She slammed her fist right into his solar plexus. Taken by surprise, he doubled up. Maddy pushed him aside and stalked out.

She did not go far. At the bend in the path she stopped and listened for any sound of pursuit. When none came, she slipped off her boots and, in her stockinged feet, crept back to Annie's cottage.

The Crowthers' dog heard her and began to bark, but he was silenced with a curse. There was no light showing at the Fleets' windows so she was obliged to throw a handful of gravel against the glass. Instantly there was the flickering flame of a candle being lit, and William's head appeared.

'It's me, Maddy,' she said in a hoarse whisper before he could call out and disturb everyone. 'Can I come in?'

'Course you can, maid. Step right in. Us'll be down directly.' William's head was withdrawn.

Maddy opened the unlocked door and stepped into the kitchen, standing uncertainly in the darkness. Soon William came downstairs, candle in hand, followed more hesitantly by Annie.

'What's happened? What be the matter, my lover?' demanded Annie. 'William, light the lamp, boy. Us don't have to grope about by candle.'

'No, please don't!' exclaimed Maddy urgently. 'I don't want them to know I'm here.'

'Them? You mean *them*?' Annie jerked her head in the direction of the Shillabeers' cottage. 'What they been up to this time?'

'They almost killed Patrick…' Once she started, the words flowed from her in a stream. The horror of the experience, her fears for Patrick, the terrible dread when she had pulled his seemingly lifeless body from the water, poured from her. Annie and William listened without interruption, knowing she needed to share the dreadful events of the day. 'I can't go back there yet,' she ended. 'Please, can I stay with you?'

'Course you can.' William spoke up. 'You stay as long as you want, and if your lot come over trying to cause trouble, they'm going to have me to deal with.' William had been something of a wrestler in his younger days; even Bart would think twice before tackling him.

A sudden exhaustion swept over Maddy. Annie noticed her droop where she sat.

'There, things be catching up with you,' she said kindly. 'You bide there a minute while I get a pillow and some covers. Won't be too comfortable there on the settle, I'm fearing, but us'll do the best us can.'

In spite of Annie's fears, Maddy was asleep almost at once.

The next day she found it odd to wake up in strange surroundings yet see the familiar scene from a different angle. Surreptitiously she watched her father and brothers set out late for the fishing.

'I bet it were a real muddle over there this morning,' said Annie. 'I'd have give good money to have been a spider in the corner watching they men trying to cope. It be baking day, too, bain't it? They won't have no bread. You'm idn't planning to creep over while they idn't there and fire the oven, I hopes?'

'No,' said Maddy grimly. 'They're going to have to get on without me.'

'Good maid,' beamed Annie approvingly. 'Well, I be glad of your company, never doubt that for a minute. Maybe, if you feels like reading, us could have a bit of *Jane*, eh? Twill be as good as a holiday. But first you be wanting to see how young Patrick be faring, I dare say,' she said gently. 'You get off to un as soon as you please.'

Maddy gave her a hug, touched by her kindness and understanding. 'No one ever had such good friends as you and William,' she said, with a lump in her throat.

'And what about the times you'm helped me over the years when I been bad? The water you'm fetched, the floors you'm scrubbed, the dinners you'm cooked? Tis us as has the good friend.' Annie sounded quite indignant. 'Off you go and give that sweetheart of youm a big kiss. That'll cure him faster than aught else.' And she gave Maddy a gentle push towards the door.

Avoiding the numerous Crowthers was Maddy's biggest problem. Quite apart from not wanting her menfolk to know where she was, she had no wish to have to satisfy Elsie's curiosity over events. Choosing her moment, she slipped along the foreshore going upstream away from the path, then, scrambling up the bank, she cut back through the scrubland behind Duncannon until she joined the path at a point out of sight of the cottages.

'Ten minutes, and not an instant more!' was Mrs Watkins' stern directive when she arrived at the Victoria and Albert. 'And definitely no funny business!'

She entered the room to find Patrick sitting up in bed reading. He looked terribly pale, but when he saw her his face lit up. Dropping the book, he held his arms open wide to her. For a while she could do nothing but hold him close, rocking back and forth with the joy of being with him. He needed a shave and the roughness of his cheek against hers filled her with tenderness.

'I feared you wouldn't want to see me again,' she whispered brokenly.

'Why ever not? It was an accident.'

She eased back from him, looking at him with astonishment. 'How can you say that?' she demanded.

'What else was it? I fell into the river accidentally and, fool that I am, not being able to swim, I nearly drowned myself. It's thanks to you that I'm still here.'

'It wasn't like that at all,' she protested, fearing that the shock of the events had affected his brain. 'Don't you remember? We were at Mill Point and my brothers—'

He silenced her with a gentle finger upon her lips. 'We were at Mill Point certainly,' he said decisively. 'That was where I slipped and fell in, and I defy anyone to say otherwise.' His eyes were clear and she could see that he was perfectly lucid. He knew exactly what he was saying.

'Oh, Patrick…' She hardly knew how to voice her feelings. 'You are wonderful… The most wonderful man in existence.'

'Of course,' he replied. 'I thought you realised that.'

'I do,' she answered, giving a serious response to his teasing. 'Good. I like to be appreciated.' He smoothed her cheek with his hand. 'Don't look so serious. Everything is fine. According to Mrs Watkins, I'll mend.'

'Thank goodness.' Maddy breathed the words, then exclaimed, 'To think of it! I didn't ask how you're feeling.'

'I preferred the way you did greet me. It was much more enjoyable. I confess I'm as weak as a kitten but otherwise I'm fine. Mrs Watkins says I've the constitution of an ox, and who am I to argue?'

'Thank goodness,' whispered Maddy again. 'When I think of seeing you there under the water, so still—'

'Don't!' Patrick's cheerful manner disappeared suddenly. His face grew more ashen and he clutched at her convulsively, his fingers grasping her flesh painfully, his face pressed hard against her breast. He was shaking violently. 'Please don't remind me. I don't want to think about it, I can't bear it.' Startled and alarmed at this unexpected reaction, Maddy tightened her arms about him reassuringly.

'It's all right,' she said. 'I'm here. It's all right.'

They remained like that, with Maddy holding him and stroking his hair, all the while whispering soothing words.

'I'm not wonderful,' he whispered eventually. 'I'm an awful coward and I know you'll scorn me for it, but I have to confess to you, I'm terrified of water. I have been ever since I can remember. Even when I cross a bridge I keep my eyes firmly away from the parapet, and as for being in a boat, that fills me with panic. There, you can scoff at me now, you who have been brought up by the river all your life. To you I must seem a miserable specimen.'

'Why?' demanded Maddy. 'There have been times when my heart's been in my mouth when the boys have been out with a northerly blowing and a strong tide running. What's more, I think you're more wonderful than ever, and I won't be contradicted. What happened to you would have been terrible for anyone. For you it was doubly so, yet you refuse to condemn my brothers.'

'It was an accident.' Patrick's hold on her became less desperate as he relaxed. 'Let's talk of something else, or better still, not talk at all. I like it like this.' And he nestled his head more comfortably against her.

Maddy gave a laugh, as much from relief as anything else. There had been a moment when she had feared she would never hold him in her arms again. Then she remembered. The river had already claimed its victim for the year in poor Biddy. If the old belief were true, it did not want another. But dared she have relied on mere superstition? No, she decided, not when Patrick's life had been in the balance. He was too precious.

'Mrs Watkins said there was to be no funny business,' she reproved him jokingly.

'This isn't funny, this is deadly serious,' he replied, and to prove it he pulled her face towards him and kissed her on the lips, gently at first then with growing ardour.

A heavy tread on the stairs betrayed the approach of Mrs Watkins.

'Time you was gone, maid,' she said in a no-nonsense voice. 'As for you, young fellow-me-lad, you can get up tomorrow if there's no fever on you, then it'll be back to work the next day.' She looked questioningly at Maddy. 'Well?' she demanded. 'What be waiting for?'

'Can I come again tomorrow?' she asked.

'I suppose so, though I can't be doing with all this coming and going, not with an inn to run.'

Maddy turned to Patrick. 'I'll see you tomorrow,' she said. 'Be sure you're a lot better by then.'

'The sight of you today has been the best tonic I could have had,' he smiled in return, and blew her a kiss.

'Daft ha'p'orth,' snorted Mrs Watkins.

On her way home Maddy saw a sight she had never expected to see. Davie was coming out of Mrs Cutmore's shop, a loaf of bread in his hand. He had a look of acute embarrassment on his face and he was holding the loaf away from his body, as if trying to disassociate himself from anything as unmanly as buying bread. He looked so funny that Maddy was hard put to it not to laugh. She dodged into a gateway out of sight, and waited until he was well ahead, to make sure she would not catch up with him.

'Your father were over yer asking if us'd seen you,' Annie informed her the instant she arrived. 'Us didn't tell un, of course. Us just said you'd be mazed to bide so close to home. That seemed to satisfy him.'

'Thanks,' said Maddy with a smile.

'You had another visitor, too. Constable Vallance. Leastways, your menfolk did.'

'The boys weren't—'

'Don't worry, he didn't take your lot away with him. He weren't looking any too pleased, mind. Had a face like thunder. Us heard him giving them a warning good and proper. Told them the injured party refused to lay charges, but that he knowd they'd been up to no good. And if they got into mischief one more time he'd be down on them and no mistake.'

'Thank goodness it wasn't any worse, though I doubt if they'll take much notice of the constable's warnings.'

'I don't know. Without you at their beck and call maybe they'll learn some sense at last.'

'Maybe,' said Maddy, but she was not very hopeful.

The rest of the day was the most idle Maddy had spent in a long time. She did what she could to help Annie about the house, they had countless cups of tea and talked, then more tea as Maddy read aloud. First it was a three-week-old copy of the *Totnes Times* that William had acquired. While he waited for passengers to be ferried across the river, he listened to her reading with interest. But when Maddy took out her copy of *Jane Eyre*, he wandered off into the garden muttering, 'That be women's stuff.' However, she noticed that his weeding kept him close to the open window. Annie noticed it too, and gave a sly grin.

'I should come in, boy, and listen proper,' she called. 'They ears of youm must be getting longer by the minute. Next us knows your nose'll be twitching and you'll be wanting dandelions for your supper.'

'I be all right here,' William grunted, but as the story progressed the regular chink of his hoe grew less frequent until it ceased completely.

From time to time, between reading and helping Annie, Maddy would peep through the window. She could see her father and the boys as they patiently cast their net upstream towards the quarry. Her conscience was beginning to trouble her. The last time she had cooked for them had been dinner the previous noon. She doubted if they had had a decent meal since then, yet there they were, working hard with no proper nourishment inside them, while she idled away her time reading and drinking cups of tea.

She was homesick too, which was ridiculous considering how close to the cottage she was. But she had never slept away from her own home before. She missed her attic, with the sharp fresh smell of tar rising from the nets stored in the room below. She missed having her familiar things about her, and her regular routine to keep her occupied. In short, she wanted to go home.

Annie noticed her growing restlessness.

'They men'll be all right, maid,' she reassured her. 'They can boil a few tatties for themselves, surely. They idn't going to starve.'

'I know, but it just doesn't feel right, me being over here doing nothing. I don't think I can last out much longer. I've been looking after them for such an age I can't stop now.'

'What if you marry? They'd have to fend for themselves then.'

'That isn't likely to happen. For one thing, I couldn't leave them.'

'Yes you could, and should if you gets a good offer. You and that Patrick seem proper fond and foolish, summat could come of that. Jack would have to do what other men does, and get a housekeeper. There be plenty of widows and spinsters needing a roof over their heads.'

'Maybe.' Maddy was not very hopeful. She feared there were not too many women desperate enough to share a roof with the notorious Shillabeers.

'You'm determined to go back then? I can see un in your face,' said Annie.

'Yes. I'll stay one more night, if it's all right with you and William, then I'll go home tomorrow.'

'Tis a pity.' Annie gave a sigh. 'But if that's what you feel be right, my lover, then us won't try to stop you. Us've enjoyed having you here and no mistake.'

For her part Maddy appreciated the time away from her family, it had given her an opportunity to sort out her thoughts.

–

Patrick was up, dressed, and sitting on the wall in the sun when she called upon him next morning.

'I'm glad to see you looking better.' Maddy greeted him with, a furtive kiss, away from the eyes of Mrs Watkins.

'I'm feeling even more better after that.' He returned her kiss energetically. 'I've been instructed to sit here and get my bones warmed through. That way, by tomorrow, I will be quite fit to heave beer barrels about, or so Mrs Watkins assures me, and she wouldn't lie about a thing like that, would she?'

Maddy shook her head, smiling; then she grew grave. 'I want to thank you. Constable Vallance called on my brothers yesterday.'

'I don't need thanks for that, it was none of my doing.'

'Fool! I didn't mean that, and you know it. My thanks are for sticking to your accident story.'

'Why shouldn't I, when that is what it was?'

Again Maddy shook her head, this time in fond disbelief. 'Was there ever such a man, to suffer as you did then refuse to accuse the wretches who nearly killed you!'

'Any man with a heart would do the same if he loved the sister of those same wretches.'

Maddy felt as if her heart would burst with love. He was steadfastly protecting her brothers, and he was doing it for her. She would have flung her arms about him if the forbidding figure of Mrs Watkins had not been hovering just inside the door of the inn.

'I don't know how the constable came to be involved,' she said. 'But I do know he uttered some dire threats to my brothers if they didn't behave.'

'I understand there were rumours flying about, as there always are on such occasions. Who's to tell where they come from?' Patrick replied. 'There was another rumour I heard, that might be easier to verify: a little bird said that you had left home and that not even your father or brothers knew where you were.'

'How did you hear that?'

'Your father came here yesterday to ask if you were with me.'

'He did that? After all that's happened?' Maddy was mortified.

'It was certainly an error of judgment on his part,' chuckled Patrick. 'He did not see me. He only got as far as Mrs Watkins. Have you ever heard her in full cry when she thinks her respectability is being questioned? I fear your father left a sadder and wiser man without knowing any more about your whereabouts. Where did you go?'

'I stayed with Annie and William.'

'You were as close as that and your family did not know? How marvellous.' Patrick roared with laughter. 'And what will you do now?' he asked, when he had gained control of himself.

'I'll go back home,' said Maddy with a sigh. 'I can't leave them any longer. My conscience won't let me. I keep wondering what my mother would have said, letting them go out working on the river with no food inside them.'

Patrick shook his head reprovingly. 'Always thinking of others, not yourself,' he said. 'But you would not be my Maddy if you were any other way.'

His Maddy. Two short words, yet how she cherished them on her way home. His Maddy… there was no other title in the world that she wanted more.

Predictably, the cottage was in a mess when she arrived. There was no fire, the hearth had seen no hint of a brush since she had left, and it seemed as if every crock in the place was dirty and littering the table. Maddy tied an apron about her waist and began work. By the time the menfolk returned home, the fragrant smells of newly-baked bread and frying bacon were wafting through the kitchen door. All five of them came to an abrupt halt on the doorstep and sniffed appreciatively.

'You'm back then,' said Jack.

'I'm back,' replied Maddy, watching with wry amusement as boots were removed before entering and hands were washed without prompting.

'Where were you?' demanded Bart, sounding almost subdued.

'With friends,' said Maddy.

Nothing more was said as they sat down at the table waiting for their food to be served. They continued waiting.

'Before we start dinner there's something I want to say,' Maddy stated, making no attempt to dish up. 'You four nearly killed Patrick. Lew was the only one who showed a grain of sense, and it's thanks to him you aren't facing a serious charge. I don't suppose there's any point in hoping that some day you'll learn to think before you act. But there's one thing that's got to happen and happen right now! You are to promise you'll keep away from Patrick. He is not to be harmed, hurt, or harassed by any of you ever again. If you do, I'll walk out of here and I swear I'll never return.' She paused, a plate and a serving spoon in her hand. The bacon was done to a turn, potatoes were bubbling on the fire, the fresh bread cooled on a rack by the open window. She saw them swallowing with hungry anticipation. 'I want your promise,' she said.

If there was any hesitation it was imperceptible.

'I promise,' said Bart.

One by one the others followed suit, leaving only Jack.

'And you too, Father,' she insisted.

'I wadn't in on this caper,' he protested.

'And I want to make sure you aren't in on any capers in the future,' she said. 'Do I have your promise?'

'Oh, all right, only get that dinner on the table, maid, afore I dies of starvation.'

From the way they cleared their plates, Maddy wondered if they had eaten at all during the previous two days.

After they had gone back to the boat, she began tidying up. As she did so she became aware of Davie hovering on the kitchen step.

'Maddy,' he said. 'You won't go away again, will you? It were terrible without you. Us missed you something awful.' Suddenly he darted in and planted a kiss on her cheek before dashing off to join the others.

He had not waited to extract any promise from her, and she wondered what her answer would have been if he had. With a sinking heart, Maddy knew that kiss bound her with the hardest fetters to break, those of loyalty, duty, and love, for she did love her troublesome, difficult family. She felt torn in half, between them and Patrick. But she had managed to ensure one thing: her menfolk had sworn not to harm Patrick, and despite their numerous faults, they always kept their word. Patrick was safe. For the moment that was all that mattered.

Chapter Eight

The tea party in the garden at Hill House was everything such an elegant occasion should be, with discreet gossip circulating along with the wafer-thin cucumber sandwiches and fingers of Madeira cake. The Fitzherberts had been accepted back into the local society for several weeks, and although Mrs Fitzherbert was in her element, Victoria was not so easily satisfied. Below the polite acceptance, there was still a chilly atmosphere, particularly where she herself was concerned.

One reason for her unpopularity among the other women was the fact that the sole eligible male in the party had not left her side the entire afternoon. Matthew Brooks was a nephew of the squire, a naval officer spending his leave in the Devon countryside with his uncle. He was young, good-looking, and energetic, and if he had appeared on the scene earlier in the year Victoria would have regarded him as manna from heaven. Now she felt indifferent.

'Being on Gib we had to go up and see the apes, of course,' he continued an anecdote about his last voyage. 'We'd been warned to keep anything we valued well out of their reach, but what did old Bonzo Markham do but hold out his cap to one. The ape put it on, tried to eat it, sat in it. We were helpless with laughter but Bonzo stopped being amused when the wretched creature refused to give it back. There he was, chasing the ape all over the place, while we were laughing too much to do a thing to help.'

'And did your friend get his cap back eventually?' Victoria asked, since some response was obviously expected of her.

'No, the ape ran up the rocks with it and that was that. Poor Bonzo had to return to the ship bareheaded. He got a terrible wigging for appearing improperly dressed.'

There was a flutter of laughter from those round about, and Victoria joined in for the sake of appearances, though she did not truly find the story funny. She wondered why not. Matthew Brooks was a pleasant young man, the rest of the company seemed to think him amusing. So why did she find him a bore?

She knew why: she was comparing him unfavourably with Cal Whitcomb. Although they had only known each other for two or three days, Matthew Brooks already had an expression of dog-like devotion in his eyes whenever he looked in her direction. Cal Whitcomb, by contrast, had been disapproving and critical of her after such a short acquaintanceship. His strength of character and maturity, as well as his open censure, had made him a worthy challenge. By comparison, adding such a willing victim as Matthew Brooks to her list of conquests hardly seemed worth the bother.

'He was most attentive towards you, my love. Everyone remarked on it,' Mrs Fitzherbert prattled during the carriage drive home. 'He had eyes for no one else. Mark my word, my love, you have found yourself a most acceptable beau.'

'If I want him,' said Victoria without enthusiasm.

'Not want him? But he is most eligible. The family is extremely wealthy and there is just himself and his sister to inherit. I had quite a chat with Mrs Bowden, she was most informative.'

Knowing how little the vicar's wife approved of her family, Victoria suspected that her mother must have used great determination to prize out so much information – one more reason for the Fitzherberts to be unpopular in the village. Not that she cared. She had an assignation with Cal Whitcomb the next day. Compared to that, eligible naval officers and tea parties at Hill House faded into insignificance.

–

'You're late,' she complained to Cal when he arrived at the agreed rendezvous the following afternoon.

'I did warn you I might not be prompt,' he said, calmly consulting the silver watch from his waistcoat pocket. 'I'm only three minutes overdue. You must have been early.'

'If you thought anything of me you'd have been here ages before I arrived,' she protested petulantly.

'And if you thought anything of me you would know that was impossible,' he countered. 'I have two farms to run, not to mention the cider business. I can't ask my animals to look after themselves nor my crops to stop growing in order that I may spend time with you.'

'If you really wanted to you could. You employ workers, don't you?'

'Yes, and they have more than enough to keep them occupied as it is. Tell me, are we going to spend our time arguing, or do I get a kiss?'

It should have been she who offered the kiss, dangling it before him as a temptation, as a promise of pleasures to come. Instead he had as good as demanded it as if it were his right. Worse still, she found herself lifting her face towards his without a murmur of dissent. His kisses were practised, yet there was something impersonal in them that both annoyed and intrigued her.

'Kiss *me*!' she demanded. 'You might well be kissing just anyone and I won't have it. I want you to kiss *me*.'

'You are accusing me of going through the motions?' he asked, surprised and amused. 'Is that what you mean?'

Victoria was not too sure what she had meant. 'You don't put your heart into it,' she said sullenly.

'Ah, that is what you want, is it? My heart? I don't promise to go that far, but will this do?'

This time she could not accuse him of being offhand. There was power and a passion in his kiss, as well as an expertise that made her body throb and her heart spin. His embrace was far removed from the furtive embraces she had previously experienced. Somewhat alarmed, she pushed him away.

'I still haven't got it right, have I?' he smiled down at her with almost sardonic amusement. 'Perhaps we had better walk a little way.'

They had chosen a secluded copse bordering the river as their meeting place, and as they strolled on, leading their horses, Cal slid his arm about her waist. She liked this much better. There was security and strength in his encircling hold, and she nestled against him, rubbing her head against his sleeve like a contented feline.

He smiled down at her again, but this time more gently. 'Do you know your trouble, Miss Victoria Fitzherbert? You don't know your own mind.'

No one had ever accused her of being undecided before, quite the reverse.

'Yes I do,' she said firmly. 'I know exactly what I want.'

'And what is that?'

'To be with you every single day.'

'Delightful as the idea is, I'm afraid it just isn't possible. It might be some time before we can meet again. Not for fear of damaging your reputation, I hasten to add, nor yet because I don't want to risk your father coming after me with a horsewhip, but because I have a harvest to get in.'

'What do you mean by some time?' she demanded suspiciously.

'It's hard to say. Probably about a fortnight.'

'A fortnight?' She moved away from his hold abruptly. 'You would ignore me for two whole weeks for the sake of a few fields of measly corn?'

'For a number of fields of top quality corn,' he corrected her.

'But why? Aren't I more important to you?'

'There you pose a very difficult question. Let me say that my mother is getting on in years and I would be a most undutiful son if I forced her into the workhouse because I preferred dallying with a pretty lady rather than providing for her comfortable old age.'

'You are obsessed with money. What if you do get into debt? Simply avoid the dunners or ignore them.' She almost added, 'That's what we do', but stopped herself in time.

'A very fine philosophy.' His tone had become grim. 'And a very selfish one. Quite apart from losing land that has been in my family for generations, which would be the inevitable result of bankruptcy, what about the people to whom I owed money? My farm workers, my tailor, the mason who repairs my buildings? If I don't pay them the money that is their rightful due, how will they feed their children? No, in my view wanton debt is nothing more than a form of theft.'

'Oh!' She was startled by the idea. Throughout her life she had been accustomed to having what she wanted and ignoring the bills which followed. It had never occurred to her to question the morality of it, much less the consequences to those to whom she owed money.

'They'd manage, those sort of people always do,' she said.

The look he gave her came close to dislike; then he said, 'Let's have no more talk of debt and bankruptcy; in my case I am determined they will not occur. We will not be able to meet until harvest is over, and there is no point in arguing.'

'I only argue because I'll miss you terribly,' she said.

If she hoped he would be persuaded to change his mind by her woebegone expression she was sadly mistaken. He gave a short laugh and kissed her on the nose.

'An admirable attempt,' he said. 'If I could abandon the harvest I would, but I can't. I will get a message to you when I am free again.'

'And what am I supposed to do in the meantime?' she demanded angrily. 'Ride up and down by myself, dying of boredom?'

'You'll manage,' he said. 'Your sort always does.'

She gave a gasp. 'That was uncalled for,' she said, closer to genuine tears than she had been in a long time. 'You – you are a hard, cruel man.'

He appeared to consider. 'Yes, I am a hard man,' he said. 'When it is necessary. I hope I'm not a cruel one, though.'

'You were cruel to me just then,' she said, her lip quivering.

'No, I was not. I was pointing out to you your thoughtlessness towards others.'

'Oh...' That seemed to be all she said to him recently, so frequently did he take the wind from her sails. 'You really like me, don't you?' She was surprised at how much she wanted reassurance.

Once more he kissed her on the nose. 'Enough to meet you again in a couple of weeks' time, when the harvest ends,' he said.

They parted with Victoria feeling unsettled and dissatisfied, as she usually did after one of their assignations. Her conquest of Cal Whitcomb was not going at all the way she had intended. The more she considered it, the more she wondered why she continued with the relationship. The nerve of him, thinking he could summon her at his least whim! When his message came she would ignore it. He could wait about in vain – and she hoped it would be raining!

For a few days she concentrated her attention upon Matthew Brooks, beaming the radiance of her smile upon him with such effect that the poor fellow was dazzled. Her resolve lasted until church on Sunday. There was Matthew, eager and boyish, in the squire's pew, and there was Cal, manly, upright and solid. There was no comparison. When his letter came, rain or no rain, she knew she would be waiting.

The message was a long time in coming, nearly a week later than she had anticipated. When she met him at the disused quarry which was one of their favourite meeting places, she flung herself into his arms.

'Oh, how I've missed you,' she cried, lifting her face for his kisses. Cal happily obliged with an enthusiasm which pleased her: He had missed her too. Victoria revelled in her minor triumph, for once she held the upper hand. This was more like it. She had not given up hopes of bringing Cal Whitcomb to heel.

'You said two weeks and it is now three since last we met,' she chided.

'I said probably two weeks. One can never be definite in farming.'

'But an extra week! What took so long?'

'It has been an extremely good harvest, the best in years. It took time to gather in and store,' he explained patiently. 'And, of course, I lent my neighbours a hand.'

'You bothered about other people when you knew how desperate I was to see you?' Her chiding tone slipped, betraying an underlying anger.

'That is the way of it in the countryside. My neighbours help me and I help them, particularly at harvest. There was a chance of thunder too, after the hot weather we've been having. I couldn't let good wheat lie to rot in the fields, could I?'

'Yes you could,' she retorted, 'if it were a choice between it and me.'

He gave a sigh and maintained his calm with increasing difficulty. 'Why do you refuse to understand? Farming is not a game that can be taken up and let fall at will. It is our livelihood and must take priority always.'

'Not where I am concerned. I refuse to come second to a load of corn.'

'Now you are being silly. Silly and immature.'

She noted the growing exasperation in his voice and realised that she was trying him too far.

'Don't think me silly,' she pleaded in a small voice. 'I try not to be, and I do want to understand. I admit I find it hard when I want to see you so desperately and you insist upon digging up a field or sitting with a sick cow or something. You always seem to have such a lot to do. You see, I've never met anyone who was not free to do exactly as he pleases.'

'That nephew of the squire's who made sheep's eyes at you all last Sunday, he's in the navy. Surely he isn't free to do what he pleases?'

'Not when he's at sea, of course. But when he has a long leave he can. All the other gentlemen of my acquaintance are exactly the same. They have nothing to do but amuse themselves the entire day.'

'Poor souls.'

She looked at him in surprise. 'You really mean that!' she said.

'I do. The thought of nothing to do, no purpose in life...' He gave a shudder.

Victoria considered him carefully, conscious for the first time that the gulf between his world and hers consisted of more than money and breeding.

He looked at her face and laughed. 'I do believe I've shocked you,' he said. 'You can't comprehend a man who wants more from life than filling in time between lunch and dinner at his tailor's or his club. Never mind, although I may not have much spare time, I promise you that what I have will be spent with you.' In a fit of high spirits he swung her up in the air, depositing her gently on the low branch of a tree. 'You can look down on me for a change,' he grinned.

Victoria enjoyed it when he behaved with such physical exuberance. There was a solidity in his grasp and in his strength which gave her an extraordinary sense of security. She put her hands on his shoulders drawing him closer, then, with what she was convinced was tantalising slowness, kissed him.

'There,' she said. 'Isn't that better than harvesting?'

'Infinitely,' he agreed, pausing to return her kiss in good measure.

'Good, then let's forget stupid old harvesting. We don't have to think of it for a whole year. We've lots of months in between to be together.'

Cal roared with laughter. 'I love your idea of farming,' he chuckled. 'I'm sorry to disillusion you, my sweet, but it is only the corn harvest that's finished. I can doubtless snatch some free time during the next three or four weeks, after that I'll be busy with the cider-apple gathering, then the cider pressing.'

She looked at him with dismay. 'How long does that last?'

'Off and on, for a couple of months. The apples aren't all ripe at the same time. The Oakwood fruit, what there is of it, should be ready in September, while the Church Farm orchards go on into October, maybe later.'

'You are making this up!' Her playfulness had disappeared, swallowed by anger and disappointment. 'You can't seriously expect me to hang about waiting for the pleasure of your company for the rest of the year.'

The laughter was also wiped from his face. 'What you do is entirely up to you,' he said coldly. 'I have an apple crop to gather in.'

'It's a lie!' She fairly spat the words at him. 'I should have seen it before. You have done nothing but lie to me. Harvesting and apple crops! They're nonsense! You're seeing some other female, that's what you're doing.'

'That is an extremely silly accusation, even for you.'

Something in his tone reminded her of the way her father addressed her mother, and the fury inside her grew.

'Silly, is that what you think of me?' she cried. 'Then I wonder you bother seeing me at all. Goodness knows you find enough excuses not to!'

'I do not need excuses,' he retorted. 'If I no longer wish to see you then I only need to say so.'

'Indeed?' she exclaimed haughtily. 'Then say it! Say you do not wish to see me again!'

'I do not wish to see you again.' His voice was cold and hard.

She looked down at him in shocked surprise. 'You don't mean that?'

'I do,' he replied. 'Victoria, you can be amusing company when you choose, but I've had enough. You either cannot or will not understand my situation and I refuse to suffer your tantrums every time I am obliged to put earning my living before seeing you. Therefore it would be better if we do not meet again.'

He lifted her down from the branch and this time she gained no pleasure from his touch.

'You don't mean it,' she repeated. 'You are cross because I was stupid. Of course you must work on your farm. I'll try to understand, truly I will. Say you'll see me again. Please! Please!'

'No.' The one word had a terrible finality about it.

She scanned his face, looking for some sign that he might relent. There was none. She found it hard to take in. Cal could not be abandoning her! She was meant to be the dominant one in this relationship, she the one to say whether or not it ended!

'You can't finish with me,' she cried, her voice rising. 'I won't let you. You will see me again, I say! You will!' She flew at him. Grasping the front of his coat tightly in her small gloved hands, she tried to shake him.

He disentangled himself from her grasp and, holding both of her wrists in one hand, gently pushed her away from him.

'Victoria,' he said firmly, 'it was amusing while it lasted, but now it is over. Admit it, we neither of us took this affair seriously.'

'How do you know?' she demanded. 'You are speaking for yourself.'

'Oh come now! You know your affections were never involved, any more than mine were. The game has run its course.'

'A game? Is that what you considered it to be?'

'Yes,' replied Cal bluntly. 'I work hard. Like you I enjoy a little diversion now and again.'

'And am I nothing more to you than a diversion?' Her lip quivered and tears began to trickle down her cheeks.

'I have enjoyed our times together,' he said, for the first time showing signs of uncertainty. 'I thought that we had an excellent understanding – that we met for the pleasure of each other's company, nothing more. If I have misinterpreted the situation and your feelings have been hurt then I am desperately sorry. But you have to acknowledge that there was never any question of anything permanent. We could have no future together.'

'I should think not,' Victoria retorted, forgetting her tears in anger. 'As if I could ever have any warm feelings for a person of your class! The idea! My father would chase you from the house with a horsewhip for such presumption.'

'I was not considering things from that angle exactly,' admitted Cal honestly. 'More your unsuitability to be a farmer's wife.'

'Oh!' Victoria gave a gasp of fury. He would not even give her the satisfaction of rejecting him for his low birth. 'You are the most insulting man I've ever met!'

'Then it will be no hardship for you if we part.' Cal was relieved. For a moment he had been afraid he had misjudged her feelings and that she was genuinely fond of him. 'Now be a good girl, call Robbins from wherever he is dozing and go home.'

He was still holding her by the wrists. With unnecessary vigour Victoria wrenched herself free. 'Stop patronising me!' she cried. 'And stop telling me what to do. I won't go home. I'll stay here until you promise to see me again. I'll make you say it! I'll make you!' Used to getting what she wanted, she did not know how to cope with this situation. Anger, fuelled by frustration, humiliation, and a totally unexpected level of distress, rose within her in an hysterical tide. 'You'll be forced to see me. If you don't I'll make sure you're ruined.' In a frenzy she tore the hat from her head, and began shaking her hair loose.

'What on earth are you doing?' demanded Cal.

But Victoria had already ripped at the front of her riding habit The buttons gave way beneath the force of her onslaught, exposing the swell of her small, rounded breasts above the lace edge of her camisole.

'What are you about?' he demanded. 'Button yourself up again, you stupid girl. What do you hope to achieve? Be reasonable.'

By now Victoria was past being reasonable. 'How dare you insult me!' She was sobbing uncontrollably. 'You wretch! You seducer! I'm going to call Robbins, then the whole world will know what a beast you are. You'll never dare show your face again, not here, not anywhere. I'll see to that.'

'Think what you're doing!' There was a rare element of alarm in Cal's voice. 'You can't appear in front of Robbins or anyone else like that. Think of your reputation!'

But it was Cal's reputation Victoria was thinking about, and how best to ruin it. All the time she had been yelling she had been wrenching at the front of her camisole, determined to expose herself completely. Unfortunately the border of broderie anglaise, ribbon, and insertion lace proved extraordinarily durable. Uncontrollably hysterical at being thwarted, Victoria stripped off her gloves and raked her nails down the front of her bosom until the blood ran, then throwing back her head she screamed at the top of her voice.

—

Maddy heard the screams as she walked along a sheep track above the quarry. Setting down the basket of wild blackberries she had just gathered, she ran in the direction of the high-pitched shrieks, her heart pounding with dread at what she might find. The last thing she expected was to come upon a decidedly ruffled Cal Whitcomb and a half-naked Victoria Fitzherbert.

'For pity's sake, Victoria,' Cal was pleading. 'Think what you are doing. Stop this racket before someone comes.'

But Maddy had already come. Without another thought she strode forward and slapped Victoria hard across the face. As if by magic the screams stopped. Somewhat belatedly Robbins was puffing up from the thicket where he had been enjoying a doze. Swiftly Maddy summed up the situation. Turning to the groom and to Cal she said briskly, 'Lose yourselves for ten minutes. This is no place for either of you.'

The two men looked at one another then thankfully did as they were told. Victoria had sunk to her knees, sobbing and nursing her slapped cheek.

'Oh, do get up,' said Maddy unsympathetically. 'I didn't hit you that hard, though goodness knows I was tempted.'

'He attacked me,' wept Victoria, making a last-ditch attempt to ruin Cal. 'He was like a wild animal.'

'He didn't and he wasn't.' Maddy's voice was matter-of-fact.

'How do you know?' demanded Victoria, her tears forgotten in her indignation.

'Because I can recognise hysteria when I hear it. There wasn't one bit of fear in that row you were making. You're having a rare old tantrum and nothing more.'

'He did attack me.' Victoria tried repeating her accusation, but it was a half-hearted effort. Then her tears began to flow again, and this time they were genuine. 'What am I going to do?' she wept.

'First we'd better get you tidy,' said Maddy. 'You can't go home like that. What on earth were you up to? Didn't you give your reputation a moment's thought? If one whisper of this ever got abroad, the local gentry would cut you for ever. They've only just started sending you invitations after your last escapade.'

'How do you know that?' demanded Victoria.

Maddy looked at her pityingly. 'In a village there's not much gets by the local gossip, which is why you'd better hope and pray you don't meet anyone on your way home. Now, let's fasten your buttons, you aren't decent with your chest hanging out like that.' It was not an easy task, for half the buttons had been ripped off. However, Maddy did what she could, with ham-fisted assistance from Victoria. She regarded their mutual handiwork. 'I suppose it's better than nothing. I've got a clean handkerchief here. I'll go and wet it in the stream to wash your face, while you do something with your hair.'

She was back within a few minutes, nevertheless Victoria's hair showed no improvement.

'Come on, make an effort,' Maddy snapped. 'I've a lot to do today. I can't spend all my time tending to you. Tidy your hair, for pity's sake, you look like the mad woman of Bedlam. If you're short of pins you can have some of mine.'

Victoria half raised her hands to her head, then let them fall again. 'I can't,' she wailed.

'You can't what?' asked Maddy, perplexed.

'Do my hair. I don't know how. My maid always does it for me.'

Maddy regarded her with astonishment, and then with something like contempt.

So much for the gentry, she thought, who claim to be our betters and to be set in charge over us. Aloud she said, 'All right, I suppose I'll have to do the best I can. Here, take the handkerchief. I presume you can wash your own face?

She was no skilled hairdresser, but she had often done Annie's hair for her when her friend's hands were bad.

As she smoothed Victoria's hair into some kind of order, the other woman said, 'Don't you want to know what happened between Mr Whitcomb and me?'

'No.'

'Why not?'

'Because it's none of my concern.'

'You took Mr Whitcomb's part without question, yet from what I've heard you don't like him.'

'I don't like either of you,' said Maddy bluntly. 'I just happen to owe Farmer Whitcomb a favour and I always pay my debts.'

'Without waiting to see whether or not he was in the wrong?'

'But he wasn't in the wrong, was he? I don't suppose you can put your own hat on, either? Here, pass it to me.' Maddy took the stylish creation, brushed off as much of the mud as she could and set it on Victoria's head. 'There,' she said critically. 'That will have to do. Let's hope I never have to earn my living as a lady's maid.'

Victoria accepted her ministrations without a word of thanks. 'Why are you doing this?' she asked. 'It's not to help me, is it?'

'No.'

'Then why? I know you've said about a debt owed and all that, but I'd have thought you'd have enjoyed seeing that Whitcomb wretch humiliated.'

Maddy considered carefully. 'Although I can imagine Cal Whitcomb guilty of all sorts of things quite easily, I don't see him as a ravager of women, even if your performance earlier on had been more convincing,' she said. 'You were in no danger from him, I'm certain, so whatever he did to get you in such a paddy is none of my business.' Ignoring Victoria's snort of annoyance she added, 'Since you're as respectable looking as you're ever going to be I suggest we call the men back.'

Cal and Robbins returned in answer to the summons, both looking awkward and uneasy. Maddy addressed the groom first.

'You'd best get your mistress home, and by the quietest roads you can manage,' she said. 'And remember, you didn't see anything because there wasn't anything to see.'

Robbins nodded enthusiastically. Whatever it was that had been going on, it looked as if Miss Victoria had come off worst, and he wanted no part in it if he could help it.

'Come along, miss,' he said. 'Let's be mounting up and getting home. We'll go the back way.'

An unusually subdued Victoria allowed herself to be helped into the saddle, and together they rode off.

Maddy was left with Cal Whitcomb – an acutely embarrassed Cal Whitcomb; and she would have been less than human if she had not relished his discomfort.

'Well,' she said, 'you got yourself into a right pickle there.'

'I did,' he agreed. 'And you have my grateful thanks for getting me out of it.'

'I came along at the right moment. Not so long ago, in the church-yard, you came along at the right moment for me. Now we're equal.'

'Please understand I never touched her.'

'You don't have to convince me.'

'No?' He sounded surprised. 'I thought you Shillabeers considered me capable of every crime under the sun.'

'Of most crimes under the sun,' Maddy corrected him. 'I've never heard you were one to force yourself upon women.'

'You missed a golden opportunity there. You could have cast all sorts of doubt upon my manhood.'

'I thought of it,' admitted Maddy. 'But with only the two of us here it didn't seem worth the trouble. Besides, I think you and your manhood have taken enough punishment from women for one day.'

He laughed, dispelling the last hint of awkwardness in his manner. Maddy was relieved. She was so used to encountering a supremely self-assured Cal Whitcomb that to see him embarrassed made her feel unaccountably embarrassed too.

'I'm sorry,' he said, when he had stopped laughing. 'You come to my rescue in a most timely manner and what do I do? Goad you over old scores.'

'That's all right,' Maddy replied. 'What are enemies for?'

He laughed again. 'Is that what we are? Enemies? I suppose we must be. In that case I say thank goodness for enemies. I can think of no friend who would have coped so ably with Miss Fitzherbert.'

Suddenly Maddy's curiosity got the better of her. 'You must have been mad, coming to such a secluded spot with her,' she said. 'Did it never occur to you to be on your guard?'

'Not really,' he admitted, somewhat shamefaced. 'I thought I had the situation under control. She was playing some game with me, that much was obvious. Unfortunately, I misjudged the young lady's temperament.'

'You certainly did. What on earth possessed you to play along with her?' Then she stopped abruptly. 'Your pardon,' she said. 'That was impertinent of me, and none of my business.'

'Now it is my turn to say "that's all right",' he grinned. 'Contrary to general opinion I am quite human. I find the company of pretty women most agreeable.'

This conversation was growing both amicable and quite personal. Maddy decided it had gone on long enough.

'Next time you wish to prove how human you are you should either choose a less hysterical companion or else keep to more public places,' she said.

'That is excellent advice. I'll try and stick to it. You are leaving now?' for Maddy was beginning to head towards the spot where she had left her basket.

'Yes, I've wasted enough time for one morning.'

She was some distance away from him when she heard him call, 'Maddy, I'm not sure if I thanked you properly. I was in quite a spot there. I'm most grateful to you for your intervention.'

'That makes us even,' she called over her shoulder.

It was not until she was nearing home that she realised he had called her by her Christian name. The nerve of the man. Was there no end to his impudence?

–

By good luck and the manoeuvrings of Robbins, Victoria managed to get home and up to her room without anyone, bar Mary, seeing her. The maidservant's silence she bought with a morning dress she no longer wanted. Once she had calmed down she was thankful no one had observed her in her dishevelled state. As an attempt to punish Cal Whitcomb it was a stupid thing to have done. She was thankful that someone had intervened, though she wished it had not been that wretched Shillabeer woman. For that creature to have seen her humiliation… Victoria wept bitter tears at the memory.

There was another reason for her tears: the end of her affair with Cal caused a deep hurt which surprised and bewildered her. She refused to accept that she had been attracted to a rough farmer, she preferred to blame her strange emotional state on the fact that she had lost an amusing diversion – her only amusing diversion in this mud hole.

This did not explain the bitter discontent she felt after church the next Sunday when she saw the Shillabeer woman walking with the fiddler from the church band. They were hand in hand, and their total absorption in one another struck her a blow of sharp envy. Why should that common creature be loved – and by quite a handsome fellow too, although he was of the lower orders – while she had been rejected? Resentment settled in Victoria's heart and stayed there, fuelled steadily by loneliness and misery.

By contrast, Maddy's heart was buoyed up by the sheer joy of living and loving. Autumn was coming on apace, a richer, more beauti-fully abundant autumn than any she had ever experienced, thanks to Patrick's influence.

The salmon-fishing season was over. For the last time that year the nets had been hung up to dry on the tall frames that stood along the foreshore, then stacked away in the room below Maddy's attic. The boat would not be needed much during the winter, and it had been hauled up into the boat store beside the house to be cleaned down, the big double doors closed protectively on it.

Maddy added up the total earnings for the summer months, and pulled a face.

'It could have been better,' she said. 'But thanks to the prices shooting up over these last few weeks we made more than I'd dared to hope.'

'Shows how scarce they salmon have been,' put in Jack. 'I can't never remember getting two shillings a fish afore. Thank gawd they fancy folk up to Lunnon be willing to pay such prices. They must be made of money.'

'We certainly aren't,' said Maddy, double-checking the figures. 'But we'll get through the winter just as long as we don't have any unexpected expenses.' She looked hard at her brothers, and they shuffled uncomfortably under her gaze.

'They'm going to behave, idn't you, lads?' said Jack confidently. 'Us'll manage fine. Bart, Charlie and me've already been promised places up the quarry. What about you, Lew boy?

'I saw Arnie Chambers this morning,' replied Lew. 'And he wants me back. I'll be in the wherrying trade again this winter.'

Only Davie had failed to find anything full time, but when Maddy went up to Rob Bradworthy's farm for the apple gathering, he went along too. The cider apples were allowed to fall from the trees, carpeting the orchard floor with jewel-bright crimsons, ambers and golds. It was back-breaking work picking them up from the damp grass, and even more exhausting heaving the full sacks onto the wagon, ready to be taken to the apple yard.

'Yer, Davie, you'm put on some muscle since I saw you last,' remarked Rob, watching him lift the sacks. 'I be a worker short – daft fool fell out of the hayloft doing a bit of courting. I could do with a man with brawny arms and a sound back for a spell, at least until the cider pressing's done. The job's youm if you wants un.'

Beaming, Davie accepted, more delighted at being called a man than at gaining steady employment for a few weeks.

Maddy beamed too, happy that a few more coins would find their way into the Delft jug, securing against the harsher, hungrier days of winter.

For a while Stoke Gabriel forgot about the summer past and the approaching inclement weather, and devoted itself entirely to the making of cider. Almost every farm had its own press and poundhouse, where the cider was made mainly for home consumption. Only at Oakwood was it considered as a money-making venture. The sweet smell of overripe fruit hung in the air as the apples grew increasingly soft and 'sleepy' – the ideal state for cider-making. Then farm lanes and yards became slippery with squashed fruit underfoot, and ancient poundhouses echoed to the rattle of the iron-ridged crushers mangling the apples into pulp.

'I fair ache across the shoulders,' complained Davie after one day's work. 'Turning the handle on that crusher be harder than the fishing 'cos there idn't no easing off.'

'Why didn't you take turns with whoever was shovelling the apples in at the top?' asked Maddy.

'Didn't think of un,' admitted Davie with a grin. 'Anyway, I suppose I should be thankful. Up to Oakwood they'm got a horse doing my job.'

'You'm near as pretty as a horse, and you smells a lot better,' said Jack, sniffing at his youngest son who was well spattered with pulp and juice. 'What do Rob use to bed down the pulp in the press?'

Davie thought. 'Wheaten straw,' he said. 'Yes, that be it, for they were arguing about whether the layers were thick enough. "A decent layer of apple pomace then a good mat of wheaten straw, that be the best way to build up a decent cider cheese." That be what Rob's old uncle were saying. Why do you ask?'

'Because 'tis oaten straw as is the sweetest and the best, in my opinion,' Jack replied.

'I offered to help Rob and his uncle but they said 'twas skilled work, and sent me back to the crusher,' said Davie regretfully.

'Thank your stars they didn't want you to help screw the top of the press down,' said Jack. 'Then you'd have known about aching shoulders, winding down that gurt block of elm to squeeze the juice out. Makes the crusher seem like a little maid's job, it do. I knows, I've done un. Tis a pity Rob uses wheaten straw.'

'Why? What's it to do with us?' asked Maddy.

''Cos oaten straw be the best, habn't I just told you? And Rob, being a generous soul, is bound to give Davie a firkin or two to bring home.' Then Jack gave a chuckle. 'But cider be cider, when all's said and done. If he offers, don't you refuse, son, do you hear?'

'I won't, Father, and that be a promise.'

They grinned, knowing that this was one promise Davie was certain to keep.

–

Autumn brought other changes: a rash of balls and parties among the local gentry, determined to have one last social fling together before they moved on to spend the winter in London or the warmer climes of the Mediterranean.

'Will you believe it, I'm entering society?' announced Patrick one day. 'The squire has taken it into his head to invite his neighbours to an evening of country dances such as he knew in his youth, and who better to provide the music than Mr Patrick Howard, musician extraordinary?'

'Just you alone?' asked Maddy excitedly.

'No, we will be the church band under a different banner. Already we've had a practice and we're coming along nicely. But I've left the best bit until last. Can you guess how much the squire is paying us? A guinea each!'

'A guinea for one night's work?' Maddy was astounded. 'Then let's hope country dance parties catch on among the gentry. You'll have your carriage yet.'

'And you shall be the first to ride in it with me,' Patrick laughed.

Before the winter finally came, the people who lived beside the Dart were to find themselves blessed with one more unexpected harvest. The working of the tides in conjunction with an exceptionally dry year resulted in some phenomenally low levels in the river, which promised to expose cockle beds not seen within generations.

'You'm all ready for tonight?' demanded Annie, although it was a question she had already asked half a dozen times. 'They say it be going to be the lowest water in the Dart within memory.'

'I'm ready,' smiled Maddy. 'You don't think I'd let an opportunity like this slip, do you?'

Annie gave a sigh. 'What wouldn't I give to join in. Think of it! Cockle beds what likely habn't never been touched. There'll be some with shells as big as pot lids. Where'm you thinking of digging?'

'Middle Back, I think.'

Annie nodded sagely. 'That's your best bet,' she said.

Patrick was less enthusiastic. 'I prefer to keep my feet on dry land, as you know,' he said ruefully. 'What I will do is to stay on the shore and play for you while you toil.'

'You'll be playing just for me?' Maddy asked.

'Just for you,' he assured her.

That night it seemed as if every inhabitant from both banks of the Dart was abroad. Just as the river prophets had predicted, the tide had dropped and dropped, revealing vast gleaming banks of mud and sand which had not been exposed for a century or more. The decreasing channel of water was choked with boats heading for the cockle beds.

Like many others, Maddy had made her way to Middle Back, a sandbank off Stoke Gabriel creek. Even under normal conditions it was a popular spot for gathering cockles, but now it was so vast it almost seemed to stretch from bank to bank. She found herself a spot on a newly exposed area and, her bare feet sinking into the cold, wet sand, began to work. By the light of her lantern she watched for the telltale spurt of water by which the cockle betrayed its presence, then she would dig swiftly for the shellfish, employing the small sharp tool normally used for scraping the boat. Annie may have been over-optimistic, hoping for cockles as big as pot lids, but the ones Maddy dug up were certainly bigger and of better quality than anything she had ever seen before.

'You knows what be going to happen?' commented her neighbour, hitching her skirt higher out of the wet. 'Us be going to take that many fine cockles to market tomorrow there won't be no selling them.'

'You're a little ray of sunshine, aren't you?' laughed Maddy. 'If the worst comes to the worst we can all live on cockles for days to come.'

'With a drop of vinegar and fresh bread and butter there idn't a better dinner,' agreed her neighbour.

'And don't forget the tea, Beattie! You'm got to have a good pot of tea with cockles,' joined in another woman, while from round about the sandbank came a chorus of agreement.

There was a carnival air on Middle Back that night, with everyone joking and chatting as they dug. Maddy regarded the scene about her. Each bending figure, illuminated in the darkness by its own lantern, was reflected in the gleaming wet sand, making a picture she would never forget.

The conversation turned to where they would sell their cockles.

'And what about you, maid?' Beattie enquired.

'I think I'll give Paignton a try to start with,' Maddy began. She got no further, for drifting across the river came the sound of a lone fiddler playing from somewhere on the Stoke Gabriel side.

'Hark at he,' declared Beattie. 'It be that Patrick from the church band, surely? No one else plays that beautiful.'

Across the sandbank the laughter and chatter ceased as everyone straightened up to listen to Patrick's music, Maddy listening with a greater delight than anyone else. She had not believed him when he said he would play for the cockle-gathering, she thought he had been joking. Listening to the sweet notes floating on the night air, she felt more than ever that this was a night to remember.

'Idn't he the grand one, to think up summat like this,' Beattie said appreciatively. 'Goose flesh all over, that's what I've got, he'm that good. He makes up times hisself, did you know?'

Maddy made a noncommittal reply.

'I heard one of his tunes once. At Miller Bond's daughter's wedding it were. I were helping with the serving and afterwards he played a piece as he said he'd made up special for the day. "A Devonshire Rose" he called it, Rose being Miller Bond's daughter's name. My, her were that pleased her cried, and so did her ma, and I heard her pa give that Patrick fellow an extra half-crown just for the tune.'

Maddy felt uncomfortable. Patrick had never mentioned making up a tune for Rose Bond. In fact, he had never mentioned making up a tune specially for anyone else, only her. A cold little dread stirred inside her. What if he had played her tune?

He wouldn't do that. How can you think it? she chided herself. He promised the tune was mine.

She was annoyed at her lack of faith in him. Surely she was confident of his love by now? But she could not stop herself from asking, 'How did it go, this "Devonshire Rose" song?' 'Bless you, maid, I can't remember. It were months since. I'd knows un if I heard un again, but I idn't good enough to sing un.' Beattie paused to listen. 'He'm started to play again. That last one were "Sweet Nightingale" but I be blowed if I knows this one. Pretty, though, bain't un?'

Maddy thought it was very pretty indeed; unlike Beattie she knew the tune well. It was 'Miss Madeleine's Air'. Her heart warmed as she heard it, and her eyes filled with tears. Patrick had kept his promise, he was playing for her alone.

For Maddy the midnight cockle-gathering seemed to put a special stamp upon the weeks which followed, when the autumnal weather came with a rush. Somehow the lashing rain and fearsome gales, usually dreaded because they presaged the coming of winter, did not seem so terrible. One benefit of her cockle money was that she bought *Wuthering Heights*, a volume fat enough to get her through the longest winter. Not that she needed books now to divert her. In the worst of the storms she had merely to let her mind go back to the magical evening, to hearing her song coming to her across the dark water, and the rough elements outside were forgotten. Even when the river overflowed, flooding right into the kitchen, it did not seem a disaster. Patrick's love was protection against everything, or so she thought.

Maddy was preparing to bake bread. The day was raw and the prospect of being indoors by the bright fire was a pleasant one. She had just emptied the flour into the big earthenware crock when she heard running footsteps coming down the path. Davie burst in, his face ashen.

'Maddy, oh Maddy! Help me!' he cried, and flung himself into her arms.

'Here, boy, what's this about?' she asked, hugging him close. 'Something terrible's happened. You'm got to help me get away, our Maddy. Constable Vallance be after me.'

Beneath her grasp Maddy could feel him trembling. 'Constable Vallance? What've you done?' she demanded in alarm. 'I can't help you until I know what's wrong.'

'I've killed a man! I've killed Farmer Whitcomb!'

'You've what?' Maddy suddenly went cold.

'I didn't mean to,' sobbed Davie, pressing his face against her, desperate for reassurance. 'I had my catapult... I just meant to knock his hat off... but he fell off his horse with such a crash and lay so still...'

'Your catapult?' Maddy swallowed hard with relief. 'You shot him with your catapult? You daft idiot, hefty men like Farmer Whitcomb don't get killed by a pebble from a catapult. As like as not you took him by surprise, that's why he fell off his horse. The fall will have knocked the wind out of him.'

'Do you think so?' Davie raised his head and looked at her hopefully. 'But he lay so still.'

'Did you go and take a proper look?'

Davie shook his head. 'I were too scared. I come running home.'

'You should have gone to see how he was, our Davie,' Maddy said reprovingly. 'He may have hurt himself in the fall.'

'He was dead, I tell you.' Davie suddenly abandoned all hope. 'He went down with such a thud and he never moved again. I killed him, and Constable Vallance'll be here any minute for me. You've got to help me get away!' His voice had been rising steadily and Maddy was forced to cut into his panic sharply.

'Of course I'll help you,' she said brusquely. 'But let's find out what you've done first. Farmer Whitcomb won't be dead from a flung pebble, but he won't be pleased, either, so I wouldn't be surprised if

Constable Vallance does call. Remember the warning he gave last time about you boys and your pranks? Perhaps you'd best go and hide up in the copse until I come. I'll go into the village to find out exactly what's happened.'

'Thank you, Maddy. You'm a good un.' Davie almost managed a smile as he wiped away his tears with the heel of his hand.

'Of course I am. Did you ever doubt it?' Maddy gave him a fond thump as she reached out for her shawl.

At that instant there came a heavy knocking on the door. With a sense of foreboding Maddy went to open it. There on the step was the burly figure of Constable Vallance.

'Is your father home, Maddy?' he asked gravely.

She gave no sign that she could guess why he was there. 'No, he's working at the quarry,' she said. 'Why?'

The constable ignored her question. 'Best send for him, maid, and quick.' He looked past her at Davie, who had shrunk back into a comer. In a very official voice he said gravely, 'David Shillabeer, I want you to come with me to answer questions concerning the death of Edward Knapman, head stockman to Mr Calland Whitcomb.'

Maddy and Davie looked at one another in horrified bewilderment.

'Ned Knapman?' Davie said in a hollow voice. 'Not Farmer Whitcomb...? It were the wrong man. Maddy, did you hear? It were the wrong man.'

Chapter Nine

Maddy felt that the scene would be engraved on her mind for ever. Yellow lamplight illumined the faces of the six people present in the cob-walled room that served as a police station. The squire and the constable regarded Davie sternly from across the desk; she and her father were seated against the wall on a bench. Cal Whitcomb sat on the other side of the room, apart and aloof.

It was the squire, as the local JP, who asked most of the questions, while the constable wrote down the proceedings with much scratching of his pen.

'This is a serious affair, Davie,' the squire said gravely. 'Ned Knapman is dead. You must tell the absolute truth, do you understand?'

Davie's 'Yes, sir' was barely audible.

'But why should my brother be involved?' broke in Maddy, determined to protect him. 'Who says he had anything to do with the matter?'

Constable Vallance stopped his writing and looked at her reprovingly. 'He was seen running away. One of Farmer Churchward's men was behind the far hedge clearing a ditch. He was close enough to hear the thud as Ned hit the ground and Mr Whitcomb's horse come to a stop. When he looked across he saw young Davie here running for dear life.'

'But that doesn't prove...' Maddy's voice faded into silence. She was not helping Davie by interrupting.

The squire cleared his throat and continued, 'Ned Knapman was struck by a stone. Do you deny that you threw the stone?'

'I didn't throw it, sir. I shot-flung it with my catapult.'

'Your catapult, eh? And do you deny that you lay in wait for Ned Knapman on the road from Port Bridge in order to strike him a blow with a stone from this catapult?'

'No… that be to say, yes… it were only a joke,' declared Davie.

'Joke or not, did you lie in wait for Ned?'

'I lay in wait right enough, only it weren't for Ned.' He looked uncomfortably towards Cal Whitcomb. 'It weren't for Ned as I waited, it were Farmer Whitcomb.'

'And what made you so certain Mr Whitcomb would come that way?'

'I'd seen him go towards the blacksmith's at Port Bridge. His horse had a loose shoe, I could hear un clear enough.'

'And you presumed he would come back the same way, is that it? Mr Whitcomb, does Davie's testimony match up with your view of the events?'

'It does, sir,' replied Cal. 'And Captain, my horse, certainly did return along that road, but I wasn't riding him. When I got to the smith's I found he was very busy. As I was on my way to an appointment I decided not to wait, but to go on foot. I left my horse at Port Bridge and sent one of the smith's children back to Oakwood for someone to fetch Captain. I did not ask for Ned specifically, but he always enjoyed riding Captain when he got the chance, poor fellow.'

'So, Davie, you decided to attack Mr Whitcomb, but you got Ned instead.' The squire's normally kindly eyes glittered angrily in the lamplight.

'I didn't mean to attack him, sir,' protested Davie. 'I only wanted to knock his hat off.'

'With this?' The squire held up a stone.

At the sight of it Maddy felt sick. It was far from the pebble she had envisaged. It was a hefty stone with cruelly jagged edges.

'This is somewhat extreme for simply knocking off a hat, wouldn't you say?' demanded the squire. 'You're a well-built lad. I would guess that with your power behind it, and if it had hit the right spot, this could have felled the horse, never mind poor Ned.'

Davie said nothing, he hung his head.

'There's one thing I can't comprehend,' stated the squire. 'If you were after Mr Whitcomb, as you say you were – and I don't need to ask why he was your target – how is it that you mistook Ned for him? There's no resemblance. Ned was shorter, dark-haired, much older…'

'I don't know, sir. I just did.' Davie's head remained bowed.

'Your pardon, squire.' Constable Vallance laid aside his pen. 'Mr Whitcomb, what were you wearing when you took your horse to the smithy?'

'Wearing?' Cal looked surprised at the question. 'Why, what I am wearing now. A brown kerseymere coat and a black hat.'

'Ned was wearing a brown coat,' said the constable, 'though his was of fustian. He had a black hat too. And he was riding Mr Whitcomb's gelding, a horse well known in the village.'

'What point are you making, Constable?' asked the squire.

'That young Davie here saw exactly what he was expecting to see. When Captain came back along the lane, ridden by a man in a brown coat and a black hat, the lad assumed it was Mr Whitcomb, and didn't look any further.'

'But surely he could see?' objected the squire. 'The hedges are getting pretty bare at this time of year. In fact, I'm surprised the boy managed to remain concealed.'

''Tis beech hedge along the lane to the Port Bridge smithy,' said Constable Vallance. 'And a beech hedge holds its leaves.'

The nausea that Maddy was feeling deepened. She had never appreciated how sharp the constable was, nor how thorough. Nothing of this affair was going to escape him, and she feared every detail would be to the detriment of Davie's chances.

The squire, too, was nodding approvingly at the policeman's comments. 'Excellent thinking, Constable,' he said. 'Now, Davie, I must know. Were you alone in this enterprise?'

'Yes!' The reply was uttered so sharply it echoed round the room.

'Had you been drinking before you lay in wait?'

'No, sir. Not a drop all day.'

'And for my final question, I want you to think hard, Davie, and answer with utmost honesty. Did you or did you not mean serious harm to either Ned Knapman or Mr Whitcomb? Think before you reply.'

'I don't need to think, sir,' replied Davie promptly, raising his head. 'I didn't mean no harm to Ned nor Farmer Whitcomb. I swear it. I'll swear it on the Bible or on my mother's grave if you want.'

At his words Maddy was conscious of a sense of relief. Her greatest fear had been that he had gone after Cal Whitcomb with a serious intent to injure him. Although it was not the sort of thing he would normally have undertaken on his own initiative, she had feared it nonetheless. To hear him swear otherwise was a burden lifted from her.

'There is no need for a Bible or anything else.' The squire pushed back his chair. 'You're a silly young fool and a great nuisance to all and sundry, but I'll accept your word. Constable, have you any further questions? Mr Whitcomb? Mr Shillabeer, is there anything you want to say on behalf of your son?'

Jack mutely shook his head. It was left to Maddy to burst out with, 'Please, sir, he's only a boy, he's not sixteen yet. And he's a great one for playing pranks, anyone will tell you that. This was a joke that went terribly wrong. Please make that clear.'

'I know Davie's fondness for skylarking only too well,' said the squire wryly. 'It shall be included in the report, eh, Constable? Along with his age. Has anyone anything else they want to say? No? Then I think we can close these proceedings. Davie, you must remain in custody here. Tomorrow you will go to Totnes, and thence before the magistrates who will commit you to Exeter assizes in due course.'

Maddy gave a gasp of dismay – but what else had she expected? A man was dead. Davie would have to go before judge and jury.

–

She could not get warm. When they returned home she built up a fire and cooked a meal nobody wanted, and still it seemed as if the chill had seeped permanently into her bones. After she had cleared away, she could not settle, too much was going round in her mind. She had to talk to someone so she went over to Annie's. As she expected, her friend already knew most of the details.

'How be you, my lover?' was Annie's first concerned enquiry. 'And how be Davie bearing up?'

'The pair of us are fair enough, I suppose. Oh, Annie, he's likely to go to prison for killing Ned and it's all my fault!' she burst out. 'I had the raising of him and I should have taught him right from wrong, but I didn't. I failed and now he'll be sent to prison.'

She felt herself seized by the arms and shaken quite violently. Unobserved by her, William had entered the kitchen and overheard what she had been saying. He stopped his shaking and glared at her angrily.

'Listen yer, Maddy Shillabeer! I don't never want to hear you say naught like that again,' he said. 'Ever since your ma died they lads of yourn, Davie included, habn't never come home to a cold hearth nor an empty table, they habn't never been in need of dry stockings nor a clean shirt of a Sunday. To do that would have daunted many a growd woman, and you'm done it since you were no more than a bit of a maid yourself. And you found time to come over here and help my Annie, too. Davie be in proper trouble, there idn't no denying, but the blame don't lie at your door.'

Maddy was too astounded to reply. If Annie had made such a speech she would have accepted it as typical of her friend's warm-hearted concern, but to hear gentle, quiet William speak out made a deep impression. He let go of her, looking sheepish.

'There, I shouldn't have gone on like that,' he said shamefacedly. 'It be naught of our business I suppose, but us be rare fond of you. To speak the truth, they brothers of youm be good boys spoiled by lack of a firm hand, but it should've been their father's, not youm. That were Jack's responsibility.'

'That be true,' agreed Annie. 'You'm anxious enough for your Davie as 'tis, maid, don't go feeling guilty on top. There idn't no need. Mind, in all fairness, it've got to be said that Jack habn't never been the same since your ma died. I habn't never seen a man so sunk in grief. Tis my way of thinking as he habn't never throwed un off. And there be no denying as Lizzie were a managing sort of woman, bless her. Twas her as ruled the household, including Jack. When her died, you seemed to step right into her shoes; I don't suppose your father ever, felt the need to stir himself and take charge.'

'He missed Mother certainly,' agreed Maddy, seeing her parents' relationship in a new light. 'He still does.'

'And now more than ever, I dare say,' said Annie. 'Where be Davie to?'

'He's at the police station, Constable Vallance wouldn't let him come home. Tomorrow he'll be taken to Totnes until he comes before the magistrates, then he'll go to Exeter.'

'If he'm biding to the police house you'd best take him up something to eat. Amy Vallance be one of the worst cooks God ever made.'

Maddy managed a flickering smile. 'Davie won't be pleased at that, he likes his food. I think I'll go up now and take him a few things. He'll need a change of shirt, and maybe a blanket. Tonight's likely to be chilly.'

She was glad to be active, she could not bear the thought of staying at home that evening, knitting socks and having dread thoughts of

Davie whirling ceaselessly in her head. Far better to stride out through the bitter cold darkness towards the village and her brother.

'Certainly you can see Davie.' Constable Vallance looked less authoritarian in his shirtsleeves than he had in his blue serge tunic. 'First I'd best have a look at what's in that basket of yours.'

'Don't you trust me?' demanded Maddy indignantly.

'No, Maddy my girl, I don't. I know perfectly well that you'd trample me underfoot and tear down this place stone by stone if you considered there was a chance of getting your brother free. I think none the less of you for it. If there's one thing I respect it's true loyalty. But just the same, I'll do my duty and check through the basket, if you don't mind.'

He was thorough in his search, though he made no objections to any of the contents, not even the candles that Maddy had included. She had feared that the constabulary issue might not be very generous and she dreaded the thought of poor Davie sitting alone and afraid in the darkness.

'What's to become of him?' she asked, as the constable returned the contents to the basket.

He sighed thoughtfully. 'He'll be accused of murder, I'm afraid.' At Maddy's horrified gasp, he added, 'I doubt if it'll come to that. My guess is that he'll be convicted of manslaughter. You'd best be prepared for him going to prison, but if you get a reasonable judge and jury they should take his age and the nature of the offence into consideration.' He gave another sigh, more regretful this time. 'How often have I warned your lot? But they wouldn't listen. Something like this was bound to happen sooner or later. Such a pity it's the youngster… Right then, if you're ready I'll take you in.'

He handed her back the basket and led her into the room where Davie had been interviewed that afternoon. At the far side was a heavy door with a small grille at the top through which glimmered a meagre light. 'Davie, lad, you've a visitor,' he said, putting a huge key in the lock and turning it. 'Your sister's here.'

'Maddy! Oh Maddy, am I glad to see you!' Davie burst out of his prison and would have flung himself at Maddy if Constable Vallance had not caught firm hold of him.

'Take it easy, lad,' he said quite kindly. 'You've to stay inside. Your sister must come in with you. I'll have to lock you in too.' He looked apologetically at Maddy. 'Just give a yell when you're ready to leave.'

The cell was little more than a large cupboard, lit by one candle stump so small it was already flickering. Maddy was glad she had thought to bring more, just as she was glad she had brought a thick blanket, for there was no heating and a fearsome draught came through the small barred opening in the wall, which served as a window.

'Oh Maddy, you came!' Davie clutched thankfully at her hand. 'I didn't think you would, not in the dark.'

'Since when have I let the darkness bother me, you silly boy,' said Maddy fondly, stroking the hair back from his forehead.

'I'm – I'm in a bit of a pickle, aren't I?' he said, his lips trembling. 'What's – what's to become of me?'

His words, an echo of her own, tugged at her heart. 'I've just been talking to Constable Vallance about it,' she said. 'He was honest with me. The accusation will probably be murder...' She put her arms about him and held him as, even in the dim light, she saw his face go grey with shock. 'Don't despair. It won't be as bad as that. Constable Vallance seems to think that you're more likely to be convicted of manslaughter, which will mean a prison sentence, I'm afraid. However, we must hope the judge and jury will be lenient because you're young, and because it was the result of a silly prank. You must help yourself by not being a difficult prisoner and by answering up honestly. And I'm sure the constable will do his best for you – he's a good man.'

'I know he be. Maddy, I can't stop thinking about poor Ned and wishing he were alive again. Tis a terrible thing to have killed a man, specially a decent fellow like Ned, and I be powerful sorry, truly I be.'

'I know. I know,' Maddy comforted him.

'You'll be there when I go to Exeter, won't you?' Davie clung to her tightly. 'It be such a way from here.'

'Certainly I will! I'm surprised that you should ask.' Maddy tried to sound indignant but failed miserably. 'Of course I'll be there, you daft pudden,' she whispered softly, holding him close. 'Did you think I'd leave you on your own? As for Exeter being a long way, it can't be more than thirty miles. I can walk that in a day easily, and I'll be thinking up ways to help you every step of the way.'

It was getting late, and Maddy knew it was time to be going home.

'You'll go before the magistrates at Totnes first,' she said. 'And when you do, I want to see you all spruce and tidy. Make a good impression. I've brought you your comb and some soap, so there's no excuse.'

'You'll be at Totnes too?' Davie let go his grip on her with great reluctance.

'Was there ever such a lad?' she said in mock exasperation. 'I'll be in that magistrates' court, never fear. Constable Vallance,' she called, 'I'll be off now.'

He opened the door and she stepped out.

'Will you make sure he washes behind his ears?' she asked him.

'I'll see he's turned out as trim as a new shilling piece,' the constable assured her heartily, locking the cell door behind her.

Davie's face appeared in the grille – white, young, and frightened. 'Maddy!' he said. 'Maddy!'

She hurried back, and stretching up on tiptoe just managed to kiss him.

'You won't be on your own,' she said. 'While you're at Totnes there'll be someone up to see you every single day.'

'You promise?'

'I promise!'

The others are going to visit him every day, whether they want to or not, she vowed silently. Even if I have to beat them senseless with the copper-stick. And that goes for Father too!

Outside the police house a figure detached itself from the surrounding darkness. It was Patrick. At once she rushed into his arms.

'I saw you go in,' he said. 'I wondered your father or some of your brothers didn't come with you.'

Maddy was surprised. She suddenly realised how much responsibility she had assumed for the whole family. It never occurred to her, or to the others, that they might visit Davie and give him comfort too.

'No, I came alone,' she said.

'Good, then I can walk you home.' He slid his arm protectively about her waist, and they began to climb the hill. 'How is your brother?' he asked.

His simple enquiry released a dam of words from within her. All the way home she poured forth her worries and concerns for Davie, pausing only when they stopped at the top of the last descent into Duncannon. 'I'm sorry,' she whispered, wiping her tear-streaked face with her hand. 'I didn't seem able to stop talking.'

'Did it help?' he asked gently.

'Yes.' Her reply was unhesitating.

'Then that's the important thing. The time ahead is bound to be difficult for you. Please remember that I am here for you to lean on. If I can help in no other way, let me at least be your support.'

His goodnight kiss was soft and tender, and she returned home feeling far more calm than she had dared to hope. In the midst of her recent troubles and worries there was still Patrick. He was there for her to lean on. She was not alone.

One thing she should have anticipated, yet did not, was the antagonism in the village against the Shillabeer family. In the days that followed Davie's arrest, she was conscious of hostile eyes following her when she went to the shop; people she had known all her life, who would normally have given her a cheerful greeting, deliberately turned away as she passed by or, even worse, spat insults at her.

'As if we haven't enough to distress us,' she cried one evening when she got home. 'Can't they see we're sick to our hearts because Ned Knapman's dead? We know Davie's responsible, they don't have to rub it in.'

'Don't you pay no heed, our Maddy,' Lew comforted her. 'They'm ignorant, that's what they be. Can't see no further than their nose end, most of them.'

'You know who'll be gloating over this, don't you?' said Bart. It had been his turn to go up to see Davie at Totnes, and he had been very quiet since coming back. 'Mr High and Mighty Whitcomb, that's who. You can bet 'tis his influence that's getting Davie sent to Exeter.'

'Oh, surely not.' Upset as she was, Maddy could not see how Cal Whitcomb could be to blame.

'Surely yes,' countered Bart. 'I reckon he and the squire got their heads together even afore they questioned Davie, determined to send him afore the judge. Think on it. It were an accident, everyone knows that. Why, then, idn't Davie just going to be sent to the magistrates' court up to Totnes?'

Under ordinary circumstances Maddy might have seen the unreasonableness of her brother's thinking, but she was sick with worry and only too happy to find a scapegoat for Davie's troubles. That was why when she encountered Cal Whitcomb soon afterwards and he enquired politely enough, 'What news of your brother?' she had no inclination to give a civil reply.

'He's been committed to the Exeter assizes. He goes next week, thanks to your evidence,' she retorted.

'I gave the facts about my own movements, nothing more.'

'Couldn't you have put in a good word for him or something?'

'Why should I?' Cal reined in his horse closer and frowned down at her. 'Your brothers have been nuisances ever since I can recall. The miracle is that no one has been killed sooner by their stupidity. Now a man has been killed. A good man with a wife and young children dependent upon him. I was the one who had to go to Mrs Knapman and tell her Ned was dead. I'm the one who, in decency's name, will have to provide for her – it will be no use appealing to you Shillabeers, you never have two ha'pennies to rub together. And I'm the one who had to walk behind Ned's coffin and see him decently buried. I'm having to do all these distressing things because your brother hasn't the sense he was born with. Maybe he is only fifteen, but that's old enough to know how dangerous a catapult shot can be when aimed at a man's head. Don't expect me to pity him.' With that he urged his horse away.

He had spoken the truth, Maddy could see that, but she refused to admit it. She seized on the one scrap of ammunition she had been able to glean from his speech.

'And whose fault is it we never have two ha'pennies to rub together?' she called after him. 'You tell me that, Cal Whitcomb!' Nevertheless, he had touched a sore spot in her conscience. They did owe Ned Knapman's wife some reparation. Someone from the family ought to call upon the widow, and by someone she knew it would be her. Ever since Davie's arrest she had been trying to pluck up her courage, and she could put it off no longer.

–

'Yer, what be doing with that?' Bart's voice made her start.

She looked down at the money on the table. 'I'm taking it to Ned Knapman's widow.'

'Be you mazed or summat?' He grasped her hand and pushed it away from the scattered coins on the scrubbed deal. 'Us'll need every penny of that from now on because of this caper. There'll be trips to Exeter to pay for, and lodgings and lost wages. Us can't go giving naught to charity.'

'It's not charity. We owe it to Mrs Knapman,' protested Maddy. 'Goodness knows it's little enough to compensate for the loss of a husband. That poor woman's got five children to rear.'

'She won't starve. Whitcomb'll see to her.'

'Where's your pride, Bart Shillabeer?' she demanded. 'You may not care that Cal Whitcomb is paying our debts for us, but I do. That money's going to Mrs Knapman and no argument. Yes, we're going to need money for Exeter, so you men can stay home at nights from now on, and the money saved can go in the jug instead of Harry Ford's pocket.' She slipped the coins into a canvas bag and stalked out.

The Knapmans lived in a cottage just beyond the farmhouse at Oakwood. Racked with nerves, Maddy walked past three times trying to think up what she would say before she dared knock on the door. An elderly woman opened it.

'Yes?' she demanded.

'Is – is Mrs Knapman in, please?' Maddy asked.

'Who wants to know? Her've enough on her plate without being bothered by callers.'

'The name is… Shillabeer. Maddy Shillabeer.'

'Shillabeer?' The woman pondered for a moment, then realisation struck. 'With a name like that you'm daring to come yer, you brazen hussy?' she yelled. 'I wonder you dare disturb decent folks as be in mourning. Get off with you, before I lets the dog loose.'

'Please, I just want a word with her,' begged Maddy.

'Well, her don't want no word with you. Her wouldn't soil her ears, wouldn't my daughter.'

'Who is it, Ma?' called a female voice from inside. Footsteps sounded and a younger version of the woman who had harangued Maddy came to the door. 'Why, 'tis Miss Shillabeer, idn't it? Come in, do. There be a cruel draught beating through the door.'

'You'm having her in, after what her kin have done?' demanded her mother.

'Her idn't responsible for her kinsfolk, Ma. None of us be. Come in, Miss Shillabeer.'

'Thank you,' said Maddy, following her into the small kitchen-cum-parlour. 'It's very kind of you to see me, but if you want the truth I do feel responsible. I had the raising of Davie, you see. I should've managed to teach him not to play stupid tricks by now.'

'There, don't take on about it. You was left very young to rear your brothers, so I've been told. Bringing up childer idn't no frolic. I knows, having five. I be sure you did your best, no one can do more.'

Maddy gave a weak smile. 'How things have turned about,' she said. 'Here you are giving me comfort when the boot should be on the other foot. You're very kind.'

Mrs Knapman shook her head. She looked tired and washed out. 'I just tries to see things the way they be,' she said. 'I don't suppose the boy did it deliberate.' Her mother gave a disbelieving snort. ''Tis true, Ma. From what folks say, he were just fooling around, as boys do.'

'He meant your husband no harm, I can assure you of that, Mrs Knapman. He's terribly sorry for what happened – we all are. If it had been possible he would have come with me today. Since it isn't, then it falls to me to say how much he regrets behaving so stupidly.'

Again the old woman snorted. 'Just as well he bain't yer,' she said. 'Prison's best place for un.'

'Ma!' Mrs Knapman was gently reproving. 'It were an accident. The lad's being punished enough. Prison must be a terrible place, specially for such a youngster. And as Miss Shillabeer says, he didn't mean no harm to my Ned.'

She pulled the youngest child onto her lap. As she lulled the drowsy infant to sleep she seemed eager to talk, but about anything rather than the tragedy that had befallen her.

'It were Mr Whitcomb as were the target of the joke, they say. I can't never understand why folks be so against Mr Calland. I knows your family have your reasons, but there's lots of other people who habn't a good word for him, yet my Ned fair worshipped the ground he walked on. Everyone held that it were the elder brother, Christopher, as were the pick of the Whitcombs, but not according to my Ned. Mr Calland were twice the man his brother were, and ten times the farmer. 'Tis a terrible thing to say and 'tidn't widely known, but if the cholera hadn't taken Mr Christopher when it did, the Whitcombs would've lost Oakwood because of his debts.'

'He was reckoned to be kind-hearted, though,' said Maddy, surprised at these revelations.

'Oh, he were kind-hearted right enough. The pity was he didn't have pockets to match. Us've had many a hard struggle because Ned didn't get his wages on time from Mr Christopher. Poor Mr Calland got a terrible name for turning off workers when he took over. Truth was there wadn't no money to pay them. He had to sell the gold watch his pa left him in order to find wages for everyone. No one as left was owed a penny. How many'd have done that?'

'Not many,' Maddy was forced to admit. It put a new perspective upon Cal's reputation for meanness. The talk of money prompted other uncomfortable thoughts.

'Mrs Knapman,' she said. 'Forgive me for asking, but how will you manage now?'

'Manage?' Mrs Knapman looked bemused, as if the idea had never occurred to her. 'Oh, us'll do fine. Mr Calland's promised I shall have ten shillings every week till the end of my days. Ten shilling! "You'm not going on the parish, Mrs Ned," he says – always calls me Mrs Ned, he do – "Tis the least I can do since that stone were meant... meant..."' Mrs Knapman's calm demeanour suddenly crumbled into tears. The sleeping child awoke and began crying too as its mother rocked back and forth sobbing.

Maddy knew this was no place for her. While the old woman was occupied with comforting her daughter, she let herself out of the cottage, leaving the bag of money on the table. She almost wished Mrs Knapman had been as aggressive towards her as her mother. It might have been easier to tolerate than her gentle forbearance. As it was, Maddy knew she would never get the sight of the unfortunate widow from her mind, nursing her child in her grief, and all because of the Shillabeer family.

–

Davie was taken to Exeter Gaol on the following Monday. Maddy went to Totnes to say goodbye. She had made light of the distance to Exeter, but no one in their family had ever been as far as the city before and it seemed as remote as China. In the hope of giving him final encouragement she waited to see him leave. She was not prepared for seeing him in iron fetters, shuffling painfully from the tiny gaol on the ramparts of the old town to the waiting cart. He went with head bowed, and she was glad he did not see her, for she knew that anguish was written all over her face.

December was the date set for Davie's trial, during the winter assizes. The great debate among the Shillabeers was whether to take one day on the road or two.

'Lodgings for us lot on the way be going to cost a pretty penny,' protested Bart.

'All the same, us'll have to pay up and look handsome,' said Lew. 'Daylight be short this time of year, and if us idn't careful us'll find ourselves stumbling about Exeter in the dark looking for somewhere to stay. It idn't too bad for us menfolk, if the worst comes to the worst us could always find a stable or summat, but us idn't having Maddy on any caper like that. Us'll get to Exeter in good time to find respectable lodgings.'

Jack was clearly impressed by Lew's uncharacteristic determination, for he overrode Bart's objections, saying, 'Right, us'll do as the boy says. Us'll overnight on the road.'

It proved to be a wet, cold trudge to Exeter. How easily it might have been a great adventure. But there was no excited anticipation; they were going to Exeter because they must and there was only unhappiness in the prospect.

Maddy had never believed there were so many people in the world as crowded the streets of Exeter. In truth, the city was normally a very modest county capital, still rural in its aspect with views of the surrounding green hills from its very centre. But the winter assizes were regarded as something of a social event, and the usual population had increased considerably, making it a tumultuous throng to Maddy's astonished eyes.

It was as well they had arrived in good time, for lodgings, respectable or otherwise, were hard to find. Eventually they found a couple of rooms at a small inn near the Iron Bridge which straddled the narrow valley between the city centre and St David's Hill. The inn was reasonable enough, although carts carrying lime passed along the road outside in a steady stream from dawn to dusk, creating a racket with their iron-rimmed wheels and leaving a film of acrid white dust over everything.

The first cart to rattle over the cobbles before dawn did not disturb Maddy. She had already been awake for hours. She was not troubled by the noise or the dirt, all she wanted was to get to the court and for Davie's trial to be over as soon as possible.

'If you'm wanting to go to the assizes you best get there early,' their landlady informed them. 'Folks like to see the procession with the judge and barristers and everyone, then there be one gurt crush to get in and hear the triads.'

'Thank you for telling us. We might go that way to see the procession,' said Maddy civilly, not wanting to betray their true reason for being in Exeter.

The landlady was not fooled. Why else would poor folk come to the city at this time, especially those who looked worried sick? It could only be because they had someone standing trial. Not that she minded. As long as they paid their bills, other folks' misfortunes were none of her concern.

Maddy and her family found the law court easily enough, a fine stone building in the old Castle Yard, girded by high walls. The steep narrow street was already jammed with people when they arrived. Maddy feared they would never manage to get into court at all, such was the crush.

'Don't you fret, my lover,' a stout neighbour consoled her, seeing her anxious face. 'As soon as the judge's coach and the others have gone through you follow on behind. Be quick, mind, and don't worry about who you treads underfoot.'

Maddy managed a bleak smile of thanks, and waited for the procession. No doubt it was quite a spectacle, with the fine coach bearing the judge in his full robes. The other bystanders seemed to think so as they cheered and shouted, but to her it was merely irritating and irrelevant. What place had pageantry in the trying of her Davie? But she did not let her irritation slow her reactions. The moment she guessed the last carriage was approaching, she pushed her way in behind it, not caring that she risked falling beneath the wheels. All five Shillabeers were carried along by the crush to the assize court. Once inside, it was strange and bewildering but somehow they found where to go.

Although there were already many people there, Maddy took no notice of them, her attention was entirely taken up by the room. How impressive it was, and intimidating, especially the high-canopied judge's chair, surmounted by the royal coat of arms. The two rows of benches close by were presumably for the jury. And then there was the dock for the accused. There was no mistaking it. She shuddered. This was where Davie would stand, cut off from her and the rest of the court by its wooden walls cruelly topped by sharp metal spikes.

The waiting felt interminable. Maddy and her family seemed to have nothing to say to one another except, 'Won't be long now, eh?' or 'They'm going to have to start soon.' Then Lew said, 'Hullo, something be up. Look who's just come in.'

Escorted by an usher, four men came in and occupied a bench at the front.

'They'm witnesses,' their neighbour informed them, the same stout woman who had stood by them in the road.

Maddy did not need to be told. Constable Vallance was instantly recognisable, and Cal Whitcomb, looking neatly formed in a dark suit.

The squire was there too, along with the man who worked for Farmer Churchward and had seen Davie run away. The fourth gentleman was vaguely familiar, although she could not put a name to him.

'Dr Barratt.' Jack leaned across and hissed the name. 'From Paignton. I suppose he were the one called in to look at Ned's body.'

Soon afterwards the jury filed into their seats. Maddy watched as they were sworn in, and her stomach tightened into a knot. Twelve men who held Davie's future in their power. Twelve men – and the judge.

Oh, let him be a kindly soul, she prayed. So much depends on him. Let him be lenient.

Her first proper view of Mr Justice Stroud came as a surprise. Her fleeting glimpse of him as he passed in the carriage had given no hint of his small stature. He was tiny and so swamped by his wig and heavy robes that she felt an hysterical urge to giggle. Her neighbour did not greet the judge's appearance with amusement, however.

'Oh gawd,' she murmured. 'Not old Stroud. Some poor soul be in for a rough time.'

'Why do you say that?' demanded Maddy.

''Cause he be the meanest judge on the circuit. A proper old devil, he be. Bain't you heard of "String em up Stroud"?'

Bleakly Maddy shook her head. Her prayers had not been answered.

There was a stirring round the courtroom as Davie was brought in. Maddy's fond eye immediately took in the fact that he was wearing a clean shirt, that he had been at pains to comb his unruly hair into some sort of order – and that he looked terribly young, far less than his fifteen years.

'Why, he'm naught but a babe,' said her neighbour sympathetically. 'And a fine-looking boy too, poor lamb.'

Maddy bit her lips hard. This was no time for tears. She had to stay clear-headed, willing Davie to have courage, and the sharp-faced judge to be compassionate.

The proceedings began.

'David Shillabeer, you are charged with that on the 15th of November in the year of our Lord 1869 you did unlawfully murder one Edward Knapman, stockman, in the parish of Stoke Gabriel, in the county of Devonshire. How do you plead, guilty or not guilty?'

'Not guilty, sir... my lord.'

Maddy did not like the way the judge's head snapped round at Davie's slip of the tongue.

Dr Barratt was the first to give evidence. He spoke clearly, with assurance, having obviously performed this sort of duty before.

'…I was called to examine one Edward Knapman, stockman… I pronounced him dead… cause of death a blow to the temple… the stone found near the body and covered with blood could certainly have been the instrument of death… would have needed some impulsion… being shot from a slingshot or catapult could certainly have given the required force, in my opinion.'

The doctor answered the questions put to him by Mr Linton, the prosecuting counsel. Then it was the turn of Mr Attwill, Davie's defending counsel.

'Could there not have been some other cause which would account for Mr Knapman's sudden fall from his horse? Did you look for other possibilities in your autopsy, or did you merely see the wound and assume it to be the cause of death?'

'I did a thorough autopsy, sir,' retorted the doctor testily. 'In my written report, if you care to read it, you will see that I pronounced Mr Knapman's heart, liver, lungs and other organs to be in excellent condition.'

Mr Attwill tried another tack. 'In your opinion this stone exhibited here was the cause of death?'

'Yes, it matches the wound exactly. In addition it is heavily stained with blood.'

'Must this stone have been flung in a catapult or something similar? Could the deceased not have fallen onto it, causing the injury?'

'It is possible,' said the doctor, adding sardonically, 'but that leaves the problem of why a fit, sober man should suddenly fall from a quiet horse to hit his head on a convenient stone.'

Mr Attwill was not doing well. He seemed a pleasant man but young and inexperienced, unlike Mr Linton who was sharp and missed nothing. The prosecuting counsel made sure that Constable Vallance gave firm evidence that there were no cuts on the horse's knees to indicate that the animal might have slipped. From Cal Whitcomb he determined that the horse was well-schooled, that Ned was a competent rider who had ridden the creature many times. Any hope of Ned's death being accidental withered before his enquiries.

Maddy listened to the cut and thrust of the questioning with dismay, particularly the verbal skills of Mr Linton. She had never realised that words could be twisted in such a way. She did not like the line of the prosecuting counsel's interrogation, especially when Cal Whitcomb was in the witness box. Much seemed to be made of the longstanding feud, the former incidents between the two families, and the fact that Cal had already brought a prosecution against Davie and his brothers. The way Mr Linton spoke of these incidents, and contrived to make Cal describe them, they grew in seriousness out of all proportion to the truth. When he finally stepped down, Cal's face was grave. He looked towards Davie and shook his head regretfully, as if sorry for the things he had been obliged to say.

The squire and the man who worked for Farmer Churchward fared no better. From the way Mr Linton manipulated their evidence it seemed as though Davie was well known in the village as a vicious thug with a malicious temper. Constable Vallance was a far more experienced witness. Maddy sensed that he was doing everything he could do to help Davie, as far as his duty would allow, but even he was not proof against Mr Linton's skilled questioning.

'A boyish prank with a catapult? But wasn't the stone used extremely large for a mere prank?' persisted the prosecuting counsel. 'Constable, in your experience, both as upholder of the law and one-time small boy, would you have used such a vicious stone if all you wanted was to knock off a hat? Would not a rounded pebble have been more suitable? More easily directed?'

Constable Vallance was forced to agree with the point.

'Tell me, Constable, how long was it between Mr Whitcomb taking his horse to the smithy and Mr Knapman collecting it?' Constable Vallance consulted his notebook. 'About an hour, according to both the blacksmith and his apprentice, sir.'

'About an hour!' Mr Linton's nasal voice rang out. 'As I recall, the weather on the fifteenth of November was exceptionally inclement. To wait for more than an hour behind a hedge in the freezing cold simply to knock off a man's hat, that is dedication to a joke indeed – or would it seem, perhaps the action of someone with a more serious object in view?' There was an excited murmur throughout the courtroom as Mr Linton smiled with self-satisfaction at having driven his point home. Maddy shivered. It was growing late, but the prosecuting counsel had not finished.

'Constable Vallance, when you went to apprehend the accused, how did he behave?'

'He made no attempt to evade me, although he was nervous.'

'Did he admit that he had flung the stone with his catapult?'

'I did not question him as to that immediately, sir. Later, when he was questioned by the Justice of the Peace, he freely admitted shooting the catapult.'

'Did he not say anything at all when you apprehended him?'

Constable Vallance hesitated. 'You understand, sir, that the accused was under the impression that he had hit Mr Calland Whitcomb.'

'So I understand from your earlier evidence,' persisted Mr Linton, 'but did he say nothing when you first apprehended him?'

Maddy could not understand why the constable looked uneasy. Whatever Davie had said was unimportant, surely?

'He said, sir...' The constable made a great show of looking in his notebook. 'He said, "Ned Knapman? Not Farmer Whitcomb? It were the wrong man..."'

A sigh went through the onlookers and Maddy realised why Constable Vallance had been ill at ease. He had seen how damning those few words would seem to hostile ears.

When the court proceedings ended for the day, Maddy and her family returned to their lodgings. She found she could neither eat nor sleep. She had come to Exeter dreading the length of sentence her brother might get for manslaughter. Now a much greater fear had hold of her.

In the dock next day, Davie's gaze ranged nervously round the public gallery. Maddy knew he was looking for her, but although she risked the displeasure of the court officials and waved, he was looking away by then and did not see her.

How alone he must feel, poor boy, she thought. I hope he realises we're here and doesn't think we've left him to face this ordeal alone.

Maddy wished fervently that prisoners could be allowed to give evidence on their own behalf. If only Davie could speak up for himself and explain... Then she reconsidered: after having seen the way the prosecuting counsel had twisted the other witnesses in knots she knew her young brother would not have stood a chance. Mr Linton would have had Davie condemning himself out of his own mouth.

The judge's summing up was a masterpiece of harshness and bias. Maddy listened in horror as he stressed the damning details – the long years of animosity, the size of the stone, the determination needed to wait so long for the victim to pass, Davie's reputation along with his brothers as troublemakers. Worst of all, he stressed Davie's own fatal words, suggesting they were an admission of guilt. Nothing was said of the boy's youthfulness, of his immaturity, nor of his fondness for pranks. The jury were gone a very short time. After such a summing-up, there was only one verdict they could give.

'Guilty, my lud.'

With deliberation the black cap was placed upon Mr Justice Stroud's wig. 'David Shillabeer,' he boomed, an oddly large voice out of such a small frame, 'you have heard the jury's verdict. You have been found guilty of the wilful murder of Edward Knapman. Therefore you will be taken from here to a place of execution and hanged by the neck until you are dead.' There was a hush in the court and then it was broken by a woman's voice crying out, 'No! Oh no! Dear God, no!'

With shocked surprise Maddy realised that it was she who was screaming.

Chapter Ten

The stark lines and plain façade of Exeter Gaol struck Maddy as even more awesome than her brief view of the cathedral – or maybe her reaction was caused by association; there was hope in the cathedral, she found no hope in the prison. Steadfastly she averted her eyes from the tower at the rear. That was where the scaffold was housed and the executions took place, an informative bystander had told her as they had waited at the main gate.

Finally they were ushered into Davie's cell.

'Special privilege, you lot being allowed in at once,' the warder informed them. 'Condemned prisoners be permitted these treats.' He sounded quite proud of the concession, as though Davie were a favoured child or a prize pupil.

The reality, however, dominated the thoughts of all the Shillabeers, a reality that was stressed by the grim little cell with its meagre table, stool and hammock – not even a proper bed. As soon as they entered, Jack and the brothers asked a plethora of questions such as: 'How be you, boy?' and 'They treating you proper?' and 'How be the food, then?' before their imaginations failed them and they were reduced to commenting upon the marvel of the gas lighting and how it worked. Their seeming callousness was not because they did not care, but because they were out of their depth. It was left to Maddy to say the things they wanted to say yet for which they could not find the words.

'We were there all the time,' she said. 'I waved but I never seemed able to catch your eye.'

'I saw you,' Davie said. 'At first I didn't and I felt proper down, but then I remembered you promised to be here and—' His face, white and pinched, suddenly crumpled as he lost his fight to appear brave. 'Maddy, I be so scared of dying.'

She was with him in an instant, comforting him as she had done when he was a small child.

'You're not to lose heart,' she said firmly. 'Things are far from hopeless. I expect Mr Attwill's already spoken to you about an appeal. It sounds very promising. Everyone in court was shocked at the verdict and said how harsh and unjust it was. Even the usher who took us to see Mr Attwill after the trial, he said it was one of the worst verdicts he's ever heard, and that anyone could see it was a clear case of manslaughter. People are talking about your case in the street, we've heard them. Folk we don't know, who we've never met before.'

'That should help then, shouldn't it?' Davie looked a shade more cheerful.

'It's bound to. Your case isn't lost yet, not by a long chalk.' Maddy was determined to be optimistic. 'I'm surprised you haven't asked what's in the basket,' she went on. 'There's a clean shirt for a start – you let me have the couple you've got and I'll wash them. But it'll be the food you're interested in. There's some toffee that Annie made for you, a few apples, and a lump of Mrs Cutmore's best cheese, and I made you a jam tart and a batch of nubbies with currants in them, just the way you like them.' Maddy emptied the basket, finishing with the fragrant yellow saffron buns.

'I brought you some peppermint rock,' said Lew. 'You'm going to need un after eating that lot.'

One by one the others added their offerings, all edible, to the pile. Davie was young enough to regard the feast with delight, and old enough to realise that it did nothing to alleviate his situation. For a brief moment his face lit up at the prospect of the sweetmeats, but soon resumed its pinched look.

'Is there anything else I can bring you when we come tomorrow?' Maddy asked.

'You're coming again tomorrow?' He said it with an eagerness that wrenched at Maddy's heart.

'Of course we are, you daft lump,' she said. 'Do you need anything?'

'Some soap. Something that smells good. Anything to shift the stink of this place.'

Remembering her past battles to get her young brother to wash, Maddy found this request almost too moving to bear. A tense silence settled on the cell, until Lew took up the conversation.

'I can't say I be impressed with this yer gas lighting,' he said. 'Tidn't no wonder you'm looking a bit wisht, Davie boy. Tis making my head spin already.'

'That's because you'm too close to un, being such a longshanks,' retorted Bart.

The conversation returned to the merits and defects of this modern marvel. Neither Maddy nor Davie joined in, but it filled in the awkward silence until the warder came, with much clanking of keys, to tell them it was time to leave.

On her way back to their lodgings, Maddy bought Davie a bar of lavender-scented soap.

'How much did un cost?' asked Bart, after he had given it an appreciate sniff.

'Sixpence.'

'Sixpence? Gawd, I wonder you didn't buy a gross at that price!'

'It's best quality soap. The lady in the shop said she uses it herself. Do you begrudge Davie a few pennyworth of something decent?' Maddy was incensed.

'No, I don't begrudge un, maid,' said Bart, quite gently for him. ''Tis just that Mr Attwill said the appeal should be heard in ten days. Well, by my calculating, there idn't no way the five of us can stay in Exeter more'n another three days at the most.'

Maddy was dismayed. For once she had completely forgotten the family budget. Their lack of money came as a shock.

'You aren't suggesting we should go home, are you?' she protested. 'Abandoning poor Davie?'

'I idn't suggesting naught,' said Bart with uncharacteristic patience. 'I be simply stating how things be. There idn't much money left, and that be the truth.'

'We'll have to do something,' stated Maddy. 'We can move to cheaper lodgings. Cut down on food...'

'Finding cheaper lodgings be easier said than done with the assizes still on. And even if us lives on bread and scrape, us can't stay no longer than three more days.'

'Very well, then we'll just have to find temporary work. One thing is certain, we aren't leaving Davie, not now, supposing we have to sleep in the streets.'

'It might come to that,' muttered Bart.

His forebodings proved to be uncomfortably accurate. Cheaper lodgings were simply not available, not if they had any pretensions to respectability. As for temporary work, that too turned out to be impossible to find.

'It idn't just the gentry as comes into the city for the assizes,' explained Mrs Polsoe, their landlady. 'Folks come in from the country at this time for the casual work, portering and such. By now most jobs'll be took. Mind you, as we're full I could do with someone myself until the assizes be over. Someone to help in the kitchen and generally make herself useful. The hours be from six until eleven of an evening. I'll give you free lodgings and a proper supper each night, and you'll stand a chance of earning some tips.' She looked meaningfully at Maddy.

'I'll take it,' said Maddy promptly, although she was sceptical about the tips. From what she had seen, the clientele of the shabby little inn did not seem the sort to have money to throw about. Nevertheless, she was grateful for the offer. It meant she, at least, could stay on.

It turned out that she was the only one in the family to find employment.

'Not even no unloading down to the quay nor digging ditches nor nothing,' complained Jack bitterly.

'That's it, then,' said Bart with an air of finality. 'Thanks to Maddy's job us've managed to stay on and be with Davie for an extra couple of days. Us can't stay no longer, though. Not all of us.'

'But we'll soon have the result of the appeal,' pleaded Maddy. 'And it means so much to Davie, us going to see him every day.'

'I idn't denying it,' replied Bart. 'And you, Maddy, can certainly stay until the appeal and… and after that if need be.'

Maddy flinched at the implication of his words. She had not let herself even consider the possibility of the appeal failing.

'Maddy idn't staying by herself,' said Lew, protective as ever. 'How about if us gives what money's left to Father, so's he can bide here while us goes home? Us can be working and earning a bit while they two cheer up poor old Davie.'

'But you won't know the result of the appeal,' Maddy protested.

'You could send us a letter, they say 'tis only a penny,' pointed out Lew. 'Think on it! Us getting a letter!' His brief attempt at cheeriness faded as he said seriously, 'And if you needs us in a hurry, maid, us can get back in a day. There'd be no need for us to spend a night on the road, not now us knows our way better.'

It was a sensible suggestion, and everyone agreed to it.

Maddy felt a wrench, watching her brothers heading off homeward in the cold darkness of morning. Part of her longed to be going with them, to the peaceful familiarity of Duncannon.

It seemed an age since she was last there. She longed to be with Patrick again, too. Just to see him, to enjoy that smile of his, to feel his arms about her; but she could not go to him yet. To desert Davie was out of the question.

The hours until they were allowed entry to the prison dragged for both father and daughter. How Jack filled in his time Maddy could only guess. Usually she passed the time wandering about the city exploring the streets and gazing into the windows of the grand shops. On this particular morning, for a change, she decided to watch the comings and goings at St David's Station. She had seen trains before at both Totnes and Paignton, but they were insignificant compared to the busy Exeter lines. The station had the added advantage of offering shelter, very welcome on such a raw morning.

She was crossing the wide courtyard in front of the station when she heard someone calling her name. Turning round she saw Cal Whitcomb hurrying towards her.

'Miss Shillabeer! I thought it was you ahead of me but I couldn't be sure. You go at a rare pace, I was hard put to it to catch you up.' He had about him the fresh ruddy glow of a man who had been hurrying.

Maddy regarded him, smart as any Exeter gentleman in his Inverness cape of heavy woollen tweed and his top hat, and was not sure she had anything to say to him. But he did not give her an opportunity to speak.

'Miss Shillabeer – Maddy,' he said, 'you are the last person I expected to see this morning but I am very glad I have. I'm not sure how to put this into words… What I want to say is how horrified and outraged I am at the verdict against your brother. I am all the more distressed that I was in part responsible as a witness for the prosecution. Had I realised the outcome, the devious way the prosecuting counsel had in twisting words, I would have been more on my guard.'

'It's not much good having these thoughts now!' she exclaimed, suddenly glad to have someone to rail against. 'You should have thought of them earlier. All the regrets in the land won't help my brother now. Did you have to paint him so black? Did you have to bring up every incident and insult that's ever passed between you? It was a boy's life you were dealing with, you know – not that it really matters to you. It'll be one less Shillabeer to trouble you. I suppose that's what counts most.'

'No!' he protested. 'Never that. I was angry with him, I'll admit. It was a terrible thing that happened as a result of his stupidity, but never for a minute did I think it was deliberate. I certainly never considered such a verdict. Manslaughter, yes, but not murder. The last thing I intended was to portray him as a black villain.'

Glaring up into his face Maddy saw that his distress was genuine. He was truly upset about Davie; but she could not relent and forgive him his testimony.

'I hope that you will be suitably contrite when they hang my Davie,' she hissed at him.

She realised that he was grasping her hand. When he had taken hold of it she had no idea, but it was not his touch that distressed her. It was the fact that she had put her deepest fears into words. *When they hang my Davie.* That was what she had said. Wrenching her hand free she turned and ran away from him, from the station, from the dirt and pungent steam of the trains. The only thing she could not run away from was the terror her own words had aroused in her.

By the time she met up with Jack outside the prison she must have managed to compose herself again for he did not seem to notice anything amiss.

''Tis funny without the others,' remarked Davie when only his father and sister entered his cell. 'You idn't going to have to leave, though, be you?' Desperation was in his voice, despite his attempts to control it.

'No, we won't leave,' Maddy promised. 'I'm getting on fine with my job at the inn, and that's my bed and board pretty well seen to. And as for Father…'

'As for me, I can bed down with the horses if needs be, I won't hurt none,' said Jack cheerily.

Davie managed a bleak smile, obviously heartened by their reassurances. Maddy looked at him and felt her heart lurch with pity and love. It was usually claimed that adversity aged a person, but on Davie it had had the opposite effect. His increased pallor along with loss of weight contrived to make him seem younger and more vulnerable each time she saw him.

'You'll never guess what I'm going to do,' she said, forcing herself to sound cheerful. 'I'm going to write to the boys to let them know how you're getting on. Imagine them getting a letter! Annie'll have a fit when she sees the postman calling.'

'I wish I could see her face.' Davie's own face lit up with something of his old liveliness, then quickly grew serious again. 'You can tell them about my appeal.'

'That I will, and won't they celebrate when they hear it's been successful.'

'*If* it be successful!' Davie was too sharp to be taken in by her false optimism.

'Of course it will be successful,' declared Maddy.

'I idn't so sure. I reckon the size of the stone be against me. I said as it were too big. I wish I'd used the tiddy pebble I wanted first, but then what be the point of wishing? It don't do no good. If it did, I'd wish I habn't never joined in the whole daft eaper in the first place.'

Maddy stiffened. 'What do you mean, joined in?' she demanded.

Davie looked suddenly wary. 'Well, thunk it up,' he said.

'Then why didn't you say thought it up? Why did you say joined in? Was there someone else with you?'

'Of course there wadn't.' His reply was a little too prompt and a little too indignant. 'As for what I said, joined in or thunk up, what be the difference? I idn't one for book-reading like you.'

'Yer, our Maddy, you leave the boy alone,' said Jack sharply. 'Habn't he enough to contend with without you starting to sound like that there Linton?'

Reluctantly Maddy let the matter drop, but she was deeply disturbed. Her father had failed to realise the significance of Davie's slip. No matter how much her brother denied it, his words implied he was not alone in the prank. And had he not said something else when referring to the stone? Something like 'I said it were too big?' Had she heard him properly? She was not sure now, but as she left the prison she felt most uneasy. The more she thought of it, the more troubled she became – and the less she felt that the whole escapade had been Davie's idea. It had too much of careful, patient planning about it for her impetuous younger brother. But it was exactly the sort of scheme he could be persuaded to participate in, especially by someone with a stronger will.

When she put her suspicions to Jack he thought them unimportant.

'No one habn't mentioned no second person,' he pointed out. 'Not even that man of Farmer Churchward's, what were quick on the scene by all accounts. He didn't say naught about seeing no one else, did he? And Davie have denied un, so I don't know what you'm fussing about.'

Perhaps he was right. Maddy tried to put the suspicion from her, but it lurked tenaciously at the back of her mind.

–

She had more than one reason for being grateful for her job at the inn. The chance to earn herself lodgings was marvellous, but being kept occupied in the evenings was equally welcome. During the day she could fill in time walking about the city, but the hours of darkness had grown intolerable. Now she cooked and cleaned, served ale, and swept floors like a thing possessed.

'My regulars idn't going to know the place soon,' remarked Mrs Polsoe after closing time, as Maddy scrubbed energetically. 'I didn't know they tables was that colour. Come up real vitty they have.' She heaved a sigh. 'I tell you what, maid, I'd as soon be wielding a brush as doing this lot.' She thumped a stubby forefinger on the papers in front of her.

'What's the trouble?' Maddy asked, wiping her hands on her apron.

'The figures be at sixes and sevens. I'd leave un until tomorrow, when my head'd be clear, but the brewery man's due in the morning and he'll expect paying. This be the bill he left me but it seems terrible dear to me. I've reckoned it up this way and that but I can't make it no less, yet something's wrong somewhere.'

'Here, let me have a look.' Maddy pulled the oil lamp closer. 'That's the draught bitter per barrel, I presume, and that the mild. What's this entry?'

'That be the bottled beer. I usually has a dozen crates from time to time – folk round here don't usually run to such fancy tastes but as 'tis Christmas I thought I'd double the order. But I didn't expect un to cost this much!'

'That's because he's charging you for two scores of crates, not two dozen,' said Maddy. 'The writing's not too clear, it seems as if it's been altered. But if you add it up, the cost is for forty crates not twenty-four.'

Mrs Polsoe made some calculations with her blunt pencil. 'So 'tis,' she declared. 'And me only taking delivery of two dozen! Us can guess where the extra money'd have gone, can't us? And who'd have altered it very carefully again before it got back to the office! Of all the cheating, conniving… I never did trust that fellow! His tailoring be far too natty for just a brewery tally man!' She paused in her ranting to beam at

Maddy. 'That were sharp of you to spot it. There was a time when that cheating toad'd never have dared try something like that on me, but I idn't the woman I was.'

'There, I think you'll find that's more like it.' Maddy pushed the amended bill towards her. 'Couldn't you find someone trustworthy to do your books for you?'

'There idn't that many as I'd trust,' said Mrs Polsoe, 'but the job be youm if you want it.'

'Oh, but I didn't... I wasn't hinting.'

'I knows you wadn't, maid, else I'd not have offered. But I idn't been in this trade for donkey's years without learning to judge character, that's why I be offering you the job.'

'That's kind of you, but I don't expect we'll be in Exeter for much longer.'

'Only until the appeal, I suppose.'

'How – how did you know?' gasped Maddy.

'I idn't deaf nor blind, girl.'

'And you'd offer me a job of trust, although my brother's in prison?'

''Tis he'm as in prison, not you. And a crying shame he be there, according to the gossip. But then if that idn't Judge Stroud all over. He'm got a terrible name. And to answer your question, yes, I still be offering you the job.'

Maddy knew she could not turn down such an offer. 'Very well, while I'm here I'll do your books for you.'

'Good. That be a load off my mind. Maybe you'd take on my six-monthly accounts up to the year's end, too, or near enough? I expect you'm going to be dashing home when the appeal's been heard. You bain't be wanting to hang about round here over Christmas, be you? But if you do, I can certainly make use of you until then.'

Mrs Polsoe was right. Maddy had given no thought at all to Christmas; of course she wanted to be home for then. And no doubt Davie could not wait to get back to the cottage and the river. The landlady would be loath to lose an extra pair of hands over such a busy period, but it could not be helped.

'Naturally I means to pay you for your bookwork,' Mrs Polsoe said. 'How shall it be? I can pay you in coin or else your father bides yer free, and you can both take all your meals here. Which'd you prefer?'

Maddy bit back a smile. Grateful as she was to the old woman, she knew how much Mrs Polsoe hated parting with money. The offer of meals was a good one, for although the food at the inn was plain, it was good and filling. To have bought the equivalent meals elsewhere would have cost at least a shilling for both her father and her. She also knew that a couple of extra dinners each day would never be missed from the busy kitchen. And as for her father's lodgings, his cot in a room shared with several others would have cost Mrs Polsoe practically nothing.

'I'll have the meals and Father's lodgings, thank you,' she said, straightfaced.

Mrs Polsoe beamed, well satisfied with the arrangement.

The day of the appeal seemed a long time in coming, but at last it arrived. Maddy and her father were at the prison with Davie, waiting for Mr Attwill to arrive. When they heard the key turn in the lock, the three of them leapt to their feet. Without his wig and gown the lawyer looked younger and more boyish, which only served to emphasise the solemn expression on his face. Jack took one look at him and appeared to age ten years. For a horrible moment Maddy feared she was going to be violently sick. It took a superhuman effort to control herself and put a comforting arm about Davie.

'You'd better give us the verdict, Mr Attwill,' she said quietly.

The lawyer also seemed to be struggling with his emotions. 'I am sorry… so very sorry…'

'What − what reasons did they give for turning down the appeal?' she asked, astonished at her own apparent calm when inside she was in turmoil.

'Simply that, there being no new evidence brought before their Lordships, they saw no reason to overturn the existing judgment.'

No new evidence! Had there been someone else with Davie that day? That would have been new evidence.

Davie's already white face had drained to an even deeper pallor and his eyes burned with horrified bewilderment.

'What does it mean?' he asked.

'It means that the Court of Appeal has refused to change the verdict,' explained Mr Attwill.

'But it wadn't murder. I didn't mean to hurt no one. No, the verdict must be manslaughter.' Davie's mind steadfastly refused to accept the awful truth.

'I'm afraid not,' said Maddy unsteadily.

'It must be!' Davie's voice rose in panic. 'If it be murder they'll hang me. They'll put a rope about my neck and choke the life out of me. Maddy, don't let them do un. Please don't let them do un to me!'

Sobbing bitterly, Maddy enfolded him in her arms, anguished beyond bearing that she had no comfort to give. Hopelessness and the sense of her own helplessness seemed to drag her down into a bottomless pit.

It was left to Jack to ask the dread question. 'When?'

'In three days. The day after Boxing Day,' said Mr Attwill.

With a shock Maddy realised the date. 'It's Christmas Eve today!' she exclaimed, grasping at one small spark. 'The season of goodwill. Maybe...?'

Mr Attwill shook his head regretfully. 'I did put forward to their Lordships that at this celebration of our Saviour's birth it might be appropriate to show leniency, but my plea was turned down.'

There was no hope. They had to accept it.

Taking their leave of Davie was the most terrible thing Maddy had ever experienced. He wept and clung to both her and Jack so tenaciously that in the end two warders had to restrain him.

'We'll be back tomorrow, we promise,' wept Maddy, knowing full well there would be few tomorrows. 'We'll be back.'

They could still hear his cries as they hurried away.

Back at the inn Maddy longed to be able to give way to her grief but she knew that would have to wait. First she must write to Bart, Lew and Charlie telling them the awful news and begging them to come quickly. Were letters delivered on Christmas Day? Would they get the message in time?

Maddy had never anticipated that writing a letter would prove so difficult. How cold the words looked, the pencilled lines austere and impersonal on the cheap paper. She wished she could convey some comfort to her brothers, but there was none to give them either.

As she returned from the post office, her thoughts went back to Mr Attwill's comments on the appeal. It had been turned down because of lack of new evidence. But she had new evidence, or at least the prospect of some. Upon impulse, she hurried towards Mr Attwill's chambers in Bedford Circus.

'I presume you have questioned your brother about this other person. What does he say?' asked the lawyer after listening to her sympathetically.

'He denies it. He says he was alone.'

'Then I regret there is no more to be said.'

'But if we got a stay of execution while Constable Vallance made more enquiries? He'd find out who the other person was, I'm sure.'

'If there was another person,' prompted Mr Attwill gently. 'And if the constable found the identity of the culprit, what then? There would simply be a second trial with probably the same tragic outcome. It would not alter your brother's case. Do not torture yourself, my dear Miss Shillabeer. Everything possible has been done to aid your brother. I fear all that is left is to be at his side to comfort him, and to help him make his peace with God.'

Mr Attwill spoke with great kindness but there was a finality in his voice that angered Maddy. What did he care? It was not his brother who was to be hanged.

Because it was Christmas Day, Maddy and Jack were allowed to spend longer with Davie than usual. The joyous clamour of the cathedral bells only served to increase the bleakness of the prison cell and the misery of its three occupants. Even the special fare that Mrs Polsoe had packed for them – some slices of roast goose, mince pies, and a bag of nuts and raisins – tasted like ashes in their mouths. Jack had brought a draughtboard he had spent some time improvising, and he tried to interest Davie in a game. But it soon became evident that the boy could not concentrate. Finding a subject of conversation proved well-nigh impossible, for eventually everything seemed to remind them of how little time they had together. In the end they lapsed into a silence broken only by the hissing of the gas lamp and occasional echo of footsteps in the corridors outside.

No one mentioned that there was only one full day left.

'If the boys got my letter this morning they might get here by tonight,' Maddy said, as she and her father walked back to the inn.

'They'd have to shift some for that,' said Jack. 'More likely by tomorrow night. Look for them then. They'll come tomorrow for sure.'

It was the only reference they made to anything connected with the execution.

The next day, Boxing Day, there was no sign of Bart, Lew and Charlie; Maddy and Jack had to go to the prison alone. It was an anguished affair, but although the tears streamed down his face, Davie did not make a scene when they made to leave. It was Maddy who found it too much to bear.

'We'll be here—' she began, but could not finish. There was no way she could say the dread words, 'In the morning.'

As for Jack, he could only hug Davie to him and say brokenly, 'You'll be all right, boy, you'll be all right.' It was a stupid statement and totally false. Davie was not going to be all right. But in his heartbroken state it was the only comfort Jack could think of.

There was still no sign of the three brothers at the inn.

Although it was long before she was due to begin work, Maddy tied a sacking apron about her waist and began to clean. She scrubbed floors and shelves, turned out cupboards, and washed windows.

'Maid, maid,' protested Mrs Polsoe. 'It idn't that I bain't grateful, nor that the place couldn't do with a turnout, but you'm going to work yourself into a collapse going on at this rate.' Gently but firmly she took the scrubbing brush from Maddy's unprotesting hand and said, 'You'm going to need all the strength you'm got, my lover, for yourself and for your pa. He'm taking it hard too, you know, and there bain't no shelves for him to scrub. You go and spend a bit of time with him and never mind working tonight. Go and have a game of draughts with him or summat.'

Maddy was stricken by this reminder. Jack needed her every bit as much as Davie. Yet she feared she could not get through the next few hours without hard work to occupy her.

'I don't think I can,' she gasped. 'I couldn't put my mind to it.'

'Nor can your pa, I dare say,' said Mrs Polsoe. 'But if you just push they draughts about the board I don't suppose he'll notice you idn't playing proper. It'll keep the pair of you occupied until they brothers of youm come.'

Maddy took the landlady's advice, and she was touched at how grateful her father was for her company. Obediently they began a game with the makeshift draughts, although it bore scant resemblance to the official rules. Part way through, Jack paused, a draught in his hand, 'Do you mind when Davie was little how he'd climb in the boat when us was busy hauling in the net and paying him no heed?' he asked. 'How many times do you reckon he lost the oar overboard trying to row proper?'

'I don't know,' said Maddy. 'Dozens, probably. Just as many times as you walloped his backside because you had to wade into the river to fetch the oar back.'

'What a boy, eh? Always up to something,' Jack chuckled, and with the game piece still in his hand, went on to reminisce. The game of draughts forgotten, they talked about Davie far into the night, laughing and crying at their memories. It helped to ease the pain, though it could not stop their eyes from straying to the clock on the wall. The hours were passing, but there was no sign of the others.

'They must be having a hard walk of it,' said Jack, when the clock hands reached midnight. 'You go to bed, maid. I'll wait up for un.'

Maddy protested, but Jack was adamant. 'You'm done enough work for three today. You needs your rest,' he insisted. One thing he did not say was that they would have to be up early in the morning. The execution was at seven, and they had been told to be there by six to see Davie for the last time.

Reluctantly Maddy went up to her room, but although she undressed and got into bed she could not sleep. How could she with the awful weight of pain pressing on her? In addition, she was listening for the clump of heavy boots on the road outside that would herald the arrival of her brothers. When finally she did hear footsteps, they passed right by as men went off to work in the morning darkness.

Where could the boys be? she wondered anxiously. Surely they had got her letter? They had had plenty of time to get to Exeter.

A clattering downstairs announced that Mrs Polsoe was astir, which must mean it was about five o'clock. Thankful to be on the move herself after the long wakeful hours, Maddy rose, washed and dressed. She could hardly do up her buttons she was shaking so, but it was not the December cold that was making her tremble. She was reluctant to go and wake her father immediately because he shared a room with other lodgers, and she did not want to disturb the other men unnecessarily. Instead she went downstairs first to see if he was already there.

She had awakened convinced that nothing could make that morning any worse, but the scene that met her eyes in the bar parlour did exactly that. Mrs Polsoe was slapping her father sharply across the face and shaking him, exclaiming, 'Wake up, you gurt fool! Wake up, can't you!' But Jack remained blissfully unconscious. An empty stone cider jug on the floor beside him told its own story.

'Oh no!' cried Maddy. 'Oh no! Not that! Not today of all days!'

Mrs Polsoe swung round at the sound of her voice. 'You see how it be, maid,' she said. 'I been trying this last ten minutes to get him back to his senses, but I fear it idn't no good.'

'Why didn't I think!' Maddy exclaimed in distress. 'I should never have left him alone last night. What a fool I was.'

'If he'd wanted the drink bad enough he'd have got it, no matter what anyone else did. I suppose you can't blame the poor soul.' The landlady looked sympathetically at Maddy. 'It do make it harder for you, though, my lover.'

Maddy gazed about her in bewilderment, almost as if she expected to see Bart and the others concealed in the room.

'My brothers aren't here yet,' she said hopelessly. 'I can't understand it. They should have got here last night.'

'I dare say it be a fair step from where you live,' said Mrs Polsoe. 'And roads be tricky this time of year. Maybe they'm having to go out of their way because of floods or summat. They'll get here, never fear. While you'm waiting I'll make you a bit of breakfast.'

The thought of food made Maddy's stomach heave. 'No, thank you,' she said. 'I couldn't swallow a bite.'

'But you can't face – you can't go through this morning with naught inside you.' Mrs Polsoe looked concerned. 'How about if I made you a nice cup of tea? The kettle must be almost on the boil.'

Maddy shook her head. 'You're very kind, but no. I don't think I could keep it down even if I had the time. I— I must be leaving soon.'

'I don't like the thought of you going on your own,' Mrs Polsoe said with increased concern. 'Maybe I could get someone to mind this place so's I can come with you.'

Again Maddy shook her head. 'You're – you're so kind,' she said in a broken voice. 'I'll be all right. Davie's ordeal… will be far worse than mine – he'll have to face it alone, won't he?' Choking back the sobs, she rushed upstairs to fetch her bonnet and cloak. When she returned, Mrs Polsoe was standing there with a determined expression on her face and a glass of golden liquid in her hand.

'You'm habn't eaten, you'm habn't had a cup of tea, but you'm going to get this down you, supposing I has to force you,' the landlady said grimly. 'You got to have something to help you through.'

'What is it?' Maddy asked, taking the glass suspiciously.

'Best brandy. Us don't get much call for it yer, but I always has some in. You swallow the lot. It'll put heart in you. And heaven knows you'll need it, poor maid,' she added in an almost inaudible aside.

Maddy took a mouthful that set her coughing and spluttering. 'I'm sorry,' she gasped, setting down the glass. 'I can't manage any more.'

'Never mind,' said Mrs Polsoe. 'Here's summat as might bring ease to your brother.' And she placed a small bottle marked 'Laudanum' on the table.

'Oh,' breathed Maddy. 'I should have thought of that.'

'Was there ever such a maid for thinking her's responsible for everything?' Mrs Polsoe raised exasperated eyes heavenwards. 'You'll most like have to slip the warder something to make sure he gets it, mind.' She put a silver coin beside the bottle. 'The brandy and the laudanum be on the house, the half-crown be out of your pa's pocket.'

Slipping the money and the bottle into her own pocket, Maddy said, 'How can I ever thank—'

'There idn't no need for thanks. Just get back here sharpish after… And should your brothers come, or him return to his senses,' the landlady jerked her head in the direction of the still unconscious Jack, 'I'll send them on.'

How her legs supported her on her walk through the dark streets Maddy did not know. Her knees shook as she staggered unsteadily towards the prison. The nightmare grew worse as she was taken to Davie's cell, for she did not know what state he would be in. She did not know what she would find. Outside the cell door, she paused and held out the vial of laudanum.

'I've brought some of this to help my brother,' she said.

'There idn't no need for that, my lover,' said the warder. 'He'm had some. Your friend saw to it. One dose last night and one this morning.'

'Which friend?' asked Maddy in surprise.

'Couldn't say. I wadn't on duty then.' The warder unlocked the cell and ushered her in.

'Hullo, our Maddy.' Davie's words were slightly slurred as he rose unsteadily to greet her. 'Where be Father?'

'He's – he's not well this morning. Too ill to come, though he sends his love.' She was astonished to see him so calm.

'Still sleeping un off, eh?' Davie gave a drowsy grin. 'Good old Father.' He yawned. 'What about the lads?'

'I wrote. I'm expecting them any minute.'

'They'll get here if they can. They'm grand fellows.' He waved a casual hand. 'I be glad you came, though. Twill be good being just you and me for a bit. I be telling you this because I won't get no other chance. You'm the best sister a fellow could have. There idn't no one as can hold a candle to you, Maddy Shillabeer, and there never will be, don't let no one persuade you otherwise.'

Maddy had told herself she would not cry, that she would be brave and strong, but Davie's words completely undid her.

'There, don't take on like that,' he comforted her. 'What be un as Annie says? What can't be cured must be endured? There idn't no cure for what be coming so us may as well endure un with a good grace.'

'How can you be so calm?' The words came out in a cry of protest.

'It were a long night, I don't deny it, but you can get tired of being terrified, you know. I suppose I just couldn't go on being frightened no more. And the stuff you sent me made a difference too, I idn't denying that, neither.'

'I didn't send anything,' wept Maddy. 'I brought some laudanum but someone else got in before me. I don't know who.'

'A true friend, whoever he be – or she. Who knows? Maybe I got myself a lady admirer at this late stage,' he grinned.

'Oh Davie!' Maddy wept harder.

Outside, the corridor rang with approaching footsteps, and Maddy went ice-cold as the door opened to reveal the prison chaplain and the head warder.

''Tis time to say goodbye, seemingly,' remarked Davie as casually as if he had been off up to Totnes. 'Give Father and the lads all my best when you see them, and thank Annie for the toffee she sent. And I'll give your love to Mother. Her'll be right pleased to learn how good you'm been to us.'

'Oh Davie!' Maddy could say nothing else as he hugged her tightly.

'Don't you go lingering about this place, do you hear?' His voice wavered for the first time. 'Get yourself far away. And you'm idn't to grieve. It were a daft thing I done, and whereas I still think the judgment were a bit hard, there be no denying I killed Ned Knapman, and he, poor soul, doubtless thought that were just as hard. Get you home, maid, back to your garden and they noisy fowls of youm and that fiddler fellow. He idn't good enough for you, but then in my eyes the Prince of Wales idn't good enough, neither. If your Patrick be what you wants, then wed him and be happy. You deserves un.'

The chaplain gave a discreet cough and one of the warders moved to Maddy's side, indicating that she must leave. There was such a lot she had not said, things she wanted to say to her brother, and there was no time. No time at all.

Somehow she found herself outside in the corridor, leaning against the wall for support.

'What about his funeral?' she asked brokenly. Why had she not thought of that? There would be arrangements to be made.

'That'll be seen to,' said the warder with such finality that Maddy could not find the strength to enquire further. 'You'm on your own?' the warder asked quite kindly.

Maddy nodded.

'There be a room downstairs where you can wait until... I could send for a woman to attend you if you like.'

'No, thank you.' She straightened up and wiped her eyes. Davie had told her to go away and that was exactly what she would do. How much he had grown up in the last twenty-four hours. If he could be serene and calm, then so could she.

Her resolve lasted until she stepped into the road. Although it was a bitterly cold morning and not yet light, a crowd had gathered round the prison gate. The sight of so many people brought her to a halt. What were they expecting? Didn't they know that a human being was about to be destroyed in there? That it was her brother who was going to be dangled on the end of a rope?

Having stopped, somehow she could not gather the momentum to move again. Davie had told her to get far away, but she could not. She had to stay as close as possible to him until the end. Fortunately her cloak was an old-fashioned one and she pulled the hood up over her head, bonnet and all, as she pressed herself against the prison wall.

She did not think she could bear the agony. The terrible anguish within her was like a physical pain from which she could get no relief. Resentment against Jack and the boys for not being there, against Mr Attwill for his ineptitude, against Judge Stroud for his inhumanity made her want to cry out. She pressed herself closer to the wall, enveloping her despair in the folds of her cloak.

The stout frieze cloth might hide her face and cut out the sights, it could not prevent her hearing the conversations taking place near her.

'Tidn't no fun now us can't see naught no more,' remarked one voice. 'When it were public hangings us used to go up Northemhay, the whole lot of us. A grand view you could get from there.'

'That you could,' agreed a second voice. 'You could see them drop and dangle from the rope as clear as clear; a proper outing it were too, with old women selling gingerbread and toffee, and tumblers and musicians and everything. Almost as good as a fair in my opinion. I can't see why they had to change things and do the hanging indoors. Taking away poor men's pleasures, that's what it 'mounts to.'

She had to get away from such ghoulish talk, yet as she tried to push her way through the crush, a clock somewhere struck seven. The prison bell began to toll and a sigh went round the crowd. It was over.

Maddy stood very still, her eyes closed, using every scrap of will-power to hold on to her self-control. Davie had said she was not to grieve. That was an impossible task, but she was determined to behave with dignity for his sake.

If only the voices round about would be quiet. She could not help hearing, although she tried not to. There were comments about Davie, discussions about the trial, talk of previous, more spectacular executions.

'I reckon I'll be going home,' said someone.

'You idn't waiting to see him taken away then?'

'No, 'tidn't worth it in this danged cold.'

Maddy's eyes flew open. 'They're taking him away?' she said. 'Where?'

Two middle-aged women regarded her with frank curiosity.

'Why, to the hospital,' said one. 'So's the doctors can cut him up.'

She had not expected this. Shock paralysed her completely. Her Davie's body was going to be mutilated. She wanted to yell, to scream, to cry out against such an obscenity, but no proper sound would come from her frozen throat. In mute despair she lashed out with her hands, beating them against the wall until they were bruised and bleeding. Then at last she began to make a noise. Softly at first, then rising to an anguished crescendo, the dreadful unearthly wailing of a soul in torment.

The crowd in her immediate vicinity moved back in alarm.

'What be wrong with her?' demanded one woman.

''Sterics,' said a second. 'Some folks can't take the excitement.'

'That bain't 'sterics,' stated a third. 'Her'm a lunatic. I idn't staying yer to be attacked by no mad woman.'

Locked in her grief, Maddy did not notice that she was alone and that the street was almost deserted. Collapsing to her knees she buried her face in her hands, rocking back and forth as she continued to wail. Not until she felt herself lifted to her feet and being shaken quite violently was she jolted out of her frenzy of distress. Someone was repeating her name over and over again. It was her father! Or one of the boys! Eager for the comfort of a familiar face she opened her eyes – to see Cal Whitcomb looking at her with concern.

'Why aren't you my father?' she cried. 'Why aren't you Bart or Lew or Charlie? Don't you know what's happening? They aren't content with hanging my Davie. They're going to let the doctors cut him up. Cut him up like so much meat on a butcher's slab. How can they do that? Answer me that! How can they?'

And with that she slumped senseless into his arms.

Chapter Eleven

Maddy recovered consciousness to find that she was lying on a bench and that she was bitterly cold, in spite of being swathed in some sort of covering. Slowly her foggy brain took in her surroundings – an unfamiliar room furnished with tables and chairs and oak settles. An eating house perhaps? Or an inn? With awareness came a terrible sense of tragedy that bewildered her at first until she remembered.

'Davie!' she exclaimed, trying to rise but hampered by her wrappings.

'Don't try to move,' said a male voice, as a strong arm helped her into a sitting position. She knew that voice. It was Cal Whitcomb's. Vaguely she remembered seeing his face before the darkness had claimed her. 'Take a sip of this,' he continued, and held a glass to her lips.

She smelled the spirits and turned her head away. The brandy Mrs Polsoe had given her still churned within her; if she drank any more she would be sick. Struggling to free herself from the enveloping folds of what proved to be a man's Inverness cape, she exclaimed, 'I must go! Davie!' But what use could she be to Davie now? A cloud of grey mist swirled in her head and a high-pitched singing filled her ears, forcing her to close her eyes and lean back.

The pungency of smelling-salts brought her back sharply, and she found herself confronting a concerned Cal Whitcomb once more.

'You must rest,' he said. 'Don't even try to move. Just lay where you are.'

But Maddy found it impossible to be still, in spite of her physical state.

'They mustn't do it,' she protested, trying to stand when it was as much as she could do to sit up unaided. 'They can't cut Davie up. I won't let them! I won't!' She wanted to sound determined, yet she could hear the strain of hysteria in her own voice.

Cal pushed her firmly back onto the settle. 'They aren't going to. That is why I'm in Exeter. Davie is to have a proper burial.'

'Let me go! I've got to go!' Maddy was too busy struggling against his restraining hands to heed what he was saying.

'Stay still, woman!' He rapped out the words to gain her attention. 'Won't you listen to me? Davie's body is not to be sent to the hospital. He is to have a proper burial in the prison grounds.'

'Proper burial?' She stared, paying attention to him at last.

'Yes, that's why I'm here in Exeter,' he repeated quietly. 'I am here on behalf of the squire – his gout is too bad for him to travel himself. I brought a letter from him appealing to the governor of the prison, who is an old acquaintance, to allow your brother a decent Christian burial. He persuaded other people of note from Stoke Gabriel to add their names too, in view of the harshness of the verdict and Davie's tender age.'

'And the governor agreed?' She dared not believe it.

'Yes. The burial will be at nine. Under the circumstances, if you are recovered in time I'm sure you would be allowed to attend.'

'I'm quite recovered.' To prove it Maddy tried to leap to her feet, only to collapse with dizziness.

'When did you last eat?' Cal demanded, then not bothering to await her reply he ordered a dish of scrambled eggs from the disapproving woman who had been hovering in the background.

'I don't want anything to eat,' protested Maddy. 'A cup of tea perhaps…'

'Where have your father and brothers got to?' Cal asked, ignoring her comments. 'We've to find them quickly if they're to be at the funeral.'

Maddy bit her lip. 'I wrote to the boys at home,' she said. 'I was sure they'd get here in time, but they didn't.'

'And your father?'

She avoided his eyes. 'He was very unwell this morning, too ill to come.'

'You mean you were by yourself when… You faced this morning entirely alone?' Cal was aghast. 'Was there no one who would have come with you?'

'The landlady of the Three Feathers – that's where we're staying – she offered. She's got a kind heart.' The words came jerkily. 'It was better alone, just Davie and me.'

Cal did not believe her. 'No one should go through such an experience alone,' he muttered angrily. 'No one. If I had known...'

The woman brought the scrambled eggs and a pot of tea and set them before Maddy.

'I'm really not hungry,' she protested.

'Eat it anyway.' He scooped some egg up on the fork and handed it to her. Fearing he meant to feed her like a child, she gave way and took hold of it. Usually she would have resented his authoritarian manner, but compared to the other events of the day it was too trivial to bother about. 'Will your father be recovered by now?' he asked, a hint of sarcasm in his voice. 'I mean, if I send a cab to the place where you are staying, do you think he will be well enough to attend the funeral?'

Her mouth full, Maddy nodded.

'Right, you stay here and finish your meal. Every last crumb,' he stressed. 'I'll go and find a cab. What did you say the inn is called?'

Maddy swallowed hastily. 'The Three Feathers, in Lower North Street,' she said.

He was not gone long, yet by the time he had returned Maddy discovered to her surprise that she had made considerable inroads into the scrambled eggs and toast. Cal regarded her near-empty plate with satisfaction as he sat down opposite her. 'I've told the cabby to bring your father here, and your brothers, if they've arrived. Then he's to wait to take us to the prison.' Again his commanding manner would normally have drawn a sharp protest from Maddy, but on that morning she was simply grateful to have someone taking charge. Davie was to be laid to rest properly, that was all she cared about now.

The food did help her. By the time she had cleared the plate and drunk the tea, her head no longer swam, her knees had stopped shaking and warmth was beginning to seep back through her chilled body.

'Kindly show the young lady where she can refresh herself,' Cal said to the woman, whose disapproval had not lessened.

They were evidently in a small, select eating house which was not yet open for business. How they had got there Maddy could not recollect, but she surmised that their unwelcome presence so early in the morning was the cause of the woman's silent censure. When she gazed into the mirror of the ladies' room, she knew differently. The face staring back at her was deathly white, streaked with dirt and tears, surrounded by hair as wild as any harpy's. Part mad woman, part woman of the streets, that was what the reflection looked like. No wonder the proprietress of this clearly reputable establishment was not happy at her presence. As she set about repairing the damage, Maddy decided that it said a lot for Cal's forceful character that they had been allowed in at all.

Within a few minutes, her face washed and her hair combed into some semblance of order, Maddy felt she looked presentable again. What had happened to her bonnet she did not know, it had disappeared entirely, but with the hood of her old cloak pulled over her head, she felt she was fit to attend Davie's funeral. She returned to the eating room just as Jack, pale and woebegone, entered. Behind him were Bart, Lew and Charlie, looking travel-stained and exhausted. They did not speak immediately, but held out their arms to take her in a mass embrace.

'You must've thought us wadn't coming, that us didn't care,' said Lew unsteadily, when at last they released her. 'Didn't get your letter until mid-morning yesterday.'

'Someone's going to pay for that,' muttered Bart fiercely. 'That letter should've come earlier!'

'Us set off as quick as us could,' Lew went on, ignoring the interruption, 'making good time until nightfall. Us wadn't so clear on the road as us thought, and in the darkness took a wrong turning.'

'Halfway to Barnstaple us were afore us found out,' put in Bart. 'And though us walked right through the night us didn't get here in time.'

'How – how...?' Lew stammered over the question he could not ask.

'He were powerful brave, you'd have been proud of him.' In her distress Maddy's fine accent crumbled. 'He sent his love to everyone... He were that strong, I should've been comforting him and instead it were him as give me comfort... Oh Davie...!' She collapsed against Lew's chest and sobbed.

'You didn't ought to have been alone, maid,' he said, patting her shoulder. 'You didn't ought.'

The three brothers shot reproachful glances at their father, who hung his head in shame.

'I be sorry, Maddy my lover,' Jack said brokenly. 'I be that ashamed of myself. I just couldn't face it... I kept remembering him as a little un, always merry and up to mischief… He were our babe, you see, and I couldn't face what they were going to do to un.' Jack turned away, his shoulders heaving.

Maddy went over to him and put her arms about him. 'I know how you felt,' she said gently. 'And so did Davie. He understood and sent you his special love. I — I think that in some ways it was easier for him without so many… us'd have been that distressed, and us'd have set one another off and that'd only have upset him… Yes, Davie understood.'

'Us gathers 'tidn't all over,' said Bart. 'Us'd not been at the inn five minutes but this cabby arrives with some tale about a funeral.'

'Yes, if we hurry there's a chance for us to be at Davie's funeral.' Maddy recovered her accent and her composure as she wiped her eyes. 'We—'

She did not finish for Bart suddenly exclaimed, 'What the hell be he doing yer!'

For the first time the Shillabeer men noticed Cal Whitcomb standing in the background. And for the first time Maddy realised that she had quite accepted his presence, with no hint of the traditional animosity. If she were honest she was extremely thankful for his presence. Without him she would probably still be keening her grief away in the gutter.

'Mr Whitcomb's been very kind,' she said, choosing her words with care. It would not do to admit how much she owed to Cal Whitcomb personally; the details of how she had collapsed with distress in the road would only serve to increase her father's pain and guilt. 'But for him, there would be no funeral.'

'No funeral? What be talking about, maid?' Bart glared belligerently at Cal. 'Trust a Whitcomb to be where he idn't wanted. You idn't going to gloat over us, boy, so I suggests you get out now, while you can!'

'You don't understand,' protested Maddy. 'Without Mr Whitcomb there would be no funeral. They would have sent Davie's body to the hospital instead.'

'Don't talk daft, our Maddy,' Bart retorted. 'What would they do that for when he be already dead?'

'I thinks I knows,' said Lew suddenly. 'I heard un somewhere, only I didn't believe un. They send the bodies of them convicted of murder to the hospital for the doctors to cut up. That be it, idn't it?'

'Oh my gawd!' gasped Bart and Charlie in unison. Jack gave a choking sound, not a vestige of colour left in his face.

'But it won't happen to Davie,' put in Maddy. 'Because of Mr Whitcomb, he'll be buried like a Christian.'

'The thanks are mainly due to the squire.' Cal spoke for the first time. 'He is the one responsible, the one who wrote the appeal to the prison governor. I'm just his messenger.'

'But you coming all this way to deliver the message, that was bound to add some weight, wasn't it, you being Davie's intended target?' said Lew shrewdly.

'A little, I suppose,' said Cal.

There was a pause, then without speaking, Lew stuck out his hand. He did it rigidly, as if he might regret it, but he did nevertheless. For a Shillabeer it was a major gesture. Cal took his hand and shook it. Slowly the others followed suit, ending finally with Bart whose handshake was the briefest.

'I think we'd better be going,' Cal said, then sensing a tension among the other men he added, 'I am afraid I must accompany you to the prison since I have the necessary papers of entry, but when we get inside, I'll withdraw. I've no intention of imposing on your grief.'

Riding in a cab was one more new experience dimmed by the circumstances. Something that Maddy would ordinarily have regarded with great excitement she now considered as merely expedient. In fact, they were not far from the prison, yet she was grateful she did not have to walk. At the sight of the plain frontage on top of the slope above the road, her knees began to tremble again, and she feared she might not be able to stand. Thankfully, this time when she entered the prison she was flanked by the reassuring figures of Lew and Charlie.

At the prison gate there was a delay. Cal went first and presented the documents which the warder appeared to query. Time and again the prison official glanced over to where the Shillabeers stood almost as if he were counting them. Maddy's heart was in her mouth. Did the prison chaplain know they were coming? Would he wait for them? To her intense relief, agreement seemed to have been reached at the gate and the warder waved them in. Maddy had a strong suspicion that she saw him pocketing something slipped to him by Cal, but she may have been mistaken.

They were led through a series of bleak courtyards and dismal passageways, each needing to be unlocked to let them through. The graveyard, when they were ushered in, proved to be neatly tended. That was all Maddy had time to notice before her eyes were drawn to the new grave yawning open in the freshly dug earth. Apart from two grave-diggers, prisoners presumably, the chaplain was already there, along with a man who proved to be the assistant governor. They looked surprised at the Shillabeers' arrival, but Cal engaged them in earnest conversation.

'What be that about?' muttered Bart. 'They'm looking at us as if us bain't got no business yer.'

'I knows what 'tis,' said Jack. 'They'm bothered in case Maddy be staying for the funeral. Maddy, maid, get yourself off somewhere, this bain't no place for you.'

'I'm staying.'

Four pairs of masculine eyes stared at her in shocked amazement. In the village, funerals were affairs for men only. Maddy had not even attended her mother's burial.

'You can't!' objected Jack. 'It idn't...' He had been going to say 'fitting', but the bleak look in Maddy's eyes stopped him. After what his daughter had endured that morning, she could surely stand up to the rigours of her brother's funeral.

Whatever the problems holding up the proceedings, they had clearly been solved, for the assistant governor gave a signal, and from a side door came two warders pushing a trolley upon which rested a coffin. A decent coffin of polished wood, Maddy was relieved to notice. Davie was not going to his last rest in plain deal or, worse still, a canvas shroud.

'Wait!' Jack's shout brought the warders, trolley and all, to a surprised halt. 'Wait,' he repeated, more quietly. 'Us'll carry him the rest of the way.'

The four Shillabeer men moved forward and stationed themselves alongside the trolley. The warders looked rather nonplussed but stood aside without comment as Jack and his sons lifted the coffin onto their shoulders and carried it to the open grave.

The service was plain and matter-of-fact, with the chaplain offering no comfort, no hope of a life to come other than what was in *The Book of Common Prayer*. He gave the impression that a convicted murderer deserved no better, just as his family deserved no comfort. It was over so quickly that Maddy felt she had not said a proper goodbye to her brother. Looking down, the coffin with its first scattering of earth seemed a forlorn final resting place for Davie, who had always been so full of life. Then she noticed a clump of snowdrops growing against the wall. Ignoring the disapproving exclamations of the warders, she picked a few of the fragile flowers and one by one she dropped them, watching through her tears as they fell on the polished coffin lid. Young and fresh, she felt they were a far better tribute to her brother than any words.

Outside the prison gate they stood in an awkward group, five Shillabeers and one Whitcomb, not certain how to bridge a gap built up over three generations. As ever, it fell to Maddy to express the family feelings to Cal.

'Thank you,' she said. 'That's a very poor way to express what we owe to you and the squire. Goodness knows, events have been terrible enough, but if they had taken Davie—' She choked, unable to finish. With a struggle she recovered herself to continue, 'Things have been terrible enough, but without you and the squire intervening they would have been unbearable.'

'It was the squire mainly. As I said, I am merely the messenger boy,' said Cal.

'That's not true and you know it,' Maddy stated. 'And before I forget, we owe you something else – the cost of the coffin. Yes we do,' she insisted as he waved a protesting hand. 'That was no prison issue, but decent, polished wood. It was what we'd have chosen for Davie ourselves.' A sudden thought struck her. 'It was you who sent the laudanum, wasn't it?' she said. 'And you were planning to attend the funeral, anyway, weren't you? Even if we hadn't met outside the prison… you'd have seen him decently into his grave.' The last was a statement, not a question.

Cal looked uncomfortable. 'No one should go to his grave unattended,' he said.

That explained the long discussion at the prison gates: Cal had had to persuade the authorities to allow six people to enter when his papers were for only one. Yes, and probably had to bribe them into the bargain. The Shillabeers looked at one another, then Jack stepped forward and cleared his throat. 'That were a great kindness,' he said. 'We be much obliged.'

'Your thanks aren't necessary,' Cal said almost sharply. 'If you want the truth, I still feel responsible for the tragedy. It was my evidence that was the most damning, though I never intended it to be.'

Jack, still bowed down by the burden of his own remorse, could find it in his heart to be magnanimous to a fellow sufferer of self-reproach.

'You spoke naught but the truth,' he said. 'It were that Linton devil. Twist the words of an angel, he could.'

'You are very kind.' Cal hesitated awkwardly, as if not knowing what more to say. Then he said hurriedly, 'If you'll excuse me, I have a train to catch within the hour. I suppose you'll be going home, too?'

They were, but not by train. The Shillabeers would leave Exeter the way they had come, on foot. Their parting was stilted and polite. Maddy wondered how this new obligation to Cal Whitcomb would affect their lives back in the village.

For all of them, departure from the city could not come soon enough. Only leaving Mrs Polsoe caused any regret.

'There'll always be a welcome for you yer,' she insisted. 'You'm to come back soon, do you hear?'

'Perhaps we will,' said Maddy, giving her a farewell hug, though in her heart she felt that she never wanted to set eyes on Exeter again.

–

The peace and quiet of Duncannon was like balm to Maddy's distressed spirits. Tired and footsore, they walked down the steep lane and there stood the three cottages on the river foreshore, nestling under the hill. There was no constant racket of passing traffic, the air was not heavy with lime dust and soot. There was just the clean salt smell of the Dart, overlaid by a scent of wood smoke. The cottage was not even dank and chill when they entered. Hot embers glowed on the hearth, there were logs stacked in the chimney comer and a fresh loaf of bread on the table – Annie and William's work undoubtedly. Eveïything was so belovedly familiar that Maddy could have wept with the sheer joy of being home again.

When Annie and William came over to welcome them back, Maddy clung to them, their friendly, much-loved faces part of the pleasure of her homecoming. In time she would tell them of the terrible happenings, it would give her ease, but not yet. For the moment she was content to hold on to them, relieved and thankful to be back among people and places she loved.

Although she was glad to be home, she quite dreaded her first excursion into the village, but far from being hostile everyone was kindness itself.

'There's plenty of folks as wants to say this but feels awkward, so I may as well be the one as speaks up,' said Mrs Cutmore, when Maddy went for tea and sugar. 'Everyone be mortal sorry for what happened to your Davie. He deserved to be punished, but not like that. It were naught less than cruel and brutal. They heathens in the hot countries couldn't have done worse. Us wants you to know as everyone feels terrible sorry for you and your pa and your brothers.'

There were other customers in the shop, awaiting their turn, and they murmured their assent. Maddy was deeply touched, the more so when she encountered similar sympathy wherever she went. She set off for home with her head full of messages of comfort to be relayed to Jack and the boys, and her basket full of small gifts — a jar of honey, a bunch of winter jasmine, a pot of clotted cream — donated by well-wishers. In the face of tragedy, the small community was gathering itself together and embracing the family with all the compassion it could muster.

Of Patrick there was no sign. That was the one disappointment in her homecoming.

Then suddenly she saw him. He was sitting on the wall at the end of the lane to Duncannon, waiting for her. As he saw her approach he jumped down and held out his arms. It was all the invitation Maddy needed. Ignoring her heavy basket, she ran to him.

'I heard that you were back... but there were too many people about...' He punctuated his words with kisses. 'That's why I waited here... where everyone's eyes wouldn't be on us. My poor love. What you have gone through. Was it very terrible?'

'Yes,' said Maddy simply. She still did not want to talk about it, and he did not press her.

'It is behind you now,' he said softly. 'And you must forget about it. I'm here with you, to help take your mind off the unpleasantness by telling you how much I love you. That is what you must concentrate upon — how much we love each other.'

It was kindly meant, and Maddy cherished the idea of concentrating only upon their love, but she knew it was impossible. For once Patrick had misunderstood. He had no concept of the true depths of her suffering. She would never forget what had happened to Davie. In time she would no doubt be able to push it to the back of her mind, but it would never leave her. She did not tell him this. He so clearly wanted to be her comfort and mainstay that she did not have the heart to disillusion him. It was preferable to savour the warmth of his love and be comforted by his presence.

'I wish we had longer.' Patrick stroked her cheek with his fingertips. 'Sadly, this is a stolen meeting. I must get back before Mr Ford discovers I'm gone.'

'Mr Ford? Don't you mean Mr Watkins?'

'No, I'm back at the Church House Inn again.' He looked half shamefaced, half mischievous. 'There was a spot of bother while you were away. You recall Lottie, the barmaid at the Victoria and Albert? Seemingly she has a sweetheart who works in Penn's Quarry, and this sweetheart made certain allegations against me that weren't true – well, not entirely – and he threatened to bring his brothers and cause damage if I remained. The fellow is built like a barn end, and I understand his two brothers are constructed on the same lines. No, it was quite understandable of Sam Watkins to part with me sooner than offend three such heavyweight customers.'

Maddy laughed. She thought she had forgotten how, but the sound crept out of her unbidden.

'And I dare say there were complaints from other quarters,' she suggested, knowing full well that Sam Watkins was of sterner stuff than to capitulate before one isolated threat.

'Maybe one or two.' The corners of Patrick's mouth twitched, then he flung his arms about her in a bear hug. 'Oh Maddy, you are indeed exceptional. Any other woman would have been up in arms at my antics, but not you. But I am good for you too, aren't I? See, I've got you laughing already.'

'So you have,' she smiled. 'Yes, you are very good for me.'

'Splendid.' His kiss was feather light on her lips. 'I hate to go, but I must. We'll meet again soon.'

'Soon.' Maddy echoed the word.

The past, particularly the immediate past, could not be swept away like dust on a floor, however. There were many things that happened every day which brought back memories of Davie.

–

'He's out there somewhere, the wretch!' Maddy declared vehemently one day after returning from the village.

'Who be?' asked her father.

'Whoever put Davie up to that trick. He wasn't in it alone.'

'You bain't still on about that, be you, maid?' Jack said gently. 'Forget un, that's what I say.'

'How can I forget it when I'm certain there's someone walking the village who as good as killed our Davie?'

The brothers stopped spooning broth into their mouths and looked at her.

'What be this you'm on about?' asked Lew.

'Some maggot her've got into her head,' said Jack. 'Her've the notion Davie weren't alone, and that someone put him up to taking a pot shot at Cal Whitcomb's hat.'

'The longer I think on it, the more convinced I am,' said Maddy firmly. 'Consider it! Knowing what a fidget Davie was, can you imagine him thinking up a prank where he had to lie in wait behind a cold hedge for an hour or more? He could have been persuaded to do it easily enough, but he'd never have thought it up by himself. And there were things he let slip, about saying the stone was too big and wishing he hadn't joined in the caper. An odd choice of words if he was by himself.'

Bart stirred his broth thoughtfully. 'You asked Davie about this?' he said.

'Of course I did, but he denied it. Insisted he'd been on his own. I even went to Mr Attwill about it.'

'Much good he'd be,' murmured the usually silent Charlie.

But Lew intervened with, 'What did he say?'

'That even if we found there had been a second person, it would not have helped Davie. It would only have meant someone else going for trial as well.'

'Then there's no more to be said.' Bart's spoon stirred more quickly.

'Yes, there is,' declared Maddy. 'We might have been able to prove that this other person was the instigator, particularly if he was older. That would make him the truly guilty party. Perhaps Davie would have just got imprisonment. I'm sure this other person exists and I mean to find out who he is. I was down mill this afternoon and the usual idlers were hanging about there as they always do, the ones Davie loved to mix with no matter what we said. I had a talk with them, hoping one of them would give himself away. No one did this time, but I'll keep on. I'm sure it was one of them. How he can live with himself is past belief. He was responsible for two deaths, Ned's and Davie's, yet he isn't man enough to own up.' Maddy stopped, aware that her voice had been rising along with her distress.

Silence followed. No one else agreed with her about the existence of a second person. Maddy did not care. She was still convinced and she would go on searching for him.

Next morning she was first up as usual, creeping downstairs so as not to wake the others. It would be some time before it was light, and she worked at her chores by the soft glow of the oil lamp. Shivering, she lit the fire, went out into the frost-sharp darkness to fetch water; then she set the kettle to boil and laid the table. She blessed the familiarity of her routine, anything which helped to get her life back to normal.

When all was ready, she called up the stairs to where Jack and his sons shared a room, then went back to stirring the porridge, one ear cocked for the usual sleepy stumblings which meant they were astir. Stockinged feet thudded on the stairs as a bleary-eyed Jack entered the kitchen, his braces dangling round his waist.

'Our Bart be out in the privy?' he asked.

'Bart?' replied Maddy in surprise. 'Not that I know of. I haven't seen him this morning yet.'

'That be odd.' Jack looked perplexed. 'He idn't upstairs and his bed be empty.'

'In that case he must have gone out the back when I wasn't looking,' said Maddy. Then she shook her head. 'No, I've just been out there myself and there wasn't any sign of him. How peculiar…'

By now the other brothers had joined them.

'Us didn't hear him get up,' said Lew. 'Where the heck have he'm gone?'

'I can't recall him saying anything about having to start work extra early,' Maddy said. 'I suppose he did get dressed?'

'Us didn't think to look.' Already Lew's long legs were striding upstairs. He was back in an instant looking serious. 'His clothes be gone,' he said, 'and the stuff in his locker. I reckon Bart have left home.'

'Left home?' The others stared at him.

'Don't be daft,' said Jack scornfully. 'Even if he did want to go, what need would Bart have of creeping off like a maid as was eloping?'

'I don't know,' protested Lew, 'but he'm gone, his things be gone and I found this. 'Tis addressed to you.' He handed his father a folded piece of paper.

Jack held it towards the lamp to read more easily.

'No!' he exclaimed. 'No!' The letter fluttered from his hand as he sank into the chair and covered his face.

Maddy was at his side in an instant. 'Father,' she cried. 'What is it? Are you all right?' But Jack's only response was to bury his face further in his hands.

It was left to Lew to pick up the letter and read it aloud.

'Maddy got it right,' he read. 'I were too scared to own up but Davie kept silent and never gave me away. He were a far better man than me and I let him hang without saying a word. That's why I can't stay, not after what I done. If it be any comfort, I be paying a terrible price, for I won't never have no peace for the rest of my days. I can't ask none of you to forgive me – I won't never forgive myself...'

'I don't understand. What do he mean?' asked Charlie.

But Lew and Maddy understood right enough. They stared at one another with tense, white faces.

'He means,' Lew explained slowly, 'that Maddy here were right when she said that someone else put Davie up to un. Someone as never owned up.'

'You don't mean it were Bart?' Charlie exclaimed in a shocked voice. 'Never our Bart!'

'Looks that way,' said Lew.

'When I spoke up, I—I never thought of someone so close to home,' whispered Maddy in distress. 'I thought it was one of that rough lot down mill. I never guessed... I said some hard words, not knowing, and now I've driven Bart away.'

'It were best he went.' Jack spoke up for the first time. He had recovered some of his self-control and sat more upright in his chair, although his face remained white and pinched. 'Yes, it be for the best. What you said was right, maid, even though you didn't know you was meaning our Bart. He were equal guilty in the killing of Ned, and as for Davie's death... as for Davie's death, he were responsible for that sure enough. He were old enough to have knowd better, instead of egging the boy on. I think it best if us don't mention his name in this house again.' He rose to his feet, hauled his braces over his shoulders and reached for his jacket.

'Where are you going?' cried Maddy.

'To work, maid. Where else? Can't be late for work.'

'But you haven't had any breakfast.' Still reeling from this new shock, Maddy clutched at her domestic routine for support.

'Couldn't eat naught, but I'll take a drop of tea. You can be pouring it as I does up my laces.' There was a grim air of determined calm about Jack as he pulled on his heavy boots. The task completed, he looked at his two remaining sons. 'As for you two, habn't you best be stirring yourselves?'

He did not wait for an answer, but drained his tea and strode out so swiftly that Maddy was obliged to run after him with his midday bread and cheese.

'Does this mean us idn't never to speak of Bart again?' asked Charlie.

'Not in Father's hearing, certainly,' said Lew.

'What's us to say if folks ask about un?' Charlie persisted.

'We'd best say he's decided to go to sea,' said Maddy. 'It's likely to be the truth, anyway. I expect he's heading down to Dartmouth to find a ship.'

'I expect he be.' Charlie nodded, content with this solution. 'Do you think he'll ever come back?'

Maddy and Lew exchanged glances.

'I doubt it, somehow,' said Maddy.

'Pity. I be going to miss old Bart.' Charlie, too, put on his jacket. 'Come on, Lew. Us idn't doing no good standing yer jawing. Let's be going.'

Lew stuffed his bread and cheese in his pocket, and turned to look at Maddy. 'I be sorry us've got to leave you alone,' he said. 'Tell you what! You'm scarce touched that gurt book of youm. Why not take un over to Annie's and have a good read? You'd enjoy un, the pair of you.'

'I might do that,' Maddy said shakily. He had a good heart, had Lew, it was thoughtful of him to be so concerned for her.

The cottage felt terribly empty after they had gone. In the lamp-light, eveiything seemed forlorn, and the smell of scorching from the neglected porridge on the fire did nothing to lighten the atmosphere of gloom. Setting the burnt pan to soak, Maddy went about her morning chores, willing herself not to think of what had happened. She succeeded fairly well until she went upstairs to make the beds. It was the sight of Bart's empty cot, and the door swinging wide on his empty locker which undid her. After Davie's death, she had thought that nothing could hurt again, but this did. This was a new and totally unlooked-for pain. Strangely, it was not thoughts of Bart's betrayal or his cowardice in not sharing the blame which filled her head, but memories of the younger, gentler Bart of her childhood. It was also grief at the loss of another brother, for from now on Bart would be as good as dead to them all.

Somehow she set about her chores, then steeled herself to go over to Annie's. Annie was a sharp one, she would have to be told something, and the sooner the better, before she started putting two and two together.

'Gone off to sea? Your Bart?' The other woman received the story with astonishment. 'You do surprise me. Your Charlie I could accept, he'm always been a bit of a wanderer. But Bart! And so sudden too. I'd have said his roots be too deep here for un to leave.'

Maddy felt herself go tense before the strength of Annie's incredulity. Maybe it was an unlikely story, one that nobody would believe, but what other explanation could she give? Then to her intense relief Annie said, 'Still, 'tis a hard time you'm all had of late. Enough to unsettle any lad. Your Bart idn't the first to want to get far away from unpleasant memories, nor will he be the last.' She put a kindly arm about Maddy's shoulders. 'You'm no need to look so wisht, maid. You'm going to miss him, I knows, but maybe this be just what the boy needs for a spell. A voyage or two and some seagoing vittles and he'm going to be glad to be back.'

Maddy knew better, though she could not say so. 'I'm sure you're right,' she said, managing a tremulous smile. 'Meanwhile, I think those of us left behind could do with a diversion. I'll bring *Wuthering Heights* over after dinner, shall I?'

'That would be grand.' Annie beamed. 'I'll be sure to have the kettle boiling.'

Before that, however, there was the morning to fill in. Long, empty hours when Maddy would have too much time for unhappy thoughts. As ever, hard work seemed to be the best antidote, and she was so busy cleaning that at first she did not realise she had a visitor.

'If I'd known how little you wanted my company I'd not have gone down on my bended knees for an hour off,' said a voice.

'Patrick!' For an instant the chair she was standing on wobbled precariously, then she was swept into the safety of his arms. 'Patrick!' she repeated.

It did not matter that she was enveloped in a hessian apron, nor that she had soapsuds up to the elbow. He was there, nothing else was important. She clung to him, pressing her face against his shoulder. 'How did you know I needed you more than anything in the world just at this moment?' she asked, her voice muffled by the cloth of his jacket.

He paused, and she was suddenly afraid he might make a flippant remark such as 'Don't you always need me?' or some phrase of that sort. She should have known better. There was nothing trifling in the way he replied, 'I had a feeling. Normally I would not have intruded upon what I know is a dark time for you, but I had this great urge to see you. I knew you would be by yourself, with your father and brothers at work, and something inside told me you should not be alone.'

'And so you came.'

'Yes, I came.'

She had been sure that nothing on that grim morning could have lifted her heart, but Patrick's arrival, and his reason for coming, achieved the impossible. That he should sense her need over such a distance, without any communication, seemed nothing short of both mystical and miraculous.

'Bart's left home,' she said. Not even to Patrick could she tell the full story.

'For good?'

She nodded.

'Maybe that was why I felt your distress.' He held her more tightly, giving her the comfort of his presence. 'I know you'll miss him, but painful though the thought is, I have to say this – perhaps you will find life easier without him.'

In the upheaval and upset of the morning this was something Maddy had not considered. Bart was definitely a disturbing influence in the family and had been for years. She did not want him gone, and certainly not in the present circumstances, but the prospect of a more peaceful life in the future did have an appeal.

Maddy raised her head and looked at Patrick. 'I don't know how you've done it,' she said, 'but you've made me feel better. Half an hour ago there was nothing but misery in my life, then you arrived and suddenly you've made me feel better.'

'It's called love, sweetheart.' Smiling, he kissed her lightly on the forehead.

Suddenly she clung to him, driven by a desperate need. 'Oh Patrick, what would I do without you?' she whispered. 'How would I live? Things have been so terrible lately! You are the one thing that makes my existence bearable.'

'Dearest Maddy, don't even think of being without me because it won't happen. We were meant to be together, for always.' His lips, at first gentle, became more insistent, as his hands about her waist grew more questing. The coarse sacking apron was discarded as one by one, with tantalising slowness, he undid the small buttons on the front of her dress. The softness of his hands on her skin brought comfort as well as arousal. In the midst of such misery he was her only happiness. As the one source of her joy, it was natural that she should go with him up the steep stairs to her attic room. There they slipped from their clothes and, revelling in each other's nakedness, made love on the narrow bed. Her need for him brought an ecstasy of passion which drove away the darkness surrounding her. She had never realised that the act of loving could give such emotional relief. This irrefutable proof of Patrick's love for her had blunted her desperate unhappiness as nothing else could have done.

Afterwards, when they lay sleepy and content in each other's arms, Patrick drew the coverlet more closely about her and asked, 'No regrets?'

'Of course not.' She was surprised at the question. 'Have you?'

'No. But I only meant to comfort you, I did not mean things to go so far. You were vulnerable and not for the world would I have you think that I took advantage.'

Maddy propped herself on one elbow, the better to look at his beloved face. 'But you did take advantage,' she pointed out. 'And I am glad that you did. No one but you could have taken away the blackness; no one but you could make me see that there is a glimmer of brightness ahead, no matter how bleak things seem now.'

'Oh, Maddy, what a creature you are for making a fellow feel good.' He went to take her in his arms again, but desisted, smiling fondly. 'No, I fear I know where that would lead, and I should have been back at the Church House half an hour ago. I must leave you for the present!' He swung his legs over the side of the bed and reached for his shirt. 'We have some serious talking to do about our future. Not yet – too much has happened of late to put you in a turmoil and it would not be fair – but soon. And then we really will be happy. Today will be a trivial incident by comparison.'

Maddy knew she should have felt ashamed for her lost virtue, but she could not. She still had much to mourn, but she also had a future, and that future was Patrick. With such a prospect ahead she knew she would survive anything.

Chapter Twelve

Now that she and Patrick had made love, Maddy felt closer to him than ever. She considered it to be a bond between them, a trust, proving that they belonged completely to one another. Not even the risk of pregnancy caused her any misgivings. When her monthly courses appeared exactly on time it was only then she experienced regret, for she would have loved to have borne Patrick's child. It was not to be, however, and gradually for Maddy, as for the rest of the family, the winter days began to acquire a regular pattern.

It was not the pattern they were accustomed to, that was gone for ever. But it was a systematic routine that they grew to appreciate. As they tried to become used to their changed lives, Jack was adamant about one thing.

'Us've all been up to squire and said our thanks, as were right and proper,' he said. 'But us still be beholden to Cal Whitcomb for Davie's coffin and that do stick in my craw, for all it couldn't be helped. I be danged if us be going to be in debt to him for one minute longer than necessary.'

In the last confused hours before leaving Exeter Maddy had sought out the undertaker who had supplied the coffin and found out how much it had cost. Once home again, it was no easy matter putting aside the money. Jack had forsworn his scrumpy without being prompted, though in truth he had scarcely touched a drop since the execution. He would glare at Lew and Charlie if they even mentioned a visit to the Church House, so that they invariably announced that they had gone off the idea and stayed at home.

It was a hard struggle saving the money, especially in winter, when extra ways of earning a few pence were scarce. They saved hard, and Maddy took one of their few family treasures, a brass telescope, into Paignton to sell. Although she got a good price for it, the amount fell short of what was needed. Then good luck, in the form of winter ague, swept through the village, giving Maddy plenty of temporary employment standing in for folk who had been struck down.

'That be it!' announced Jack in triumph one evening when the contents of the Delft jug had been counted. 'Us can pay Whitcomb, and I don't mind telling you it be a load off my shoulders. Us'll pay un tomorrow first thing.'

'How?' asked Lew.

'What do you mean, how?' demanded his father.

'How'm you going to get the money to un? Be you going to knock on his door and say "Yer tiz" or what?'

'You idn't expecting me to go up Oakwood?' Jack was appalled at the idea. 'I idn't setting foot on that land, I tells you straight.'

'Then you'm going to have to traipse up and down the lane until you finds un then, aren't you?' pointed out Lew.

'No I idn't.' Jack was firm. 'Because one of you be going to pay him the money.'

'Don't be looking at me!' Lew backed away. 'I idn't being the first Shillabeer to soil his boots on Whitcomb mud.'

'Nor me,' declared Charlie.

'What do you think will happen to you if you call at Oakwood?' asked Maddy. 'That the ghost of Grandfather Shillabeer will strike you down?'

'Course not,' replied Jack uncomfortably. 'But no Shillabeer—'

'Never mind, I'll take the money in the morning, and if pigs start flying and cows climb trees you'll know who to blame,' she said.

'If aught of that nature be likely to happen then I be staying indoors.' Lew's grin held an element of relief. 'Seagulls overhead be bad enough, but pigs and cows...'

'Gurt fool!' chuckled Maddy, pelting him with a sock that was drying on the line over the hearth. He responded, Charlie and Jack joined in, and in the ensuing battle she observed that this was the first friendly horseplay they had indulged in for a long time. Little by little the wounds were healing.

Early next morning Maddy walked over to Oakwood Farm and, seizing the highly-polished brass knocker, she rapped boldly on the front door. No lightning struck! The River Dart remained flowing in its natural course at the enormity of this event. The only happening was footsteps that sounded within. The door was opened by a gaunt-faced maidservant whose mouth dropped open with amazement at the sight of Maddy.

'I would like to see Mr Whitcomb,' said Maddy. Then, when she got no response she repeated, more loudly, 'Mr Whitcomb? Is he in?'

'I'd best fetch the missus,' said the maidservant uneasily, and scurried back into the depths of the farmhouse.

From within, Maddy heard Mrs Whitcomb's voice raised in irritation.

'Have you taken leave of your senses, Ellen? What would one of the Shillabeers be doing here? I suppose I'd better go and see who it really is.'

Slippered feet scuffed along stone flags, and the short, stout figure of Mrs Whitcomb emerged through an inner door. She came to an abrupt halt when she saw Maddy. 'Lord preserve us!' she declared. 'One of the Shillabeers, as bold as brass!' Pulling herself up to her full stature, she advanced towards the front door, stays creaking, the white curls fringing her widow's cap bobbing. 'What do you want?' she demanded.

Maddy regarded the indignant woman. 'I wish to see Mr Whitcomb, if you please,' she said politely.

'I don't please, and nor does he!' was the response.

'I really must see him, it will only take a few minutes,' Maddy insisted.

'Oh, you must, must you? What about?'

Something warned Maddy to guard her tongue. Mrs Whitcomb did not seem to know that they owed money to her son. Maddy began to doubt that Mrs Whitcomb knew how much her son had become involved with the Shillabeer family lately; she decided to be careful what she said. Mary Whitcomb had a reputation for having a sharp tongue, and the last thing Maddy wanted was to cause Cal trouble.

'I need to see Mr Whitcomb on business,' she said.

'I know all my son's business, but I know naught of this,' declared Mrs Whitcomb, standing firm.

Maddy was growing tired of the older woman's attitude. 'Mrs Whitcomb,' she retorted, 'your son is expecting me to call. There is a small matter between us that needs attending to. If he is not at home then kindly say so, and I will return at some other time.'

Mrs Whitcomb seemed taken aback at this brisk approach. 'He's not here,' she said, in a less belligerent tone. 'He'll be back in for his breakfast presently. You'd best come in.' Then, in case Maddy thought this was too great a concession, she added, 'I'm not having Shillabeers tramping up to my door all hours of the day and night. Once is once too often.'

She led the way into a low-ceilinged, well-furnished room. The smell of polish overlaid an atmosphere of chilly formality common to best parlours, unused except for special occasions. Maddy wondered why she was being afforded such an honour. She soon found out.

'You may as well sit,' said Mrs Whitcomb, indicating an upholstered chair beside the unlit hearth.

From her seat Maddy had an uninterrupted view of two glass-fronted cabinets against the opposite wall. They were packed with silver, delicate porcelain, and gleaming crystal. Maddy, as a representative of the Shillabeer family, was being shown what fine possessions filled the Whitcomb home, treasures far beyond the reach of a bunch of hobbeldehoy fishermen. Because she knew she was expected to comment on the display, she held her tongue, causing Mrs Whitcomb to speak up for herself.

'My son had those cabinets made specially for me,' she announced with pride.

'Did he indeed?' said Maddy.

'And everything in them he bought for me,' Mrs Whitcomb went on.

Maddy was determined not to appear impressed, even though she longed to get close enough to examine the beautiful things. She remarked, 'You are fortunate in your son. He is certainly generous.'

'Is?' snapped Mrs Whitcomb in irritation. 'Is? It wasn't Calland who gave me these. It was my other son, my Christopher, who was taken from me by the cholera.'

If there was any doubt about the difference in Mary Whitcomb's attitude towards her two sons, it was swept away by the disparity in her voice. Maddy was extremely thankful she had not betrayed the full reason for her visit. Cal's mother clearly already held him in little enough esteem. A door banged at the rear of the house and firm footsteps echoed along the passage.

Mrs Whitcomb winced. 'Can't he do anything quietly?' In a louder voice she called, 'Calland, you've a visitor.'

Cal Whitcomb entered the front parlour, his face glowing with the chill of the morning. 'Mad— Miss Shillabeer!' he greeted her with surprise. 'This is an unexpected pleasure.'

'Good morning, Mr Whitcomb,' replied Maddy, hoping his mother had not noticed his slip of the tongue. 'I'm sorry to disturb you, but there is a matter I must settle with you. A private matter,' she added with emphasis.

'Ah yes,' said Cal, ignoring his mother's expression of blatant curiosity. 'And you aren't disturbing me, I assure you. But why on earth are we in the front parlour? It's as cold as the tomb in here. Let's go where it's warmer. Can we offer you a cup of tea?' He moved towards the door, to hold it open.

'Thank you, but no.' Maddy could see that Mrs Whitcomb was about to explode with indignation at this offer of hospitality. 'My business will only take a minute, then I must be on my way.'

'If you are sure? Then to business. A private matter I think you said.' He looked pointedly at his mother, who withdrew with a sniff of protest. Closing the door after her he listened, his head on one side, until the shuffling of her slippered feet faded, then he turned to Maddy and smiled. 'I can guess the reason for your visit,' he said. 'There is no need, you know.'

'Yes there is,' said Maddy. 'We are in your debt, and the Shillabeers always pays what they owe.'

'Particularly when it is to a Whitcomb, eh? You see how well I am coming to understand your family!'

'Then you should know we would insist upon repaying you.'

'This tit for tat repaying is getting out of hand. We really must stop returning the honours in such a way or we'll never cease.'

'This time it is rather more serious,' said Maddy quietly. 'We have more than one reason to be grateful to you. You made sure our Davie had a proper burial, and if we were to thank you from now until Doomsday for that alone it would never be enough. But we can pay you back for the coffin. It was exactly what we'd have chosen... if we'd had the time...' Her voice broke. Unable to go on, she emptied her purse into a china bowl on the table. 'It's all there,' she said, pulling herself together. 'Count it.'

Cal shook his head. 'There's no need,' he said quietly, not even looking at the bowl full of sovereigns and silver coins. 'How are you faring these days? I hear your eldest brother has gone off to sea. Things must be very different for you now.' There was such compassion in his voice that Maddy felt a lump rise in her throat.

'We're managing,' she replied with difficulty. She had a sudden desire to confess to him the true reason for Bart's departure. The crazy impulse only lasted a moment. Firmly she quelled it, and pulling her cape about her she said, 'Now that our business is done I will interrupt your morning no longer. I am sure we both have a great deal to do.'

'Then I must thank you for coming. Will you please offer my thanks to your father and brothers for their promptness. I never regarded it as a loan, but if they feel more comfortable this way, then so be it.'

'They do,' Maddy assured him. 'And so do I.' She held out her hand. 'Thank you, Mr Whitcomb, and goodbye.'

'Goodbye, Miss Shillabeer.' He shook her hand, then gave a sudden grin. 'In our forgetful moments we are much less formal with each other, aren't we?' he said.

'But this isn't a forgetful moment, is it?' she replied, looking pointedly at the door through which Mrs Whitcomb had departed. 'Nor, I fancy, is this the best time or place to be informal.'

'Very true.' He was still smiling as he escorted her to the door.

Maddy entered the lane somewhat bemused by the events of the morning. Although she had been nonchalant in front of her father and brothers about coming to Oakwood, in truth she had been apprehensive. Now it was over she felt relieved. She had braved Mary Whitcomb in her home, and repaid Cal the money they owed him. But, strangely, it had never once occurred to her that she was in her ancestral home, the house which rightfully should belong to her family. As she was pondering on this unexpected omission her thoughts were suddenly interrupted.

'He paid for your brother's coffin, then?'

Maddy jumped. 'Who...?' she gasped, then she saw Ellen, the Whitcomb's elderly maid, leaning over the side gate to the farm. Rugs were hung on the washing line, and she had a cane carpet beater in her hand, but there were precious few other signs of activity.

'How did you know?' Maddy demanded.

'Listened at the window,' said Ellen, quite unconcerned. 'Gawd, her'd go fair mazed if her ever found out.' She inclined her head towards the house. There was no mistaking who she meant. 'You and him speak really easy together. That idn't the first time you two'm had a chinwag, not by a long chalk.'

'What if it isn't?' Maddy raised her head haughtily and glared at the maidservant.

Ellen merely gave a toothless grin. 'Don't worry, I idn't going to say naught. I idn't one to get poor Mr Cal's ears chawed off. If that idn't typical of him. Don't make no fuss, yet he'd do a good turn for anyone. Even a Shillabeer.' Then, shaking her head in wonderment at such generosity, she raised the carpet beater with sinewy arms and began thrashing the rugs.

Maddy went on her way conscious that Cal had at least one ally in his home.

She was nearly at the turning to Duncannon Lane when she saw the unwelcome figure of Victoria Fitzherbert coming towards her on horseback. Of late Maddy had ceased to be wary of her approach, she had had other, more serious things to worry about. She saw Victoria rein in her horse and deliberately manoeuvre it across the narrow lane. Maddy refused to be intimidated. She held her ground.

Victoria's smile, from her higher position in the saddle, had a strangely triumphant air about it.

'You are the Shillabeer creature, I believe,' she said. 'I'm sure I recognise the plain face and the shabby clothes.'

'You know perfectly well who I am,' replied Maddy, tensing herself for whatever was to come. 'There is no need to play games with me.'

'I should think not!' Victoria pretended to be shocked at the idea. 'I would not even consider associating with you. I am only speaking to you now in order to relieve my curiosity.'

Maddy had no intention of asking the cause of Victoria's curiosity.

'Don't you want to know why I am curious?' Victoria demanded.

'No, though I dare say you'll tell me anyway.'

'I want to know how you have the nerve to walk abroad in daylight. Most folks would be too bowed down with shame to leave the house if they had had a brother hanged for murder.'

Maddy refused to flinch. 'I have every right to walk abroad, in daylight or the middle of the night if I choose,' she said.

'But to have a brother hanged,' persisted Victoria. 'Did you see him dangling from the end of the rope? Oh no, such things are carried out behind closed doors now, I believe. I understand the face goes purple first then quite black, and the tongue protrudes most fearfully.'

Maddy was forced to grit her teeth to control herself. 'You have an over-lurid imagination,' she ground out. 'I'm surprised your mother doesn't dose you with something to cool the blood. The juice of watercress is very effective, I'm told.'

Victoria gave a tinkling laugh. 'I've no need of your filthy remedies,' she said. 'I was merely telling you what actually happens.' Then she said in an arch voice, 'I suppose you want to get by.'

'I presume it amuses you, getting in other people's way,' Maddy retorted. 'It's surprising what trifling things entertain some folk.'

'Oh, I have no difficulty in entertaining myself,' replied Victoria. 'And not in any trifling way, either. I have discovered that this place is much more amusing than I had realised. Much, much more amusing.' And she laughed aloud, as if at a private joke. But she moved her horse to let Maddy pass.

Maddy seized the opportunity, walking past with all the dignity she could muster. Victoria's attitude puzzled her. Apart from taunting her about Davie, there had been something more in her manner. Gloating... Yes, that was it. Victoria had been gloating over something. But what? Maddy could not understand such strange behaviour and before long she ceased to try. Let Victoria Fitzherbert do what she liked. She was just a silly, spoiled creature, not worth thinking about.

–

The winter seemed interminable. After weeks of unseasonable mildness the weather deteriorated with a vengeance. Torrential rain fell and bitter winds swept down the valley. Jack and Charlie returned from the quarry each day soaked, cold, and tired. As for Lew, there was never any knowing when he would come in from wherrying; the only certainty was that he would be totally exhausted after grappling with the gales and the fierce tides. Closer to home, the river lapped over the garden wall more than once, and life for Maddy became a constant round of heaving sandbags to keep the water from the house and mopping up and drying out when her preventative measures failed.

'It takes so long to get rid of the smell, that's what I hate,' she declared, sniffing irritably at the dank stench of saltwater that continued to hang about the kitchen after the most recent inundation. 'I lifted the rug and moved as much furniture as I could before the water came in, but it's made no difference. This place still stinks and there's no getting rid of the damp.'

'There, that might make a difference.' Lew, who had just arrived home, slung a couple of extra logs on the fire. 'As for the smell, all I notices be that meat pudding on the hob. I be ready for un, I can tell you.' He slumped wearily by the fire.

'You look tired,' said Maddy.

'Is it any wonder? Three hours or more it must have taken us to tack down Long Reach, with the wind and tide against us. There idn't a muscle in my body as don't ache.'

'This won't last much longer,' said his father confidently. 'Spring'll be on us afore us knows it.'

Jack's words echoed the thoughts that had been in Maddy's head for some time. She waited until they had eaten and were taking their ease by the fire before she fetched her little black accounts book from the dresser drawer.

'What'm you doing, getting that thing out for?' protested Jack mildly as she put it on the table.

'Because it's necessary,' replied Maddy, pressing the stiff pages open. 'You said yourself that spring's on its way. We've a few things to see to before that. There's the net licence for a start.'

'All right,' said Jack resignedly. 'As soon as the sailing's a bit easier us'll go to Totnes and see about un.'

'Good.' In pencil Maddy wrote down the licence fee. 'How about the nets? Do you think they'll do?'

'I don't know why you'm asking, maid. Habn't you checked yourself?'

'I did have a look at them,' admitted Maddy. 'They need some repairing but I think we'll get through the season with them. I'd like your opinion though. You're the expert.'

Jack gave a derisive snort. 'So you tries to tell me.' Then he gave a grin. 'As it happens I did give them a going over the other day, and I agrees. Put down tar on that list of youm and a couple of balls of twine to begin. Then there'll be caulking for the boat – I reckon us'll have paint enough put by. There, what's that come to? Can us afford to start the season?'

It was a question he asked every year. Maddy did her brief calculations and checked them with the money they had in hand.

'We should manage,' she said.

'They salmon, they'm had their sea-year and they'm coming home to spawn,' said Jack confidently. 'I reckon they'm going to be early this season.'

How he could know about the movements of the salmon out in the Atlantic they did not know, but no one questioned his pronouncement. They had grown accustomed to relying upon his instincts born of a lifetime on the river and having the blood of countless generations of salmon fishermen in his veins. He was seldom wrong.

'It won't be easy this year, with one thing and smother,' said Maddy. 'We'll do it, though, with a bit of luck.' Deliberately she closed the accounts book and looked at the others. Now came the part she was not relishing.

'You know what I'm going to say,' she said. 'We're two men short for the net. Who are we going to get to...?' She tried to say '...replace Davie and Bart' but the words stuck in her throat.

A brief silence followed, charged with emotion. The Shillabeers had always fished together. It had been a matter of pride to them. Maddy looked questioningly at Jack, but unexpectedly it was Charlie who spoke.

'Best look for a third man while you'm about un,' he said, staring steadfastly at the scrubbed surface of the table. 'I got a place on one of they boats carrying stone from the quarry. Thought I'd take a look at Lunnon, like. It be only for a couple of trips,' he added defensively when no one spoke.

But it would be for more than a couple of trips; Charlie was the one with wanderlust, inherited no doubt from Greatgrandfather Shillabeer. Now Maddy thought about it, she wondered that he had stayed at home so long.

Jack's mind must have been working on similar lines, for he expressed no surprise. He said, 'I suppose 'tis only natural to want to see a bit of the world at your age.'

'When do you go?' asked Maddy.

'Monday. On the morning tide.'

So soon! Another one of her brothers going! Maddy's heart ached at the thought.

'We'll miss you,' she said.

'Us won't have time to miss un,' broke in Lew. 'They quarry boats be to and fro all the time. He'll be back in no time, bawling for his dinner as usual, won't you, boy?'

Maddy shot a grateful look at Lew. 'Trust him to find some cheerful comment.'

'When did you fix this up?' she asked Charlie.

'Some time back.' He seemed reluctant to discuss his new life, but that was typical of Charlie. Quiet and taciturn, he always kept his thoughts to himself.

'We'll have to make sure you've got everything you'll need,' Maddy said, being practical. 'Thank goodness I've almost finished that new pair of stockings.' She paused. 'In the meantime, perhaps we should get back to the question of who we are going to get to make up our crew. We daren't leave it any longer or the best men will have found places.'

'George Davis, he'm a cousin of your mother and a good enough man, if us can get him,' suggested Jack. 'And he'm got a boy coming up to the right age too. They be family, more or less.'

'Who for the third?' asked Lew. 'How about that Lennie, as were a friend of Davie's?'

'Not that useless article!' Jack objected. 'Us'd never know if he were coming till he got yer.'

For a good hour names were put forward only to be rejected. Finally they decided on a nephew of William's.

'Always supposing they'll come with us,' said Jack gloomily. 'If not, I suppose us'll have to take who us can get.'

The days before Charlie left home were filled with hectic activity. Fortunately the men approached to complete the crew were agreeable. Then there was the trip to Totnes for the net licence.

'You don't need me to come with you,' protested Maddy. 'I've got Charlie's things to iron.'

'I do need you,' insisted her father. 'You'm better at the reading than me. 'Sides, I don't know why you'm being so particular about Charlie's things for. No one on the quarry boat'll care if his drawers be crumpled or no.'

'I suppose not,' Maddy smiled. She knew that, as ever, her father needed reassurance over anything official.

'And afore that boy goes traipsing off to Lunnon us'd best get the nets tarred. 'Tis a heck of a job at the best of times, without being one pair of hands short. Thank goodness we'm in for a dry spell.'

Before the tarring could commence, the nets had to be repaired. They were spread out along the foreshore, above the tide-line, the better to see the tears and the frayed patches. As Jack had said, they were in for a dry spell, and to make the most of it all three men worked on the repairs when they could. With the twine they painstakingly refashioned areas of net which were worn or torn. Jack was meticulous over his salmon nets. It was not unusual for him to insist upon repairs being done again if they did not meet his exacting standards.

'That idn't going to hold no weight of salmon,' he would declare angrily. 'There idn't no point in catching fish only to see them burst free 'cos you can't braid up a bit of net proper.'

When Jack was completely satisfied, the tar boiler in the old thatched shippen was lit. And he took full charge as the sharp familiar smell filled the air. Boiling tar was a dangerous occupation, and anyone fooling about in the proximity of the boiler got a hefty clout, no matter who it was.

Once each long hempen net was soaked with tar, it was a tricky job to hang it from the drying frames on the foreshore. Heavy and sticky-wet, it all too easily became entangled and covered everyone within range with melted tar. Every spare pair of hands was needed to carry the nets. Even Maddy, well swathed in sacking, joined in, helping to hook up the nets using poles, so that they hung up to dry like swathes of coarse black lace. A hard task, but a necessary one, for it was the tar that preserved the hempen twine. When dry, the nets were stored in the room above the boat store, filling the cottage with the clean pungent scent that to Maddy meant the approach of the salmon season.

'Just in time,' said Jack, as a drift of rain swept across the river. 'There's the boat to see to now, but I can manage un in the boat store.'

Charlie left on the Monday morning's tide. Jack and Lew were already at work, but Maddy stood on the garden wall and waved as he sailed by.

How quiet the house was without him, which was strange, because Charlie had never had much to say for himself. Jack, too, became more silent, spending his spare time in the boat store working on their small craft, making it watertight for the coming season. Usually the approach of March brought with it a sense of excitement as everyone awaited the opening of the season, but not this year. Maddy knew that, without three of his sons and with a new and untried crew, for once Jack was not looking forward to snaring the great silver fish.

Nevertheless, promptly on the morning of the fifteenth of March, the first day of the season, he was up betimes, the net stowed in the stern of the boat, his attention divided impatiently between the lane at the back of the cottage and the river at the front.

'Where'm they to?' he demanded irritably. 'Dang it, they'm late.'

'Who'm you on about? George Davis and the rest or the fish?' asked Lew. 'For if 'tis the salmon, I reckon they'm here bright and early. I saw one jump not ten minutes since.'

"Tis the crew as is late,' retorted Jack, his irritation growing. 'A grand start this be.'

'Don't be so impatient,' said Maddy. 'The river's dropping fast but it's got a way to go before you can set the net. George and the others'll be here presently, you'll see.'

She was right. Soon afterwards two men and a boy came down the lane. They called a greeting to her and went on down to the foreshore where Jack and Lew were already standing by with the boat. Within minutes Lew had tethered one end of the net to a stout beech trunk, and the men had pushed the boat, with Jack at the oars, further into the water. The new season had begun.

From time to time during the next few hours Maddy paused in her chores to watch as they made their systematic way downriver, though from her position in the garden it was difficult to judge how things were going. Once Lew looked towards her and gave a 'thumbs up' sign, but even at that distance she thought the gesture showed a lack of enthusiasm. Her heart went out to her father. The first time out together was bound to be difficult for any crew, but Jack would be finding this trip extremely painful. Last season he had fished with his sons, this year he was with comparative strangers.

Maddy continued to observe the river, but now she was watching for a change in its flow. She knew her father would stop fishing just before the tide turned, to have the net out on a rising tide caused all sorts of problems hauling it in. But Jack was far too experienced to be caught out. He would have the net stowed, and he and Lew would be home soon, wanting their meal. Busy in the kitchen, she heard George and the other two walk past. They did not shout any greetings in passing this time, nor did they speak to one another. Maddy thought this was ominous. When Jack came in, his face lowering like a thundercloud, her enquiry about how the day had gone died on her lips.

'A parcel of danged fools, that's what I be burdened with!' declared Jack, sitting down and removing his boots with unnecessary energy.

'Things wadn't so bad,' said Lew. He looked tired and dispirited. Maddy had a pang of conscience. Her thoughts and sympathies had been for her father, she had overlooked the fact that the morning's fishing would have been just as painful for Lew.

'Wadn't so bad?' protested Jack vehemently. 'When I had to tell they idiots what to do every step of the way? The boy I expected to be green, but George don't seem to know naught from nought. And as for that nephew of William's, I be rare disappointed in he, and I don't care who knows it.'

'They'm good men,' insisted Lew. 'And George's boy be as bright as they come. They just idn't used to your ways yet. With us it were different. Us'd come with you since us was in petticoats, and us knowd what was wanted without telling. Give these new lads time, 'tis all they need.'

'And what you two need is some hot food inside you,' said Maddy, setting down the plates. She knew her tone was overbright but she could not help it. She felt she had to lift their spirits somehow.

Jack merely grunted, but Lew managed a smile. 'You'm right there,' he said. 'Tasty! Just the job. Yer, stand back everyone, let me get at un.'

Maddy waited until they had eaten before she asked the vital question.

'Was the catch any good?'

'Nothing special,' replied Jack, concentrating on his plate.

'How many's nothing special?'

'A dozen.'

'A dozen salmon?' Maddy regarded him in amazement. 'You're sitting there like a wet wash-day and you caught twelve salmon on the first day of the season!'

'They wadn't no size. Us'd only get about one and threepence each,' replied Jack gloomily.

'There's no pleasing some folks,' protested Maddy fondly. She looked across at Lew, who gave her a conspiratorial wink. They both knew that it was possible to go days, even weeks, without catching anything. A haul of twelve salmon, even small ones, was very acceptable.

As the season continued, Jack grew to accept his new crew and became less critical of them. The annual urge to hunt for salmon was too strong in him ever to think of giving it up, and if this meant that now he must have outsiders in his boat, then so be it. Something of the old pattern returned to the days, but the evenings were a different matter.

'Place be as quiet as a tomb,' Jack complained. 'And he don't help.'

The object of his complaint was Lew who, trim and spruced up, was going out.

'Why shouldn't he go out? He's going courting,' Maddy protested.

The object of Lew's affections was the brown-eyed daughter of the wherry master who employed him each autumn and winter.

Jack snorted. 'They'm chapel. What you want to get involved with chapel folk for?'

'Because they'm good, decent people,' replied Lew, then added with a spark of mischief, 'And because Mollie Chambers be the prettiest girl in the village.'

'I suppose that's a good enough reason for deserting your old father every night,' Jack agreed.

''Tis only supper once a week,' corrected Lew. 'That's all her mother'll allow. Though when the nights start lightening I be hoping for better things.'

'Then you'd best be off sharpish. You idn't going to keep in her mother's good books by letting the supper spoil,' advised Jack... When the door closed behind Lew, he said, 'He'm going to be the next to leave. If he'm got his knees under the table it must mean her folks approve.' Then he gave a tremulous sigh. 'It would've been different if the others had got wed and gone. You expects your young uns to leave home that way, 'tis only natural...'

'If Lew marries Mollie they won't be far away,' said Maddy. 'They'd always be calling here, and think of the grandchildren. You'd never be short of visitors.'

'We'm a long way off that stage,' Jack pointed out.

Silence settled on the kitchen, broken only by the ticking of the clock and the crackling of the logs in the hearth. From time to time Jack shifted restlessly in his chair until finally Maddy put down her knitting.

'Shall I read you more about Heathcliff?' she asked. 'You enjoyed it the last time I read to you.'

'If you like.' The response was lacklustre, but she fetched *Wuthering Heights* just the same. As she searched for the right page, Jack suddenly said, 'Book-reading be all very well but it idn't near as good as real company. What about that mountebank fellow you keeps company with? Why don't he never come?'

Maddy was so astonished she almost dropped the book. 'You wouldn't object?' she asked.

'If the Chambers can have Lew to supper up to their place I don't seen why us can't have that Patrick fellow yer sometime.'

Patrick's astonishment matched Maddy's own when she told him. 'You're asking me to supper? At your home? Does your father know about this?'

'Of course he does,' Maddy laughed. 'It was his idea.' Then she grew serious. 'He gets terribly lonely in the evenings now. He doesn't seem to want to go out much any more and...'

'And he considers my company is better than no company?' completed Patrick.

'Something like that,' admitted Maddy, smiling. 'Please say you'll come.'

'How could I refuse such a chance – any chance – to be with you?'

'We'll see you on Friday then.' She nestled her head more comfortably against him, conscious of the impending difference in their relationship. So far their romance had been carried on against a background of disapproval from her family. Now, seemingly, that was to change.

When Friday evening came, Maddy felt absurdly nervous, and her unease was not improved by her father's restlessness.

'Rabbit pie!' he commented, looking at the fare she was providing. 'And what be that to follow? Junket and cream? By harry, maid, 'tis only a potman from the Church House we'm expecting, not the Queen.'

'The rabbits for the pie didn't cost anything, because Lew caught them, and I decided we could afford to be a bit extravagant on the pudding,' replied Maddy defensively. 'I thought you liked junket and cream.'

'I likes un well enough when I can get un,' said Jack grumpily. ''Tis a sorry state, though, when I has to wait until a mountebank potman comes afore I gets the chance.'

Her father's mood did not bode well for the evening. Then Maddy began to worry about Patrick's reactions. His encounters with her family had at times been violent. Had he really wanted to come this evening, or had he accepted merely to please her?

The kitchen looked cosy and welcoming, with the firelight reflecting on the polished copper pans and the shining Delft. A freshly laundered white cloth covered the table, which was set with the best china and cutlery she could muster. She had even placed a jug of primroses in the middle, something which had caused Jack to snort derisively.

'Here I am, pretty as a picture and fit for company,' announced Lew, mincing down the stairs. 'I've even washed behind my ears. Look.' He bent towards her, pulling at his earlobe to give her a better view.

'You mazed fool! Poor Mollie Chambers, she doesn't know what she's taking on.' Laughing, Maddy tried to push him out of her way, but he insisted upon thrusting his ear towards her. In the heat of their mock conflict, Maddy almost did not hear the knock on the door.

'I was afraid I'd come on the wrong night,' said Patrick, when she let him in.

'I don't know about the wrong night, you must have thought you'd come to the madhouse with all this noise,' Maddy said. 'It was Lew acting the fool.'

'When it comes to being a fool our Lew don't need to act,' said Jack, holding out his hand. 'Come on in, boy.'

Stepping over the threshold Patrick grasped his outstretched hand, and Maddy heaved a silent sigh of relief. The brief moment of horse-play had caused her father to suspend his misgivings about their visitor. Her spirits rose more when, after having shaken hands with Lew, Patrick took a bottle from his pocket.

'A small contribution towards what I know is going to be an enjoyable evening,' he said.

'Honey wine,' said Jack appreciatively. 'Well, there idn't naught wrong with your taste, boy. I habn't had honey wine since I don't knows when. Come and sit by the fire and us'll take the top off un while Maddy gets supper on the table.'

Maddy glanced at Patrick and he smiled at her, a reassuring smile that said 'Everything's going to be all right.'

And everything was all right. At first there was little conversation, the excellence of the supper saw to that. No one could ever accuse Patrick of being poor company and, after the dishes were removed and the honey wine set out, he soon had the others in fits of laughter. Maddy was delighted to hear her father chuckling, she had not seen him look so animated for a long time. She enjoyed, too, the firm grasp of Patrick's fingers as he held her hand beneath the table. This was an evening she had never expected to happen, to have Patrick sitting by their fireside, with her father's approval.

'I really must go.' Patrick gave her hand one last surreptitious squeeze, then rose to his feet. 'I'm afraid I've sadly outstayed my welcome.'

Jack looked up at the clock. 'It can't be that late!' he exclaimed incredulously. 'Why, it don't seem two minutes since you got here, boy. You'm given us a merry time and no mistake.'

'No, the giving was on your part,' contradicted Patrick. 'I can't remember when I last spent so enjoyable an evening. Being something of a wanderer, with no longer any folks to call my own, it's a rare treat for me to sit beside a proper fireside and be treated as one of the family.'

He could not have said anything that would have appealed more to Jack, who was still missing his lost sons sorely.

'Family be a great thing, boy.' Jack put his hand on Patrick's shoulder. 'Sadly us don't always appreciate it till 'tis too late. If you'm a mind, you must come again.'

'I will, you can be sure of it. And my thanks for your hospitality and your kindness.'

Patrick said his goodbyes and Maddy saw him to the door. There were no lovers' farewells, just an exchange of smiles that were brief and tender. Maddy did not mind. The evening had gone better than she could ever have anticipated. True, her father had never once referred to Patrick by name, only as 'boy', but she sensed a last residual reserve in this rather than disapproval.

'That fellow of youm, he'm rare amusing, there idn't no getting away from the fact,' yawned Jack, reaching up to wind the clock, as he always did before bed. 'Once you gets to know him he seems a brave enough fellow. Don't be too long afore you invites him again.'

'I won't, and thank you, Father.' Maddy was delighted. She became aware, though, that Lew had said little. 'Don't you like Patrick?' she asked bluntly.

'I agrees with Father. He'm some amusing, and that be a fact.'

'But do you like him?' she insisted.

'Tidn't no use asking me summat like that,' Lew said. ''Tis if you likes un, that be the important thing.'

Maddy was not fooled. Beneath his diplomatic response she sensed he did not like Patrick. She felt a momentary distress, but it swiftly disappeared. He would soon come round. Once he really got to know Patrick, how could he help himself?

–

'Your Lew's in well with the Chambers these days, I hears,' remarked Annie one day. 'Us'll be hearing wedding bells soon I shouldn't wonder.'

'Perhaps, in time,' replied Maddy. She knew that her brother had good reasons for not rushing things.

'Us'll wait a while until the talk about Davie dies down,' he had said. 'Not that I be ashamed of him, nor do it make no difference to Mollie. But her ma be still not too happy about her girl marrying into a family as has a hanging in its history. Only natural, I suppose, so I think 'tis only right to let things settle down a bit.'

Maddy hoped sincerely that things would 'settle down a bit' for the pair of them, for although he said little, she knew Lew was desperately fond of his Mollie.

'And what about you, then?' Annie's voice broke into her thoughts. 'I hope you'm getting your bottom drawer together too, for you'm going to need un afore long, if I be any judge.'

'Get along with you!' said Maddy scornfully.

'Don't you scoff at me, my girl!' Annie pretended to be indignant. 'My eyes idn't playing tricks. That Patrick of youm be down here of a Friday night for his supper regular. If that idn't a sign of a wedding to come I don't know what be.'

'If you're looking for a chance to buy a new bonnet soon then I'm afraid you're going to be disappointed,' Maddy laughed.

She did not admit that, of late, she had begun to be of the same opinion. No longer was it a question of deserting the family if she wed. If she married Patrick they could live with Jack, for there was plenty of room. She was sure her father would not object. Already he was beginning to say in a jovial tone, 'Any day now I be going to have a serious talk with that fellow of youm. I wants to know his intentions.'

And what were Patrick's intentions? He had never actually mentioned marriage, but his remarks always referred to the wonderful future that they would share one day. Recalling the things he said, and the way he was always so tender and loving towards her, it was no wonder that her thoughts were beginning to turn happily towards wedding rings and church bells.

It was one wash-day when Maddy thought she caught a glimpse of Lew going past the door as she was prodding clothes into the copper in the lean-to beside the cottage. Through the clouds of steam she could have sworn she saw him, but when he neither came in nor called out to her she decided she must have been mistaken. Hadn't he said he was going down mill to settle up with the Totnes agent for the salmon? He would never have come home so promptly, not when he had a chance to call in on Mollie. But as she was carrying the basket of wet laundry into the garden, she definitely heard his voice.

It was coming from Annie's house. She paused, puzzled as to what he was doing there. At that moment he emerged from next door with Annie. Seeing her, their serious expressions grew even more grave.

Maddy put her washing down. 'What's the matter?' she demanded. 'What's happened? Something's happened to Father!'

'No, Father be fine,' said Lew, helping Annie over the rough path. 'Just wait for us indoors. We'm coming as fast as us can.' He looked unusually agitated.

It seemed an age before the pair of them finally entered the kitchen. When they did they looked at each other with seeming helplessness, as if each willing the other to speak.

'You tell her,' Lew urged Annie. 'I habn't got the heart.'

'For pity's sake, one of you tell me what's been going on!' cried Maddy.

'You'm best sit yourself down, my lover, for us've got a bit of bad news,' said Annie gently. She took a deep breath as if steeling herself for what was to come. 'Maddy, my maidie, there idn't no easy way to say this so I'll come straight out with it. That sweetheart of yourn, Patrick, have run off.'

'Run off?' Maddy sank onto the nearest chair.

'That idn't the worst, neither. Oh, Maddy, I wishes I wadn't the one to tell you this but... he'm eloped with that haughty Fitzherbert wench!'

Patrick gone? Eloped with Victoria Fitzherbert? It was unthinkable! Ludicrous! Maddy could not, would not, believe it.

'What sort of stupid joke is this...?' She looked from Annie to Lew. Their eyes showed distress and love and pity. 'It's a joke,' she said. 'It's got to be... Please say it's a joke.'

But no one admitted to joking. The only response was silence.

Then she knew it was true.

Chapter Thirteen

Maddy sat very still. Patrick had eloped with Victoria Fitzherbert. Patrick, who just the night before had held her in his arms and told her that she and no other was his beloved Rustic Damozel. He must have gone straight from her to— No, she could not bear to think of it. He had betrayed her in the cruellest way – with kisses and sweet words. All the time he had been pleasuring her with soft caresses and loving whispers he had been planning to run off with Victoria. She was too numb with shock to feel any pain yet, bewilderment was her sole emotion. Her head knew the story was true – Annie and Lew would never have come to her with such a tale if they had not been certain – but her heart refused to accept it.

'Tell me the details,' she said bleakly. 'I want to know.'

Annie looked up at Lew. ''Twas the boy yer as heard un, and he came hastening to me.'

'I heard about un down mill,' Lew said. 'The place were buzzing with un, and I were afeared you'd find out by chance. That's why I come to Annie. I reckoned her'd know the best words.'

'There idn't no best words, not for news like this,' said Annie grimly.

'Tell me, anyway,' insisted Maddy, her voice expressionless. 'I must know.'

'According to the tale down mill, when Mary, the Fitzherbert wench's maid, went to wake her, the bed was empty. Just a note on the pillow saying as her'd gone off with the man she loved. At first no one knowd which man her meant, her never seemed to fancy no one special. Then Mr Fitzherbert questioned Mary, real fierce about it he were, and the upshot were her admitted her mistress had been seeing that Patrick on the quiet.'

'Then it's just Mary's word that Victoria's eloped with Patrick!' Relief roused Maddy from her stupor. 'The maid must have been mistaken or else she's lying.'

Annie shook her head sadly. 'Patrick's things have gone from the Church House, and no one have seen him since late last night.'

'That doesn't mean anything.'

'He took his fiddle, and Lucy Ford's pony and trap has disappeared.'

'A coincidence,' Maddy cried contemptuously. 'Who would think of eloping in a pony and trap? They'd be overtaken in no time.'

'It'd get them to Newton or maybe Torquay, some busy place like that, where they could get the train,' Lew pointed out. 'Anyway, Mr Fitzherbert have gone after the pair of them, swearing like nobody's business and lashing about with his whip.'

'Then he's gone on a fool's errand,' declared Maddy. 'As like as not that wretched female's not eloped at all. You know what she's like for making mischief. She certainly won't be found with Patrick.'

Again Annie and Lew exchanged concerned glances.

'There's more'n Mary's word,' said Lew. 'They was seen together a few times. Folk thought it were chance, with that Victoria always riding about the place, but now—'

'Lies!' cried Maddy. 'All lies!' Then she put her head in her hands and wept, because try as she might to disbelieve what she was hearing, she kept remembering Victoria's odd behaviour last time they met. She feared she knew the reason now for that gloating self-satisfied expression. No wonder Victoria had been triumphant, she had got her revenge for past conflicts with a vengeance, by inflicting the greatest hurt she could upon Maddy. She had stolen her lover.

The door flew open with a crash, and there stood Jack.

'Be it true?' he demanded. 'What I be hearing about that mountebank and the Fitzherbert wench?'

'It be true, right enough,' said Lew.

Jack strode over to his weeping daughter and, ignoring his working dirt, enfolded her in his arms. 'He'll pay, my maidie,' he swore. 'No wretch causes my girl this sorrow and gets off scot-free. He'm played fast and loose once too often and, by harry, idn't he going to rue the day.'

'What are you going to do?' cried Maddy through her tears, as Jack released her and made for the stairs.

'I be going after the pair of un,' he replied.

'But Mr Fitzherbert's gone already,' said Lew.

'Fitzherbert? He idn't naught!' Jack was disparaging. 'Plenty of noise and little else. He won't find un.' And he stamped up the stairs.

He was back in a few minutes dressed in his Sunday suit, an old haversack over his shoulder. Helping himself to some bread and cold bacon and to a few coins from the Delft jug he said, 'I'll likely be home late. Don't wait up.'

Lew leapt to his feet. 'Hang on a minute,' he cried, 'I'll come too.' But Jack shook his head.

'This be my work, boy. You bide yer, and have charge of the boat. I suppose Fitzherbert have took his horsewhip? Horsewhip!' He snarled in disgust. 'That be too good for the villain. He'll feel my fist, aye, and my boots, too, when I catches up with un. They'll teach un a harsher lesson than any horsewhip.'

'Father! Please!' Maddy, too, had leapt from her seat. She meant to plead with Jack not to harm Patrick. It was an automatic response. Her love for him was so deeply ingrained that, no matter how much he had hurt her, she could not bear to think of him being injured. But Jack, misunderstanding, did not give her a chance.

'Don't you worry about me, my lover,' he said. 'I'll be all right.' And he hurried from the cottage, slamming the door behind him.

There was an unreal quality about the rest of the day for Maddy, as if none of this was happening. When she saw Lew slicing the loaf, however, and hacking off lumps of the bacon joint, she tried to stir herself.

'Your dinner!' she exclaimed. 'You haven't had your dinner.'

Gently but firmly she was pushed back into her chair, and a cup of hot sweet tea was thrust into her hands.

'I be managing fine,' said Lew, his mouth full. 'I won't starve, don't you fret.'

'The tide be falling,' said Annie. 'You'll need to get to the boat soon, won't you, boy? Well, you go with an easy mind. I'll stay on yer. Maybe William'll lend a hand, with you being a man short. 'Tis his slack time. You give un a shout as you go—'

With bread and bacon still in his hand, Lew thanked her and hurried out.

'And how about you, maid?' Annie turned to Maddy. 'Why don't you go upstairs and have a lie down? I dare say you could do with a spell by yourself, but I'll be yer if you needs me.'

Gratefully Maddy did as she was bid. Solitude was exactly what she needed, a chance to ponder on this awful thing that had befallen her.

In her attic bedroom Maddy sat on the edge of her bed trying to make sense of what had happened. Then suddenly she found herself grappling with a bewildering succession of emotions that gripped her with such intensity her limbs trembled. Distress, a sense of betrayal, love, confusion, disbelief – each ran its course, leaving her understanding no better, and no more at peace.

Patrick loved her. Hadn't he said it? Proved it over and over again? Why, then, had he run off with Victoria? Maddy was not vain, she could see the attractions only too clearly. Victoria was pretty, elegant, and sophisticated. She was also gentry and Maddy could understand how that would appeal to Patrick. But why had he given no hint, no sign?

Meticulously she went over every occasion when she and Patrick had been together during the last few weeks. He had been as warm and loving as ever. There had never been the least suggestion that someone else held his affections. Surely she would have noticed if there had, loving him and knowing him as she did?

But perhaps she did not know Patrick as well as she thought. Certainly she had never believed him capable of such treachery. Of course, she had known and understood about his flirtations, but it had never occurred to her that he might seriously betray her with another woman. How wrong she had been! How stupid! How gullible!

A great surge of anger and pain welled up inside her. Suddenly she wanted to purge her life of everything connected with Patrick. Her one memento was the silver Janus ring. Distraught, she pulled at the neck of her dress only to find that the ring was not there. Sometime during that very morning the ribbon must have come undone and she had lost it. It seemed to emphasise everything else that she had lost. Could the Roman deity have been the god of betrayal too?

She sank back on the bed, longing for the release of more tears, but she remained resolutely dry-eyed. For a while she lay there, tense and miserable, until she could bear the inactivity no longer. When she went downstairs she found Annie in the kitchen, her swollen hands struggling manfully to peel some potatoes. She looked up as Maddy entered.

'There idn't no call for you to stir yet,' she said kindly. 'You have a bit longer if you needs un.'

'I'm all right now, thanks. Here, let me take over.' Maddy held out her hand for the potato knife; then when Annie was reluctant to pass it over she said, 'I'd prefer to be up and doing, honestly I would.'

Annie nodded with understanding and pushed the bowl of potatoes in her direction.

'Goodness knows if Jack'll be back tonight, but it'd be as well to have something ready, I suppose,' she said. 'And your Lew'll need feeding when he gets in.'

'Lew always needs feeding.' Maddy peeled the potatoes with fierce concentration. 'Annie, I haven't thanked you yet for being so kind.'

'I habn't been kind.' Annie was in no doubt about it. 'Today be the worst day's work I ever done, telling you news like that. I'd understand if you want me out of the way, but if you feels you needs a bit of company I'll stay and gladly.'

'Stay, oh please stay!' replied Maddy fervently. She could not bear the idea of being alone with her thoughts; it had been what had driven her down from the seclusion of her bedroom – that and the fact that giving way to a broken heart was the prerogative of the rich; the poor had work to do and meals to cook.

Annie had half risen from her seat, now she sank back again, happy to be of some use. 'Before I forgets, I found a fairing on the floor, I supposes it must be youm. I put un in the glass dish on the mantel.'

'Fairing?'

'Yes, a ring with two faces on. My, I habn't seen one of they in years. Us used to get them up to Totnes Fair off a gypsy pedlar when I were a girl. Fourpence I think they was in them days. He used to try to fool us they were real silver. I asks you a silver ring for fourpence! Base metal, more like.' Smiling at the memory, Annie did not notice Maddy flinch.

A tawdry ring bought from a cheapjack, not something of ancient significance. Maddy's grip on the potato knife tightened. Patrick had not even been truthful about that.

During the rest of the afternoon she was grateful for Annie's cease-less chatter and for the familiar tasks involved in preparing the meal. Not that she found concentration easy. Often she had no idea what her friend was talking about, and more than once she had to check that she had not forgotten some of the ingredients in the stew she was making; but somehow she got through the afternoon with a semblance of normality.

'The men'll be back soon,' said Annie. 'I'd best get something cooking for my William.'

'Tell him I'm sorry for keeping you for such a long time, but you've no idea how thankful I've been for your company.'

'Get on with you!' Annie gave her a fond smile. 'You habn't heard more'n one word in five as I've said.'

'Maybe not, but you were here to say them. That made all the difference.'

'If it did then I be content.' Annie kissed her on the cheek and made her slow way home.

When Lew came home he looked surprised and relieved to find Maddy in her usual position, tending the cooking pots on the fire.

'I didn't expect this,' he said. 'I thought I'd be toasting myself a bit of cheese. Be you sure you feels up to cooking and such?'

'Of course I do, if you feel up to eating it.' Her reply was braver than she was feeling, but Lew was fooled.

'That's the girl!' he exclaimed. 'And when didn't I want my vittles?'

As soon as he had washed, he tackled his stew with enthusiasm. While he ate he talked about every bit of inconsequential gossip he had gleaned during the day, everything but the one thing Maddy knew everyone would be talking about. She gave up any pretence of trying to eat and pushed her stew away, scarcely tasted.

'You may as well tell me what's being said,' she sighed. 'I'll just find out from someone else.'

Lew nodded glumly. 'Folks were talking about un down mill when us took the fish ashore – 'twere to be expected, I suppose. I had a word with Matt Efford, as plays the clarinet in the church band, and he reckons the carryings-on began way back at the country dance the squire gave for the gentry.'

'As long ago as that?' Maddy was appalled. 'But that was early in the winter, before...' She almost said 'before Davie's execution' but she still could not speak of her brother's death. 'Before Christmas,' she amended.

'It were some time back,' agreed Lew, noting her hesitancy and sharing her pain. 'Matt were playing for the dancing, along with that Patrick rogue, and he reckons that Victoria were making up to the wretch. Oh, discreetly, mind. Asking about the music and would he be free to play up at the White House one day, but Matt says her were leading un on, anyone could tell. Course 'tidn't the first time a lady of quality have set her cap at a rough fellow, and I don't suppose 'twill be the last.'

233

'Quality? She isn't quality!' Maddy rapped out the words.

She was remembering that, after the success of the squire's country dance, there had been quite a vogue among the local gentry for folk music. Patrick had played the music, and inevitably Victoria would have been there to listen, to dance – and to flirt.

A whole winter of deception, when Maddy had thought Patrick loved her, yet his eyes had already been straying. The duration of his duplicity dealt her a new hurt, one that made her want to cry out in pain, for this affair must have been flourishing during the time of Davie's trial and execution, when she was away from the village. Knowing that the pair of them were together while she was in such despair caused Maddy to bite her lips in anguish. Yet, afterwards, when she returned from Exeter, Patrick had been so kind towards her. What had that been? A charade? A ruse to cover his affair with Victoria? Maddy's head was throbbing with it all, she could no longer think clearly.

To hide her distress she busied herself with what was left of the stew. 'I'm keeping some on one side for Father,' she said. 'But shall I leave it on the fire or not? There's no knowing when he'll be back; he's bound to be tired and hungry, poor man, he'll need something hot. On the other hand, if I leave it too long it'll dry up and be spoiled.' She was gabbling, she could not help it; anything to smother the awful anguish within her.

If Lew noticed anything amiss he made no comment. 'Why not take the pot off the fire completely?' he suggested. 'I brung plenty of logs on my way in, us can have a decent blaze going and the stew heating in no time, even if Father comes home in the middle of the night.'

His advice proved sound; it was dawn when an exhausted Jack returned home. Maddy, who had found sleep impossible, was downstairs, encouraging the dull embers in the hearth into flame the instant she heard his boots on the path. Lew followed soon after her.

'I didn't find un,' said Jack dispiritedly as he slumped in front of the blaze. 'Just as well, maybe, I'd likely have killed the wretch, and us've had enough trouble in that quarter of late.' He rubbed his face wearily. 'When I got as far as Newton Abbot I asked at the station if anyone'd seen a fancy miss and a fellow with a fiddle. No one had, but they recalled Old Man Fitzherbert right enough. Roaring like a bull, by all accounts, and not thinking clear.'

'How do you mean?' asked Maddy.

'Because he only bothered about asking at the railway. By the sound of un he'm determined they'm gone to Lunnon, he was heard ordering his carriage to take the Exeter road. Not having no carriage, I hung about a bit to see what I could see, and I did find Lucy Ford's pony and trap, which were more than Fitzherbert managed, for all his bellowing. It were stabled at an inn down by the market, but no one knowd where the couple who'd brung un had gone. I could find neither hide nor hair of them after, though I tried along every road out of town. They could've gone anywhere, in my opinion – Plymouth, Exeter, or maybe Bamstaple-Bideford way. They could be hiding out up to Dartmoor, plenty of places there where folks wouldn't be noticed. No, I don't reckon they'm making for Lunnon, somehow.' Jack yawned, then looked at Maddy. 'And how be you faring, maid?' he asked belatedly.

'Well enough, thank you, Father,' she replied.

'That be my maid.' He rose and patted her on the shoulder. 'I daresay this has bothered you some, but that bit of rubbish, he idn't worth getting in no state over. Best you found out about un now 'stead of later, eh?' He gave another, wider yawn. 'I think I be off to my bed. Thank goodness the ebb tide be latish today, I might manage a couple of hours' sleep.'

'Just leave they dishes, they idn't going to run away,' said Lew after he had gone. 'You go on up too. I'll see to the fire. As Father says, us can lie on a bit this morning.'

Maddy managed the ghost of a smile and went upstairs to bed. She lay there, dry-eyed and wakeful, uncertain whether to be glad or sorry that the eloping couple were still missing. What good would it have done her if they had been found? Victoria might have been dragged back to Stoke Gabriel, weeping and wailing, but Patrick could never have been forced to return. He was lost to her for ever, and this increased her torment, for Maddy knew that, despite the way he had treated her, if he had appeared at the door that very minute she would have welcomed him back with open arms.

The next thing she knew it was bright daylight. Having overslept was a blessing in disguise; in the frantic activity to catch up and get Lew and her father out before they missed the tide she had little time to think about her own sorrows. It was different after they had gone. Once alone, she began to consider the problems ahead of her. One of the most distasteful would have to be tackled that morning – going into the village where everyone would know what had happened.

A few short months ago, after Davie's troubles, she had had to face the reaction of the villagers. Then they had shown anger, hostility and, ultimately sympathy. Now it would be harder to bear, for they would show her pity. Patrick had done what Davie, for all his tragic fate, had never achieved. He had shamed her! He had made her that most pathetic of objects, a female past her prime who has been deceived by a man. There was no help for it, though. The sooner she faced the world the better.

Commiseration was in the air, she could feel it as she walked down the steep hill towards Mrs Cutmore's shop. A few folk sniggered as she went by, but most showed sympathy for her in their eyes, although few referred to what had happened. Only one old woman, who had known Maddy since her cradle, clutched at her with a claw-like hand and said, 'You'm better off without un, my lover. That sort brings naught but trouble.'

Maddy thanked her for her kindness, readjusted the set smile she had fixed upon her face, and continued about her business. It cost her dear to go on smiling and making remarks about the unsettled weather when all she wanted was to bolt home and hide her humiliation. She must have succeeded in giving an impression of equanimity, however; as she moved away from a group of women, having just passed the time of day, she heard one of them remark, 'Her'm taking it well, at any road.'

'Yes,' replied another. 'Sensible maid, be Maddy Shillabeer. Her'm got her head on straight.'

Is that what they really think? wondered Maddy. Do they honestly imagine that I don't mind that the man I love has run off with another woman? If only they knew. If only they knew!

Although Maddy had been into the village, it was through Annie that she learned the most recent gossip. 'Mr Fitzherbert idn't back yet,' her friend informed her. 'He'm staying up to Lunnon until he finds un. Leastways, that were the message he sent.'

'He seems certain they've gone to London.'

'Where else? There be this place up to Scotland, Gretna or some such name, where I hears you can be married without the parents consenting, but somehow I don't think that Patrick be turning out to be the marrying sort.' She saw a shadow of pain cross Maddy's face and carried on hurriedly, 'Besides, there being so many people in Lunnon, who's to notice two more?'

'Father thinks they may have made for Plymouth or Bristol.'

'Too close to home.' Annie shook her head emphatically. 'You mark my words, they'm up to Lunnon. Everyone says so.'

'If they are then I don't fancy Mr Fitzherbert's chances of finding them.'

She was right. Mr Fitzherbert returned home alone at the end of three weeks.

'In a right high dudgeon he be,' announced Annie. 'Do you knows what he did? Took all Miss Victoria's things, her pretty dresses and everything, and made a bonfire of them in the garden. Tended it hisself, too, until there wadn't naught but ash left. Then he got the servants together and told them that from now on he didn't have no daughter, and that anyone as mentioned her name'd be dismissed on the spot. He means it too. Even Mrs Fitzherbert idn't allowed to speak of her.' Her expression grew sad. 'Seems terrible harsh, though, to deny your own flesh and blood. I idn't saying that the maid idn't a headstrong piece, and selfish to boot, but her'm young. And I fancy her'll be repenting sore after her'm much older.' She glanced at Maddy. 'I don't suppose you can be expected to have much sympathy for the wench.'

'Not much,' Maddy admitted. 'But she's been brought up to get whatever she wants, she can't be blamed for that. In this case, whether she'll continue to want what she's got is another matter.'

Annie nodded approvingly. 'That be a fair way of thinking, in the circumstances,' she said. 'There idn't many in your shoes as'd be so generous.'

Maddy felt she did not deserve such approval. Perhaps she should hate Victoria, yet somehow she could not. Self-willed and selfish the girl might be, yet there was also a vulnerability about her that Maddy found pathetic. Wandering the country with an itinerant musician was not going to be easy for a girl who could not even dress herself or do her own hair. To her surprise Maddy found that she pitied the silly girl. Her resentment was directed against Patrick, despite the fact she still loved him. After all, Victoria did not owe her anything, but surely Patrick owed her loyalty at the very least.

Outwardly Maddy went back to her everyday life as if nothing had happened. It was a matter of self-respect for her to dress the same, to act the same as she had always done. Things had been different when Davie had died. Then she had felt able to give way to her emotions. Now, though, her pride was involved as well as her heart, and she refused to show how much Patrick had humiliated her.

Surprisingly, most people were taken in by her outwardly calm demeanour, even Annie, who was usually most perceptive. 'But that don't bother you none, eh?' she would say when some news of Patrick and Victoria, usually unsubstantiated, found its way back to the village. 'You'm grateful you'm shot of yon Patrick and no harm done, I daresay.'

And Maddy would nod and pretend to agree. Only at night, when she was alone in her attic, did she allow herself to admit her misery. Now she fully understood the meaning of the phrase 'a broken heart'; it described perfectly the numbing, aching pain that was always with her. She would lie wakefully in the darkness, suffering, yet still unable to find relief in weeping.

One morning, noticing that her supplies of flour were low, she went to the mill by the quay to order a sack of flour. On the way home she decided it would be more pleasant to take the path across the fields. The last person she expected to meet on her walk was Cal Whitcomb. He, too, looked surprised, but not displeased.

'This is an unexpected pleasure,' he said. 'May I walk with you?'

'Certainly,' said Maddy. She knew it was unlikely that he was wandering aimlessly about the countryside, so she added, 'if it will not divert you from your business.'

'My business is at an end, thank you,' he said, falling into step beside her. 'I have been down looking at the old quarry.'

'You aren't thinking of opening it up again, are you?' she asked incredulously.

'No,' he replied. 'Not exactly. I'm thinking of setting up a second cider press, you see, and I need stone to extend the building.'

Two presses, thought Maddy. His cider business must be prospering. Aloud she asked, 'And did you find your stone?'

He shook his head. 'It would be too difficult to get out, and take too many men. Penn's Quarry is closer to Oakwood, of course, but these days they seem to concentrate upon sending stone up to London to build more roads. They aren't interested in providing a few tons to extend a farm building. No, I must look elsewhere. Not that there is any urgency. This is a plan for way in the future.'

'Then I will mention it to no one.'

'I know I can depend upon your discretion. You have already proved it.'

As he spoke he had a mischievous twinkle in his eye which prompted Maddy, remembering her visit to his home, to ask, 'And how is your mother?'

He laughed aloud. 'Very well, thank you, and all the better for not knowing that you and I deal quite amicably together on occasions.' Then the laughter faded from his face as he said, 'Yes, I know you have discretion and tact, but more than that, you have great courage.'

Maddy stiffened. Something in his tone disturbed her. 'I don't know what you mean,' she said.

'Yes, you do.' His response was quite brusque. 'You are the bravest creature I know, Maddy Shillabeer, but I beg you, do not go on being brave, covering up your feelings for the sake of appearances. You must give way to what is inside you. Those who think you don't care or "have got over it" are fools who cannot possibly know you. When someone cares for another the way you cared for that Howard fellow, how can they be expected to shrug off their feelings in a minute? Like most of the village I always considered him to be a rogue and a vagabond, not fit to tie your bootlaces, but that makes no difference. Admit you grieve for him, before you make yourself ill by keeping your distress to yourself.'

Maddy was struck dumb. Cal Whitcomb was the last person she would have expected to have seen beneath her protective charade. Looking up she saw concern on his face, but it was the sympathy in his expression that proved too much for her.

Although it had been his perception of her own state that had shaken her, irrationally it was against his criticisms of Patrick that she railed. She might resent her fickle lover's behaviour, but no one else was going to find fault with him.

'How dare you speak in such a way about Patrick!' she cried. 'You and the rest of the village, you know nothing about him. I don't care what you say, he is not bad! He is not! In addition, you are impertinent. What right have you to meddle in my affairs, Mr High-and-Mighty Whitcomb? Concerned for me, were you? In future, I'd be grateful if you would mind your own business.'

She spun round on her heel and stalked off, leaving a grimfaced Cal looking after her. Her indignation lasted until she had climbed over the next stile and was hidden from his view by a high hawthorn hedge. Then she crumpled up against the hedge bank and, for only the second time since Patrick had deserted her, she gave way to tears. The much-needed storm of weeping swept over her, leaving her limp and tired, but the tension in her nerves and muscles had gone. The unhappiness remained, though. It would be a long, long time before that went away. Until that happened she had no alternative but to try to carry on as normal.

In the midst of everything, her rudeness to Cal Whitcomb troubled her. Maybe he had been outspoken, but she sensed he had been trying to help. It was with relief that she encountered him a few days later on the Aish road. At the sight of her he half checked his horse, then seemed to change his mind and made to ride on.

'If you could spare a minute, Mr Whitcomb, I would be most grateful,' she called.

He reined in the gelding and said stiffly, 'Good day, Miss Shillabeer. How can I help you?'

'By accepting my apologies for being so rude at our last meeting. To be honest I don't know what got into me, shouting insults at you like that. I am very sorry.'

He fidgeted with his riding crop before replying, 'I should think that what got into you was rightful indignation. I was personal, rude, and downright impertinent.'

'Oh no,' Maddy protested. 'You were showing concern for me, and I replied by turning on you like a shrew.'

'I think I upset you very much, and that was not my intention. I should not have interfered.'

'I am glad you did. You were right, I had been holding my feelings too close within myself. Getting angry at you... had a most beneficial effect.'

He looked relieved. 'You have no idea how glad I am to hear it. I have had many uneasy minutes since then worrying in case I had made things worse.'

'You did not do that.' She could have added that nothing could have made things worse.

He smiled, 'That is a weight off my mind, and having been inter-fering once I may as well continue and say the sun will shine again for you one day, you know. Never doubt it.'

How often had she told herself that. After Davie. After Bart. And now after Patrick. 'I know it will,' she lied, and bade him farewell.

–

If the sun were ever going to shine, it was taking a long time, in Maddy's opinion. The high summer sun may have burnt the surrounding cornfields golden and ripened the swelling apples in the orchards, but it did not enter her life. Her chief cause for optimism during those long warm days was her father. It had been an extremely good salmon season, which had cheered Jack considerably and now, in August, with the end of the netting approaching, he was beginning to accept that he had a good crew. Enough, at any rate, to ask them to join him for the following year. He was beginning to go out again. If Lew or one of his friends suggested a pint of scrumpy up at the Church House Inn, he accepted with enthusiasm. He was beginning to take more care about his appearance too.

Lew noticed the change and teased his father. 'I be the one as is reckoned to be courting,' he joked. 'Be you trying to put me in the shade?'

'Cheeky young devil!' Jack aimed a half-hearted blow at his head which Lew laughingly avoided with ease.

There was a cheery camaraderie between father and son these days that Maddy was delighted to see. At first, she put it down to Lew being the last boy left at home, but sometimes she caught a knowing glance passing between them as if they shared some mischievous secret.

'Men!' she exclaimed on such occasions. 'Always up to something!' Maddy watched her father growing more and more like his old self, and she rejoiced. With Lew now accepted as Mollie's recognised suitor, and Jack growing more cheerful by the day, she felt the future must hold better times for them if not for her.

'I be glad you'm both staying in for a change, 'cos I wants a word with the pair of you,' Jack announced one evening.

'You make it sound as if we're out gallivanting seven nights in the week,' protested Maddy. 'Come on, what's this mysterious word that's so important?' She was intrigued; he looked decidedly sheepish. He was also trying to suppress a grin, so it could not be anything disastrous.

'The truth be – in truth – I be thinking of getting wed again,' Jack blurted out.

There was an astonished silence, then, 'What?' cried Maddy.

'I— I wants to get wed.' He sounded hesitant, almost as if he were asking their permission.

'Well done, Father!' declared Lew.

So many questions crowded into Maddy's head that they tumbled out in a stream. 'Who is she—? How long have you been courting—? Why haven't you mentioned her before—? Have you fixed a date—? Oh goodness, I'll have to clean the house out before she comes.'

'Hold hard! Hold hard!' exclaimed Jack. 'Don't start no cleaning just yet. And let me answer one question afore you throws another at me. To start with, her'm called Joan Carey.'

Maddy had never heard of her. 'She's not from Stoke Gabriel, then?' she said in surprise. That her father had chosen a new wife was astonishing enough, that he had chosen a 'foreigner' from beyond the village boundaries was astounding.

'No, her'm a widow woman from Paignton.'

'But how did you meet her?' As far as Maddy could recall her father had not been to Paignton for months.

'Her'm working up to the Church House Inn. Lucy Ford be her cousin, and her'm come over to help out, them having been short-handed lately.'

So that was it. Maddy had heard that Lucy Ford had a relative helping her, but she had never met the woman.

'The Church House!' Maddy turned on Lew. 'Then you knew!'

'I did have an inkling, what with Father smelling of April and May,' admitted Lew. 'And Mrs Carey always filling his cider mug way over the brim.'

'And you never said anything!' Maddy protested.

'Wadn't up to me to speak out. 'Twere Father's business.'

Maddy had to admit he had a point. 'How come we've never seen this Mrs Carey? Not even in church,' she demanded.

Jack shrugged. 'Her'm got married childer over to Paignton as her goes to see of a Sunday. Doubtless her goes to church there.'

'How long has this been going on? Why didn't you tell us anything?'

'I didn't tell you naught, 'cos there wadn't naught to tell, not until recent, anyhow. What be the matter, maid? Don't you approve?' He sounded so anxious that Maddy was filled with remorse.

'Did I sound a bit sharp?' she asked. 'I'm sorry, I didn't mean to. It's just that… well, you have taken the wind out of my sails, rather. As for approving, of course we do, if she'll make you happy. If she doesn't…'

'Our Maddy'll go for her with the copper-stick while you and me hides behind the door,' Lew finished for her.

Maddy gave him a thump, wondering if, like her, he was remembering their mother, and thinking that here, yet again, was a mayor change in their lives.

'What's the right thing to do?' she asked, suddenly anxious. 'Is it up to us to ask Mrs Carey to tea so we can meet? Or is it more proper for her to say when she wants to come?'

'I don't knows about no ettyket,' said Jack. 'I think it'd be best to find out when Joan be free and act according. And if it be your courting night, boy, then you'm going to have to go without for once.'

'We'd better have Mrs Carey on her own first, don't you think?' Maddy asked, as Lew pulled a face. 'So we can get to know each other. We can have her family over some other time.'

'Lor, us can't be having her lot in one go, there idn't room. Her'm seven childer living, all married and increasing fit to beat the band, far as I can gather,' said Jack.

'I knows you'm been complaining about a lack of company of late, Father,' commented Lew. 'But idn't you going to extremes? At this rate I can see us sitting down to eat in shifts, like the Church Tea.'

In answer Jack aimed another mock blow at his son's head, which Lew again nimbly avoided.

'Do you know what we've forgotten?' Maddy's appalled voice stopped them both in mid-battle.

'What?' they both asked in alarm.

'To toast the happy couple! Lew, get the best glasses down while I hunt out the wine. We've got some of last year's elderberry that should be perfect.'

'Idn't it a bit odd, us doing this without no bride?' Jack asked.

'Us be only practising this time round,' said Lew, setting out the glasses. 'This way us gets two celebrations instead of one.'

'Ah,' said Jack approvingly, watching as Maddy poured out the rich ruby-red wine. 'I'll drink to that.'

Maddy was happy for her father, truly she was, but she was human enough to have some misgivings. Firstly came the natural pang of regret at the thought of another woman taking her mother's place. But this was the way of things, her mother was dead and her father could not be expected to live a bachelor existence for the rest of his days. Less easy to come to terms with was the fact that she would be losing her status in the home. For years now she had been in charge of the housekeeping, and that was going to change. How would she tolerate being subservient to someone else after all this time? She confessed to herself she was not looking forward to finding out. But before that the first hurdle had to be tackled. Her new stepmother had to be invited to tea.

On the day that Mrs Carey was to visit them Maddy set out the fresh white cloth and the best china, remembering how she used to prepare in just such a way for the coming of Patrick. Her father had always scoffed at her putting flowers on the table; on this occasion, when she set out a jug of Michaelmas daisies, he merely said, 'They'm handsome, maid.' He was restless with nervousness, too, and even Lew was fidgety. Maddy guessed they were all thinking the same thing. What if they did not take to one another? She, Lew and Jack – and Charlie when he was home – had their ups and downs, though on the whole they existed amicably as a family. That was one aspect of the new order she hoped was not going to alter.

Jack walked up to the Church House Inn to fetch his betrothed. At the sound of their approach Lew leapt to his feet. Maddy whipped off her apron, simultaneously checking she had not forgotten to set out anything vital and that the kettle hanging on its crook over the fire was boiling.

'And yer her be,' announced Jack proudly as he entered with his Joan. 'This be the future Mrs Shillabeer.'

Maddy's first impressions were favourable, for Mrs Carey proved to be a trim, neat little woman, with brisk movements and lively eyes.

'Joan, my handsome, this be Maddy,' continued Jack, 'and that long length of naught you know.'

Joan Carey greeted Maddy with a brisk, firm handshake. 'I be glad to meet you,' she said. 'Jack have told me a deal about you.' With Lew, however, it was impossible to be so formal. She took his hand also and said, 'I don't knows about a length of naught, boy, but you looks as though you'm cheaper to keep a week than a fortnight.'

'Oh, I idn't much trouble,' said Lew. 'A bed under the table and a dry crust from time to time, I don't needs no more.'

Joan looked at the table, laden with buttered lardy cake, splits spread with jam and clotted cream, and rich fruit cake. 'Maddy, my maid,' she said. 'I can sees you'm set out a rare tea for us three, but if you pardon me for saying so, where be the boy's dry crust?'

'Don't worry,' said Maddy. 'I'll fetch him one from the fowls' dish presently.'

Lew let out such an anguished wail that everyone laughed.

'Don't you take no heed of they two, they'm mazed,' Jack told Joan delightedly. 'Sit you down yer, I dare say you'm ready for summat to eat.'

All awkwardness dispelled, they settled down to tea. Maddy's initial anxieties about this big step her father was taking evaporated before his air of pride and the fond way he kept looking at his beloved. From her own point of view she felt relieved her prospective stepmother seemed such a pleasant, good-natured woman. Mrs Carey was bound to have had her own anxieties at meeting them, and Maddy hoped that they, too, had disappeared. There was, however, one matter which still troubled her. She decided it was best to settle it promptly, and this she did under pretext of showing Mrs Carey the garden.

'I hope you won't be annoyed,' she said. 'I mean you no disrespect by it, but please understand that I remember my own mother very clearly, and I feel no one else, no matter how agreeable, could ever take her place. Would you mind if, after you are wed to my father, I don't call you Mother?'

'Lor' bless you, cheel,' declared Joan Carey. 'I don't mind a bit. There'm enough as calls me Mother as 'tis, I don't needs no more. You call me Joan, maid, and I'll answer. There, be that the only thing as was troubling you, or be there aught else? For us may as well get things sorted out now as later.'

'There's nothing else,' said Maddy.

'Then if that be all I reckons us'll bide together proper handsome.'

'I'm sure we will,' Maddy agreed.

There were changes ahead for the Shillabeers, that was certain, but after so much bad luck and misery, Maddy felt that, at last, things were taking a turn for the better.

Chapter Fourteen

The pungent smell of burning assailed Maddy's nostrils from across the garden. Dropping the rake with which she had been cleaning out the fowls, she ran to the house to find the kitchen full of black smoke and the potato pan boiled dry. As she pulled the pot off the fire Joan appeared from upstairs.

'My dear days!' she cried. 'All they tiddies spoiled and the pan as well, I shouldn't wonder. Why didn't you keep an eye on un?'

'How could I? I was seeing to the fowls,' objected Maddy. 'I thought you were watching them, seeing that you were indoors.'

'I were indoors, I don't deny, but I were upstairs doing the bedrooms. You knows I always does they of a Thursday.'

And a Tuesday and a Saturday, too, if you get the chance, thought Maddy, for her new stepmother was proving to be a compulsive cleaner. Aloud she protested, 'You only did the bedrooms a couple of days ago.'

'I do un when they needs doing, I doesn't wait for no special day no matter what state they be in.' The implied criticism plus the slight emphasis on the I made Maddy's hackles rise.

'I've had no criticism about the cleanliness of the bedrooms in the past, doing them once a week,' she protested.

'What do men know about cleanliness?' said Joan scathingly. 'Most wouldn't notice if they had to shovel their way in.' Then a look of horror spread across her face. 'Oh my gawd, just look at the mud! Habn't you sense enough to take off they boots of youm afore you traipsed muck across the floor?'

'I didn't stop because I thought the house was on fire,' retorted Maddy indignantly. 'How was I to know it was just the potatoes you'd forgotten?'

'The potatoes *I'd* forgotten?' Joan's voice rose.

The next few minutes were lively, and finished with Maddy stalking out, dirty boots and all, and returning to the fowls in a fury.

When she had cooled down she recognised that the burnt potatoes had been no particular person's fault, they had been the victims of having two women in the same kitchen. Nor were they the first such casualties in the few months since her father's marriage. But the hinted suggestion that she had not kept the bedrooms clean had rankled. The trouble was that town-bred Joan was trying to maintain urban standards in the country. Maddy, who had been accustomed to fighting both country dirt and river mud all her life, had long ago accepted that a certain amount would find its way indoors. Joan had not yet reached this conclusion and was waging a hopeless war in the cause of spotless floors.

For most of the time Maddy got on well with her stepmother. She felt sympathy for her, too; life at Duncannon must have seemed far more quiet and isolated than anything she had experienced in the bustling resort of Paignton. She was also some distance from her children and grandchildren, yet Joan never complained. It was only in matters of cleanliness that her tongue grew sharp.

'Her habn't been turning out again?' complained Lew later as he prepared to go to Mollie's house for supper. 'I can't find my white muffler nowhere, and I be going to he late.'

'Look in your locker,' Maddy advised. 'That's the proper place for it in Joan's opinion, not hanging on the bedpost.'

'I put un there to dry off after I got caught in the rain,' he protested. 'Lor,I idn't saying naught about the woman, her'm a nice body, truly, but her don't give the spiders a minute to settle.'

'And when were we infested with spiders?' retorted Maddy indignantly, caught on the raw.

'I never said us was infested,' replied Lew soothingly. 'I just meant as those us did have was contented little souls.'

Maddy had to laugh. 'All right, perhaps I didn't dust away every single cobweb. I never seemed to have the time.'

Lew gave her a sympathetic smile. 'It can't be easy for you, having to move over for someone else,' he said.

'It's not.' Maddy could admit it to him alone. 'Joan is very good. Most of the time we manage well enough. It's only when something untoward happens, such as today, when the potatoes burned.'

'You'll get used to un, given time,' said Lew.

Maddy doubted it. She had found an independent streak in herself she had never realised she possessed, a streak which resisted being told what to do by anyone else. This was a problem she feared time would not solve.

Time had not solved her love for Patrick, either. How long had it been since he had gone? Four – five months? Yet she still missed him, and although the agonising pain of losing him had eased to a dull ache, it remained with her. No one had any definite news of his whereabouts or of Victoria's. Rumours abounded, and from time to time Mr Fitzherbert, despite his pronouncement that he no longer had a daughter, would ride off somewhere in a flurry of oaths and sparking carriage wheels. But soon he would return alone in a more foul mood than before.

For the first time in her life Maddy began to learn what it was to have time on her hands. With only two men in the house and two women to look after them there were often not enough domestic chores to go round, even allowing for Joan's mania for housework. Maddy, as the now-subservient female, would wander over to help Annie or to read to her. She took to knitting stockings for William, since, with two sets of needles busily employed in the Shillabeer household every evening, Jack, Lew, and Charlie, who was still working on the stone barges, were more than well provided for. But Maddy was restless. Looking back she could remember innumerable times when she had longed for a lessening of her duties, and time to herself. She could have as much as she wanted now, and she found she did not like it. In fact, she resented it.

–

'I don't suppose it be easy for you,' remarked Annie when they had finally closed the pages of *Wuthering Heights* and were having a cup of tea.

'What isn't easy?' Maddy asked.

'Having another woman in the house after all these years.'

'We'll manage well enough,' Maddy said, determined to be loyal.

'I dare say it can't be easy.' Annie took a sip of tea. 'But when things is bad look on the bright side; your father couldn't have taken up with a better woman than Joan. Her'm sober and hard working, and though her tongue can be sharp her idn't no shrew. And things can't always be simple for her, you know, coming into the house where there's already a grown woman in charge.'

Maddy knew that she spoke the truth yet she could not help still feeling restless.

'It's as if I'm no use any more,' she complained to Lew.

'No use? How d'you make that out?' he had replied. 'When Mollie and me are married you'm going to be the only one left at home. Then you'm going to find out how much use you be.'

Was that to be her future? As a companion to her father and Joan for a few years and then, as they grew steadily more frail and elderly, their sole support and succour? Lew had been right, she would certainly be needed then, but it was not the idyllic future she had dreamed of with Patrick.

Soon she and Joan, both women used to being occupied every minute of every day, were reduced to looking about for things to do, particularly when the inclement weather prevented them working out of doors.

'You'll be holystoning the logs and scrubbing the fowls soon,' commented Maddy one day as Joan began polishing the already gleaming brass yet again. She had meant it as a joke, but her stepmother took it the wrong way and made a retort about hoity-toity females who had nothing better to do than be sarcastic. The result was one of the squabbles which were becoming more frequent. The trouble was that they were cooped up together too much – the incessant rain saw to that.

Then the wind swung to the north-east, turning the rain to snow and bringing with it searing gales. No one could remember such severe and continuous storms. The large estate of Sharpham, across the river, lost stand after stand of fine mature trees, and the river ran swift and murky, carrying along with it great baulks of timber which smashed into small boats and anything else that got in their way. It became too dangerous for the quarry boats to sail and since the stone could not be moved there was no point in cutting more; in any case the work was becoming more and more dangerous in the icy conditions. Jack and most of the other workers were sacked. Lew was out of work too.

'There idn't no boats going in or out of Dartmouth, so there idn't no cargoes to bring upriver, nor to carry down,' he explained. 'Mr Chambers'll send for me soon as he can, but for the time being his boat be laid up. Laid up and snowed up,' he added with wry humour.

It was a situation that had arisen before from time to time; on this occasion week slipped into week. Joan's face began to grow grave, and

Maddy knew the reason why. Her stepmother had taken charge of the housekeeping money, but Maddy was well aware how difficult things were becoming.

'There, I can't find no more.' Jack turned out his pockets and produced a few pence. 'What about you, boy?'

Lew's search unearthed a shilling and a sixpence. The entire family's finances, plus the contents of the Delft jug, came to a little over five shillings.

'That be all us got,' said Joan anxiously. 'What be us going to do?'

'Well, this weather idn't going to change for a spell, so us habn't no hope there,' Jack pronounced gloomily. 'And if there were aught in the way of jobs going, don't you think us'd ave taken un? We'm going out every day looking, idn't us, boy?'

'Certainly us be,' said Lew. 'Us idn't the only ones, that be the trouble. I reckon at least half the men in the village be out of work, thanks to the weather.'

'We know you try hard,' said Maddy. 'No one was suggesting otherwise.'

'If there idn't work for men there might be summat for females,' said Jack. It was evidence of the seriousness of the situation that he should swallow his pride enough to suggest such a thing.

'There's nothing casual to be had. I know. I've looked,' said Maddy. Ironically, in this bad winter there had been no usual mild epidemic that might have given her occasional work.

'What be stopping you looking for summat full time, then?' stated Joan, adding defensively, 'I don't know why you'm looking so surprised. I can't go out to work, can I, not with the house to see to? If anyone goes it must be Maddy.'

Strangely enough the idea of looking for a full-time job had never occurred to Maddy. Accustomed as she was to being tied to the house she had thought in terms of the part-time or casual employment that she had always done. She was no longer needed in the house, was she? She had been ousted from that position and was now free to take up work anywhere.

'I haven't heard of anything round here,' she said. 'I could ask the parson's wife or the squire's. They might know of someone up-country who needs a servant.'

'No!' Jack spoke so emphatically that everyone looked at him in surprise. 'You idn't working for no strangers,' he said firmly. 'When

I mentioned you females finding work I wadn't thinking of no one going away. There've been enough childer lost to me of late, I idn't losing no more. Oh, the boy there will get wed directly and leave home, I dare say, but that be different. I idn't having my only maid wandering off goodness knows where. Her'm biding yer, and her'm going to go on biding yer, and that be final.'

Maddy was touched by his unusually determined attitude; nevertheless, she noticed that, although he accepted marriage as a legitimate reason for Lew leaving home, he clearly considered there were no such prospect for her. She agreed with him, but the thought stung just the same.

'Right, I start looking for work tomorrow,' she said.

It seemed reasonable to begin the search for employment among the larger houses in the village. She went out as far as Aish and Waddeton and Sandridge. The one place she avoided was the Fitzherberts' residence; but it made no difference, there was no work to be had. It was tricky tramping about the countryside, the surface of the snow had frozen to a glacial treachery, causing her to slip and slide at every step.

She had to admit that perhaps her appearance was against her, swathed in cloaks and shawls as she was against the biting cold, her boots bound with sacking to get some grip on the icy lanes. Rejected by the gentry, she hoped the farmers' wives would be less fussy about the looks of those who offered themselves into service, but here again she was disappointed. With the severe conditions restricting their dairying and their marketing, no one, not even Janie, Rob Bradworthy's wife, could offer her employment. The thought never entered Maddy's mind to try at Oakwood; the idea of working there was too preposterous to be considered.

Exhausted by her arduous wanderings and dispirited by her lack of success, Maddy would have headed straight home if, by chance, she had not passed the Victoria and Albert. Mrs Watkins was sweeping dirt out through the open door, a sour expression on her face. The sight of the landlady doing such a menial task brought Maddy to a halt.

'I'm looking for work, Mrs Watkins,' she said. 'Do you need any help? I'm strong, reliable, and willing to tackle anything.'

'You'm idn't wanting to live in, I hopes?' Mrs Watkins leaned on her broom and glared at her.

'No, thank you, I'd prefer to live at home.'

'Thank gawd for that. Last stupid wench never knowd which bed were her'n. Got in with the ostler once too often. I had to pack her off back to her mother. When can you start?'

'Tomorrow morning.'

'Right, be here at seven.'

'And the wages?'

'Five shilling and your dinner, and make that seven o'clock sharp, mind.'

'When do I finish?'

Mrs Watkins looked surprised. 'When you'm done,' she said.

Five shillings a week was poor wages by anyone's standards, even including the food, and Maddy had a strong suspicion she would earn every penny.

She was right. She had never doubted her ability to work hard, but by the end of the first day she wondered if she would survive. She had gained some experience of inn work at the Three Feathers in Exeter, but that bore no resemblance to the hard labour she now endured.

As well as being a hard taskmistress, Elsie Watkins was short-tempered, liable to lash out if things were not to her liking. Maddy tolerated the curses and insults, but when Elsie aimed a blow at the side of her head she decided enough was enough. She saw the clout coming and dodged. Leaping to her feet she faced up to her employer, her fists clenched.

'You strike me one blow, Elsie Watkins, and it's two you'll get back!' she exclaimed.

Mrs Watkins retreated, disconcerted by the unexpected threat of retaliation. 'Then just you see you does the work proper, that's all,' she blustered.

There were no more threats of violence, but that did not make the work any easier. A less determined soul would have given up, but somehow Maddy managed to stand it. The family needed the money.

''Tis too much for you, maid,' protested Joan time after time, as Maddy slumped exhausted in front of the fire. 'I knows I was the one as suggested you should find work. I regrets it now, truly I do. I never meant naught like this.'

'I can put up with it.' Maddy tried to smile reassuringly.

Joan shook her head. 'Give un up, my lover,' she urged. 'Us'll manage somehow. 'Sides, better weather's bound to come soon.'

Eventually Maddy did give up her job, in quite a dramatic fashion. One morning Elsie Watkins decided the stairs were not being scrubbed to her satisfaction. There was nothing wrong with them, of course. Maddy had got them white as a hound's tooth, but Elsie was in a bad mood and refused to be satisfied.

'If you can't clean un proper first time, then you'm going to have to do un again,' she snapped and, raising her foot, she deliberately kicked over the bucket.

Maddy was on her knees at the bottom of the stairs when the bucket toppled over and she caught the full force of the dirty water.

'You get they stairs properly clean, do you hear?' snapped Elsie. Saying not a word, Maddy picked up the empty bucket and went out into the yard to fill it, not at the pump but from the rain tub, where she had to break thick ice first. Then she marched back indoors.

Elsie was gathering up empty tankards when she entered, and at the sight of Maddy stalking through the bar parlour instead of heading for the stairs, a frown darkened her face. 'What do—?' That was all she had time to say before Maddy emptied the entire bucket of icy water over her head. Elsie could do nothing but gasp at the shock of it, while the customers were convulsed with laughter.

Leaning over the counter, Maddy took a florin from the till and held it up. 'I've taken my wages,' she said. 'You owe me two and a penny for two and a half days' work, but I'll let you off the odd penny.' With that she strode out, collecting up her cloak and scarves with one sweep of her arm as she went. She was so furious she did not notice the cold even though she had gone quite a way before she pulled on her outdoor clothes over her sodden dress and apron.

At the sight of her, Joan gasped. 'Maid, the state of you!' she exclaimed. 'You'm a sheet of ice!'

Maddy looked down. Her apron had frozen solid, and her skirts were stiff with the cold. She was forced to stand in front of the fire to thaw before she could undress with Joan's help, for her fingers were completely numb.

'You'm idn't going back there, that's for certain,' Jack declared when he heard the story. 'Us idn't standing no more capers like that from yon Watkins woman.'

'I don't think she'd have me.' Maddy grinned at the recollection of the wet and gasping Elsie.

'Maybe not,' agreed Jack, beginning to smile too.

Surprisingly, Maddy suffered no ill effects from her soaking, though Elsie Watkins took to her bed for two days. The story put out was that she had taken a chill, but the entire village put her illness down to sheer temper. Unemployment again stared Maddy in the face, and though she tried hard there was nothing available. The only money coming in now was the few pennies for the equally few eggs.

'They fowls be all us has left,' said Joan. 'They'm going to have to go.' But Maddy was reluctant. Although it was sometimes necessary, she hated killing her beloved hens, and besides, once they were gone, so was a source of income, no matter how meagre.

'Give it a few more days,' she said. 'Something might happen.'

What did happen was a slight shift of wind. It blew as fiercely as ever, but having backed round more to the west it lost its bitter edge. The rims of the icy snowdrifts began to crumble, and the lanes ran with melt-water, making them as impassable as before. Some shipping began to move, but not enough for Mollie's father to call Lew back to work. As for the quarry, the conditions there were still too dangerous for it to reopen. In an attempt to earn some money, Jack and Lew did risk going out on the swiftly flowing river to do some handlining, but the catches were poor. Then the whisper went round the village that the iron ore man was buying again.

Iron mining had been a thriving business in Devon, until the recent development of the Welsh industry. That had caused most of the mines scattered throughout the region to close. However, occasionally a local demand for ore would send the traders out to see what could be bought from the abandoned mines. The gleaning was usually done by women, so the instant she heard the rumour Maddy kitted herself out with a basket and barrow and an old mattock head whose angled blade was exactly right for digging up bits of surface ore.

'You'm idn't really going to do un?' protested Joan, watching her wrap herself up protectively in sacking. 'It sounds terrible hard, dirty work.'

'The dirt will wash off, and compared to working for Elsie Watkins, this will be a picnic,' Maddy said, and she trundled her barrow to the old mine.

Gathering the ore did not involve digging in the old workings themselves. Although they had been abandoned for no more than two or three years, they had become extremely dangerous. Instead, the women picked up the nuggets of iron ore that were scattered about the surrounding field. That was the theory. In reality, the surface ore had embedded itself in the earth, or got overgrown with grass and weeds, or was resting at the bottom of mud-filled ruts. Anything, in fact, but lying conveniently on top of the ground waiting to be picked up.

A difficult and messy task it was, hacking lumps of the red-brown stone from earth that had not quite thawed. Before long, Maddy's hands were raw from gripping the short stub of mattock handle and she was caked in mud. As for her back, she tried not to think of it. Remembering her light-hearted words earlier that morning, she began to wonder if she had been too optimistic. The one thing which kept her going was the thought that each load of muddy stones in the basket meant a few more coins in the Delft jug at home.

The work did not end at the Mine Field. When she had gathered as much as she could shift, Maddy pushed her barrow back through the village to the Mill Pool. She was not alone. Other women were taking the same road. Not all had barrows, some carried their ore in baskets or sacks. There was no cheerful banter as there would have been after harvest or apple gathering. Everyone was too exhausted. Once by the waterside, Maddy and the other women washed the mud from each lump of ore. The salt water got into the cuts, grazes, and chilblains which every woman bore, and more than one was obliged to straighten up for a moment and tuck her smarting hands under her armpits, her lips pressed together with the pain.

A cottager living near the quay acted as agent, weighing the ore and handing over the money. It was a pitiful amount for such strenuous effort, but as Maddy walked wearily homewards she found the jingle of coins in her pocket comforting.

There was no knowing how long the demand for ore would last, so Maddy was back at the Mine Field betimes next morning to make the most of it. The second day was no easier than the first, harder in some respects for hands that were already raw. And it was certainly muddier, since the field was considerably churned up from the previous day's activities. By the time Maddy was pushing her full barrow in the direction of the Mill Pool again, she could barely shuffle along from fatigue.

In this state she encountered Cal Whitcomb. She was so well caked with mud she hoped she might be unrecognisable. It was a vain hope.

'What the hell have you been doing?' he demanded angrily, causing his gelding to prance uneasily.

The vehemence of his greeting brought her up short. Tired as she was she rapped out, 'I will thank you not to use such language to me, sir!'

At her sharp response he had the grace to look disconcerted.

'You are right. I apologise most humbly. But I ask you again. What have you been doing?'

The wording might have been more courteous but his tone remained indignant.

'I haven't been on your land, if that is what is troubling you,' retorted Maddy.

'Been on it? You're taking half of it away with you, by the look of things.' He was gazing not at the contents of her barrow as he spoke, but at the mud which clung to her makeshift sacking overalls.

'If you can find a cleaner way of picking ore I would be glad to hear of it.' Her indignation at his comments made her speech more precise.

'Picking ore? Is that what you've been doing?' he asked, although he could plainly see her full barrow. Then he demanded with greater indignation, 'Is that the best you can do, woman?'

'Who are you calling "woman" in that way?' cried Maddy angrily. 'And since you ask, yes, it is the best I can do. It has been a very hard winter, in case you haven't noticed, and some of us like to eat.'

Cal's mouth tightened, whether with remorse at his rudeness or greater fuiy she could not tell.

'Tip that rubbish away,' he rapped out, pointing to her barrow with his riding crop. 'And come up to Oakwood first thing tomorrow morning. I'll find you something to do.'

Maddy's anger boiled over at such condescension. 'You will find me something to do?' she repeated mockingly. 'And what makes you think I want anything that you might find for me?'

'It would be better than picking ore,' snapped Cal.

'That is your opinion. It is not mine.' With great dignity she grasped the handles of her barrow and left him, her head erect.

'The offer stands,' he called after her.

But she did not turn her head.

Anger gave momentum to her feet, and she was past the Baptist Chapel and well on her way into the village before she began to cool down. She accepted that her reaction owed much to humiliation that Cal should have seen her in such a state. Relations between them had eased considerably over the last year, but she was still reluctant for a Whitcomb to see a Shillabeer at a disadvantage.

She was further on her journey, at the top of Mill Hill, before the full enormity of the encounter struck her. Cal Whitcomb had offered her a job. He had said he would find her something to do. Once before she had fancied he had been on the point of offering her work, but that could have been her imagination. There was no imagining it now, though. His offer had been definite. A Whitcomb proposing to employ a Shillabeer; a Shillabeer working for a Whitcomb. She did not know which was the more incredible. At home she made no mention of Cal's extraordinary behaviour. There was no point since, naturally, she had no intention of taking up his offer.

There was hardly any sleep for her that night. Every bone and muscle in her body ached too much for that; worst of all were her hands. In spite of Joan anointing them with soothing ointment and binding them with clean rags, they were an agony to Maddy that did not diminish with the hours. She had plenty of time to think, and as the hours went by, another day picking over the Mine Field began to seem less attractive, while working for Cal began to appear more feasible. But, no, a Shillabeer working at Oakwood was out of the question.

While searching for stray hairpins next morning, Maddy chanced to take the glass dish down from the mantelshelf. There, looking in two directions at the same time, was the Janus ring. As she fingered it, a vision of deep blue eyes and a laughing mouth came to her, along with the ghost of a sweet song played on the fiddle: 'Miss Madeleine's Air'. Did Patrick ever play it these days? Or was it destined to be banished from the world because it no longer interested him, just as he had banished her from his life once she had forfeited his interest?

Maddy felt the pain inside her as sharply as ever as bittersweet memories assailed her. Patrick had taken so much from her, yet he had also given her much: confidence, the ambition to better herself, a sense of her own worth; though looking at her reflection in the mirror she had to admit there were precious few signs of any of those qualities these days. She was dressed for picking ore, her shabby dress impregnated with red mud, dirty sacks tied about her, her hair scraped back in its old style because… because what was the point of making an effort?

Continuing to stare at her shabby image in the looking-glass, Maddy felt the stirrings of anger. Was she the sort of woman who existed only if she had a man to lean on? A weak shadow of a creature with no character of her own? Disgust at herself made her clench her fist tightly, inadvertently crushing the Janus ring out of shape. But perfect or distorted, surely his powers were the same? He was still the god of beginnings… She decided she had to make yet another new start; there was no alternative, and this one she must not let slip away.

It was as well that Joan was over at Annie's when Maddy left the house, for she would have commented that the well-brushed dress and cloak, the clean apron, and the softly-dressed hair were scarcely suitable for a day picking ore.

When Maddy reached Oakwood Farm she stopped. As she opened the side gate into the yard, she acknowledged that she felt nervous in spite of herself. Supposing Cal had not meant his offer? Supposing he had changed his mind? The one way to find out was to risk humiliation and go and look for him.

Boldly she entered the farmyard. The first person she met was Ellen, who was making for the kitchen door, a basket of eggs on her arm.

'Back again?' said the maid. 'You'm a glutton for punishment, I give you that.'

'I'm looking for Mr Whitcomb,' Maddy said.

'Didn't think you was visiting her!' Ellen jerked her head in the direction of the kitchen. 'As for Mr Cal, he'm to the poundhouse – that'n there, across the yard. And if anyone asks, as far as I be concerned you'm idn't yer.'

'Very wise,' said Maddy, and was rewarded with a toothless grin.

The sound of voices echoed from the stone-built poundhouse. The time for pressing apples was long gone. Nevertheless, when Maddy stepped inside the cool, dark building, the sweet scent of fermenting fruit still filled the air. As testament to the vast amount of apples they pulped, Oakwood Farm boasted a huge granite crushing wheel that needed a horse to shift it, a far cry from the manually-driven roller which had caused Davie's muscles to ache so. Beneath the wheel was an equally large stone basin which held the fruit to be crushed. They were both clean and idle now, while alongside stood the great wooden press which was used to squeeze the juice from the pulped apples. Noting its size, Maddy wondered at Cal's plans to set up a second one some day. It showed the extent of his ambition, for his existing press must have been easily the largest for miles around.

There was no one about in that part of the building; the nimble of men's voices was coming from the next room. Moving to the doorway, she saw Cal with two other men. They were siphoning cider into a fresh barrel from one of the sixty-gallon hogsheads which stood against the wall. Not wishing to interrupt, she stood in silence.

One of the workers saw her first. Such was his astonishment at the sight of her that his jaw fell open and he lost his concentration, letting the precious cider spill.

Cal gave a curse. Then he, too, saw her. He showed no surprise. 'I will be with you directly,' he said, turning his attention back to filling the hogshead, as if her presence were the most natural thing in the world. He completely ignored the open astonishment on the faces of his workmen. Not until the job was done did he dismiss the men and come over to Maddy.

'They'll enjoy being the first to spread the word that there's a Shillabeer about the place,' he said, indicating his departing workers with a jerk of his head.

'The second,' corrected Maddy. 'I met Ellen on the way here.'

'Ah, then she'll fend off the worst of the attack. I might even get my dinner in peace.'

At his words, Maddy felt awkward. She was certain he was regretting offering her a job, understandably so when she considered how much trouble it would cause with his mother. Not certain what to say next she remarked, 'You're late racking your cider.'

'This has already been racked three times,' he said, referring to the careful drawing-off of the cider from the sediment which collected at the bottom of the barrels. 'But this is destined to be Oakwood Farm Superior, that's why it is getting an extra racking. After that it will be matured for a good three years.'

'That should be superior indeed. I've never heard of a cider being kept that long.'

'You see now why I'm considering expanding the poundhouse. I need the extra storage room. I've other ideas, too. I want a second press, as you know. And the mill doesn't crush enough fruit; it's time it was replaced. As far as I can tell it's been here since my great-grandfather's time. *Our* great-grandfather,' he corrected with a grin. 'And I want to do away with the horses too and have everything driven by steam.'

'Steam?' exclaimed Maddy, astonished at such forward thinking.

'I intend to drive only the machinery by steam. The workers will still have to move by themselves,' he said, straightfaced.

'That's a relief. I thought you were trying to put me off working here.' Maddy paused. 'There's no need for you to think up daft stories, you know. If you've changed your mind about employing me, you've only to say so.'

'I haven't changed my mind. I'm just relieved to see you, particularly after I was rude to you.' He suddenly threw out his arms in a bewildered gesture. 'How is it that when I want to help you I begin by insulting you?'

Maddy pondered for a moment. 'It's a sop to your Whitcomb blood, so that you can then help a Shillabeer with a clear conscience.'

His laughter rang up to the rafters and echoed round the large barrels lining the walls. 'You could be right,' he chuckled. 'Come along and I'll show you where you are going to work.'

Maddy had been vaguely aware of female voices sounding nearby. Cal led her to a neighbouring outbuilding. The moment they entered, the laughing and talking ceased, and the three women who had been working there looked at them with mute astonishment.

'I don't believe my eyes!' exclaimed one of them at last.

'I think you all know Maddy Shillabeer,' said Cal calmly. 'She's come to work here.' Three pairs of jaws dropped as far as the men's had done. Cal ignored them. 'I'll just tell you briefly what your duties will be,' he said to Maddy. 'Susan and the others can be more specific. At the moment we're busy bottling the new season's cider.' With a sweep of his arm he indicated a table laden with grey stone flagons. Picking up one which had been already filled, he said, 'There, that's a gallon of Oakwood Farm Regular ready for market, complete with the Oakwood Farm label.' Briefly he ran his finger over the paper label, a gesture filled with pride. 'And here we're bottling the Superior,' he went on, putting down the stone jar and moving to another table.

'Glass bottles!' exclaimed Maddy in surprise. 'I've never heard of that for cider before.'

'There's never been a cider of the quality of Oakwood Superior before. It deserves something special. It's a family recipe that was handed down from my great-grandfather.'

'That would be *our* great-grandfather again, would it?' asked Maddy. Old habits died hard, and she found herself thinking it was typical of a Whitcomb to build a business on something which should have belonged to her family, and employing her to help him into the bargain.

Cal grinned and shook his head. 'This time the great-grandfather is entirely mine, old Granfer Whitcomb, who was a notable cider-maker in his day, they say.'

'Oh…' Maddy felt somewhat abashed. To cover her discomfort she asked, 'Do you sell all your cider in such small quantities?'

'No, we've customers in Totnes and Newton Abbot who take it by the hogshead. Not enough of them yet, but I plan on getting lots more.'

Maddy had been doing some calculations. 'You say you're bottling the Superior now,' she said, 'but you told me it has to stand for three years. Surely you haven't been in business that long?'

'And you think I might be cheating my customers with this batch, eh?' His eyes were bright with humour. 'No, I would not risk my reputation. Oakwood Farm Superior, when it reaches the market, must be absolutely prime.'

'Then how…?'

'I haven't been selling cider for three years, but I've been making it for a lot longer. This lot was put down years back, never fear.'

She should have known better than to question him. Was not Cal Whitcomb's ambition and business sense a byword? Trust him to have begun planning his cider company a long time ago.

'If you have no more questions, I'll leave you to Susan's tender mercies.' He turned to leave, then paused. 'There are canvas aprons hanging up over there,' he said, pointedly looking at her own clean apron and neat brown woollen skirt.

Knowing he was silently referring to her muddy state after picking ore, Maddy almost made a sharp retort, but bit it back in time. He was her employer now, therefore she must guard her tongue. She suspected she had already taken rather too many liberties as it was, but she had no intention of letting him get away with his inference entirely.

'We haven't discussed wages yet,' she said. 'Or is a canvas pinny all I'm getting?'

'You'll get the same as the others, seven shillings a week, working from eight o'clock until six o'clock on weekdays, and you finish at noon on Saturdays. You get an hour off for your dinner – it gives you time to get home. And breakages have to be paid for. Will that do?'

Maddy nodded, wanting to thank him, yet again not knowing how.

'How come you'm working yer?' demanded Susan, when he had gone.

'There was a job going so I took it,' replied Maddy.

Susan looked disappointed, she had been hoping for a more exciting explanation. But she refused to give up the drama of the situation.

'Do this mean that the Whitcombs and the Shillabeers bain't daggers drawn no more?' she asked.

'If it do, I idn't going to be the one to tell Ma Whitcomb,' said one of the others. And everyone laughed.

'Us'd best get back to work or us'll have the maister after us, and he can be every bit as hard as his ma when he'm a mind,' said Susan.

'Is he difficult to work for?' asked Maddy.

'As maisters go he idn't bad. The wages be a bit stingy, but he pays prompt. Mind, he'm a Tartar if you don't work proper. Just let him catch you spilling more'n you should, or if he gets one whiff of soda in the bottles 'cos they habn't been rinsed proper, and my word, thunder and lightning habn't naught on he. Us washes the bottles in the shippen there.' Susan indicated a small lean-to at the end of the shed. 'This weather us takes turns with the washing.'

Maddy was surprised. She expected to be delegated to that task, since it seemed the least pleasant.

'It be nice and warm in there,' explained Susan, seeing her puzzled expression. 'The boiler be there for the hot water. Can't have un in yer, it'd get too warm for the cider and us'd have the bungs shooting out all over the place. There, that be enough jawing. Get a pinny and start filling they one-gallon flagons.'

Maddy enjoyed her first day's work. Compared to her recent employment it seemed almost a rest cure, and though it might have become monotonous after a while, the women had organised themselves to change tasks at regular intervals to break the tedium. Corking the bottles of Superior intrigued Maddy the most, for the corks had to be forced in by a handheld machine, then secured with wires. Afterwards they were covered with tinfoil.

'Fancy, eh?' said Susan, seeing her interest. 'Do you see 'tis green tinfoil matches the leaves on the label? Thinks of everything, do the maister.' Then she looked grave. 'Us'd best see how you gets on afore us puts you on bottling the Superior. Get that wrong and us could be given our marching orders.'

Somehow Maddy doubted it, nevertheless she accepted the decision without comment. It was easily the most interesting job and as a newcomer she could not expect to be allocated to it yet.

The most trying aspect of the day was the inquisitiveness of her workmates. The fact that she was working there had aroused their curiosity, and their stream of questions, although good-natured, seemed endless. Maddy parried them all with equal good humour, while at the same time admitting to herself that some of their queries struck home uncomfortably. The one about her father's reaction to her working at Oakwood, for instance. That was something she would find out before nightfall, and she was dreading it.

Maddy had time to go home to eat at midday. Jack was out in the boat hand-lining, and she was thankful to find herself alone with her stepmother. Joan regarded her tidy appearance with raised eyebrows.

'You habn't been picking ore, then?'

'No. I've got myself a new job.' Maddy hesitated. 'I'm getting seven shillings a week up at Oakwood, bottling cider.'

'Seven shillings a week regular!' Not having been bred to the long-standing feud, Joan grasped the most important point first. 'That idn't bad. And it be easier than ore picking any day. Your father idn't going to be too pleased, of course, but it can't be helped. Tis far better'n you killing yourself lugging lumps of iron ore or getting lung fever from being soaked working for Elsie Watkins. No, he idn't going to be pleased, but for seven shillings regular he'm going to have to put up with un.'

Joan's casual acceptance of the momentous step she had taken cheered Maddy. All the same, she was quite relieved to have a few hours' respite. She wondered how Cal was faring. She feared it would take more than the skinny presence of Ellen to deflect his mother's fury from him. She was right.

'Could hear her clear across the yard.' Susan, who lived some distance away and therefore ate her dinner by the warmth of the shippen boiler, was only too happy to regale the others with the events of the last hour. 'The things her called him – and you, Maddy,' she added with a grin. Then her face grew serious. 'There idn't many men as'd put up with un, and that be the truth. Going on like that! Tidn't as though he were a drunkard nor a womaniser nor naught. Course, the other son were her favourite, everyone knows that, but 'tidn't no cause for her blaming maister because his brother died of the cholera and he didn't.'

'It must be difficult for un, the maister I means,' said one of the other women. 'He'm all her's got and he'm responsible for her. He can't live elsewhere, not with the farm and everything to hand, and I doesn't fancy his chances of persuading her to move.'

'That's why he'm never married, if you asks me,' said Liza. 'What man'd want to bring a bride into a house along of her?' Maddy listened to the conversation and felt guilty. Because of a kindness to her, Cal Whitcomb was having an unpleasant time. He was not the sort to crumble under the onslaught, she knew, but it was not right for him to be uncomfortable because of a good deed. Sadly there was nothing she could do about it save give up her job, and she could not afford to do that. Somehow she did not think Cal would want her to.

'You'm joking,' was Jack's immediate reaction when she told him she was working at Oakwood. When he realised that she was serious, his anger exploded. 'Working for a Whitcomb? What do you think you'm about, maid? Be you'm off your head or summat? How you could even consider such a thing be more than I can fathom. A daughter of mine up to Oakwood! You'm idn't going back and that be for sure. Things be bad but they idn't that desperate.'

'Yes they be,' broke in Joan before Maddy could protest. 'The maid be bringing in seven shillings a week. It be honest, regular, and us can't afford to turn un away.'

'Yes us can,' retorted Jack furiously. 'Whitcomb money bain't never honest. True enough, us had to rely on Cal Whitcomb up to Exeter, but that were an emergency, and us paid un back.'

'And idn't this an emergency, not having enough money for food beyond tomorrow? I don't see no problem.' Joan was adamant. 'Maybe you'd rather see your own daughter slaving her heart out for a pittance. If so, you'm a funny sort of father.'

'You don't see it our way,' put in Lew. 'Maddy have – well, her've betrayed the family in a way. I idn't saying as Cal Whitcomb wouldn't be a decent enough fellow and a good maister if he were anybody but a Whitcomb, but he *be* a Whitcomb, and there idn't no getting away from the fact.'

'Load of stuff and nonsense, if you asks me,' retorted Joan. 'Making this fuss about summat that happened afore any of us was thought of, never mind born. The Whitcombs have Oakwood and the Shillabeers have this cottage, that's the way it be; you may as well forget everything as went afore and make the best of un.'

'Make the best of un! Forget everything as went afore!' Jack was almost beside himself with rage. 'You think us should ignore being cheated out of our inheritance? You don't understand naught about un, woman! The farm and all as goes with it should've gone to my father and thence to us, and it would've done if my Uncle Matt habn't bewildered a poor old man with weak wits into leaving the place to him. That's how the Whitcombs got un, through cheating and treachery. And you say us should ignore that?'

'I don't understand naught about cheating and treachery, any more'n I knows much about inheritance and such,' said Joan calmly. 'But I knows one thing: farms don't run themselves. Where were your father while all this were going on, Jack Shillabeer? Who were doing the ploughing and sowing and harvesting and tending the stock? It seems to me as your grandfather wadn't the least bit weak witted. It seems to me he left the farm to the son as'd done the work while t'other were gallivanting about the world getting neither wiser nor richer, from what I've heard. And it also seems to me that if your father had inherited Oakwood, there'd have been precious little of un left by now, him having the reputation for not being able to keep a coin in his pocket long enough for un to get warm.'

A stunned silence greeted this heresy. Even Maddy, whose side Joan had taken with such energy, was shaken. A belief which had been instilled in her since birth was being rocked to its foundations. But shocking though Joan's words had been, there was a deal of sense in them; too much for comfort. Looking towards her father and brother, she noted that Lew seemed less confident now. Even Jack, renowned for his obstinacy in everything connected with the old feud, looked uncomfortable, as if he were grappling with doubts.

Joan set aside her knitting. 'Shall I make us a cup of tea?' she asked. 'Us wants to be in bed betimes, don't us? Specially Maddy. It'd look real bad if her were late on only her second day working to Oakwood.' She paused and regarded her husband questioningly. When there was no further argument, she reached for the kettle, giving Maddy a triumphant wink as she did so.

Maddy rose to fetch the tea caddy with a feeling of gratitude; she had never expected her stepmother to be such a spirited champion. Whether Joan's views on the old feud were right or not, she knew that they shared the same sense of relief – the seven shillings a week were secure. She could go on working for Cal Whitcomb.

Chapter Fifteen

Maddy soon found that working for Cal Whitcomb was no easy option. He demanded perfection, and everything connected with Oakwood Cider had to be first class, particularly the Superior. Woe betide anyone who failed to notice a flawed bottle or who did not twist the wire over the cork securely. He was a stickler over waste, too, quickly commenting on spoiled labels and discarded foil. Most of all, though, he hated to see his precious cider spilled.

'I don't slave over the cider-making to have you wash the floor with it!' he was wont to roar at anyone who was careless. A repeated offender would find her wages docked; as a result the workers in the bottling shed soon developed a steady hand and a good eye.

'Don't take it to heart,' Maddy consoled a tearful Susan, who had just felt the force of his fury over a dropped bottle of Superior. 'I'm sure he didn't mean it.'

'But he said if it happened again I could look for work elsewhere,' wept Susan.

'I'm sure it won't happen again, you aren't usually clumsy,' said Maddy. 'But if it did, I'm convinced he wouldn't dismiss you. He's just in a bad mood this morning, that's all.'

'He'm idn't half getting short-tempered these days,' commented Liza. 'I reckon he'm taking on too much, what with two farms and the cider business. He'm trying to run everything single-handed and it be too much for one body.'

It was as if Cal had beard her, for one morning soon afterwards he came into the bottling shed and announced, 'I'm looking for a checker and overseer. Who feels they could do the job?'

'What would we be checking and overseeing?' asked Maddy.

'The work would involve checking the deliveries of empty bottles for cracks and flaws, counting them, making sure they are properly washed, and checking the filled bottles of Rough, Regular and

Superior. The job is worth an extra one and six a week; whoever takes it will earn their money because I will hold them responsible for the good condition of everything that leaves the bottling shed.'

Faces that had looked hopeful at the mention of the extra one and six now grew doubtful.

'And there is the paperwork,' went on Cal.

'That be me out,' muttered Susan. 'Never was no good with a pen.'

'Me neither,' agreed Liza.

'I can figure a bit,' said Gertie, the fourth woman present. 'If it idn't too difficult, that is.'

'It would be keeping account of stocks of materials, and being responsible for letting me know when to reorder, also noting the number of filled bottles sent out each day, breakages and things of that nature.'

Gertie shook her head. 'That be beyond me,' she said.

They all looked towards Maddy.

'Seems like it be up to you, maid,' said Susan.

'Do you think you could do it?' asked Cal.

'Yes.' Maddy had no doubts on that score. 'But I'm the newest one here, it hardly seems fair.'

''Tis fair if the rest of us idn't up to un,' insisted Susan, then she said in a whisper, 'He'm only going to bring in gawd-knows-who if you don't take un, and us don't want that, do us?'

Cal was not supposed to hear this aside, but his lips twitched. 'Well, Maddy, are you going to take the job, or do I have to find gawd-knows-who?' he asked.

'I'll take it,' Maddy said.

'Good. Come up to the house as soon as you get back from your dinner and we'll discuss the details.'

When he had gone, everyone burst out laughing. 'Lor', to think he heard me!' chuckled Susan. 'I didn't knowd where to put myself when he said un – "Do I have to find gawd-knows-who?"' She mimicked Cal's voice, then fell to laughing again.

Maddy wiped her eyes, then clapped her hands. 'Come along, ladies, this will not do,' she said in a schoolmarm voice. 'Back to work instantly, if you please.'

'Lor', if her'm going to be this uppity us'd be better off with gawd-knows-who,' muttered Liza in mock mutiny, and that set them laughing again.

Jack greeted the news of Maddy's promotion with a sniff. He never mentioned her job at Oakwood, nor did he seem to take much interest. Joan, on the other hand, was delighted.

'There, if things idn't taking a turn for the better all round!' she beamed. 'The weather be on the mend, the menfolk be back at work, and now Maddy be getting an extra eighteen pence a week. It were a good day when her was took on at Oakwood, and no mistake.'

Jack ignored his wife's remark, and occupied himself busily looking for his tobacco pouch. Maddy smiled to herself. She knew he was pleased at her advancement but that nothing on earth would induce him to admit it.

Later that afternoon, when Maddy arrived at Oakwood farmhouse, Ellen demanded, 'You'm sure you got the right door?'

'Yes,' grinned Maddy. 'Mr Whitcomb wants to see me.'

'You best come in then.' Ellen held the door wide. 'Now, be you front parlour company or be you kitchen company?'

'I think I'd better be passage company until Mr Whitcomb comes,' Maddy smiled.

'He might be some time. He'm gone to look at a bit of wall as collapsed down Church Farm. Bolted his dinner, he did. Won't do him no good. I tells un till I be blue in the face but he won't listen. I think you'm best in the front parlour. That should get her riled up good and proper.' Ellen gave a grin that was pure mischief and ushered Maddy into the well-furnished parlour.

'You put her where? She could be up to anything, being a Shillabeer.' From beyond the closed door Maddy could hear Mrs Whitcomb's cry of indignation, followed by the shuffle of slippers and the appearance of the lady herself.

'My son said you were to come here, you say?' she demanded, with barely masked disbelief.

'Yes, Mrs Whitcomb. He wants to discuss something with me.'

'I can't think what that might be.' Cal's mother glanced swiftly round the room as if checking that her possessions were safe. Then her pride in her treasures overcame her suspicion and she went over to one of the cabinets and opened the glass door. Adjusting a plate a fraction of an inch she said wistfully, 'That's a beautiful set. Worcester, every piece hand-painted, and that's pure gold round the rim. A birthday present from my boy, it was, and never used. I intended to have it out for his wedding, but my funeral is the only airing it'll get.'

'What about Mr Cal's wedding, won't you use it for that?' asked Maddy. She had no illusions who Mrs Whitcomb meant by 'my boy'.

'Oh him!' Cal's mother dismissed him impatiently. 'He doesn't appreciate fine things the way his brother did. He'd be happy with tin plates and cloam cups. Do you know, his father left him a fine gold watch with a beautiful chain. But will he wear them? Not Calland. He prefers a battered silver thing he's had for years.'

Maddy recalled Ned Knapman's widow telling her something about Cal's gold watch. Had he not sold it to pay the wages of men his brother had rashly taken on? Looking about her at the cupboards full of expensive china and silver, Maddy was certain there were plenty of things on those shelves that could have been sold to pay the men. But Cal had preferred to sacrifice his watch, and secretly at that. She was sorely tempted to tell Mrs Whitcomb a few home truths about both her sons; but it was not her place to speak up and reluctantly she held her tongue.

'I can't stay here all day. Mr Whitcomb will be with you soon.' Mrs Whitcomb bustled out, white curls bobbing round the black lace of her widow's cap.

A few moments later Ellen entered, carrying a large duster. 'Her'm says I be to dust the parlour,' she said. 'Really 'tis 'cos her'm feared you'm going to run off with her gew-gaws.' She began her task, but it did not interfere with her chatter. 'Her going on about Cal's watch,' she said, proving that she had been listening at the keyhole. 'I knows what happened to un and why, and so would her if her'n had an ounce of sense. But then Mr Cal couldn't never do naught right in her eyes. Too like his father: Mr Kit born again, that's what he be, but just in his looks. His quickness and sharp tongue be from his Shillabeer blood.' She glanced sideways at Maddy to see her reaction to this remark. When there was none she continued, half to herself, 'Daft besom, her had a good husband and her didn't want he, and her'm got a fine son and her don't want he, neither. Her'm the sort as only wants what her can't have, that be Mary Whitcomb for you.'

'You've been with the family for a long time then?' asked Maddy.

'I come from Church Farm with Mr Kit when he were wed.' A nostalgic smile softened Ellen's gaunt features. 'He always said he brung three things to his marriage – the parlour pianny, the family Bible, and me. Just as well I did come,' she went on more briskly. 'At least there were someone to see they two was looked after proper.'

Maddy guessed she was referring to Cal and his father. Despite its comfort and prosperity, Oakwood Farm had clearly not been a happy place for a long time.

Ellen rubbed hard at an imaginary fingerprint on one of the cupboard doors. 'They fal-lals and trinkets! Mr Christopher were forever buying them for his ma, whether the money were there or not. I idn't calling him, mind. As nice a fellow as you could meet, but he were a man of straw.'

'He didn't have his brother's strength of character?'

'No, not by a long chalk. He meant well, but he weren't up to naught.' Ellen paused, her duster in her hand. 'I tells you, Mr Cal have told me there be a home yer for me till my last breath, so I sleeps easily at night. If Mr Christopher had said the same thing I'd be lying awake worrying, 'cos I knows I'd be knocking on the workhouse door sometime or another. That were the difference atween the two.'

Firm footsteps sounded on the passage flags, and Cal entered. At the sight of Ellen he frowned. 'What are you doing, dusting when there is a guest in the room?' he demanded.

Ellen ignored his stern tone. 'Shillabeers idn't guests, and any road, don't blame me. This wadn't my idea.'

'It doesn't matter whose idea it was, kindly take your duster and be off.'

With an indignant sniff Ellen did as she was told.

As he closed the door behind her, Cal grinned. 'I don't know why I bothered to send her packing,' he said. 'She'll listen at the door. The best informed member of the household, is Ellen.'

'She's devoted to you,' said Maddy.

'That's true. It doesn't stop her giving me a good scolding if she thinks I need it, though. You are entitled to scold me too, at this moment, for keeping you waiting.'

'I don't think I'll risk it, I haven't Ellen's courage,' Maddy replied.

Cal chuckled. 'I don't believe that for a second.' Then he grew serious. 'Now to business.' He produced a black ledger, and for a while the conversation was about deliveries, checking, and keeping tallies. 'There,' he said at last. 'Do you think you understand everything?'

'I think so,' said Maddy.

'If you've any problems, come to me.'

'Thank you.' Maddy hesitated. 'I appreciate being given this job, you know, especially with times being hard and the fact that I'm a Shillabeer...'

'Surely it's high time that old feud was forgotten? It's been feeding on resentment and prejudice for long enough, don't you agree?'

'I do, though I suppose it's easier for our generation. Our parents feel it more because they were closer to the dispute.'

'Does your father disapprove very strongly about you working here?'

'Yes,' said Maddy with a smile. 'But as my stepmother approves equally strongly, he keeps quiet and pretends it isn't happening.'

'How fortunate for you,' Cal said ruefully.

'Your mother disapproves of me being here, I know.'

'And sadly she does not do it as silently as your father. But as you say, their generation was more involved in the quarrel, and I suppose it's natural for my mother to feel bitter since she blames the money going away from the farm for ruining her life.'

'The money? You mean my wages?' asked Maddy in surprise.

'No,' smiled Cal. 'Some of it was the money which Great-grandfather left your grandfather.'

'But my grandfather got nothing!'

'I am sorry to contradict, but that isn't true. My grandfather, Matt, inherited Oakwood but your grandfather, John, was left eight hundred pounds.'

'Eight hundred pounds! He was left eight hundred pounds?' Maddy was astounded. No one had ever mentioned any inheritance at all, let alone one involving so much money. Certainly there was no evidence of such riches now.

'You don't believe me? I have the will locked up in my strongbox if you want to see the proof.' He would have left the room to get it if she had not detained him.

'I believe you,' she said.

'You knew nothing of this money before?'

She shook her head.

'How amazing! Did you think that Great-grandfather was so unfeeling that he left your grandfather penniless?'

'The general opinion in our family was that the old man had grown weak witted and that Matt, your grandfather, put pressure on him to make the will in his favour.'

Cal laughed. 'Weak witted? Why, the story is that the old man was querying the doctor's bill on his deathbed. I can't verify that, mind, but upstairs I have documents which prove everything else. From what

I was told, John had said more than once that he had no interest in the farm or farming. His father took him at his word and left Oakwood to Matt, and eight hundred pounds to him. Not the value of the farm, perhaps, but it was a goodly sum and all the money available. And that was the root cause of our problems.'

'Problems?' This was the first time Maddy had heard of difficulties at Oakwood. The stories she had been fed had claimed it was a prosperous place, thriving while her side of the family declined into poverty.

'Yes, that money should have been the working capital for the farm. My grandfather had a very hard time of it with no buffer against poor harvests or falling prices or any of the other farming hazards. Despite his efforts, he would have gone under if he had not married a girl with a bit of money of her own. Times got somewhat easier and my mother was born, but it was still a hard struggle.'

'You said that my grandfather's eight hundred pounds was part of the money.'

'Did I?' Cal looked unconvincingly vague.

'Yes, you did. What other money was there?'

'Nothing of importance. You don't want to hear it.'

'Yes, I do,' Maddy insisted.

'Well, if you are sure,' Cal said with reluctance. 'Sometime after Great-grandfather's death – quite a while, it must have been, for my mother was about seventeen or eighteen by then – your grandfather got into financial difficulties. I do not know the details, only that it was a business venture that went wrong and there was a risk of him going to prison. Rather than let that happen his brother, Matt, bailed him out. It was just a matter of a few hundred pounds but it happened at a time when there had been a run of poor prices. As a result Oakwood found itself on the brink of disaster yet again.' Maddy was astounded. Her grandfather must have gone through a fortune. 'And – and how did Oakwood survive?' she asked hesitantly.

'The same way it survived before, by an advantageous marriage. My mother was obliged to wed my father.'

'Obliged?'

'What else could she do? If she refused then the farm was lost and the family ruined.'

'She did not do so willingly?'

'I believe there was a young man whom she cared for, but my father was prosperous, though a fair bit older than she was; she had no option but to wed him.'

Maddy was stunned into silence. The story explained much of Mary Whitcomb's stubborn resentment against her side of the Shillabeer family. Because of them she had lost her chance of happiness and been forced to marry a man she did not love. Maddy could sympathise with her feelings, she too knew about lost happiness.

'The ironic thing was that my mother's sweetheart went to Australia and made his fortune as an engineer,' Cal continued. 'When he came home he could have bought Oakwood from his loose change.'

'Then if she had waited...'

'But she wasn't allowed to wait.'

Mary's bitterness had obviously continued throughout her married life. Moreover, she had let her rancour poison her relationship with her younger son simply because he looked too much like his father. This was something Maddy found harder to understand. Then she remembered: Mary Whitcomb had been born a Shillabeer, and if there was one thing the Shillabeers were good at it was bearing a grudge.

If what Cal had said was true, her grandfather had fostered a feud against his own brother for no better reason than... Why had John felt such bitterness towards Matt? Because he was jealous of his brother's steadiness and ability to survive? Because he was resentful at having to go cap in hand to him for help? To mask his shame at his own failure? Suddenly the reasons for the feud that she had unquestioningly accepted since childhood seemed less straightforward. John had rejected his right to Oakwood, and instead had been amply provided for financially. He had no cause to complain, and still less to resent his brother for the rest of his life. Maddy was sure her father knew nothing of this story and she wondered what he would make of it. Poor soul would probably be even more bemused by it than she was.

—

Jack's immediate reaction to the tale was predictable. 'Pack of lies,' he snorted.

'Farmer Whitcomb have the papers to prove un, seemingly.' Lew was less dogmatic. 'Us could ask to have a look at them.'

'Wouldn't give un the satisfaction,' Jack retorted.

'Eight hundred pounds,' said Joan wistfully. 'Your father could've set up a thriving shop with that money, Jack. Something like Cutmore's only with more choice on the shelves...'

'Did you know anything about this money, Father?' asked Maddy.

'Not a word of truth in un,' Jack retorted.

By his refusal to give a straight answer she felt certain that the news of the inheritance had come as a shock.

'...Or he could've bought three or four good houses.' Joan could not get her practical mind away from the possibilities of such a sum of money. 'Nice places where he could've asked a decent rent and got respectable tenants, not the sort as hide in the privy come rent day. He could've been set up for life, and us too.'

A silence fell upon the room. Financial security, the dream of them all, could so easily have been theirs.

Suddenly Joan gave a deep sigh. 'There idn't no point thinking on un,' she said. 'What's gone's gone, and us idn't never going to get un back again. Us must just be thankful as Oakwood Farm did fall to the Whitcomb side or, along with everything else, us'd be short of Maddy's eight and six into the bargain.'

Jack's response was to snatch up a lantern and mutter something about going out the back. Maddy felt sorry for him. It was hard enough for her to come to terms with the fact that it was Grandfather John who had been the chief cause of the dissension all these years. How much more difficult it must be for her father to accept it. No one mentioned the fact that Matt's intervention had saved their grandfather from going to prison. The family had coped with enough disclosures for one night.

These new revelations had a profound effect on Maddy's attitude towards the Whitcombs. She had long ago dismissed the idea that Cal Whitcomb was a villain, yet at the back of her mind had lurked the notion, instilled in her since childhood, that no Whitcomb was completely trustworthy. That had gone completely now, replaced by respect for a family who had managed to pull itself back from the brink of ruin more than once. She even felt a grudging sympathy for Mary Whitcomb. Cal's mother was a trying woman, but she had had some cause. Maddy's compassion for her would have been absolute if only she did not have the knack of making other people's lives miserable, particularly her son's.

There was no time to dwell upon the past, however. The future, in the shape of the forthcoming salmon season, demanded everyone's attention; it was then that Lew made his announcement.

'Mollie and me, we've decided to wed. There be a cottage empty up by the school us've spoken for, and us reckons to set the date next month.'

Everyone stared at him.

'Be you mazed, boy, getting wed just as the salmon be coming upriver?' demanded Jack.

'I've heard it be possible to fish and be a married man at the same time,' Lew replied. 'I haven't tried un, mind, but I knows them as have, and they seem to manage.'

'Saucepot!' Joan aimed a mock blow at his head. 'This be a bit sudden, bain't un? You sure there idn't no reason for the haste?'

'Reason? What reason could there be?' Lew asked innocently, then his good humour faded. 'Idn't no one pleased? I thought you liked my Mollie.'

'We do.' Maddy leapt up and gave him a hug. 'It's just that you've taken us by surprise. Married in a month! That doesn't give us much time to get our wedding finery together.'

'Go on! With the money you'm earning up to Oakwood you can afford to rig yourself out in silks and satins,' teased Lew.

'That'll be the day,' Maddy retorted.

'I don't knows about getting rigged out,' said Joan. 'But I'd best go over to Mrs Chambers first thing tomorrow and offer some help. Poor woman'll be at her wits' end, having to do a wedding feast in a month, and at this time of year. Couldn't the pair of you have chosen a time when things was plentiful?'

Lew's reply was a sheepish grin, confirming what everyone suspected: there was a pressing reason for such a speedy wedding.

A wedding so early in the year might have been imprudent, though necessary, but such a cheerful celebration raised everyone's spirits, seeming to mark the end of the long harsh winter and the beginning of a more hopeful spring. Joan was in her element, dashing between Duncannon and the Chambers' house to help with the preparations.

'I can't think what to wear,' was Annie's lament when Maddy called one evening. 'What about you?'

'I haven't decided yet,' Maddy replied. Then they both burst out laughing, for they knew the indecision was pure wishful thinking.

Annie would wear her fawn twill, while Maddy would wear the dress with the blue-green stripes.

'I suppose I'll be wearing the same old bonnet, too,' said Annie, regarding Maddy out of the corner of her eye.

Maddy grinned, knowing only too well what that look meant. 'I'll retrim your bonnet, if you like,' she said. 'I thought I'd go up to Totnes next Saturday afternoon, when I've got time off. I could get you flowers or feathers or whatever you want then.'

'Would you, maid? That would be real kind.' Annie beamed appreciatively. 'I know folks don't hardly ever see my old bonnet no more these days. Most have forgot what it looks like, but it don't seem proper, going to a wedding without a bit of new about you somewhere. What about you? What'm you doing?'

'Retrimming my bonnet too, I expect. I'll see what I can find.'

What she found was a length of ribbon the exact shade of her dress, and her eyes. Even in the gloom of the haberdasher's shop, the silk gleamed like sunlit water. The description 'aquamarine' came into Maddy's mind. No one mentioned the word to her any more. There was no one to compare her eyes to the translucent jewel, not now that Patrick had gone from her life. For a moment she considered refusing the ribbon. What was the point of finery if there was no one to appreciate it? Then resolutely she pushed the idea from her. She refused to live her life in the shadow of a lost love. At Lew's wedding she would wear her Sunday dress and a bonnet trimmed with aquamarine ribbons, and she would feel good because she knew she was looking her best. She did not need compliments to prove it. In this optimistic mood, she purchased the ribbon, selected some very pretty russet artificial flowers for Annie, and left for home.

It happened that her way lay past the draper's shop, and in the window was displayed a bolt of cream wool. Spurred on by her buoyant mood, Maddy entered the shop.

She left the draper's clutching a parcel containing the cream wool, half delighted, half appalled by her extravagance. With every step she tried to justify her rashness to herself. She needed something to wear over her dress, it was too thin for this time of year; her cloak was too threadbare; and her shabby old crocheted shawl was not fit to wear at her brother's wedding. However, if she teased the edges of the square of cream wool into a fringe it would make an elegant shawl, one she could wear on Sundays during the summer, one that would be warm and practical and well worth the money she had laid out... This was what she told herself all the way from Totnes to Stoke Gabriel.

On the morning of the wedding, her doubts evaporated. The blue-green of the dress and the matching bonnet looked good on her and the softness of the new cream shawl draped across her shoulders added the right touch of elegance.

'Lor, they'm going to reckon us've got some quality come to this wedding,' remarked Joan, pausing in her hectic activity to admire Maddy's finery. 'Now where did I put they spoons? Every spoon us've got, that's what I promised Mrs Chambers, and I'm blessed if I can find a danged one. Go see if Annie be ready, there's a good maid. Lucy Ford's promised her pony and trap'll be at the top of the lane for her at a quarter to the hour. The menfolk can carry her that far. Thank goodness this be Charlie's week to be home. Us couldn't do with him being up to Lunnon just now.'

'Not you, Lew. You idn't to carry me,' declared Annie, entering the kitchen in her best fawn gown and newly trimmed bonnet. 'You'm to save your strength.'

'If you says so, Annie,' said Lew. 'I'll follow close behind, and you can explain to me what 'tis I've to save my strength for.'

'I reckon us be sadly behind with the telling of that tale,' said his father. 'Can us get started, or us'll be late to chapel. And whatever else you'm been early at, boy, you'm idn't being late there.'

'I don't knows what you mean, Father,' said Lew in well-simulated bewilderment. No one believed him.

The Chambers being Baptists, the ceremony was held in the chapel at the top of the village. It was a good wedding, everyone said so. Standing before the minister, exchanging their vows, Lew and Mollie looked up at each other with such love that Maddy had a lump in her throat and tears in her eyes for much of the ceremony. Afterwards the young couple led their guests downhill to the old schoolrooms, to continue the celebrations.

Despite the harsh times, trestle tables spread with crisp white cloths groaned under the weight of the food. Friends and relations had all contributed, making sure there were boiled hams and roast beef, a huge cheese, and cakes and buns in plenty, as well as the inevit-able bowls of rich clotted cream. And of course there was an ample Supply of cider. Maddy noticed with interest that the barrel bore the Oakwood mark. Jack noticed it too.

'Tidn't naught to do with me,' he said. 'If Arnie Chambers wants to spend his money on this puny stuff then 'tis his business.'

Despite his disparaging tone, he managed to force down plenty of the 'puny stuff'. Maddy watched him with fond amusement. If his singing gradually became off-key and his dancing unsteady, there was no denying that Jack was enjoying his son's wedding. Maddy had to admit that she was having a good time too. As the bridegroom's sister, she had plenty of dancing partners. In addition, there were appreciative looks coming her way, particularly from a couple of middle-aged farmers, both widowers.

'They do say as one wedding makes another,' Annie hissed in her ear as her two admirers vied for her attention.

'You aren't thinking of getting married again, are you?' replied Maddy innocently. 'Why, there's years of wear left in your William.'

'Oh you!' Annie gave her a good-humoured poke in the ribs. 'I tell you this, mind. The state that husband of mine be in, not to mention your pa and Charlie, I don't fancy they three carrying me down that lane tonight.'

'I think you're going to go down a lot quicker than you came up,' agreed Maddy.

Things were not as bad as they feared. Although definitely inebriated, the three men, firmly directed by Joan and Maddy, managed to get Annie home again without mishap.

'That were some proper wedding,' breathed Joan contentedly, after they had manoeuvred Jack and Charlie in turn upstairs to bed. 'Give the Chambers their due, chapel or not, I couldn't fault naught.'

'Nor could I,' replied Maddy, not quite truthfully, for she was remembering the music. The fiddler had come from Dittisham, across the river, and he had been good, but he had not been Patrick. Was it the music that had not quite come up to expectations, or was it because she still loved Patrick and wanted him back? She could not tell. Then weariness overcame her and she fell asleep before she could ponder the question more deeply.

Quite a few villagers went to work next morning feeling subdued. Maddy admitted to some tiredness, but by the time she had walked to Oakwood Farm on the fine spring morning, her fatigue had gone.

'For someone who was celebrating half the night you look remarkably fresh.'

The sound of Cal's voice made her turn round.

'It wasn't half the night exactly,' she said. 'Although I dare say there are some this morning who feel that it was and are regretting every minute.'

'Not on good Oakwood cider, surely.'

'On too much good Oakwood cider certainly.'

'I'm glad you resisted the temptation. Much as I want to increase consumption of our brew, I would prefer to have a sober overseer dealing with the bottles.'

There was a clip-clop of hooves and a rumble of wheels as a horse-drawn wagon came into the yard.

'Here's work for you already,' said Cal. He looked about him impatiently. 'Where are the men? I want that cart loaded up and the deliveries on their way as soon as possible. Late deliveries can be cancelled deliveries, and I can't afford to lose business.'

Maddy took this to be a hint that she, too, should be at work. By the time the loaders had stirred themselves she was prepared, book and pencil in hand, ready to check the numbers of crates, bottles, and stone jars which were put on the cart.

She found she enjoyed her new duties, despite the fact that they were taxing and meant extra work. It gave her great satisfaction seeing the crates dispatched and knowing it was up to her to ensure that the contents of every one was of top quality. If the number of deliveries fell, as they did from time to time, she felt the loss of customers personally. She found that she thrived on responsibility; the more she had, the more she liked it.

Cal, the perfectionist, seemed satisfied with her work and rarely criticised her. He seldom had cause, for she was extremely conscientious. Increasingly he grew to rely on her. 'Can you deal with it, Maddy?' he would say when some minor problem arose, or 'I'm needed over in Lower Meadow, a cow's got stuck in the ditch. Can you write the orders in the book for me?'

Gradually, almost without realising it, she found herself in complete charge of all orders and deliveries. There was more bookkeeping, which she liked, but fitting in her other duties at the bottling shed became difficult. Loath to complain in case Cal demoted her back to filling bottles, she struggled on, taking to staying late to catch up with the bookwork.

The nights were getting longer, which meant most times she could manage to do her extra work by natural light, but on one occasion, a gloomy, rainy day when she was further behind than usual, she was obliged to light the oil lamp in the partitioned section at the end of the storage area which served as an office.

'Who's there?' demanded Cal's voice instantly. The door burst open and he strode in, to come to an abrupt halt. 'Maddy, why on earth are you still here?' he asked in surprise.

There was no alternative, she had to confess. 'I have some bills to write out, and there are some orders that haven't been copied in the book yet. I'm sorry to be slow but today's deliveries were late going out – one of the horses cast a shoe – and then it was urgent that I checked over the new bottles, Susan and the others needed them, and—'

'Stop! Stop!' he exclaimed, holding up his hand. 'By the sound of it, you're running my business by yourself. Have I really given you so much to do?' He looked quite stricken.

'Most of the time I can cope, when things run smoothly.'

'But they don't always run smoothly, I know that much. Is this the first time you've stayed to work late at bills and ledgers and such?'

'No,' she admitted.

'And are you overseeing the bottling shed as well as the orders and the bills?'

'You know I am.'

'And how much am I paying you for this? Eight and six a week?'

'Yes.' She was sure he knew that too. Cal might forget some details but not how much he paid his employees.

'It's too much!'

'Surely not!' she declared indignantly.

'I wasn't referring to your wages, but to how much work you're doing.'

Maddy gave a sigh of relief and he looked at her seriously.

'I am a selfish devil,' he said. 'I didn't realise how much of a burden I was putting on you. It's the old story of the willing worker, I'm afraid.'

'Should that not be the willing horse?' asked Maddy.

He laughed. 'I would never have dared to phrase it like that. But something must be done. You can't work here in the office and the bottling shed too. Gertie has some knowledge of figures. She shall take over from you as overseer.'

'What if she does not want the job?' protested Maddy. 'She refused it when it was first suggested. That was why I took it.'

'She'll soon get to like it. Tell her it's eight and six a week or the sack. That should help her make up her mind. You can show her what to do.'

Maddy gasped at his cavalier attitude. When Cal Whitcomb wanted something, he certainly let nothing get in his way.

'As for you, you can stop work now,' he went on. 'I can't have you burning good lamp oil all night, even if you are behind with your work. Finish it in the morning.' Without waiting for a response, he bade her a brusque 'Good night' and turned out the lamp, leaving Maddy in near darkness.

She was not sure whether to be annoyed or amused at this abrupt behaviour, just as she was not sure his dismissing her had really been for economy's sake or concern for her welfare. On her way home a more serious question occupied her thoughts. If Gertie were now going to be paid eight and six, would her own wages be put back to seven shillings again? If so she did not relish the task of telling Joan.

She need not have worried. Next payday, when she lined up for her wages with the rest, only one coin was laid out for her to sign for – a golden half-sovereign.

One aspect of working more in the office was that she gained a better insight into the business and how well it was doing. The order book did not change much, and the wagon regularly left the yard laden with crates of cider, just as the larger dray left, equally regularly, carrying the big hogsheads. In her eyes everything seemed to be satisfactory. Cal thought otherwise. Every week he would go through the books with her, and inevitably he finished with an exclamation of disgust.

'We're not progressing as we should,' was his constant cry. 'Look, not a single new customer in this last month. What on earth can the agents be about? I pay them enough commission to sell my cider, heaven knows!'

'You're making a reasonable profit,' Maddy pointed out.

'That's not good enough. I want this business to grow and expand. I want to be one of the largest cider producers in South Devon, and beyond, and I won't do it on a mere reasonable profit.'

Maddy took note of the grim determination on his face. There was no doubting his ambition, that was certain.

'Then you must look for new ways of increasing your sales,' she said.

'How?' he challenged.

'Advertise more.'

'I've already taken out adverts in the local publications.'

'Then you must make people notice Oakwood Cider in other ways.'

'How?' he repeated.

She floundered briefly, then collected her thoughts. 'You could repaint the delivery cart and have "Oakwood Farm Cider" written on it in good bold letters, maybe with a decoration of oak leaves too. You do need a distinctive trade mark, you know, and the oak leaves look good. It's a pity the dray is only hired or you could have that repainted too. No one could miss seeing that, going through the countryside piled high with barrels and "Oakwood Farm Cider" on the side.'

'So I need to devise myself a trade mark and to buy a dray and a team of horses.'

'I didn't say that,' protested Maddy.

'Not exactly, but they are good ideas all the same. You have persuaded me that buying a dray will definitely be worthwhile.'

'Oh dear,' said Maddy in dismay. 'Please don't let me persuade you into anything.'

He smiled. 'Don't look like that. I have to be honest and confess that I have been considering purchasing one for some time. It makes sense – one outright payment instead of always hiring. I would be sure it was fit for the road, too, and have no repetition of the incident when the wheel came off going down into Totnes. As for extra horses, I've more than enough work for them. They'd earn their keep.'

Maddy did not doubt it.

'And what other inspired notions have you to improve our flagging sales?' he asked.

'You make it sound as though you're on the brink of ruin,' she grinned.

'That's something I have no intention of being,' he said firmly.

Remembering the sarcastic remarks made by her family in the early days of cider production at Oakwood, she suggested mischievously, 'If things are as bad as that you should sell the stuff yourself. You could hawk it about the towns and villages, or open a shop or something.'

'That's going a bit far. I have no fancy to become a cider peddlar, thank you, even if I had the time.'

'Then I'm afraid that's the best I can do in the way of new ideas.'

'In that case I'd better get back to work, and try to keep the farms and the cider company in business by myself.'

When he had gone, Maddy reconsidered the sales figures. They were fair enough, but she had to admit that there was much room for improvement. However, she knew Cal was not one to let things remain static in his drive for more customers. She wondered what new schemes he would employ.

It was about a fortnight later when he entered the office and announced, 'I have a new job for you.'

Maddy waited expectantly. For some time she had been anticipating him asking her to take over his correspondence. To her surprise he dropped a set of keys on the desk in front of her.

'What are these for?' she asked.

'The shop.'

'What shop?'

'The cider shop. I've rented premises on New Walk, in Totnes. You are to be in charge. I want you to go up tomorrow and make a list of what we'll need in the way of furnishings and equipment – nothing elaborate, mind – and work out what it will cost.'

'A shop?' Maddy repeated weakly. 'With me in charge?'

'That's right. I want us to be open within the month, to catch the summer thirsts.'

'But I don't know anything about running a shop.' Maddy's voice was close to a wail.

'You will learn,' said Cal with complete confidence. 'After all, it was your idea.'

'I wasn't serious! It was a joke!'

'There's many a true word spoken in jest.' He put two halfcrowns on the desk beside the keys. 'This is for tomorrow's expenses.' Already he was halfway to the door. 'There's no need for you to come in tomorrow to tell me what you've arranged. The morning after will do.'

With that he was gone, leaving a stunned and breathless Maddy gazing after him. How could she run a cider shop? She had no idea where to begin. She had no experience – or at least very little. She had looked after Mrs Cutmore's shop once or twice when the shopkeeper had been ill. That was experience of a sort. And she had a good idea of basic bookkeeping, and she would be selling only one commodity, cider... Surely she could manage that!

As she picked up the keys and the five shillings, there was already a tingle of excitement running down her spine. Something new and different faced her; it presented her with responsibility and a challenge, two things she was discovering she could not resist.

So Cal wanted a cider shop, did he? And he wanted it open within the month? Then he would get both his wishes. She would accept the challenge. First thing in the morning she would be on the earliest boat going upriver.

Chapter Sixteen

Maddy's first view of the shop did not inspire her with confidence. It had been easy to plan and make momentous decisions about the new venture whilst sitting beside the fire at home. Now that she was faced with the dingy shop front, matters were very different. Its position was its sole advantage, being situated on New Walk, shaded by chestnut trees and close to the River Dart, just right for catching both town and quayside trade. Apart from that, with its peeling paint and boarded-up windows, the building had precious little to recommend it. Under her breath she cursed Cal Whitcomb for expecting her to produce a flourishing concern from such rundown premises.

I won't manage it by standing here on the pavement, she decided.

The first thing which greeted her upon opening the door was an overpowering smell of damp and vermin. Lighting an old lantern she found on a shelf and hitching her skirts clear of the filthy floor, Maddy began her exploration. The front shop proved to be of a fair size. Behind it there was a store and another smaller room which housed a disproportionately large and rusty cooking range. Presumably at some time this had been an eating house. Maddy wrinkled her nose at the thought of eating anything produced under these conditions. But somehow she was going to have to get it clean enough to be a place where people could enjoy a drink. Gazing about the dilapidated shop she felt discouraged, and directed a few more uncomplimentary thoughts at Cal for dropping such a task in her lap. Moving her lantern, she caught a glimpse of a sleek grey body slithering under the protection of a pile of boxes. Angrily she flung a piece of wood at the disappearing rodent.

'The rat-catcher, that's who I need!' she declared aloud. 'Immediately! Him, and the glazier! There'll be no dealing with this place until they've both been.'

Somehow, having made this decision, her determination was restored, making other decisions easier.

Having first found the town rat-catcher and then a reliable glazier, she trudged up and down Totnes's steep Fore Street more times than she could count in search of her other requirements. With a notebook and pencil in her hand she entered side alleys she had not known existed, and hurried along unfamiliar narrow lanes, haggling and bargaining at every stop in an attempt to get the best prices.

Cal was not totally appreciative of her efforts.

'Good heavens, woman, do you think I'm made of money?' he exclaimed as he read her estimates.

'If it hurts you that much to loosen your purse strings you can always have your customers drinking among the rat droppings!' she retorted. 'Don't worry, they won't notice in the darkness, not with the windows still boarded up.'

'I thought you said you'd booked the glazier.'

'I have, but he isn't coming until tomorrow. You can cancel his visit. And while you're about it, you can cancel any thoughts of me running the shop. Your customers mightn't know any better, but I've had a good look at that place and I refuse to work in such conditions.' Tiredness made her irritable, and she was disappointed at his lack of appreciation of her efforts.

He had the grace to look ashamed. 'I'm sorry,' he said. 'I shouldn't have shouted at you like that. You've obviously worked very hard. It was just seeing all the expenses in a lump sum like this.' He ran a weary hand over his face. 'It's a mistake to talk business after we've both had a hard day. I said that this could wait until the morning.'

Now it was Maddy's turn to look abashed. 'I didn't think it could,' she said. 'I need to be back in Totnes first thing tomorrow to let the rat-catcher into the shop. I wouldn't have had time to come here first.'

He gave a faint smile. 'That was when you still intended to run my shop, eh?'

'That was before you decided my estimates were too high. If you think you can do any better yourself, why don't you try?'

Cal looked back at the paper in front of him. 'That's me put in my place well and truly,' he said dryly.

Maddy sat in silence. Perhaps it was not the most respectful way to address one's employer, but he had asked for it by being so unreasonable. While she sat there, Cal reached out and rang a bell. When Ellen appeared he said, 'Tell Joshua to harness up the pony and trap, will you?'

'You'm idn't going out again at this hour?' the maid said disapprovingly.

'Yes, I am,' replied Cal. 'And to save you catching a chill listening at the keyhole, I'll tell you that I'm taking Miss Shillabeer home.'

'Miss Shillabeer now, be un?' Ellen's disapproval grew.

'There's no need to drive me home!' exclaimed Maddy. 'It's no distance.'

'I think there is a need,' replied Cal. 'You've had a tiring day and if you're to be up at Totnes early tomorrow then you must get some rest.'

'I'm still in charge of the shop, am I?'

'I don't know. It depends on you.'

'No, it depends on you and if you accept my estimate of expenses.'

'I accept it, most humbly. I should have known better than to query it. From now on you are in complete charge of setting up the shop, and I shall not interfere.'

'That be settled then,' observed Ellen, who had been listening to the exchange without shame. 'You'm still needing the pony and trap. I'll go and speak to Joshua.'

The next few weeks were the most eventful in Maddy's life. No two days were alike, as workmen came and went and the shop gradually emerged from its decayed state and began to look presentable. Cal was as good as his word and did not interfere. He made one of his rare visits a couple of days before the shop was due to open. Through the newly-glazed windows Maddy saw him approach, stop and look at the shop front, then frown. She knew the cause of his disapproval – it was the sign writer, skilfully and meticulously putting the finishing touches to the name board above the window.

'I hope you approve,' she said, going out to greet him. 'I did mention it to you.'

'You mentioned it, certainly. I just didn't anticipate anything so ornate.'

Together they gazed at the board bearing the legend 'The Oakwood Farm Cider Shop' surrounded by a garland of oak leaves.

Having finished the final curlicue, the signwriter came down from his ladder to join them. 'There, Miss Shillabeer, wadn't I right to persuade you to have the gold lining?' he said, regarding his handiwork with satisfaction. 'Makes all the difference, does gold lining. 'Tis worth the bit extra. Adds a real touch of quality, it do.'

Maddy was careful to avoid Cal's eyes, especially at the reference to the 'bit extra'. The name board was her one cause for anxiety. 'It was my only extravagance,' she said. 'And you've got to admit it does look good.'

'Oh yes,' agreed Cal drily. 'Adds a real touch of quality, it do.'

She led the way into the shop. Cal looked about and nodded his approval. 'You've done a lot in a short time,' he said. 'But without this your hard work would be in vain.' He laid a paper on the new counter. 'The licence. Signed and sealed at the magistrates' court this very morning.'

'It's got my name on!' exclaimed Maddy.

'That's right. You're the licensee.'

To the best of her knowledge, with the exception of the parish register at birth, Maddy had never had her name on an official document before. Seeing 'Madeleine Elizabeth Shillabeer' written in authoritative copperplate filled her with an unexpected pride, as if she had suddenly become a person of consequence.

'How did you know my middle name?' she asked.

Cal shrugged. 'I made enquiries,' he said.

'You've been discussing me with folk?' she asked in some alarm.

'No, of course not! Don't look so disapproving. It was your step-mother who told me. I had to know your full name, otherwise I could not have applied for the licence on your behalf.'

Maddy was somewhat mollified. Pleased as she was at this new development in her life, she did not like the idea of him discussing her with all and sundry. She would have asked Cal more about her responsibilities as a licensee if, at that moment, his foot had not hit against a bucket that stood on the floor. Water splashed over his boot, but it was not that that caused his frown. He regarded first the bucket, along with its accompanying soap and scrubbing brush, and then the sacking apron which Maddy had hastily discarded upon his arrival and thrown on the counter.

'You've been using these?' he demanded.

'Of course.'

'You mean you've been scrubbing the floor?'

'Certainly. Who else would do it?'

'Heavens above, Maddy, when I asked you to take on the shop I did not intend you to do everything including the skivvying!'

'It needed doing and it seemed quicker and easier to do it myself,' she replied.

'It may have been quicker, but it certainly could not have been easier. You are to get someone in to do the dirty jobs, do you hear? I don't know why you didn't think of it before.' Maddy refused to admit that the reason had been her determination to set up the shop on exactly the budget he had allowed. Her pride refused to let her ask him for more money.

'Very well,' she said. In truth, clearing up after the painter was a clean and easy task compared to some of the filthy jobs she had already tackled about the place, but she kept quiet about those.

Cal, however, was eyeing her suspiciously. 'I fear I've been lax,' he said. 'I should have kept a closer eye on you. I fancy you may have been slaving away here on my behalf, working far harder than you should have done. It's to stop, do you hear? You are now the licensee of the Oakwood Farm Cider Shop, a person of importance. It's beneath your dignity to scrub floors.' While Maddy was trying to decide whether he was joking or serious he suddenly rapped out, 'How do you get here each day?'

'I come by river.'

'I presumed that much but how?'

'The tide was right today; I rowed myself.'

'And I suppose you're going to row yourself home again.'

'Of course. It costs good money to be ferried to and fro all the time. I thought I'd take advantage of the handy tides while I could.'

He clutched at his hair in a gesture of exasperation. 'Was there ever such a woman? Just because you are in my employment doesn't mean I expect you to be a slave. I know I have a reputation as a skinflint, but surely I'm not as bad as that!'

Maddy regarded him blankly, surprised at the underlying note of distress in his voice. 'I never said you were a skinflint,' she said. 'You gave me a job to do, and I'm trying to do it within the budget you set. Admittedly it isn't easy at the moment, not with getting everything started, but I've worked harder many a time, and for less money.'

He returned her gaze, slowly shaking his head. 'Whatever my drawbacks as an employer,' he said, 'I can certainly pick the right worker for the job. And having picked the right worker, I have no intention of letting her wear herself out. This very day you will find yourself an assistant to help you and do the menial work. From now on Joshua will bring you to work in the pony and trap, and fetch you back in the evening.'

'I can't do that!' Maddy protested. 'What will people say?'

'They will say that Farmer Whitcomb isn't quite the miser he is made out to be.' He drew his brows together in a mock frown. 'You are going to argue, I can see it in your face. Well, I won't stand for it. You will be driven to Totnes each day, like it or not.'

'I do like it... and thank you,' replied Maddy. 'I'll admit I was not looking forward to the river journey in the winter.' She was grateful for his consideration, and also rather surprised. That Cal knew of his own harsh reputation was obvious, but she had not realised how much it stung him.

'That's settled then.' Having dealt with the matter, Cal clearly dismissed it from his mind and turned his attention back to the shop. 'When do you think you will be ready to open?'

'Monday next. That is if I can have the cider delivery on Friday, or Saturday at the latest.'

'First thing on Friday it will be. Let me have your order as soon as possible, please.'

Maddy went to a drawer in the counter and took out a piece of paper. 'Here it is,' she said confidently, her voice giving no hint of the hours of trepidation and uncertainty that the single sheet had cost her.

'I had a feeling you would have it ready,' he said, scanning the list. 'I'm glad to see that you mean to begin modestly, with no wild extravagances. Is there anything else you'll need for the opening?'

'I don't think so, thank you. Will you be coming?'

'Of course. Do you think we should do something special? Maybe cut a ribbon across the door frame, or smash a bottle of Superior on the step?'

He was joking, but Maddy's reply was serious – and somewhat nervous. 'I've already attended to that,' she said. 'No, not a ribbon or anything of that sort. I've put an advert in this week's *Totnes Times* saying there is a free pint of cider each for the first ten customers, and that the one hundredth customer on opening day will receive a free bottle of Superior.'

She waited tensely for his reaction.

'Giving away a free bottle of Superior! That will definitely attract more custom than smashing one on the doorstep,' he said with approval. 'A hundred customers – that's a goodly number for one day. Do you think you'll achieve that many?'

'I hope we do. People will come out of curiosity if naught else.'

'And having sampled our wares will realise the worth of Oakwood Cider and become lifelong customers, is that the plan?'

'Something of the sort,' said Maddy, hoping she was right.

–

The weather could not have been more advantageous for opening day. From early morning the sun shone down relentlessly out of a sky of unrelieved blue; by the time Maddy flung open the shop door she already had an uncomfortable damp patch between her shoulder blades. The first customers who jostled for the privilege of free cider were dockers from the nearby quayside, hot and thirsty from finishing loading slates onto a boat that had had to be away on the early tide.

'That went down proper handsome,' declared one man, downing his free pint in a single swallow. 'Would've tasted just as sweet even if I'd had to pay for un.'

'Why don't you buy the next one, then you'll find out for sure?' suggested Maddy, to much laughter.

Serving the cider and listening to the men's comments, Maddy learned her first lesson. The dockers worked according to the tide, not the clock. Therefore, whenever possible, the shop would have to open likewise.

'We've got a fair crowd,' said Cal with satisfaction. He had been in the shop since half an hour before opening, his censorious eye going over the shelves neatly stacked with bottles of Superior and stone flagons of Regular, and at the standing hogsheads of draught cider, both Regular and Rough. Only when he had given a nod of approval had Maddy unlocked the shop door.

'We've this heat on our side, and there are several boats in being loaded and unloaded,' said Maddy. 'Along with novelty, we've a few advantages today.'

'And what about a top quality cider?'

'There is that, of course,' Maddy admitted laughing. 'Let's hope it's enough to keep the customers coming.'

'What else would we need?' demanded Cal.

'Luck.' said Maddy.

The first day was an unqualified success. The bottle of 'Superior' was handed over to the hundredth customer by mid-afternoon, forcing Maddy to offer another bottle for the one hundred and fiftieth, then the two hundredth, both of which were claimed before they finally closed.

'Off you go home, Nan,' said Maddy, addressing the girl she had employed to help her. 'You've done well today.'

''Tis good of you to say so, Miss Shillabeer,' Nan gave a huge yawn. 'But idn't you coming too? If you'm half as weary as me you won't hardly know how to put one foot in front of the other.'

'I'll admit I'm very tired, but I've to total up the money before I leave,' said Maddy. 'You can go now. Be sure to be here good and early tomorrow.'

'I will, Miss Shillabeer, don't worry.' Nan made for the door, but came to an abrupt halt with a squeak of alarm. 'Oh lor', 'tis Mr Whitcomb. I be going out the back way.' And she fled towards the rear of the shop.

'Why did Nan dash out like that?' he asked as he entered.

'She's frightened of you.'

'Is she? Sensible girl. You did well to find her.' He placed his hat on the counter. 'I wish more of my employees held me in the same dread.'

'If you're referring to me then you're a little late in your wishing.' Maddy had scarcely looked up at his entrance, she was engrossed in counting the piles of money in front of her. Then, suddenly the full implications of his presence struck her. 'You didn't have to fetch me yourself!' she exclaimed. 'Joshua could have brought me to Oakwood to let you know how things have gone.'

'Let's just say that I was too impatient to wait.' He nodded first at the pile of coins and then at the shelves. 'It would seem that we had a good day.'

Maddy looked at the depleted shelves that would need restocking before they opened in the morning. 'A very good day,' she agreed. 'But the real test will be how much trade we're doing at the end of three or four months.'

'Do I detect a touch of pessimism?'

She shook her head. 'No, just weariness.'

'Since you've finished totalling up, let's put the money in the strongbox and be on our way. Immediately!' he stressed when she showed signs of finding further tasks to do.

It was a long slow climb out of the town, but Maddy did not mind their snail's pace. She was so fatigued that she was content to sit in silence. When her initial weariness had eased, she began to take pleasure in the journey. She had walked this way many a time, and now here she was, Maddy Shillabeer, riding these selfsame lanes up beside Cal Whitcomb.

'You're very quiet. Is something wrong?' asked Cal.

'No, I was just thinking how life has changed of late, with me working for you and everything.'

'Yes, things are somewhat different. Your family seems to have accepted the new state of affairs remarkably well. I wish I could say the same for my mother.'

'She still doesn't approve of having a Shillabeer about the place? That's a pity. Much of the credit for changing my father's attitude must go my stepmother. She has always thought the feud was stupid and has kept saying so in no uncertain terms. Perhaps you should encourage your mother to marry again – if you could bear the idea of a stepfather, that is.'

Cal let out a shout of laughter that made the pony start. 'If we wait for that to end our family quarrel then we will be waiting on Judgment Day,' he chuckled. 'My mother reckons that marrying my father was once too often.'

'Then you must marry, and provide her with a houseful of grand-children to take her mind off things.'

'It sounds an extreme and chancy way to end the feud.'

'Why? Are you against matrimony?'

'Not at all, and I suppose it is time I was wed – if I can find the right woman.'

'I would not have thought you hard to please. I know you are susceptible to a pretty face.'

'I am and I don't deny it, but pretty faces don't come into it. Marriage for me will be a matter of business. It is how things have always been for us Whitcombs. Advantageous marriages are how we have survived and prospered. But when I do find a suitable wife, she must be certain in her own mind that she wants to wed me. I will have no one who is being forced into it by others.'

'I wish you happiness,' said Maddy. She was regretting the flippant remark of hers that had introduced the subject, for Cal's matrimonial prospects sounded bleak.

'And what of you?' demanded Cal in a more cheery voice. 'What marriage plans have you?'

'None at all,' she replied firmly. 'I intend to devote my life to making a success of the Oakwood Farm Cider Shop.'

'Since that is much to my advantage, I won't argue with your sentiments,' said Cal, 'but I hope you don't expect me to feel guilty at being the cause of such self-sacrifice.'

'I don't,' Maddy assured him cheerily.

They had reached the top of Duncannon Lane now and, bidding Cal good night, Maddy hurried homewards. As she went she felt curiously depressed. It was sad to think of Cal destined for such a cold and loveless future. He was a good man, and he was worthy of much more. As for herself, all hopes of marriage were so firmly behind her now that she could think of them with hardly a hint of pain. If she set her thoughts towards the future and her new career, she was certain she could snuff out for ever the last shadowy ache that lingered near her heart.

–

The cider shop flourished through the long, hot summer, and Maddy was kept busy and content. And then as a crisp autumn set in, Mollie presented Lew with a fine healthy son.

'A seven-month babe be un?' remarked Joan in an aside to Maddy when they went to admire the new arrival. ''Tis a miracle he didn't go full term, else he'd have been a little giant.' Then her sceptical expression softened as she gazed at the babe and cooed, 'But idn't he a fine boy, bless him? And the image of his daddy.'

'What are you going to call him?' asked Maddy, amused at her stepmother's mixed reactions.

'John Lewis Shillabeer,' pronounced Lew proudly. 'Mercifully both his grandads have John in their names, us won't have no falling out there, and of course he be Lewis after me.'

'John Lewis Shillabeer!' Jack sounded as proud as the new father, but it was more than passing on his Christian name that was pleasing him. 'Yer, boy, do you realise summat? Us've four Shillabeers now – you, me, Charlie and the babe. You get us another un like this one quick and us'll be back to having a family crew for the salmon fishing in no time.'

'Really, Jack Shillabeer, if you idn't the limit,' declared Joan, amidst the laughter. 'Would it be too much to let this child be christened and his poor mother churched afore you talks about having any more?'

'Oh, I don't mind,' said Lew gravely. 'I'd be happy to have another soon as you please. There idn't naught to this child-producing as far as I can see...' If he meant to say any more he did not get the chance, for he was immediately belaboured with good-humoured energy by both his stepmother and mother-in-law.

'Now us'll have to start looking for a husband for our Maddy,' puffed Joan, out of breath after the attack.

'You needn't bother, thank you,' said Maddy. 'I'm happy as I am.'

'You can't mean to look after a shop for the rest of your life,' Joan protested.

'Why not? There's more than enough to keep me occupied, believe me.'

Maddy meant it too. All her energy these days was going into running the cider shop. Sadly, however, although the summer trade had been excellent, with the coming of the cooler days, customers became fewer. Despite her efforts, business did not improve. By the time Christmas came and went, the takings were hardly enough to cover Maddy's wages, let alone Nan's and the upkeep of the shop.

'I had such hopes,' said Cal, shaking his head as he looked at the last month's accounts. 'It was a good idea that does not seem to be working out.'

'It's early days,' Maddy said, trying to sound optimistic. 'If we can just last out until the warmer weather.'

'That's a big "if".' Cal continued to frown at the figures in front of him. 'We can't afford to make a profit in summer simply to exist in winter.'

'What do you propose doing?'

'Cutting my losses.'

'You aren't thinking of closing the shop, surely?' asked Maddy in alarm.

'What other solution is there?'

'I don't know, but there must be one.' She hated to think that she had failed, and after only a few months, too. 'What have I been doing wrong? If I could discover that, it might make all the difference.'

'You mustn't blame yourself. It was a good idea, as I said, but one that has not succeeded. The trouble is that there are too many cider shops in Totnes already. I should have taken that into account before I dashed off and leased the shop.'

'If there are others managing to make a living, why can't we?' Maddy was determined not to give up. 'We must make the Oakwood shop stand out in some way, that's what we've got to do. We've got to have something to draw people in.'

'It's no good.' Cal, too, was determined. 'I can't afford to keep running the shop at a loss. Nan will have to be dismissed, I'm afraid. Don't worry about your own position, I'll find something for you somewhere.'

'I don't want something found for me somewhere, thank you,' Maddy retorted, her pride stung. 'You did that before, if you recall. I'll be employed on my merits or not at all.'

Cal sighed. 'Now you are annoyed, which doesn't help matters. I'm sorry if you aren't pleased, but my mind is made up. The shop closes at the end of the week.'

Maddy was horrified. 'So soon? Can't you give me a bit longer? Enough time to think of something? Cider is chilly comfort on its own in this weather. Could we perhaps serve it mulled—?'

'There's no point in going on about it,' declared Cal with increasing firmness. 'My mind is made up. We close in—'

'Pasties!'

'I beg your pardon?'

'Pasties! They're what we need! The perfect accompaniment to cider. Hot, freshly-baked pasties.'

'We close at the end of the week,' he persisted, trying not to hear her, but Maddy refused to be ignored.

'Think about it,' she begged. 'Hot, savoury pasties baked on the premises – we've that old range in the back room. Imagine what a draw the smell alone would be on a cold day.'

'I'm a cider-maker, for pity's sake! What do I know about cooking pasties?'

'You don't have to know anything about cooking them. If needs be, I'll make them, but it would be better to get someone in to be solely responsible for the baking.'

'I thought it might be going to cost me more money somewhere.'

'It would be well worth it. And while we are about it, we could make the place a bit more welcoming for folks who want to consume their cider and pasties on the premises. Bare tables and such are all very well on a hot summer's day, but in the depths of winter folk need a bit more comfort.'

'Upholstered armchairs, perhaps? Turkish carpets on the floor?'

'You don't need to be sarcastic. All I was thinking of was a bit of extra cheer.' The more Maddy considered the new idea, the more enthusiastic she became. She knew her arguments were sound, but she had to persist with them for a long time before Cal finally relented.

'Very well, you can have more money for this latest scheme of yours. I will give you three months to make the business profitable, and not one day longer. I simply can't afford it.'

Three months was not long, but Maddy was filled with enthusiasm and she refused to consider failure. Acquiring a good pasty-maker was unexpectedly easy. A word with Joan produced an aunt – or was it a second cousin? – of one of her stepmother's numerous daughters-in-law who was a fine cook and in need of employment. The relationship might have been confused, but there was no doubt about Mrs Collins' lightness of hand where pastry was concerned.

'And I likes to have a proper filling, with a decent bit of meat in un,' she insisted, offering Maddy a sample of her wares. 'I can't abide a pasty as is all tiddy.'

'Nor can I,' agreed Maddy, as well as she could with her mouth full. 'When can you start?'

'Soon as I've got every speck of rust off that there range *and* given the back room a really decent scrub out,' stated Mrs Collins.

Maddy hid her smile. The new cook was clearly a perfectionist, and that was a good thing. Much of the success of the new venture was going to depend on her.

While Mrs Collins, aided by Nan, sanded and scrubbed, Maddy made a few changes to the shop. American cloth in a cheerful red check added a touch of colour to the tables, a humble length of coconut matting took the bareness off the floorboards, and brass lamps instead of the utilitarian hurricane variety gave the place a welcoming air without making it look too feminine. With the stove in the comer burning cheerily, and the appetising smell of freshly-cooked pasties wafting on the air, the Oakwood Cider Shop suddenly became very attractive to passers-by.

The first customers were the crew off one of the foreign ships. They looked tired and cold, and Maddy guessed they had come upriver on the overnight tide. While six of them made a beeline for the stove to warm themselves, the seventh, presumably the captain, came up to the counter. 'Food!' he said, holding up seven fingers. 'Drink!' And he held up seven fingers again. That seemed to be just about the sum total of his English but he had made himself perfectly clear.

The pasties and the cider disappeared faster than Maddy had thought possible. 'Good!' said the captain. 'More!'

'Cider,' said Maddy very clearly, refilling the mugs held out to her. 'Pasties,' she said in the same tone, as Nan set more on the table.

'Cider,' repeated the captain. 'Pasties.' His weather-beaten face broke into a smile. 'Speak English. Good.'

The foreign sailors, the crew of the *Haarlem*, proved to be faithful customers during their stay. They were in two or three times a day for the short time their boat was tied up alongside the quay.

'I reckon they comes 'cos cider and pasties be just about the only English words they knows,' said Nan.

'They won't starve, then,' smiled Maddy. 'And they won't get anything more wholesome.' She was sorry when they came in for the last time.

'Go home,' said the captain, with an expression of exaggerated sadness. Then he stretched his face into a beaming smile and said, 'Come back. More pasties. More cider.'

Cal happened to enter the shop just as the *Haarlem*'s crew were leaving. 'Who were they?' he asked. 'They seemed a lively lot.'

'Just high spirits,' said Maddy. 'They're off one of the Dutch boats, and very good customers they've been. They've also developed a taste for Devon cider while they were here, they've just been buying some to take home.'

'Maybe I should set up an export business… I'm only joking,' he added hurriedly.

'I hope so. There's enough to do running this one.' Maddy looked through the steamy window after the departing Dutchmen. 'It's a pity they had to go, they were a nice lot, although they barely had a dozen words of English among them. They proved that the taste for pasties and cider is international. If the Dutch enjoyed them, then folks from other countries will.'

'In that case I *had* better seriously consider exporting,' said Cal.

On this occasion Maddy was not sure whether he was joking or not.

'Lots of time to think of that in the future,' she said firmly. 'At present we've got plenty of good local customers to rely on.'

'We are getting plenty, are we?'

'Yes!' Her reply was definite, yet secretly she was anxious. Their trade had been building up nicely since the introduction of the pasties, but what if their current success was based entirely upon being something new in town or the chance arrival of a foreign boat? She shook off her doubts. The cider shop would never face failure again. She would not let it, supposing she had to drag folk in off the street and pour the cider down them.

Fortunately Maddy did not have to resort to such extreme measures. When the first flush of novelty died down, trade remained good and steady, enough for Mrs Collins to demand – and get – a girl to help her. The customers were mainly local and regular, exactly the sort Maddy had hoped for. Some came to eat and drink in the shop, but many more took their cider and pasties away with them. Every midday, errand boys came in, a selection of small empty firkins slotted on ropes across their shoulders ready to be filled with Regular or Rough, and baskets on their arms to be piled high with pasties, to be taken off to the timber yards, the riverside wharfs, or places of work throughout the town. More foreign vessels followed the *Haarlem* to the quayside, and their crews soon found the Oakwood Cider Shop simply by following their noses. As many of these vessels returned regularly to the Dart, Maddy found that the shop soon also had a faithful international clientele.

The three months allotted by Cal to prove the shop a success came to an end.

'Will we have to close now?' asked Maddy.

Cal regarded the accounts for the previous twelve weeks gravely. 'I think we'll give it another month or two, to see how things go,' he said.

'What?' cried Maddy indignantly. Then she saw that he was grinning.

'You didn't really think I would close the shop, did you?' said Cal. 'Not with these profits?'

'I was prepared to argue again,' she said.

'That's not necessary, believe me. I'm extremely pleased with what you've done; it is entirely your work, make no mistake.' He was not one to give praise readily and Maddy felt absurdly pleased at his words.

Her pleasure was somewhat blunted when he continued, 'The shop has improved our sales of cider considerably, now we must consider ways of increasing them even more.'

'More? Are you never satisfied?' she demanded.

'No,' was his blunt reply.

Maddy shook her head in disbelief. 'What else can be done to sell more cider?' she asked.

'Frankly, I don't know,' said Cal. 'I'm relying on you for some good ideas.'

Maddy's response was an indignant splutter. 'I fear you'll have to wait a long time,' she said.

Any anxieties she might have had about the continuing success of the shop faded as time went by and a stop 'up to Oakwood's' became a regular habit for both land and river folk.

A group of wherrymen had gathered in the shop one afternoon, lounging comfortably at a table in the window. They had finished eating and drinking, and were preparing to leave when one of their number arrived belatedly. Maddy recognised him as a Dartmouth man, one who daily made the trip upriver with goods and passengers.

'What time do you call this, Bill?' one of the other wherrymen greeted him cheerily. 'Us'd given you up good and proper. You'm going to have to get up earlier of a morning, boy, and no mistake.'

'Don't talk to me about getting up early,' complained Bill. 'Save my life, Maddy, my handsome, and fetch me a pasty and a pint of Rough fast as you can.'

'You sounds weary,' said another of the men.

'Weary? So would you be if you'd near enough missed the tide. Coming up Home Reach there I thought us wadn't going to make un, with the current pulling back at us. Talk about a struggle.'

'Tidn't like you to be behindhand. What happened? A last-minute cargo?'

'No, there was a bit of bother as us set out. Nasty business. Fellow got drownded just as us was getting under way. Had to lend a hand, of course, us being close by. Twas only Christian.'

'What happened?'

'That be hard to say, though I saw un go. Out in a rowing boat, he were. Lord knows why, for he were about as handy in a boat as the widow's cow. He leaned over the gunwale as if trying to get something, and next thing us knows, over he went, boat and all. Gawd, did he holler! Two or three of us tried to get to un, but there was a stiffish breeze blowing, and going about wadn't easy. Us was too late. Fished un out, right enough, but he were dead.'

'Local man, was he?' asked a wherryman. 'Anyone us knows?'

'No, and that be another mystery. He were a musician fellow, by all accounts, as had lived upriver some time back – Galmpton, Stoke Gabriel way. Left in a hurry, the rumour goes. Got up to summat he shouldn't, I dare say.' Bill took an appreciative gulp of his cider. 'Still, the river have got its heart for this year, and early on too. Tis tragic for that young fellow, but it means the rest of us can sail easy for a long spell.'

'Indeed it do.' The other men nodded solemnly.

Maddy heard all this. She could not help it. There were no names, no description, but it was Patrick, of course. Who else? Patrick, who had only gone as far away as Dartmouth, and who was now dead.

Nan, standing beside her, had overheard too. 'You comes from Stoke Gabriel, Miss Shillabeer. It might be someone you knows.'

'It might,' said Maddy numbly.

Nan looked at her curiously. 'Yer, you'm gone dead white,' she said. '"Tis this talk of drownings and such. It have proper turned you up, I dare say. I can't abide un, neither. You go and have a sit down in the kitchen. I can manage yer.' And she gave Maddy a gentle push towards the door.

Mrs Collins took one look at her and thrust a chair in her direction. 'Make a cup of tea, maid,' she instructed the girl who helped her. 'Miss Shillabeer idn't well.' Turning to Maddy, she said with concern, 'Is there aught else I can get you? A drop of sal volatile maybe?'

'No, thank you.' Maddy managed a wan smile. 'The tea will do fine. If I sit quietly for a while I'll soon be all right.'

Mrs Collins nodded and, taking her at her word, went back to her duties, leaving Maddy in peace.

Patrick was dead. She thought of him as she had last seen him, with laughter glinting in his eyes, a smile making his face even more handsome. It had been a false smile, a perfidious smile, but somehow that did not matter any more. It had been wiped away for ever, never again to charm, to enchant – or to hurt. Patrick was dead, drowned in the treacherous Dart. To Maddy's stunned mind, it seemed like the quenching of a bright star.

What on earth had he been doing in a boat, he who feared water more than anything? She would probably never know. Not that it mattered. Knowing would never drive away the tortured images in her mind as she pictured his terror as he sank below the cold waves. But she had to try to blot out the and stir herself, for she had duties to perform and the shop to run.

'You'm sure you'm all right, Miss Shillabeer?' asked Nan with concern when she re-entered the shop. 'You'm still looking terrible wisht.'

'I'm fine,' declared Maddy. 'What I need is a bit of work.'

'If you says so.' Nan looked doubtful, as well she might, for Maddy was far from convinced herself. If only she could stop her limbs from shaking.

How she would have fared during the rest of the afternoon there was no knowing, but soon afterwards the door opened and in came Cal. 'I thought you might like to finish early today,' he said. 'I've got the gig outside.'

'But we don't close for hours yet,' Maddy protested.

'That doesn't matter. Nan can cope, she's very efficient. Where's your cape?'

He did not listen to her objections, but slipped her cape about her shoulders and propelled her firmly towards the waiting trap.

'You've heard the news,' he said. 'I can see it in your face.'

Maddy nodded.

'I'm sorry,' he said.

'So am I.'

What an understatement! She had thought herself past having any feelings for Patrick. That was not true. He had hurt her badly, but he had been like a comet that had crossed her path and altered her life for ever. Patrick was dead, but she realised, with much distress, that the embers of her love for him were far from extinguished.

–

News of Patrick's death spread round the village in no time. Many people declared it was just payment for the trouble he had caused. The more charitable decided that it was a harsh end for such a young man, no matter what he had done. As for Maddy, she kept her own counsel, avoiding the subject.

Of Victoria there was no sign. Strangely enough, although Mr Fitzherbert had travelled as far as London and beyond in search of his daughter, he seemed unwilling to ride the few miles to Dartmouth for news of her. 'I knew the rogue would abandon her one way or another!' he was heard to exclaim. 'I've done everything I can. She's likely got herself into a mess: let her get herself out of it!'

It was left to one of the river boatmen to inform the village that Patrick had indeed had a female companion – a haughty piece by all accounts – whose description matched Victoria's, but she had left Dartmouth after his death, owing three weeks' rent. Her whereabouts were unknown.

What were the pair of them doing in the seaport? That was what puzzled Maddy. And, knowing Patrick's fear of water, she still wondered what had enticed him on to the river and to his ultimate death.

Chapter Seventeen

Grief over Patrick's death remained with Maddy like a dark shadow. It might have been easier if she could have expressed her distress aloud, but people had long thought she had got over him, and now she could not bring herself to mourn in public. She kept her pain tight within her. How grateful she was for her work. At the cider shop she could submerge herself in activity for hours at a time. It was during the brief lulls at work that the harsh reality came back to haunt her.

'Could you do with another assistant?' Cal asked one day.

'Not really,' she replied in surprise. 'Why do you ask? Don't you think I am coping well enough?'

'What a defensive woman you are! I meant no hint of criticism, I promise you. I've merely noticed how you dash about like a scalded hen, and I wondered if I was overworking you.'

'You are not,' said Maddy firmly, then softened the brusqueness of her reply with a 'Thank you'. After a pause she added, 'I like to keep occupied, that's all.'

'As long as it is just a fondness for over-activity.'

She sensed sympathy beneath his keen regard, and that made her feel awkward. 'Is there any reason why I should not keep busy?' she asked.

'Busy, no. Over-busy, yes. For I am thinking of putting extra demands upon you.'

'We can't extend the shop,' she replied promptly. 'I've considered it carefully, and there is no direction in which we can expand. In addition, Mrs Collins is working to full capacity now, the kitchen just isn't big enough to take on anything more.'

'I'm glad to learn that you've been giving my business affairs such careful consideration,' he said, grinning. 'But it isn't the expansion of this shop that I have in mind, it's starting another one.'

'Another one? Where?' demanded Maddy.

Cal gave a shrug. 'I don't know yet. I'm only toying with the idea. We won't discuss the matter for the moment. For one thing, I need to get the plans clear in my head, and for another I fancy you have more than enough to cope with at present.' Maddy wished he did not seem to be able to read her mind; it was disconcerting, to say the least.

'Mr Whitcomb's gone then,' remarked Nan, observing his retreating back with some relief.

'Don't say it like that,' said Maddy. 'He won't eat you, you know.'

'I idn't so sure.' Nan's expression of alarm dissolved into one of self-satisfaction. 'I bet I knows where'm heading right now, any road.'

'The Seven Stars to fetch his horse?' suggested Maddy, her attention focused upon restacking cider mugs on a shelf.

'Not he. He'm off for a bit of courting.'

'Who? Mr Whitcomb?' Maddy almost dropped one of the mugs in her surprise. 'He's been very cunning if he is, there's no word of it about the village.'

'The folk of Totnes be one up on the folk of Stoke Gabriel in that case. 'Tis reckoned he'm got his eye on Miss Hannaford. You know, the corn merchant's daughter – has the gurt warehouse over to St Peter's Quay.'

'Oh, that Hannaford!' said Maddy. She did not know either the daughter or the corn-merchant father, but their employees were valued customers in the shop.

'Yes, that Hannaford,' affirmed Nan. 'He'm courting a pretty penny there, her being the only child.'

'Probably just rumour,' said Maddy, turning back to the stacking.

'Maybe, but he spent last Sunday with her. Saw him up to St Mary's with my own eyes, and in the Hannaford pew. Him and his mother. Leastways, I think 'twas his mother. Stout, cross-looking little body as he sometimes drives into town? All white curls and fancy bonnets?'

'That sounds like Mrs Whitcomb.'

'Well, if his ma be invited too, that have got to mean summat, don't it?' insisted Nan.

'You could be right,' agreed Maddy. It seemed as if Cal might have found his advantageous bride. For his sake, she hoped Miss Hannaford proved to be a nice girl.

It was not long before rumours that Farmer Whitcomb was paying court to a wealthy young woman reached Stoke Gabriel. As far as the gossips were concerned, Miss Hannaford's financial expectations rose with each telling. According to them the marriage settlement was already being worked out and the betrothal would be announced any day. But time went on without anything happening. Nor did Cal make any comment about the matter. Indeed, for a man facing impending marriage, he seemed remarkably calm.

And why shouldn't he? Maddy asked herself. It's not as if this were a love match. No affections are involved.

The thought depressed her. Her love for Patrick, for all its unhappy consequences, had given her an insight into what marriage could be. It seemed a shame if Cal Whitcomb had to settle for less.

Cal himself appeared far more concerned with the idea of opening a second cider shop. For a while the subject had not been mentioned, then quite out of the blue one day he said, 'I think Paignton would be a good choice, don't you?'

'For what?' asked Maddy.

'For another shop.'

'You're really considering opening another one?'

'Of course.' He seemed surprised at the question. 'Did you think I was joking?'

'I wasn't sure.'

'I'm deadly serious. What do you think of Paignton? I will give you my ideas why I think it is a good situation, and you can play Devil's advocate. Firstly, it is a busy town, with much expansion and building going on. Also, it is becoming increasingly popular as a holiday resort since the railway came. This time I have done my homework thoroughly and investigated the existing cider shops, and they are mainly in the older part of town up by the church. I think we should have our shop in the newer district somewhere near the railway station.'

'It would be expensive,' said Maddy. 'Not to mention difficult to get. I hear the properties round there are much sought after.'

'True, but I have heard of one that may be empty before long. No doubt we'll have to pay a high rent for it, but it will be worth it. Just think of what a range of customers we would have – workers, townsfolk, holidaymakers, travellers going to and fro on the trains.'

'Ah, but would we? What sort of a place would appeal to all those sorts of people? For, make no mistake, if it is too grand then the workmen will stay away. Too rough and ready and travelers and townsfolk will be put off. And as for the holidaymakers, they will patronise us for only a few weeks in the year. If we aren't careful, we could try to please everybody and end up by attracting no one.'

'A very good point,' Cal said heartily. 'I am sure you'll think of an excellent solution.'

'Me?' Maddy's voice rose to a squeak. 'I can't run this shop and set up a new one as well.'

'I don't expect you to. Nan can have charge of this place, or do you think it is beyond her capabilities?'

'No, Nan can cope right enough, with someone else to help her.'

'Right then, that's settled. Admit it, never for one minute did you entertain anyone else starting the new shop. You always knew it would be your job.'

At first Maddy began to deny it vehemently, then her protestations faded. 'Perhaps you're right,' she admitted ruefully.

'I'm always right,' said Cal. 'You will still be in overall charge of the Totnes shop, of course. Nan can run it, but I want her to be responsible to you.'

'I'm not destined for an idle life, I see.'

'No, you'd be miserable with nothing to do. It is decided? You approve of Paignton as our next business venture?'

'That decision must be yours,' said Maddy, alarmed at such responsibility.

'Then I have decided. We will open a shop at Paignton and we will both go there tomorrow to look at properties.'

As he rose to leave, Maddy was beset with sudden misgivings. 'You are sure about this?' she asked. 'You don't think you should wait until the Totnes shop has been established a little longer?'

'What good would that serve? It would only give competitors a chance to get ahead of us with our own idea. Correction. *Your* idea.'

'Does that mean I get the blame if it fails?'

'It won't fail, not with cider the quality of ours and pasties as tasty as these.' He pushed aside his empty mug and the plate bearing the crumbs of the pasty he had just eaten.

'The cider will be no problem, but if we're to provide pasties made on the premises, I had better start looking for another cook.'

'That will be no problem either,' said Cal with complete confidence. 'Isn't your stepmother a Paignton woman? And didn't she find us the inestimable Mrs Collins? A word in her ear and I'm sure she can provide us with yet another treasure.' With a wave of his hand he left the shop, leaving Maddy rather daunted by these new demands but already feeling a growing sense of excitement at the challenge ahead. Although she had the experience of the Totnes shop to draw upon, this would be a different venture. The more varied clientele would present new problems.

–

'You'm got a day off tomorrow or summat?' asked Jack, watching Maddy painstakingly pressing her skirt hem.

'Not a day off exactly,' said Maddy, as the heated flat-iron raised steam from the damp cloth covering the woollen fabric. 'I've got to go to Paignton with Mr Whitcomb first.'

'And what be you'm off to Paignton for on a working day, may I ask?'

'A bit of business. I can't tell you yet, Father, because it's confidential, but you'll know about it soon enough.'

'Oh, I will, will I? Well, I suppose I must be content with that. But be you'm going alone with Cal Whitcomb?'

'I'll be alone, of course. Who else would be with us?'

'I don't know now, do I? I were just wondering. And I suppose afterwards he'm going to drive you over to Totnes?'

'I don't know. Joshua might be in the driving seat, it depends on whether we go in the trap or the gig.' Maddy carefully set her iron to reheat at the fire and regarded Jack. 'Now then, Father, what's behind these questions?'

'I'll tell you what be behind them, my maid. I idn't at all pleased at the time you'm spending alone in Farmer Whitcomb's company. He'm your maister, I knows that, you'm bound to see a fair bit of un, but he is seeing you over to the shop, and you'm having meetings up to Oakwood to sort out the accounts and such, and there be times when he takes you to work or brings you home. Now you'm traipsing over to Paignton with un for the morning, and alone again. I reckon it be getting beyond a joke. Tidn't right for you to spend so much time alone with un. You'm getting yourself talked about, our Maddy. I accused you of that once afore, years back, and you fair jawed my ears off. Well, you habn't got no cause to jaw this time 'cos the facts be plain and clear. And I be telling you, it have got to stop.' Jack leaned back in his chair, quite out of breath after his long and impassioned speech.

Maddy regarded him with astonishment. 'But Mr Whitcomb is my employer, you've pointed that out yourself,' she said. 'How am I to avoid being alone with him?'

'That be something you'm going to have to work out yourself, maid,' Jack replied.

'That's being unreasonable. I can't possibly have a chaperon trailing after me while I'm at work. Tell him it's impossible, Joan,' she appealed to her stepmother.

But Joan's attention never wavered from her perpetual knitting. 'Your father have got a point, my lover. Folks be beginning to take notice, and that idn't never a good thing.'

'Notice of what?' Maddy demanded. 'That I work for him and have to spend a fair time in his company? Why, his betrothal is expected to be announced any day. Doesn't that scotch the rumours?'

Joan gave a derisive snort. 'Course it don't, girl. Cal Whitcomb be the sort as can cope with two women at the same time, anyone can see that.'

'Oh really!' exclaimed Maddy crossly. 'Am I expected to give up my job, my very good job,' she emphasised, 'simply to satisfy the village gossips?'

'No one's suggesting you gives up your job,' put in Joan hastily. 'But us'm talking about your good name yer, and that be important. Surely there must be some way round un?'

'I can't think of one,' retorted Maddy.

'If that be the case then there idn't naught else for un,' said Jack. 'I must go up Oakwood and have a word with Cal Whitcomb myself.'

'Please don't do that!' cried Maddy, appalled at the embarrassment it would cause her. Nevertheless, she recognised the unusual degree of determination in her father's voice. He meant what he said, even to the incredible possibility of setting foot on Oakwood soil himself.

'These yer visits to the house at Oakwood to reckon up the bills and whatnot, couldn't they be done at the shop in Totnes, with this Nan person you talks about on hand?' suggested Joan.

'I'm sure I could get Mr Whitcomb to agree to that,' said Maddy more calmly. 'But how could I persuade him not to drive me home afterwards? Perhaps if I left work earlier on a Friday and did the accounts with him in the office at Oakwood rather than at the house? That would solve one problem, and I'm sure he wouldn't mind.

There'd be plenty of folk about the place then, we wouldn't be alone. Would that satisfy you?'

'That'd be fine.' Jack's face beamed. 'There, I knowd you'd come up with summat. All you'm to bother with now is finding a way of stopping Farmer Whitcomb driving you about the countryside the rest of the time and us'll be content. The last thing us wants is for you to stop working. Us be real proud of the way you'm getting on, bain't us, Joan? But not if it costs you your good name.'

Maddy smiled absently, turning back to her pressing, her attention no longer focused on removing creases. How to discourage Cal from driving her to and fro was not what troubled her, it was the prospect of the future. Cal was involving her at a much earlier stage with this new shop, enough to take her to Paignton to look at property. She feared he intended taking a closer interest in this latest venture, which would mean their spending more time together, almost certainly alone, and this was what occupied her thoughts.

There was only one solution. She would have to put the matter frankly before Cal and request his co-operation. The prospect embarrassed her in the extreme, but she could think of no other way out.

The morning dawned fine and clear, the sharpness of autumn in the cool air. As she climbed the lane, Maddy was determined that her latest problem was not going to spoil the day. She felt quite excited at the prospect of riding into Paignton instead of walking. In addition, her outfit was new, the product of nights of sewing, ably assisted by Joan's nimble needle and Annie's advice. It had been the dark, rich damson shade of the fine woollen cloth which had first attracted her attention. She had bought a length instantly, the first indulgence of her new affluence.

The matter of style had been a far more difficult decision, until Annie had produced a paper pattern, obtained from the squire's house – no doubt surreptitiously – by her sister, Kitty. It had been of a two-piece; the skirt was full at the back, and the jacket had a peplum which Annie had assured Maddy was all the rage. How she knew, Maddy had no idea, but she took her word for it and began the nerve-racking task of cutting out. The completed garment turned out far better than she had dared to hope, especially when trimmed with matching braid.

'There, her'm going to be taken for gentry in that, and no mistake, idn't her, Annie?' said Joan proudly.

Annie's answer was slow in coming, for her attention was on Maddy's head.

'What you'm needing, girl, be a hat,' she said. 'Not a bonnet, they'm gone out with the Ark, but a hat. One of they smart ones shaped like a pork pie, maybe with a bit of a veil.' She spoke with complete authority on such matters of high fashion, in spite of being bound to her cottage for most of her days.

Rather to her surprise Maddy had found herself calling in at the smart milliner's just below Totnes' East Gate later that week and, even more to her surprise, coming away with a trim little hat in exactly the right rich hue.

Now, as she made her way to the top of the lane where Cal would be waiting for her, Maddy was delighted with her recent extravagances. She knew she looked good. Not since the days of Patrick's frank approval had she felt so confident. She would not object if Cal Whitcomb also displayed some admiration. However, as she approached, he was occupied in calming his horse, a new bay, that had been disturbed by a dog yapping at its heels.

'Wretched animal,' he remarked after the now fleeing dog. 'I'll have a few sharp words to say to its owner. Unruly brutes like that can cause accidents. You're prompt, I'm glad to see. We've a deal to do this morning. Shall we be on our way?' He handed her into the gig – and any moment for admiration was gone.

Maddy's disappointment was fleeting as she realised it was for the best. She was going to have to tackle him on an awkward enough subject sometime during the day, and it would be better not to have the affair further complicated by compliments.

It was a hectic morning. They saw five different properties, scrutinised them thoroughly, discussed terms and dates with the eager agent.

'We have sufficient information, I think,' said Cal, wafting the sheaf of papers in his grasp. 'We will inform you of our decision in due course.'

The agent withdrew, the light of optimism shining in his eyes.

'I don't know about you, but I think the shop opposite the station seems the most likely property,' said Cal, after the man had gone. 'However, let's not make up our minds too hastily. We can discuss it over luncheon. Where shall we go? The Royal serves a decent meal.'

Maddy came to an abrupt halt. 'You mean us to go to a hotel to eat?' she asked.

'Of course.'

'Together?'

'I certainly don't intend us to sit at separate tables. Why, what's wrong?'

'If you have no objection, Mr Whitcomb, I would prefer to go straight back to work,' said Maddy in some agitation. News that they had been seen dining together would definitely give the gossips something to talk about.

'When you call me Mr Whitcomb in such a way I know something is wrong. Can't we discuss it over our food, along with the other matters?'

'I would prefer to discuss it on the road to Totnes, if you please,' Maddy insisted.

'Oh, well, if we must we must, I suppose,' he said reluctantly.

Somehow Maddy could not bring herself to approach the subject until they had left the houses of Paignton behind them. In her head she tried to work out the right words with which to approach the awkward topic, and all the while the country miles were slipping past.

'If you don't say something soon we'll be in Totnes,' remarked Cal. 'Are you going to tell me what's troubling you before we get there, or will I be obliged to drive round and round?'

'People are talking,' Maddy blurted out.

'I believe they are,' said Cal. 'It's a characteristic of the human race.'

'Please don't joke. This is difficult enough for me as it is.'

'I'm sorry. Please tell me what people are talking about.'

'Us!'

'Us?' He looked at her with incredulity. 'What do you mean, us?'

'You and me! Folks are noticing that we spend a lot of time together and that often we're alone. My father's growing upset about my good name and says it must stop, so if we could do something about it – check the accounts in the office instead of the house, say, and things like that. That's why I couldn't eat with you in Paignton, it would have been the last straw, and already my father's threatening to come up to see you.' As the gig's wheels had been speeding on the downhill slope, Maddy's words had gathered momentum.

Fortunately Cal seemed to get the gist of her garbled speech. 'I see,' he said, taking the bay in hand and slowing the horse to a steadier pace. 'Your father is not suggesting that you leave my employment, I hope?' he said at last.

'Oh no.'

'He just wants me to provide a chaperon of some sort when we are together?'

'Or arrange for us not to be together – at least, not alone.'

'I see,' said Cal, and he grimaced. 'That's going to be difficult, considering our future plans for expansion. I hadn't considered it, but we will certainly be in each other's company frequently. It was foolish of me not to have given your reputation more careful thought.'

'I'm being a nuisance. I'm sorry,' said Maddy quietly.

'Pray do not go missish on me. It will help nothing,' said Cal brusquely. 'You are not being a nuisance, there's no reason for you to be sorry. I've been treating you like a man when, clearly, you are not.' He lapsed into silence again, his brow furrowed in concentration.

'I know!' he exclaimed at last. 'The perfect solution! We will get married!'

'What?'

They were approaching the turning for the last hill into Totnes.

'Drat!' declared Cal. 'We're almost there and we need more time to talk. We'll take a diversion, if you've no objections.'

Numbly, Maddy shook her head as, instead of taking the left turn to the town, he swung the gig past the tollhouse and towards open countryside and the village of Berry Pomeroy.

'Tell me, what is your opinion of my scheme?' he demanded, the manoeuvre completed.

'I think it's preposterous,' retorted Maddy.

'No, it's not,' was the calm reply. 'You haven't given it due consideration. Think on it. It's the ideal solution. No need for chaperons trailing after us, no cause for the village gossips to be busy. We can carry on working together, disturbing no one, not even your father.'

'What about Miss Hannaford?'

For a moment Cal looked blank. 'She has nothing to do with it,' he said impatiently.

'The village gossips think otherwise, they have you about to be married.'

'They are about as accurate in that as they are in their tale that you and I are having an illicit affair. Miss Hannaford is my mother's idea of a good match for me, and I am her mother's idea of a good catch for her. I don't recall them consulting either Miss Hannaford or myself for our views. She is a pleasant girl, but her heart is set upon London and lively society. The last thing she wants is to be a farmer's wife.'

'Whereas I would not object?'

'You wouldn't be just a wife, you would be my business partner.'

'Nevertheless, you can't propose to marry me just like that.'

'Why not?'

'Because… because…' Maddy floundered. 'Because you must make an advantageous marriage and I've neither money nor expectations.'

'There are different sorts of advantageous marriages. True, it would have been useful to have wedded money, but the longer I consider it the more I think marriage to you would be most beneficial. You have an excellent head for business, you work extremely hard, and you have a flair for coming up with excellent ideas. Look at how Oakwood Farm Cider has expanded since you've become involved. An aptitude such as yours is worth more than any dowry. Also, we get along together very well. You would be an ideal wife for me.'

'And what of me?' It took every bit of Maddy's self-control to keep the plaintive note from her voice.

'Your advantages would be mainly financial. As a business partner rather than an employee you would share in the prosperity gained by making Oakwood a thriving business. I'd make sure you had a proper marriage settlement, legally drawn up, ensuring you the full financial entitlement that is your due. You would have security until the end of your days – no small benefit for anyone. Moreover, you would be a married woman. I mean no disrespect, but it's a regrettable fact of life that spinsters are looked down upon socially, no matter what their personal abilities. Marriage to me would save you from such a fate. And, casting undue modesty aside, I venture to say that to be Mrs Whitcomb of Oakwood Farm is to be a person of some standing in the neighbourhood.'

'There already is a Mrs Whitcomb of Oakwood Farm,' Maddy pointed out.

'Ah!' For the first time Cal's self-confidence faltered. 'She knows I must marry sometime.'

'But to a Shillabeer? If you took me home as your bride, there would be the Devil to pay.'

'There would,' agreed Cal. 'But I am prepared to pay him if you are.'

Maddy had given up any hopes of receiving an offer of marriage from anyone, yet here was Cal asking her to be his wife. Strangely enough, her immediate reaction was one of disappointment. Disappointment for what? That Cal had not wooed her with pretty speeches? That he had not chosen a moonlit garden to make his proposal, and had failed to go down on one knee? How foolish could she get? This was no romantic declaration, this was a business proposition, and as such she had to admit he had set out his terms fairly and squarely. Yet the regret remained with her.

Cal's thoughts must have been running along similar lines, for he said ruefully, 'As a proposal that was an extremely cold-hearted affair, wasn't it? Please forgive me. Even for a first attempt that was pretty abysmal. I'll admit that expedience was the spur which prompted me to ask you to marry me. It would be mutually beneficial, but there was more to my offer than mere business. I have come to admire and respect you, Maddy, and we are never bored in each other's company. The idea of sharing my life with you is a pleasing one. This would be no love match, we both know that, but all in all I think we stand a tolerable chance of dealing happily together.'

A tolerable chance of dealing happily together... Unbidden, thoughts of Patrick came into Maddy's mind, of what it felt like to harbour joyous dreams of a marriage that was a love match. Swiftly she thrust such treacherous thoughts from her. Those dreams were irrelevant. It was Cal's offer, here in the present, that she must consider.

'Your proposal was completely unexpected,' Maddy said.

'I believe that is what young ladies say in the best novels,' said Cal. The sudden humour eased the tension that had been building up between them.

'I'm glad I didn't disappoint you.' Maddy found herself relaxing and her thoughts beginning to clear. 'You certainly put forward an excellent case for me becoming your wife. But I am sure that, with a modicum of concentration, we could find ways of protecting my good name to the satisfaction of my father without going to such extremes.'

'No, we couldn't!' said Cal emphatically. 'There is one thing I am determined upon and that is that Oakwood is going to progress. I have many plans and ambitions for the future, and with you to help me I am confident we will succeed. I would be less confident, however, if at every turn we had to stop for your chaperon to catch up, or to obtain permission from your father for some move or other. Marriage is the best, the only, solution.'

'Perhaps.' Even to her own ears Maddy did not sound convinced.

'I don't expect an immediate reply,' said Cal. 'I accept that my proposal came out of the blue. Take your time, and think the matter over carefully.'

'I will.'

They had been bowling along, taking no heed of where they went. Maddy was quite surprised to find they were passing Berry Pomeroy church and its neighbouring farm. Something about the protective girdle of chestnut trees struck a familiar note. She feared they may have been driving round and round the same narrow lanes. Cal looked at her, and grinned.

'I think the folk of Berry Pomeroy would know us again, don't you?' he said. 'I'd better get you back to Totnes.'

Maddy was glad they spoke little on the return road, for she had more than enough to occupy her thoughts. They were almost at the bridge crossing the Dart when Cal said suddenly, 'You aren't annoyed with me, are you? For proposing marriage, I mean.'

'Of course not. Whatever I decide I shall always regard it as a compliment.'

'Good. I would hate anything to spoil things between us.' His sigh of relief surprised her. Despite his outward self-assurance, Cal Whitcomb was not always as confident as he seemed. Maddy realised that there were many things she did not know about this man whom she might marry – and might not!

That night, any hope of sleeping on the problem was a lost cause. Maddy remained steadfastly awake, pondering over the situation until it was a relief when dawn came and she had to get up.

'You sickening for summat?' asked Joan, noting her pale face and heavy eyes.

'No, I'm fine, thanks,' Maddy replied. 'I've just got something on my mind.'

Joan regarded her even more keenly. 'If 'tis summat serious, you can always come to me, you knows that, don't you, maid?'

Maddy smiled, guessing the way her stepmother's mind was working. 'It's not the sort of serious you're meaning,' she said. 'And yes, I know you'd stand by me in trouble and I truly appreciate it. But, as I say, this isn't trouble really. Simply something important that I've got to sort out for myself.' Then she wondered if it might not be better to talk over Cal's proposal with her stepmother, who could be relied upon to bring practical common sense to any situation. In the event, Joan did not wait to be asked.

'If 'tis so important it have kept you awake all night then my advice be to make your mind up prompt, make un up good and proper, and don't let yourself have no regrets. They long drawn out tangles, they wears out a body until you don't know if you'm coming or going, and the decisions you makes in the end idn't no better for all the chawing over.'

Joan's brisk, no-nonsense words were exactly what Maddy needed to hear. What point was there in humming and hawing? The advantages of the marriage she knew perfectly well. What were the disadvantages? Having to share a home with Mrs Whitcomb seemed to be the worst, and she felt that even that could be overcome. And of course there would be the inevitable difficulties of a loveless marriage. Nevertheless, it would be founded on mutual respect and interests. She could think of plenty of marriages that were based on far less yet seemed successful enough.

If she did not wed Cal, what then? While she was working, her future would be agreeable enough, but as her father and Joan grew older, it would fall to her, as the unmarried daughter, to care for them in their old age. And what of her own old age? Who would there be to care for her? She had no wish to be a burden to Lew and Mollie, or to Charlie if he found a wife. Marriage to Cal would mean security, a comfortable life, status, and a thoroughly enjoyable way of life helping in the business. She would be acquiring a decent, considerate husband into the bargain. Many a woman had married for a fraction of such advantages. Thinking in those terms, she had no problem at all in making up her mind.

Next day, Maddy greeted Cal with the words, 'Yesterday you made me an offer. You made it on the spur of the moment and you probably regret it now. If you do, would you kindly say so?'

'I regret nothing,' declared Cal with some indignation. Then his face broke into a delighted smile. 'Does that mean you agree to marry me?'

Maddy was overwhelmed by a sudden shyness. 'Yes,' she said, almost inaudibly.

They were in the storeroom at the shop. Again an unromantic venue, but the one place where they could talk privately.

'I'm relieved you've been so quick in coming to a decision,' said Cal, his face beaming. 'I feared you would keep me on tenterhooks for ages. Would it be convenient for me to call upon your father tonight, to ask for your hand?'

Mention of Jack introduced a snag.

'I'm not convinced my father will give his consent.'

'No? I thought he had grown more amenable towards us Whitcombs.'

'He has, but I'm not sure it stretches as far as accepting one as a son-in-law.'

'Hm...' Cal looked thoughtful. 'Might it not be a good idea to have a quiet word with your stepmother first? She always strikes me as a sensible woman. I fancy she wouldn't disapprove of our marriage. It might be of help to have her forewarned and on our side when I come.'

It was an excellent suggestion. She was glad that Cal had not suggested defying her father. Legally she was of age to do as she pleased, but Cal recognised and respected her strong family ties.

'I'll speak to Joan,' she said. 'Between us we'll talk Father round.'

'Then I can come tonight?'

'Yes, of course.' Maddy felt she had to ask the next question. 'When will you tell your mother?'

'As soon as possible.'

Maddy did not envy him. Whatever objections Jack might express, she felt that they would be mild compared to Mrs Whitcomb's views.

A silence fell upon the storeroom, one tinged with embarrassment.

'Well,' said Cal. 'We're betrothed, or as good as. It just needs your father's consent. And there's the ring! I'd forgotten about that. I have my Grandmother Whitcomb's. It's a pretty thing of chased gold and diamonds, but old-fashioned. No doubt you would like something modern.'

'There is no need for a ring,' said Maddy, flustered. 'I wasn't expecting anything like that. Let's not bother with one.'

'You know I already have a reputation as a skinflint. To have a fiancée without a ring would just confirm my meanness. You shall definitely have a ring. Whether you wear it or not is up to you.'

'Then I think I would prefer your grandmother's ring, if it will fit.'

'We can soon have it altered if it does not.' He seemed pleased at her choice, but still vaguely ill at ease. 'There's one more matter we mustn't neglect,' he said. Then he brushed her cheek with his lips.

Straightening up he regarded her speculatively, all trace of awkwardness gone. 'That was a pretty poor effort for the sealing of a betrothal. I can do better than that.'

Grasping her about the waist, he pulled her closer and kissed her again, this time full on the lips. His kiss lacked the sweet tenderness of Patrick's, yet there was an energy about it and a sense of enjoyment that she did not at all object to. In fact, she was somewhat startled to discover that she found it positively agreeable – which was just as well seeing that she had agreed to marry him.

'I think there is room for improvement,' Cal observed, as he gently released her. 'But, God willing, we have many years ahead of us to achieve perfection.' The way he was smiling at her confirmed that he, too, had found the experience far from displeasing. Painfully aware that her cheeks were flaming, Maddy smiled back. Suddenly he reached out and took her hand. 'You'll never regret your decision, I promise you that,' he said, squeezing her fingers. Then his mood changed, and he gave a wry smile. 'I think I must go and inform my mother that I am to become a married man.' He released her hand. 'I shall see you again this evening, at eight?'

'At eight,' agreed Maddy, already feeling nervous about the interview between him and her father.

–

Joan's immediate reaction to the news betrayed far less astonishment than Maddy had expected. 'You'm thinking of wedding Farmer Whitcomb, be you?' she said calmly. 'My, if that idn't good news.'

'You don't seem surprised,' protested Maddy.

'I'll think up a parcel of objections if that's what'll please you. But if you wants the truth, I've thought once or twice recently as you'd make a good pair. Mind, what your father'll say about un I idn't going to guess.'

'Cal's coming this evening to ask his permission. You will be on our side, won't you?'

'I don't know as I'll be on anyone's side; but I can see this be a good match and I'll make no bones about saying so.'

'Thank you.' Maddy was relieved. Somehow she had felt her stepmother would ultimately approve, but she had required far less persuasion than Maddy had anticipated.

'Right then,' said Joan, returning to more mundane matters. 'You look out the best tablecloth while I'll see if us've got summat decent to drink. If not, one of us'll have to run up to the Church House.'

Jack had plans of going up to the Church House on his own account.

'You'm going to have to bide home tonight,' his wife informed him. 'Us be expecting a visitor. Farmer Whitcomb be coming.'

'Cal Whitcomb? Coming yer?' Jack's face suffused with sudden annoyance. 'What the devil do he want?'

'I thought you agreed he'm a decent enough fellow,' said Joan.

'Not when he comes bothering folk of an evening.'

At her father's words, Maddy relaxed. His irritation was born more from missing his pint of cider than from animosity towards Cal. Her relief was short-lived.

'And as for Farmer Whitcomb being a decent enough fellow,' went on Jack, 'I daresay he be, but that don't mean I wants his boots resting on my hearth. Maddy works for un, that be plenty of dealings with the Whitcombs.' Then his face cleared. 'What be he'm coming about, maid? Did you have a word with un about guarding your good name?'

'I did, Father.'

'Then no doubt he'm coming to discuss un, man to man. That idn't so bad. I habn't no objections to talking to the fellow if 'tis for our Maddy's benefit.' As he leaned over to unlace his boots, Joan and Maddy exchanged anxious glances over his bent head. Poor Jack was in for a shock, and there was no knowing how he would react.

From the moment he arrived, Cal seemed to dominate the room. It was more than his size, impressive though that was, it was his demeanour. He was a picture of self-assurance from the crown of his well-brushed hair to his highly polished boots. Although he did not betray any hint of nervousness, Maddy was beginning to learn how tightly he kept his inner emotions hidden.

'Mr Shillabeer,' he said, after having accepted a glass of elderflower wine. 'I won't beat about the bush. I have come to ask you if you will kindly grant me Maddy's hand in marriage.' Jack's jaw dropped.

'Jack, boy, Farmer Whitcomb be wanting to wed our Maddy,' Joan prompted eventually. 'Say summat, for pity's sake.'

'No!' declared Jack, finding his tongue with a vengeance. 'No! That's what I do say. My Maddy marry a Whitcomb? I won't hear of un.'

'Father, please don't be too hasty,' begged Maddy. 'Give the matter some thought.'

'I don't need to think. My answer be no.' Jack's mouth had set in a grimly determined line. ''Sides, I thought you was betrothed to some wench up to Totnes.'

'Idle gossip,' said Cal. 'It's Maddy I want to wed.'

'Well, the answer be no. And I idn't going to change my mind.'

'I'm sorry you think that way, Mr Shillabeer,' said Cal. 'I had thought our two families had drawn closer together.'

'Maybe they have, but I don't intend having them that close.'

'I assure you I can offer Maddy a future of comfort and security,' Cal persisted. 'I will happily give you details of my financial standing, though I expect you are familiar with the value of my two farms.'

'Be you suggesting I've been poking my nose into your affairs?' demanded Jack. 'I wouldn't stoop so low, not even though Oakwood near enough came to us.'

'Oh Father!' protested Maddy again, 'For pity's sake don't go raking over those old coals!'

'I expressed myself badly,' said Cal. 'I was not implying any inquisitiveness on your part. Far from it. I merely meant that my assets, in the shape of land, outbuildings and stock, are clear for everyone to see. Then there is the cider business, with its press and poundhouse and the equipment and other buildings. As for the shop, Maddy will tell you that it is flourishing.'

'I don't care how flourishing it be, you idn't marrying my girl, and that be final.'

'No it isn't,' declared Maddy. 'Aren't I allowed to have my say? Don't my wishes count for anything?'

'Speak away, maid. You won't change nothing,' said Jack.

'I want to marry Cal. Doesn't that mean anything to you? What objections have you got other than prejudice? None! It's not as though he has a reputation as a drunkard or a lecher or anything of the sort. And he is sufficiently prosperous to give me a comfortable life until the end of my days.'

'You'm comfortable yer!'

'For how long? Yes, things are easy enough now because of the money Cal pays me for running his shop, but what happens when that stops? For make no mistake, if you refuse to give your consent, I could not continue to work for him. I'd be far too embarrassed and ashamed.'

Maddy looked across at her stepmother, willing her to offer some support, but Joan avoided her gaze.

'You'd soon find summat,' said Jack with unshakable obstinacy. 'You'm a willing maid.'

'I don't want to be a willing maid, I want to be a married woman!'

'Then find someone else to wed!' roared Jack. 'For I tells you straight, you'm idn't marrying no Whitcomb, I don't care if he'm rich enough to pay the national debt and have a character whiter than the angels. I hopes that be clear,' he said, addressing Cal.

'Perfectly clear, I thank you.' Cal had risen to his feet, his face grim. 'I had better take my leave. Obviously my presence here is an embarrassment.'

'It idn't that, boy, 'tis simply a waste of time,' said Jack. 'There idn't no way a daughter of mine be going to wed a Whitcomb. Not now, not never.'

'Spoken like a true Shillabeer,' commented Joan, joining in the conversation for the first time. 'Any match between one of us and a Whitcomb be out of the question. Twould be going against years of family feeling. All the same, 'tis a pity in some ways. It might have been nice to have had one of our lot living up Oakwood again after so many years. Tis where the Shillabeers first come from when all be said and done. Their ancestral home, I suppose you might say. But if 'tis not to be...' She heaved a regretful sigh. 'You had a hat, I think, Mr Whitcomb?'

'Yes, it's on the chair. Thank you, Mrs Shillabeer.' Cal, white-lipped, accepted his hat and prepared to leave. 'Maddy, we have much to talk over, but under the circumstances I think it's best left until tomorrow, don't you?'

Maddy nodded, conscious of a deep sense of disappointment. She had expected her father to express some disapproval but she had not been prepared for such stubborn intransigence.

'Hold your horses!' Jack's voice, suddenly less belligerent, made them turn. 'Just 'cos I idn't keen on you wedding my daughter idn't no reason for you to go rushing off. Never let it be said as Jack Shillabeer sent a man away when there was some drink left in the bottle.'

Maddy and Cal looked at one another in surprise, neither of them certain how to react to this change in Jack's tone. They looked towards

Joan for guidance and, almost imperceptibly, she nodded her head, a glint of satisfaction in her eyes. Obediently they returned to the hearthside where Jack poured out fresh measures of elderberry wine.

'You told your mother?' he asked, quite convivially.

'I have,' said Cal.

Jack gave a chuckle. 'I bet her wadn't much pleased! A Shillabeer living up Oakwood! That wouldn't suit Mary Whitcomb no how! Yer, Joan girl, idn't us got naught to eat to offer Mr Whitcomb? What about that cheese us had earlier – it were rare tasty – with a bit of new bread to help un along? And while you'm about un, fetch another bottle of this elderberry. Unless there be aught else you'm preferring, Mr Whitcomb?'

'No, thank you. The elderberry is excellent,' replied Cal, sounding rather stunned.

Maddy was not surprised at his reaction, she had seldom seen such a complete about face as her father was exhibiting. As she got up to help Joan by setting out the bread and cheese, she gave her stepmother a grateful wink. She had to hand it to her, Joan had known exactly what to say to change Jack's mind.

Joan's cunning and Maddy's optimism were both justified. Before the evening was over – and by the time the second bottle of elderberry wine had been emptied – Jack was calling Cal by his Christian name. And by the time Maddy went to bed that night, she knew that she was destined to be Mrs Calland Whitcomb – with her father's full consent.

Chapter Eighteen

To call the betrothal of Maddy and Cal a nine-day wonder was an understatement. Everyone in the village was full of it and never seemed to tire of discussing the extraordinary prospect of a Whitcomb from Oakwood proposing marriage to a Shillabeer from Duncannon. Even Lew and Charlie got over their initial surprise to offer their genuine congratulations. In one quarter, however, there was a deep and ominous silence on the subject.

'Her'm closed her mouth tight as a cat's bum when her were told, and her habn't uttered a word since,' Ellen informed anyone who would listen.

Conditions at home were clearly taking their toll on Cal. He was beginning to look white and drawn, and Maddy felt guilty at being the cause. She slipped off the pretty gold and diamond ring which adorned the third finger of her left hand.

'Here,' she said, dropping it into his palm. 'It would be easier if we forgot the whole idea of getting wed. It's not fair you should have to put up with so much. Let's end the engagement and have done.'

'Is that what you really want? Are you using my mother as an excuse? I wouldn't blame you if you were.'

Strangely enough, when she was facing him, any doubts she had about the marriage disappeared. 'Of course I'm not,' she said. 'If I were having second thoughts I'd say so openly and not make your mother the scapegoat.'

'Then let's put this back where it belongs.' He slipped the ring onto her finger, but did not release her hand. 'I confess I am finding her a bit difficult at the moment. I thought our engagement would bring about one of her interminable tirades, I'm well used to those. This perpetual silence has caught me unawares. But never fear, I intend that you and your family shall be invited to Oakwood soon. It should have happened long since, and I am ashamed at the delay. But the invitation will come, never doubt it.'

He was as good as his word, and a neatly penned note inviting Mr and Mrs John Shillabeer and Miss Shillabeer to tea at Oakwood Farm the following Sunday was duly delivered.

'How did you manage it?' asked Maddy.

Cal's grin was wide. 'I merely announced that I was inviting you, with or without her co-operation. Then I told Ellen to get down the Worcester tea service and make sure it was washed in time for Sunday. That did it. The idea of the service being used at all was bad enough, but the thought of Ellen being let loose on it, that was too much. My mother is now speaking to the world again, though not to me if she can help it. And I regret to say that on Sunday you and your parents will have to make do with Crown Derby, the Worcester service is staying on display.'

It would be true to say that no one was looking forward to Sunday afternoon, with the possible exception of Ellen, who was hoping for some lively exchanges. However, even her face dropped when she opened the door to them. 'Habn't you brought the babe?' she said. 'I were looking forward to having the little one yer.'

'My brother and his wife and baby aren't coming,' Maddy informed her.

'I suppose they wadn't invited.' Ellen gave a sniff. 'Three Shillabeers at a time be enough as far as her be concerned. Still, if you and Mr Cal gets to un fast enough us'll soon have childer of our own.'

'First things first, Ellen,' rebuked Cal, appearing in the flagged hall, as immaculate as ever in brown broadcloth and snowy linen. 'There is the small matter of the wedding to see to before such things. Please come in, Mr and Mrs Shillabeer, and you too, Maddy.'

Stiff and uncomfortable, they followed him into the best parlour, Jack running his finger round his highly starched collar, while Joan hissed in Maddy's ear, 'I wish I habn't laced my stays so tight, they'm killing me.'

The welcome they received from Mrs Whitcomb fairly crackled with frost. She was sitting bolt upright on a high-backed armchair, her small plump feet resting on a footstool. 'For all the world like the Queen herself,' Jack said later. As if to continue the regal illusion, she extended a hand to her unwelcome guests. Maddy recognised it as a deliberate attempt to intimidate her family, and she exchanged a sympathetic glance with Cal, fearing an afternoon of discomfort. Her stepmother was already obviously nervous and overawed, but she had not anticipated her father's reaction.

'Afternoon, Mary,' he said, grasping the outstretched hand and pumping it vigorously. 'I hopes you'm feeling vitty.'

The room temperature dropped by several degrees.

'I don't recall giving you permission to use my Christian name,' said Cal's mother haughtily.

'Don't be daft, woman, we'm cousins. I idn't going to call you Mrs Whitcomb.' He settled himself in the chair indicated by Cal. 'Now then, Cousin Mary, what do you think about these two getting wed? I reckon 'tis a grand thing.'

'I dare say you do,' was the sour reply. 'You Shillabeers have got into Oakwood at last, which is what you've always wanted.'

'I must admit that such a thought did pass through my mind, but the more I dwelt on un the more glad I were that our Maddy have found herself a good steady man as'll treat her well. And I expect you'm equally glad your son've found a decent hard-working maid as'll stand by him through thick and thin.'

'No, I'm not!' was the unequivocal reply. 'He could have done a lot better for himself; but then it's the sort of thing he would do.' Mary Whitcomb's gaze rested on Maddy's hand. 'That ring's familiar. Where did you get it?'

'From Cal,' replied Maddy, stung by the accusation in her tone.

'It was mine to give,' said Cal. 'Grandmother Whitcomb left it to me in her will.'

'No doubt she did.' The provocative note of doubt was unmistakable. 'I'm merely surprised you've still got it, and not mislaid it as you did your father's gold watch.' Mrs Whitcomb turned to Maddy. 'Don't think you're going to have an easy life married to him. He's got no thoughts in his head save making money. A workhorse, that's what he wants you for.'

'Our Maddy won't mind that,' put in Jack before his daughter could reply. 'Her frets if her'm idle. And as for Cal thinking of naught but business, you'm done well enough out of it, I see.' He was looking at the display cabinets as he spoke, and immediately it was evident that the old lady was torn between indignation at his comment and pride in her treasures. As always the longing to show off her possessions won.

Rising from her chair, she said disparagingly, 'He didn't buy me these, they were gifts from my other son, my dear Christopher...'

She gave them the full grand tour; not a teacup, not a silver spoon was left out, complete with its accompanying history. And at every opportunity, she sang the praises of her dead son, wherever possible to the detriment of Cal. Maddy found herself growing more and more angry at this attitude, but she held her tongue. Any outbursts of hers would only make things more difficult for Cal and almost certainly cause problems for the future. The most she could do was to slip her hand into Cal's. She meant it as a fleeting gesture of sympathy, but Cal's fingers curled about hers and held them firm.

'The tea service decorated with the hand-painted birds is Worcester,' said Mrs Whitcomb, pausing in front of the final cabinet. 'That's pure gold inside, you know. A birthday present from my Christopher. He would have bought me the dinner service to match if he had lived. Ordered, it was, but that one cancelled it.' The look she gave Cal was toll of animosity.

'A good thing he did, from what I've heard,' said Jack.

'I beg your pardon?' Mrs Whitcomb stiffened.

'Well, it wasn't no coincidence that when Cal, yer, took over the farm, the men started getting paid regular. With yon Christopher in charge it weren't nothing to hear your workers grumbling 'cos they wadn't getting no money. They all said he were a nice fellow, mind, but getting wages out of him, that were another matter. And no wonder if he were buying you gew-gaws like this.'

Mrs Whitcomb fairly spluttered with indignation. 'How dare you say such things!' she cried.

'Now what've I done?' demanded Jack, as Joan muttered at him to keep quiet. 'I habn't said one word as idn't the truth. Everyone knows as Christopher Whitcomb were a terrible payer, and that after he died it was his brother as paid the wages right back. How d'you do un, boy?' he asked. 'That were where your pa's watch went, I'll be bound.'

'Father!' protested Maddy, in an agony of embarrassment as Cal looked uncomfortable. She was horrified that Jack could be so tactless. Then she noticed the expression in his eyes. It was far too innocent to be true. He was stirring things up deliberately.

It was fortunate that at that moment Ellen came in with the tea tray. Her face was crumpled in a wide, toothless grin, for she had heard every word.

Tea was not a comfortable meal. Maddy was in agonies, fearing what her father might say next, but to her relief he seemed to have decided to behave himself. Cal was the perfect host, attentive to his guests. He appeared to ignore his mother's barbed looks and words, though occasionally his gaze strayed out through the window, as if he were eager to escape to where the late afternoon sun shone on a garden rich with the colours of autumn.

His mother noticed his restlessness. 'Oh, go out, if that's what you want,' she snapped. 'Can't sit still for a minute, he can't.'

'Yes, you two young uns don't want to be stuck indoors with us old fogeys,' said Joan, abandoning her awestricken silence at last. 'Go and get a bit of fresh air.'

'Would you care to go for a stroll?' Cal asked Maddy.

She needed no second invitation. The contrast with the tense gloom of Oakwood's parlour made the brightness of the sunshine doubly welcome. For a moment she stood on the garden path, basking in the warmth. Then she could hold back no longer.

'How can you stand it?' she demanded. 'I'm sorry, I know I'm being rude, but I could hardly bear to sit there and listen to her sniping at you all the time. Yet you never made a reply.'

Cal gave a shrug. 'I hardly notice it any more.'

'Why do you put up with it?'

Again he shrugged. 'What else can I do? I can't leave her on her own. How would she manage? She has no one but me. You must understand that she is a very unhappy woman. She only ever loved two people – the young man she wanted to marry when she was a girl, and my brother, and she lost them both. Her life has been sad and unsatisfactory and, since Christopher's death, very lonely. Letting fly at me is the one relief she has. At times she goes too far and I confess I have to curb my tongue, for what good would it do to have a shouting match? It would just deepen existing wounds and make matters worse.'

'There are few who would have such forbearance,' said Maddy.

'I merely accept the situation as it is. I am only worried that Mother might make things difficult for you.'

'She won't do that,' said Maddy with assurance. She knew perfectly well that Mary Whitcomb would go out of her way to be unpleasant, but somehow she would have to learn to cope. 'When we are married I expect I'll spend a deal of time with you or else at one or other of our shops. I doubt if your mother and I will get under one another's feet much.'

It was extraordinary how easily she could say 'When we are married' and refer to 'our shops'. And equally extraordinary was the way saying those words gave her a comfortable feeling inside. It was as if she and Cal had been betrothed for an age instead of a few weeks.

Side by side they explored the garden. They were just turning towards the mixed orchard, the one where, a lifetime before, her brothers had thrown yew clippings over the hedge, when they were brought to a halt by someone calling Cal's name. One of the farm hands was hurrying in through the gate.

'Sorry to interrupt you, maister,' he said. 'But us be growing rare bothered about old Boney. He idn't showing no improvement, if anything he's weaker. Us'd be real grateful if you'd come.'

'Boney?' Maddy raised her eyebrows questioningly.

'Our ram.' Cal looked regretful. 'Any other beast and I'd trust my shepherd to cope, but Boney's a valuable animal. We're depending on him to build up our flock. I'm afraid this means I must leave you. I'm very sorry.'

'Please don't apologise. Off you go and see to poor old Boney. I'll walk in the orchard for a while, if I may, then go back indoors.'

With a grateful smile he set off after the farm hand, his hurried stride betraying the anxiety he felt for his precious ram. Maddy watched him go, then changed her mind about walking in the orchard; the sun was sinking behind the trees, taking its warmth with it. She went indoors.

'What, he'm deserted you already?' teased her father.

'Yes, and for a sick ram, too,' Maddy said with a grin.

'A ram?' Mary Whitcomb saw nothing amusing in the situation. 'That means he'll be traipsing back through the house smelling of the farmyard.'

'Of course he will,' said Jack. 'What else would he smell of? He'm a farmer, idn't he?'

Mrs Whitcomb's reply was a derisive snort.

'That boy can't do aught good in your eyes, can he?' Jack declared. 'Gawd, Cousin Mary, there idn't no understanding you! It were tragic, you losing your other son like that, and I knows how that feels, for our Davie be dead, and it don't look like our Bart'll ever come home. But it makes me think all the more of the three childer I got left. You'm only got one son surviving, and a good son too, yet it seems to me you don't want un. You prefers your memories and a few cabinets of trinkets. Have you thought where you'd be without Cal? You'd not be yer to Oakwood, that be sure, you'd never run the farm on your own. Whether you sold un or put in a steward as'd cheat you left, right and centre wouldn't make no difference. You'd likely end up one of they lonely widow women as lives over to Paignton, drinking tea and driving about in donkey carts all day 'cos they habn't got naught to do with their lives. I tells you straight, if I was give a choice atween a few shelves of fancy china and my own flesh and blood, I knows which I'd choose and no hesitation.'

'How dare you say such things!' cried Mrs Whitcomb for the second time that afternoon, but on this occasion there was a tremulous note to her indignation.

'I says it 'cos it needs saying,' replied Jack with surprising gentleness. 'No one else would. Your Cal be too soft-hearted and 'tidn't no one else's place. But we'm kinsfolk, whether you like un or no. We'm Shillabeer talking to Shillabeer. Think on what you got left, maid, not on what you'm lost, else you'm going to end up with naught and that'd be a terrible pity.'

For a moment it looked as though Mrs Whitcomb would explode with fury. Then her face crumpled and tears began to trickle down her plump cheeks.

'No one has ever had the audacity to speak to me like that before, Cousin Jack,' she said, her voice barely audible in her distress. 'Go away! That's all I ask. Go away and leave me alone, the lot of you.'

It was a very subdued trio who left Oakwood. Even Ellen was unusually quiet as she ushered them out. Cal caught up with them as they reached the gate.

'I do apologise for deserting you,' he began, then he noted their faces. 'What's wrong?' he asked.

'Your ma be a bit upset. Twere my doing,' admitted Jack. The side window opened and Ellen poked out her head. 'Her called you Cousin Jack, did you notice?' she remarked. 'That have got to mean summat.'

'It have,' agreed Jack. 'Maybe I idn't sorry, then.'

'What happened?' Cal asked Maddy quietly.

'My father did a bit of straight talking, I'm afraid. I'm not sure whether he did the right thing or not, but it's too long to explain.

Perhaps your mother will tell you everything. If not, Ellen certainly will. I must go, my parents are waiting.'

'Very well. I'll come to the shop tomorrow. We'll talk then.'

Cal stood at the gate and watched them go.

Neither Maddy nor Joan spoke much on the way home. They had both been surprised and moved by Jack's impassioned comments to Mary Whitcomb.

'Didn't know he had such words in un,' whispered Joan in Maddy's ear.

'I don't suppose they'll do any good,' Maddy whispered back.

'You know, all my life I been desperate to live up Oakwood,' observed Jack, ignoring the private mutterings of his womenfolk. 'And now I've been there I be glad I don't. You can't see the river from Oakwood. Fancy that! I habn't never realised un afore. I don't reckon as I could live out of sight of the river, I wouldn't be able to breathe. I hopes as you can manage un when you'm wed, maid.'

'I'll have to, Father,' Maddy replied. She, too, wondered how she would fare, living out of sight or sound of the river. She would miss it terribly, she was certain, but it would be one of many new things she would have to get used to.

–

Next morning Cal came to the Totnes shop as he had promised.

'Well?' demanded Maddy, anxiously scrutinising his face. After the previous day's events she was not sure whether to anticipate news of peace and harmony from Oakwood or outright warfare.

'Ellen took great delight in telling me everything that happened yesterday,' he said. 'No detail was left out, I promise you. I didn't know your father had it in him.'

'That's what Joan said. How has your mother taken it?'

'I can't say that all is sweetness and light at home yet, but when I said I fancied mutton chops for my breakfast, there was no argument. Usually she would complain that there was good ham needing eating up, or some such.'

'I hope it means some improvement is on the way. But let's forget family matters for the moment. I've got something I want you to read.'

Maddy produced a newspaper and spread it on the counter. It was a copy of *Trewman's Exeter Flying Post*, a newspaper not often seen in their part of Devon. 'A customer left it behind this morning,' she said. 'Look at this page.'

'Fear of measles among the royal family?' asked Cal, deliberately misunderstanding.

'You can read that afterwards. Look at the piece in the right-hand column.'

'"Preparations go ahead for the First Annual Meeting of the Devon County Agricultural Association". Is that the one you mean?'

'Yes, there's to be a big agricultural meeting in Exeter in May next year.'

'I've already heard about it. It's been mentioned at the Farmers' Mutual Assurance Society several times. I thought I would go if I could spare the time. Would you care to come too? Who knows, we might be married by then.'

'So we might.' For a moment Maddy was sidetracked by the prospect, then she thrust it aside, along with the thought that they had not yet discussed their marriage plans. 'Yes, I would love to go,' she said. 'Not just to look, to exhibit.'

'I did consider that,' said Cal. 'But I fear I haven't got a cow of a good enough standard—'

'I didn't mean exhibit your animals,' Maddy interrupted. 'Look at this paragraph: "As well as classes for stock it is hoped that there will be competitions to judge the excellence of local agricultural products such as butter, cream, honey, and cider." And cider,' she emphasised. 'You can't claim that your cider isn't good enough.'

'Let me see!' He moved closer in order to read the paragraph over her shoulder. 'You're right! It does say cider! No one mentioned that at the Farmers' Mutual. What a clever girl you are.'

'Yes, I am, aren't I?' she agreed. 'That's one thing we haven't tried, entering exhibitions. Just think how it would look on the labels – "Oakwood Farm's Gold Medal Cider". And the Devon Agricultural Meeting would just be a start. I've heard that agricultural meetings and shows are starting up all over the country, some are already quite well-established. Soon every county will have its own; we could compete in each of them.'

'At that rate there wouldn't be room on the labels to portray all our medals, we'd have to have bigger bottles.' Cal's face was alight with enthusiasm. 'What a partnership we'll be. There'll be none to match us.' He grasped hold of her energetically as if he were about to kiss her.

'Please!' she gasped, her face scarlet, for they were in full view of everyone in the shop.

'My apologies.' He released her promptly but with reluctance. 'I forgot where we were.'

'What do you propose to do now?' she asked, awkwardly smoothing down her apron. 'About the Agricultural Meeting,' she added hastily in case there was any doubt.

'It says here the Secretary lives in Totnes. I'll call in on him on my way home and find out the conditions of entry.'

He did not offer to take her home. Since her father's complaint he had been meticulous about such things, and she knew that Joshua would come for her when it was time to close the shop.

Things would be much easier when they were married, she decided; at least, in some areas.

–

Harvest time in the fields was over. The corn had been gathered in and duly celebrated with hymns in church and with more lively goings-on at the various harvest suppers held in farmers' barns throughout the parish. But in villages like Stoke Gabriel, the year's work on the land was not finished. The cider apples were beginning to fall, scattering the orchard grass with their splashes of bright colour, varieties that had been grown for as long as anyone could remember, with names as colourful as the vivid fruit – Crimson King, Pig's Nose, Star O'Devon.

'Things are looking good,' Cal announced, watching the first of the fallen apples being delivered to his yard. 'Demand for our cider has increased to such an extent that I'm going to have to double the quantities of apples I buy in this year.'

'That's marvellous,' said Maddy, delighted at such progress. 'What will you get? Sweet Alfords?'

'Yes, if I can. I like to go for the most flavoursome apples. There's a crop of Woodbines in an orchard up towards Staverton that I hope to buy too, although the farmer's asking an extra ten shillings a ton.'

'Woodbine? I've never heard of that one before. Is it a new variety?'

Cal laughed. 'Hardly. It seems the farmer's wife has pretensions towards refinement, and she won't let him use the old name of Slack-Ma-Girdle.'

'I suppose Woodbine does sound better in polite society,' Maddy chuckled. 'But it's not half so descriptive.'

'I've to drive over there tomorrow. Why not come with me and see what an orchard of refined cider apples looks like?' Cal suggested, adding swiftly, 'Nan can mind the shop, it will be good experience for her. And as for a chaperon, perhaps your stepmother might like a little outing. You will soon be busy with the Paignton shop. Enjoy some leisure while you can.'

Maddy was touched by his concern. During their betrothal she had enjoyed several such 'little outings' – invariably chaperoned by Joan. And while she took much pleasure from seeing the countryside, she found that she derived greater enjoyment from learning about Cal's business in greater detail. It did not matter that the gathering and buying in of fruit did not directly concern her, nor that she did not need to know what varieties were required to make the best quality cider, she found every aspect of it fascinating.

'The builders are still busy at the Paignton shop, so I can't do much there yet,' she replied. 'Yes, I would like to come with you.'

'It were kind of your Cal to take us with him,' declared Joan, when they returned home after their trip to Staverton. 'I enjoyed that. He'm proper thoughtful. You'm got yourself a good man there.'

'I know,' said Maddy. The more she was getting to know Cal, the more she was beginning to appreciate his many excellent qualities. She was, indeed, very lucky.

'And the excursion have done you good, you'm got some pretty colour in your cheeks,' Joan said approvingly. 'Cal were right, you'd do well to take advantage of all the fresh air you can get. Once you open that new shop you'll get less chance than you do now.'

The advice was timely, for when the builders and carpenters had finished, Maddy went into action.

Very conscious that they would be catering for a more varied clientele, it had been Maddy's idea to divide the new premises into two, allowing those who preferred to sit in comfort with their pint of cider and their pasty to do so, while those who declared they 'didn't want naught fancy' could enjoy simpler surroundings. Maddy was on tenterhooks in case it did not work. She chose colours and fittings she thought appropriate – with one eye forever on her budget. With the Totnes shop she had needed Cal's approval for almost everything; now it was all left to her, and she was nervous of such responsibility.

She need not have worried. The new enterprise was a success from the beginning, mainly due to her hard work. She was first to arrive in the morning, last to leave at night, her keen eyes never missing an opportunity for improvement. She had anticipated a fair amount of local trade, but before long she was delighted to find they were acquiring seasonal business as well. Cal had been right; their proximity to the railway station was certainly attracting customers from the increasing number of people who came to winter at the resort.

'Six boxes of pasties we sent up by train today,' she told Joan when she arrived home one stormy evening. 'Along with the flagons of cider to wash them down. They were private orders – folk sending a few local delicacies to friends and relatives up in London.'

'All that way?' Joan was amazed. 'I can see you opening Oakwood shops up-country afore long. But there idn't no need to start this minute. If you keeps dashing about from hither to yon you'm going to be wore out long before the wedding.'

'I've plenty of time to recover if I do, with the wedding not until June,' laughed Maddy. Then she grew serious. 'I hope Charlie will be home. I'd not like to be married without both my brothers there.'

'As far as Charlie be concerned, 'twill depend on the weather and the stone company's sailings,' said Joan. 'Still, as you say, 'tis a fair way off. You come and sit by the fire. Your father be fond of a treat, going up to the Church House on a bitter night like this.'

'Lor', 'tis a rare old storm out there,' said Annie, entering the kitchen. 'The rain've stopped, though.'

'The wind habn't,' retorted Joan. 'Come on in, and let me bar that door. The draught be cutting through yer like a knife. Have William gone?'

'Yes, he and Jack and Joe Crowther have gone up the hill together. Mazed fools when they can bide in comfort.' Annie settled herself in front of the burning logs. She nudged Maddy conspiratorially. 'I got summat for you, maid. Our Kitty've called, and her brought a couple of paper patterns. One of them'd make a lovely wedding dress.'

'I thought I told you, I'm getting wed in my new two-piece.'

'But that be wool,' protested Annie, producing the patterns from her pocket. 'You'm going to swelter in wool come June. Yer, have a look at they.'

For the next hour or more the three of them sat by the fire arguing amicably about wedding clothes, their skirts turned back over their knees to get full benefit of the warmth.

Suddenly Maddy sat bolt upright. 'What was that?' she said.

'What was what?' asked Joan. 'Be someone coming?'

'No, I'm sure I heard a cry.'

'I don't know how you managed that.' Joan was sceptical. 'I can't hear naught but the wind howling and the river roaring.'

'I know I heard something,' insisted Maddy.

Then came the sound of the Crowther's dog barking. Not the usual excited yap he gave when a fox or cat dared to cross his territory, but a deep disturbed baying.

'Maybe you'm right, maid,' Annie said. 'Us'd best go and have a look. You two go on ahead. I'll come as best I can.'

Gathering up shawls and lanterns, they went out into the stormy darkness, to encounter Elsie Crowther, followed by a string of children. 'I were coming to you,' she said, the wind almost whipping away her words. 'Something have set the dog up good and proper, and he won't settle. There, look at the mazed beast!'

By the scant light of their lanterns they could see the dog running back and forth along the edge of the river, barking at something unseen in the swiftly flowing water.

'I saw something,' cried Maddy. 'Someone's out there! Look!'

The three women held their lanterns aloft. Their light was not strong enough to penetrate far, but the meagre beams caught something white being tossed by the seething waters some yards away from the shore. It was a fleeting sighting, then whatever it was disappeared in the watery darkness.

'Tis a bit of bleached driftwood,' insisted Joan.

But both Elsie and Maddy were more familiar with the river.

'That were a face! No two ways about un,' declared Elsie. 'Some poor soul be in trouble out there. Yer, where'm you off to?' she demanded, as Maddy rushed away from the water's edge.

'To get the boat.'

'You'm idn't going out there!' cried Joan and Elsie in horrified unison. But they hitched up their skirts and ran after her towards the boat store just the same.

Maddy flung open the large doors. Buffeted by the wind, the women and children struggled to drag the boat out and across the foreshore, Joan scolding Maddy for her foolhardiness every step of the way. As they pushed the craft into the water Maddy feared her stepmother was right. The gale was whipping up the swift incoming tide so that the water seemed to seethe and boil. Only a fool would take an open boat out in such conditions, and in darkness too. But she had seen a face out there in the tumult, and in that one brief glimpse she was convinced that the face had registered despair.

The boat was already bucking and pulling on the waves as Maddy scrambled aboard and set the oars in the rowlocks.

'You'm idn't going to manage on your own,' cried Elsie, already tucking up-her skirts to climb in with her.

Joan pulled her back. 'You'm got little ones to think on,' she said. 'I be going.' With a helping hand from Elsie, and Annie, who had now reached them, Joan scrambled into the bow of the rowing boat. She knelt there, clutching at the gunwale with one hand and holding the lantern aloft with the other.

Conditions were bad enough when they were in the relative shelter of the bight of Duncannon. As Maddy began to edge the boat upstream, further from the shore, the full force of the storm hit them. It needed all her strength at the oars to maintain control. Joan's lantern, at her back, was of no use to her and in the darkness she used sheer instinct and experience to judge where she was; too much one way and they would be tossed ashore, perhaps against some rocky outcrop; too much the other and they would be swept into the turbulence of midstream, where their craft would stand no chance on such a night.

'I saw something,' yelled Joan above the screaming of the storm. 'Head further away from the shore.'

Obediently Maddy pulled on the port oar as well as she could. It was a dangerous manoeuvre, she knew, for she could feel the current tug more strongly at the boat. Her admiration for her stepmother grew with every minute. Maddy was afraid. It was more than the bitter cold that was causing her teeth to chatter, it was sheer terror, yet she knew the river well and was accustomed to being in boats. Joan had no such advantage; her experience on the water was restricted to accompanying Jack on the occasional summer's evening. Nevertheless, the older woman had volunteered to come, and now she remained crouched in the bow, peering into the gloom with never a protest or hint of panic.

'There be something right ahead. Oh no!' At Joan's cry they were overwhelmed by utter darkness. The lantern had gone overboard. There was movement in the bows, making the boat more difficult to handle than ever, but just as Maddy was about to urge her stepmother to sit still there was a thump. The boat had hit something.

'Tis a maid,' cried Joan. 'I got her!'

But catching hold of the drowning woman was one thing, getting her into the boat was a very different matter. For what seemed an age Joan struggled to pull the waterlogged body aboard. Maddy grappled with keeping the boat as stable as possible, conscious that she was growing more and more exhausted and that the most strenuous part of her task was yet to come.

'We aren't – going – to manage!' gasped Maddy. 'Can you – keep a hold – as she is?'

Joan's reply was a sob of assent.

Maddy began the perilous task of turning the boat, hampered by its heavy, trailing burden. The instant she got it turned, heading against both the current and the wind, she feared her arms were going to be torn from their sockets, for the craft bucked and leapt like a wild thing. Strenuously she hauled on the oars until her muscles felt like strands of red-hot wire with the effort, but with every pull the tide tossed them back upstream. The sodden body, still grasped by Joan, acted as a sheet anchor, hampering them even more. In a brief glimpse over shoulder, Maddy saw that Annie, Elsie and the children had a fire on shore to guide them in. Biting her lips with determination she made a greater effort. She tried to ignore the deepening chill round her feet as water came into the boat. She knew that, although she was trying to pull harder, her strokes were actually growing weaker as fatigue took its toll.

Heroically Joan attempted the near impossible by bailing whilst continuing to grasp the woman.

'Us idn't getting – no closer,' she gasped. 'I be going to have to – let her – go.'

'No! Hold on!' Somehow, in that agony of effort, pain and fear, Maddy managed to grunt out the three words. Common sense told her that the unknown woman was probably dead by now, but it made no difference. She was determined that the three of them would get back to shore. But even determination such as hers had its limitations. The oars felt like lead in her hands and they were making no headway. She knew she was barely keeping the boat under control in the roaring tide.

Through her exhaustion she heard Joan's shout, 'They'm coming!' She was too tired to wonder who 'they' were, until she was suddenly aware that the boat had become comparatively lighter and freer. Then miraculously another craft came close and her father's anxious voice shouted across, 'You'm all right now. Us'll throw you a line and tow you back.'

Manning the other boat with Jack were William and Joe Crowther, and in the stern was a dark heap which she guessed must be the unknown woman. Somehow they had managed to haul the body aboard their craft, freeing hers of its burden. Catching the flailing line was no easy task but after several attempts, Joan managed it. Then came the journey back to land. Although there were three strong oarsmen in the other boat, Maddy knew they could never tow another craft unaided in these conditions. Every part of her throbbed with pain, cold and fatigue, but she bent over to the oars again to give them her utmost assistance.

The crunch of shingle beneath the keel was a most welcome sound. She felt her icy fingers being gently prised from the oars, and strong arms lifting her. Then she was enveloped in warmth and light and she knew she was safely home again. After that, everything went black.

It was the sharp pungency of smelling-salts that brought her back to consciousness.

'You'm going to be right as rain presently,' Annie's voice said reassuringly.

'Joan! Where's Joan?' were Maddy's first words.

'Yer, maid. More or less in one piece.'

With difficulty, Maddy opened eyes that stung with salt spray and saw her stepmother, pale but managing to smile, sitting opposite her. William and Joe were there too, looking concerned.

'And Father?'

'He'm just carried that poor soul upstairs,' said Annie.

'Poor soul? You mean the drowned woman.' Oddly enough Maddy had almost forgotten the stranger who had been the cause of it all.

'Yes, but her idn't drowned. Her'm still alive, though Lord knows how... But not for long, I fear. Not in her condition. Elsie be tending her.'

As Annie spoke, Jack came hurriedly downstairs.

'How be her?' asked Annie.

'Very poorly,' replied Jack. 'I wondered if I should go over to Paignton for the doctor or summat, but Elsie reckons her be beyond doctors and it be the parson her needs.'

'I'll go for un,' said William.

'And I'd best get back to the childer, seeing as my Elsie seems likely to be here for a spell,' said Joe.

When they had gone, Jack looked at Maddy and Joan. 'I don't know if I should be proud as punch of my maids for being that danged brave,' he said, 'or leather the daylights out of the pair of you for near scaring me to death.'

'I'm sorry if we gave you a fright, Father,' said Maddy, 'but we couldn't just let her drown.'

'Us'd never have slept easy again for the rest of our lives, and you knows it,' put in Joan.

'Even so, 'twere foolhardy.'

'Maybe it were,' put in Annie, 'but I'll tell you something near as daft, and that be you two sitting there soaked to the skin. I took the liberty of setting some dry clothes to warm over the chair there. And there be some broth heating.'

'I'll go and make sure us've got plenty of water and kindling, then,' said Jack. ''Tis going to be that sort of a night, I reckon.'

Maddy was so stiff and racked with pain she wondered if she could change out of her soaking garments, and judging by the groans coming from Joan she was suffering too. Somehow she struggled into dry clothes, and slowly began to feel their warmth and that of the fire seep into her chilled bones.

Elsie came downstairs just then, a large jug in her hand. Seeing Maddy and Joan, she beamed.

'You'm a deal better, 'tis obvious,' she said. 'A pair of drowned rats wadn't in it, the way you was looking.'

'What about the woman?' asked Maddy.

Elsie grew grave and shook her head. 'Not much more'n a girl, and no wedding ring. Tis the old story. Her'm paying for un now, poor soul. Baby's on the way, but you can tell the maid habn't got the strength, even without being fished out of the Dart. 'Tis a mystery how her got in the river, but I don't suppose us'll ever find out. Her'm too weak to talk. Skin and bone, her be, and that dirty even the river habn't washed her clean. That's why I'm come for some warm water, see if I can tidy her up a bit. Tidn't right for her to meet her Maker all mucky.'

'Well come up and help.' Joan made to rise from her chair, but Elsie pushed her back.

'You bide by the fire and get some hot broth in you,' she said. 'You won't help no one by asking for lung fever. I can manage for now.'

It would have been good to sit by the fire, recovering from their ordeal, if the increasing cries and groans from upstairs had not reminded them that the night's drama was not over.

'I reckon us should go up and help, don't you?' said Joan eventually.

'I'll bide yer, minding the fire and keeping the water boiling,' said Annie. 'I finds they stairs hard going.'

Maddy knew exactly what she meant when she tried to climb the steep staircase. Her legs were too stiff to obey her, and she finished up on her hands and knees, with Joan following her in a similar manner.

Elsie was standing over the double bed usually occupied by Jack and Joan. In it now a gaunt, emaciated female tossed and turned in the agonies of childbirth.

'I wish William'd hurry up with Parson,' Elsie whispered. 'Her'm idn't going to last till the babe be born. 'Tis a miracle her'm kept going this long.'

Maddy went over to the bed and, picking up a towel, gently began to dry the pitiful creature's still-wet hair. Unexpectedly, the girl's eyes opened and she looked straight at Maddy.

Instantly Maddy stopped her drying.

'I know her!' she exclaimed. 'We all do! She's Victoria Fitzherbert, that's who she is!'

Elsie and Joan gazed down at the bed in amazement.

'Why, so it be!' Elsie exclaimed. 'I never recognised her, her'm that changed.'

'Yer, in that case us'd better fetch her folks,' said Joan. 'Maddy, my lover, your limbs be youngest. Can you make it downstairs and ask your father to go?'

But before Maddy could move, she found her hand clutched by Victoria.

'They won't come... turned me away...' The girl's voice was barely audible.

'They never did! What sort of folk be they?' demanded Joan in a whisper, scandalised at such heartlessness.

'I came here... nowhere else to go... then I saw the river...' The words faded, though her hand continued to grip Maddy's.

The three women tending her exchanged shocked looks across the bed. She had tried to drown herself! What Maddy and Joan had thought to be her struggle for survival had been the exact opposite.

'The river wouldn't take me! It pushed me back!' Victoria's sudden cry of despair shook them all.

'Un didn't want you, my lover,' said Elsie, gently smoothing Victoria's brow. 'The river have took its due for thus year. Un don't want no more.'

The irony of the situation was tragic: it had been Patrick, Victoria's lover and presumably the father of her child, whom the Dart had claimed.

Another burst of birth pains overtook her and she writhed on the bed in agony. As she did so, the neck of her nightgown – one of Maddy's – came open, revealing a favour hanging on a damp, grubby piece of ribbon. It was a Janus ring, identical to the one Maddy kept in her drawer. At that moment any lingering animosity that she had for Victoria faded and all she felt was a deep pity. How easily she might have been the betrayed girl in her place, deserted and desperate. But no, Maddy knew she would never have found herself in Victoria's plight, for there was no way that Jack and Joan would ever have turned her away from their door.

Carefully easing Victoria's fingers from her wrist, she hobbled downstairs and went in search of her father. Readily he agreed to fetch Mr and Mrs Fitzherbert, though he feared that their daughter might not survive long enough to see them.

Contrary to Elsie's prediction, Victoria was still alive when her child was born. It was a boy, perfectly formed but far too small to have survived. Joan swiftly wrapped the tiny body in a piece of clean sheet and laid it in a basket on the floor. 'Never had no chance, poor little mite,' she said. 'Oh, why don't William get yer with the parson!'

Her stepmother's speedy action had prevented Maddy from seeing the child, and she could not tell if he had resembled his father or not. She was glad. There was enough tragedy about that night without further reminders of Patrick.

Below stairs the door slammed in the wind, and the parson's voice echoed up the stairs. 'I know my way, Annie.' In a moment he was with them in the lamplit bedroom.

'Thank goodness you'm yer, Mr Bowden,' said Joan. 'Her'm sinking fast. I don't know how her'm lasted this long, and that be the truth. I reckon her'm waiting for you, that be all I can figure.'

Joan's words proved uncannily accurate, for as Mr Bowden approached the bed, Victoria's eyes flew open. They were huge and overbright with fever.

'Must tell... been very wicked.' Her voice was no more than a faint rasp.

'The Lord is compassionate to those who truly repent, my child,' said the Reverend Bowden gently. 'And you have suffered much for your sins.'

But Victoria grew agitated. 'Not the baby... not that. Patrick... I killed Patrick.' If she was aware of the gasp of horrified surprise from the others, she gave no sign. Her troubled eyes were fixed on Maddy. 'You loved him too... must know, I didn't mean to kill him... We doubled back to Dartmouth. I had some money... gave it to Patrick for tickets... boat to America... he spent it... so angry I threw his fiddle into the river... Didn't know he'd try to rescue it... poor Patrick...' Her voice had faded to nothing as tears of sorrow and weakness trickled unheeded down her cheeks. For a moment it seemed as if she had slipped away, and the parson began to pray. Then unexpectedly she rallied and a faint smile lit her face. 'He was the gypsy and I was the lady,' she said quite strongly. 'I fell in love with a raggle-taggle gypsy and I ran off with him and...' She got no further. The light faded suddenly from her face and her eyes glazed over.

'Her'm gone, poor maid,' said Joan, gently closing the pale eyelids and drawing up the sheet.

'Such a pity we did not have time to persuade her the young man's death was not her fault,' said Mr Bowden, rising stiffly from his knees. 'She might have died more easy in her mind.'

'I couldn't fathom what her were saying right at the end,' added Elsie. 'Going on about gypsies. There wadn't no gypsies. Her were rambling.'

Maddy knew what Victoria had meant. Patrick had never been quite at ease in the real world. His life had been a series of make-believe episodes, always with a woman involved. With her, he had been the worldly fellow in love with a simple rustic maiden, relishing opening her eyes to the wider world about her. Later, after Davie's death, he had played the mainstay and comfort. From what she had heard about his brief affair with Lucy Ford, at the Church House, he had been the ardent admirer happy to appreciate the jewel that had no place in such a sordid setting. With Victoria, as in the old folk song, he had evidently played the wandering gypsy whose vagabond life was irresistible to the lady of quality.

Scenes from a play, with himself as the central character – that was all Patrick's love affairs had been. Looking back, Maddy did not regret having loved him. As for taking him seriously, the unfortunate Victoria was proof of the folly of that. Maddy had prided herself that she understood Patrick completely. What arrogance and foolishness. The village gossips had been right, she had had a lucky escape. After an age of trying to bring herself round to their way of thinking, she suddenly found herself agreeing with them. And with that wisdom came an unexpected sense of freedom.

Chapter Nineteen

Victoria's body was removed from Duncannon soon after dawn. Wrapped in a blanket, her slight corpse, and that of her stillborn child, were carried up the narrow path to the waiting cart by Jack, William, and two undertaker's men. Her parents had steadfastly refused to be involved, but if they thought they were free of the affair they would soon be disillusioned, judging by the grim expression on the parson's face as he followed the sad little cortege back to the village.

Maddy closed the door behind them feeling so stiff and weary she could scarcely hobble about the house; any thought of going to the shop was impossible. It was the first time she could ever remember being unfit for work, and she despised herself for her weakness.

'You'm idn't the only one,' said Joan, easing herself painfully back into her chair. 'If I gets as far as the privy and back today I reckons I be doing well. Mind, us put in a fair effort last night. No wonder us be paying for un this morning.'

'Yet we managed to keep going until Victoria died.'

'That were 'cos us had to. Elsie couldn't have managed on her own, not with the birthing and everything. Yes, us were fine until we stopped.' Wincing, Joan straightened out her stiff limbs towards the fire. ''Twere a disgrace her folk not coming, wadn't it?'

Maddy nodded. The picture of a furious Jack returning home alone remained vividly in her mind.

Joan gave a snort of grim laughter. 'My, what wouldn't I give to hear what Parson has to say to they wretches.'

She did not have to wait long to find out. Annie arrived soon after, full of news as always, agog to spread the latest bit of gossip.

'They'm gone!' she, announced triumphantly. 'Mr and Mrs Fitzherbert got in their carriage and rode off, no one knows where. "Pack up the house and you'll be told where to send the furniture presently." That be all the servants was told. I don't suppose even

345

the Fitzherberts'd have the nerve to stay-yer-abouts, not after Parson'd finished with them. They was still abed when he got there, and they said they wadn't coming down to un. That didn't bother Parson. Stood at the bottom of the stairs, he did, and bellowed up such a sermon at them, in a voice as'd have done Moses proud. He could be heard clear down in the scullery. What he didn't say to them! And every word of un thoroughly deserved. Soon as he were gone they was dressed and off in their carriage.'

'And good riddance, I'm sure,' said Joan.

'How do you know this already?' asked Maddy curiously, for it was not yet noon.

'From Mrs Bond, the miller's wife. Her were off to see her sister over to Dittisham as usual – my William rowed her across. But you habn't heard the best bit.' Annie dropped her voice conspiratorially. 'Afore the Fitzherberts left the village, Robbins, their groom, called at the parsonage all secret like, with a bag of gold to pay for the funeral. There's some as says it were Mrs Fitzherbert herself as come, and that it were a box of jewels her left, but don't set no store by that tale, for Mrs Bond had the truth of it from the parsonage maid. It must have been Mrs Fitzherbert as sent the money, though, for the maid said Robbins was eager to be back afore his master missed him.'

'Victoria will at least have a decent burial. That's something,' said Maddy quietly.

''Bout the only thing the poor soul did have, come the end,' added Joan. 'I habn't never liked to say un, maid, but you had a narrow escape there with that Patrick fellow.'

'I agree with you,' said Maddy.

She had had time to think things over, and having heard Victoria's tale, she realised that he had deceived the unfortunate girl far more treacherously than he had deceived her. Poor naive Victoria. She could not have known that Patrick had never had any intention of sailing to America. Nothing would have got him on the water – except the safety of his precious fiddle.

'No doubt it were hard at the time, but it have worked out grand in the end,' put in Annie. 'Now you'm to marry Farmer Whitcomb, who be worth a dozen of that other one whichever way you looks at un. My, won't he be proud of you. For make no mistake, he'll hear the story. The whole village be singing your praises, going out in such a storm to save a maid as caused you naught but grief.'

Maddy tried to point out that at the time she had no idea whom she and Joan were saving, but it was no use. Annie was too busy anticipating how pleased and proud Cal would be.

Annie was wrong. Cal was neither pleased nor proud when he called later that day at the cottage to see how Maddy was.

'Stiff and aching, though improving by the minute,' she assured him...

'I'm glad to hear it. I heard you were nearly drowned.'

'An exaggeration,' said Maddy, preferring not to think of what might have happened if her father and the others had not come to the rescue.

'But you put yourself in extreme danger in a foolhardy cause. It was sheer stupidity, going out in those conditions.'

Maddy stared at him, bewildered by his words and his angry tone. 'Are you suggesting that we should have stood by and watched the unfortunate woman perish?'

'I am suggesting that you should have shown more prudence and forethought. You gave no consideration to the consequences – to me, to our future. We have made such plans for the years ahead, yet you gave them not one thought when you leapt into the boat.'

'No, I did not,' cried Maddy angrily. 'The risk to the greater sales of your cider never crossed my mind. It was very remiss of me, but that was how it was.'

'That was not what I meant, and you know it.' Cal's face was white and grim.

'No, I do not!'

'Do you really think I would put my business interests before the welfare of someone in trouble?'

'Wasn't that what you were saying?'

'No.' His voice was low. 'I never realised that you continued to hold such a poor opinion of me. I thought such views were long gone. I know our marriage is a matter of expedience for us both, but I hoped it had at its root mutual respect.'

'It has!' cried Maddy. She would have said more but he held up a hand to silence her.

'There is nothing more to be said on the subject,' he said grimly. 'I will merely confirm your low view of me by asking if you will be at work tomorrow.'

'Yes, I'll be there, but…' Maddy could have saved her breath for Cal turned and left the cottage without a backward glance.

Maddy was very upset. She and Cal quarrelled often enough at work, but this was different. There had been a disturbing personal undertone to it that she had not understood. What had the quarrel really been about? She had a distressing feeling that they had been talking at cross purposes.

'Were that Cal Whitcomb leaving?' asked Joan, hobbling in from a visit to Annie. 'I thought I heard his voice. I didn't want to disturb you so I bided over to Annie's for a bit longer.'

'You could have saved yourself the bother,' snapped Maddy.

'Oh, had words, have you? It takes some men that way.'

'What does?' Maddy demanded, but Joan was busy tending the fire and did not seem to hear her.

Next morning she was back at work betimes. Cal did not visit the Paignton shop often, usually he left its running to Maddy. As a result it was three days before they met up again, three very tense days as far as she was concerned. Upon his arrival he was his usual efficient self, checking that everything was well with his latest venture. Then he drew her aside into the back room, his grip firm on her arm, making it impossible for her to resist.

'I owe you an apology. It has taken me all this time since we last met to think up the right words.'

'There's no need for an apology. We had a pointless quarrel. Let's forget it.' She would have returned to the front shop, but his hand still held her arm securely.

'There is a need,' he insisted. 'I should have been very proud of you, yet I did nothing but berate you for being foolhardy.' He hesitated, as if continuing to search for the right words. 'If you want the truth, you scared the life out of me, going out on such a night. I know it was for the most noble of causes, but you might so easily have been drowned.'

'Is that why you were angry? Because you were concerned about me?'

'Of course I was. How could you think otherwise?' He sounded quite hurt. 'The general view in the village is that if you had been anyone but a Shillabeer, you would have been swept to your death. No wonder I was alarmed.'

'Oh…'

'Is that all you can say?'

Maddy nodded. Cal had been concerned for her safety! For her! She felt absurdly pleased. No, the emotion she was experiencing was far greater than that. It was deep and joyful happiness. In that instant she knew she loved him.

It was not a new love, that was the astounding thing. Now she had acknowledged it, she knew it had been with her for a long time, warm, comforting, and familiar within her. It was incredible that she had failed to recognise it. What had made her so blind? Immediately she knew the answer. Patrick! She had been dazzled by him. It had taken Victoria's tragic death for her to see him as he really had been – a charming scoundrel. But now she was free to love again – and to be loved.

Thinking how angry Cal had been because she had gone out onto the river, she felt hope begin to flicker. Surely such a strong reaction had to mean he had some feelings for her.

'I do believe I've struck you dumb,' Cal said, beginning to smile. 'I must try to remember the secret for when you argue with me over spending money.' His smile softened. 'Of course I was alarmed by the tales of your exploits, how could you doubt it? We've a lifetime of plans and schemes and ambitions ahead of us that I could never achieve on my own.'

At his words the flicker of hope faltered and died.

Of course he had feelings for her, respect, admiration, friendship, but they fell far short of love. How foolish she had been to expect it. Hadn't he always been honest, stating quite clearly that their relationship was based upon business and expediency? She loved Cal but it was stupid of her to hope that he might return her affections. It was only too evident that he did not.

'If these plans and schemes and ambitions are to come to anything, I'd better get back to work,' she said, her briskness hiding her pain.

'I take it that's a hint for me to get back to my duties, too,' he said. 'I can see I'm marrying a slave-driver.'

'No, merely someone who intends to keep you up to the mark,' she said, hoping her lightness of tone matched his.

'All right, I'm going!' In mock haste he made for the door, but he paused when he reached it. 'I am forgiven for my rudeness and stupidity?' he asked.

'There wadn't naught to forgive, you gurt lummox,' Maddy said, taking refuge in imitating Ellen.

Laughing, he hurried from the shop. Maddy stood at the window and watched him go. She could not help herself, she had to follow his progress every step of the way. Not until he had disappeared into the livery stables opposite to fetch his horse could she bear to tear herself away.

I love him! She said the words over and over to herself. It felt the most natural thing in the world, but what difference would it make to their marriage? For some difference it would make, of that she was certain. It was too early to ponder over future difficulties, however, her acknowledgement of her feelings was still too new. For the moment she was content with murmuring 'I love him' to herself, and firmly shutting her mind to the time ahead.

Next morning Maddy began her working day at Paignton, intending to spend the afternoon at the Totnes shop. When the gig arrived soon after midday, she was surprised to see Cal in the driver's seat instead of Joshua. Her heart leapt with pleasure at the sight of him. Just being with him would be happiness.

'I dare say your father will not approve, but Joshua could not be spared today so I am playing coachman,' he said, handing her into the vehicle. 'Besides, surely not too many eyebrows will be raised. We are betrothed, after all.'

'I'll sit with my glove off and my engagement ring in full view, shall I?' suggested Maddy, and he laughed. She was grateful for his laughter, it eased the tension that lingered between them.

'It's too cold for that,' he smiled. 'Shall we let the gossips have their fun, and be done? I'm glad of this chance to be with you. We are seldom on our own these days, thanks to decorum, and there are things I must talk over with you.'

Maddy found herself tensing. Setting common sense aside, she hoped against hope to hear him say something affectionate or tender.

'What with one thing and another we haven't made any hard and fast decisions about the Devon Agricultural Meeting,' he said, as they eased into the traffic going along the Totnes road. 'Time is getting on and we mustn't delay much longer. There are to be three classes for cider – ordinary, rough, and what they call "speciality". I think our Superior would be suitable for the speciality class, don't you? It includes vintage and sparkling ciders.'

Maddy swallowed her disappointment. 'That class sounds exactly right for the Superior. It should certainly be entered,' she said.

'And what about the others? Our Regular will definitely compete in the ordinary class, but I'm not sure if our Rough is up to it.'

'Enter it!' said Maddy without a moment's hesitation. 'If nothing else, it will bring Oakwood Cider's name to the attention of the judges so they will recognise it next time.'

'Right, we'll enter all three!' replied Cal with gusto. 'That was exactly what I wanted to hear. You never let me down, do you?'

'I try not to,' Maddy said quietly.

'You don't need to try.' He patted her hand, and she wished that he had not.

Loving Cal was proving to be a bitter-sweet sensation. Just riding in the gig with him was too comfortable and intimate for her peace of mind. The warmth and solidity of his body against hers was stirring up a mixture of emotions she had never thought to feel again.

The idea of marriage was beginning to distress Maddy. The trouble was that her love for Cal was growing with each passing day. It was as if, having admitted her feelings, her emotions had suddenly burgeoned like a young vine, quite beyond her control. Being with him gave her the greatest happiness. There was none of the heady excitement that had characterised her meetings with Patrick, just a warm joyous delight which filled her to the exclusion of all else.

Not to betray her feelings for him, that was what she found difficult. To compensate she grew a little more brisk, a little more businesslike, a little more distant when they were together.

Sometimes, when she was having to try harder than usual to mask her emotions, Cal would look at her with concern. On one occasion he said to her, 'You are happy, aren't you Maddy? I'm not working you too hard?'

'Of course I'm happy.' Her response was crisp and swift. 'Why do you ask?'

'I just wanted to be sure,' Cal responded, a look of concern remaining in his eyes.

Maddy grew to hate any day when she did not see him. It was like time lost, a dismal grey space in her life, yet she could not control her feelings. Falling in love with Cal had changed everything. Unwittingly she had upset their down to earth agreement by giving her emotions free rein. She had begun to imagine married life where she loved and he did not. Could she bear such an existence? She was beginning to feel that the answer must be no.

May was upon them almost without them knowing, and with it the approach of the Agricultural Meeting.

'We have a major problem,' Cal said, with an abruptness that made Maddy start.

'What is it?' she asked with concern.

'We do not have a chaperon for when we go to the Meeting.'

'Am I coming to the show with you?'

'Of course. Did you think I would go without you?' He looked surprised. 'I'm afraid my mother will not contemplate coming, so I wondered about your father and stepmother, as my guests, of course.'

'I'm not sure about Father, but I know Joan will jump at the idea,' said Maddy.

She was right on one count, Joan was delighted at the thought of going. Jack hummed and hawed at first, but Maddy could see he was keen to go too. 'I'd best make up the party,' he said at last. 'I hear there'll be a band of Scottish soldiers there, they as wear skirts and show their bare legs. I'd best find out if it be a proper spectacle for my womenfolk.'

That was one problem solved, but there was still a week or so to go before the Meeting.

On Friday afternoon, when she had gone up to Oakwood as usual to go over the books, Cal had greeted her with, 'Never mind the accounts for the moment. There's something you must see.'

Grasping her by the hand he had led her into the store next to the poundhouse. 'There!' he said triumphantly, indicating a rack of bottles and stone flagons set aside from the rest. 'Our entries for the Meeting. I've selected the samples with the greatest of care.'

'I see you've allowed some extra.'

'Of course. Accidents do happen.'

'Might it not be an idea to send the cider up a couple of days before the show? Just to give it time to settle before the judging?'

'An excellent idea! I was planning to take it up by train with us, but your idea is far better. What other good notions have you got in that head of yours?'

'I do have one, though you may think it extravagant.'

'I am learning that some extravagance does no harm occasionally. What is it?'

'We want to get Oakwood Cider better known, don't we? And the best way to do that is to offer free drinks. Not large ones, of course, but folks can never resist something for nothing, even if it's just a taste. If Joshua takes the exhibits up, couldn't he take them in the wagon along with a hogshead of, say, Regular as well? He'd need help, of course, and we'd have to take mugs from the shops which would no doubt run them short...' Her voice faded as she regarded his expression. 'You don't like the idea, I can see it in your face.'

'Nonsense. I think the idea is perfect.' Exuberantly he swept her off her feet and swung her round, to the amusement of a couple of storemen stacking bottles. When he finally set her on her feet again it was with a hefty kiss on her cheek. It took every bit of Maddy's self-control not to fling her arms about him and kiss him back with all the passion that was building up within her. She wanted to respond so desperately that her need for restraint distressed her far more than she could have imagined. She knew then that she could not marry him.

Putting her hands against his chest she pushed him away. 'It's time we stopped this foolery and got on with the accounts,' she declared.

Looking at her scarlet face, Cal misinterpreted the reason for her sharp words. 'You don't need to bother about those two in the corner,' he said cheerfully. 'They're blind, deaf, and dumb, the pair of them. Aren't you?' he demanded.

'That us be, maister,' replied one of the men, grinning. 'Us can't notice naught, you get on with your courting, if you wants. Don't mind us.'

'There!' said Cal with satisfaction. 'They didn't see a thing.'

'We should get back to work,' Maddy insisted primly. As she left the storeroom, she was conscious of Cal pulling a face and of the men laughing.

'Petticoat rule, that's what you'm got now, maister,' called one of them.

Maddy wished she could have joined in the good-humoured raillery. It was the sort of thing one expected in the weeks before a marriage – but there was not going to be any wedding. How and when to tell Cal, though? As soon as possible, she decided. That would be the fairest and kindest way.

Cal remained in a light-hearted mood. Tucking her arm through his as they crossed the yard, he heaved a sigh of contentment.

'I'm really looking forward to our trip to Exeter,' he said. 'I feel it in my bones that we shall do well, and it will all be due to you. You are my talisman.'

Maddy tried to protest at this but he would have none of it.

He was in such high spirits that she had not the heart to hand him back her betrothal ring just then. She would choose some other, more appropriate time.

But that time never seemed to arrive. His hopes were set on the competition at the Agricultural Meeting and he talked of little else. It was to be the expansion of Oakwood Cider's fame. That he wanted, and needed, her support was obvious, and put Maddy in a terrible dilemma. She could not desert him, not before Exeter, yet to break off their engagement after the Devon meeting would be terribly close to the wedding date.

Despite her other doubts, Maddy had great faith in Oakwood Cider, and she was convinced they would win at least one award. This helped to colour her decision. If she waited until after Exeter, then Cal would have the consolation of the medals she was certain he would win. After all, it would only be his pride that would be bruised by the cancellation of the wedding, his heart was not involved. Nevertheless, as time went by, Maddy continued to have qualms about her course of action. But then, she observed, it did not matter when she told Cal, she was bound to suffer.

May brought with it unpredictable weather, complete with thunderstorms and hail.

'Thank goodness it have cleared,' said Joan as they went up the lane on the day of the meeting. 'But I be right glad I bothered to pin my skirts up, for it be muddy underfoot. I can let un down when us gets on the train. Fancy, us riding on a train!'

There was a surprise awaiting them at the head of the lane. Alongside Cal in the hired brake, clad in a much ruffled shoulder cape and exceedingly ornate bonnet, sat Mrs Whitcomb.

'Mother finally decided she could not bear to miss the fun,' said Cal, his eyes sparkling with mischief.

Maddy was forced to smother a smile, knowing full well that Mrs Whitcomb had never had any intention of being left behind, not if the upstart Shillabeers were going.

'If this idn't grand,' declared Jack. 'A proper family party, that's what us'll be!'

Beneath her elaborate bonnet, Mary Whitcomb's plump face glowered, and Maddy had a greater struggle not to laugh.

She was thankful for her stepmother's presence on the journey to Exeter, for Joan's excited prattling made up for the silence of her companions. Cal's introverted mood was due to the possible repercussions of the competition on his business, while his mother's glumness was due to her disapproval of the company. Jack and Maddy's silence, however, had a deeper, more tragic cause, for the closer they got to Exeter, the more they remembered their last visit, and the execution of Davie.

Maddy found it worse when they transferred from the train to a cab, for at first their journey took them through streets that were agonisingly familiar. Then, thankfully, they reached a part of the city she did not know and she began to relax. The traffic was so heavy that they were obliged to alight several hundred yards from the entrance and to walk the rest of the way.

When they arrived inside the park, Joan gave a wail of near-panic. 'I idn't never seen so many folk afore. Yer, let me clutch hold of you, Jack, for if us gets separated I wouldn't never find you again.'

'We'll soon get our bearings, never fear,' smiled Cal. He consulted the programme, which included a printed plan. 'Look, the bandstand is marked by the big tree in the centre. If we get parted, that's where we'll meet up. Maddy and I are going straight to the tent where the cider is to be judged. The judging does not take place till this afternoon, but we've our exhibit to set up. What of you, Mother? You are welcome to come with us, if you won't find it too tedious.'

Mrs Whitcomb had a difficult decision to make. She must either be bored or else accompany the hated Shillabeers. In the end Jack made up her mind for her.

'You come along with us, Cousin Mary, and us'll go and see what's to be seen, eh?' Tucking her hand under his free arm, he set off, calling over his shoulder, 'Us'll meet you two by the tree about noon.'

'We'll go and find Joshua and our wagon,' said Cal, consulting his programme again. 'I see the horses and wagons are ranged round the outer walls of the park, they'll be there somewhere.'

They found the Oakwood wagon easily enough for it was festooned with oak leaves.

''Twere Miss Shillabeer's idea,' replied Joshua to Cal's raised eyebrows.

'I thought it would make us distinctive,' said Maddy.

'Just as long as we don't get mistaken for Robin Hood and his merry men,' replied Cal, clearly not sure about the idea.

'I think it do look proper vitty,' said Mrs Joshua, who had come along to help serve the free cider. 'And folks'll pick us out in an instant. Us've set up a table for the mugs and such, and us've got the barrels ready on the wagon.'

'You may as well start now.' Cal looked about him approvingly. 'We couldn't have a better spot. Being near the horses well catch both masters and grooms, farmers and yardmen. No matter what befalls, by the end of today Oakwood Cider should be known throughout the county.'

'I'll tell you what will have befallen,' said Maddy. 'Oakwood Superior will have won the gold medal.'

'Such confidence!' Cal smiled down at her, then he turned his attention back to Joshua and Mrs Joshua. 'Are you ready? Have you everything you need?'

'Yes, thank you, maister,' they replied in unison, obviously enjoying every minute of this new experience.

Before Maddy and Cal had gone many yards, a small crowd had already formed at the Oakwood wagon, enjoying the free cider. Smiling, they made their way to the exhibition tent, which was warm and smelt of bruised grass. Long tables were spread with white cloths, the areas marked off with labels bearing the names of the different exhibitors. One of the very large cider manufacturers began setting out its exhibits, and Maddy watched with awe as aproned cellermen arranged row after row of bottles under the direction of a top-hatted gentleman. They seemed so assured and competent that for the first time Maddy's confidence wavered. Maybe they had overestimated the quality of Oakwood Cider, and they were due to be humiliated. Finally the large company set up a finely painted board bearing their name and the successes of their product at other shows.

'Very fancy,' remarked an old farmer who was setting out his bottles in the space next to theirs. He gave a cheery grin although his heavily starched high collar threatened to throttle him. 'But they don't impress me none. I reckon us be as good as they. When you comes down to un, cider be about apples and experience, bain't un? Pretty painted boards and newfangled equipment don't make a ha'p'orth of difference.' Maddy smiled back, feeling heartened. The old farmer was right, small producers had just as much chance as the large ones where the quality of cider was concerned. Turning to their space on the table, she helped Cal to set out the bottles, adding the carefully printed labels that she had laboriously penned to indicate their classes. As a final touch, she added a few sprigs of fresh oak leaves. She was determined to make their presentation as good as possible – it was one final service she could do for Cal before she broke off their engagement.

They made their way back to the bandstand and met up with Mrs Whitcomb and the others. Jack was full of the wonders they had seen during the morning.

'Just think,' he declared, as they made their way to the luncheon tent. 'In all my life I habn't never set eyes on a real lord afore, yet yer they seems thick as fleas on a dog.'

His comments were cut short as the heavens opened, and everyone made a dash for the tent. They were a damp and bedraggled party as they ate, trying to avoid the drips coming through the leaky canvas, but Joan and Jack laughed at the discomfort and even Mrs Whitcomb's complaints were muted. Cal, however, scarcely touched his food.

'You wait until after the judging,' he said, when Maddy urged him to take another slice of cold beef. 'Then I'll be ready to eat a horse.'

Although she knew the competition meant a great deal to him, she had not realised how much. She, who thought she knew him well, could still be surprised at how much he concealed his true feelings. Then she allowed herself a self-deprecating smile. Hadn't she thought she knew and understood Patrick? And look how wrong she had been about him.

'Are you coming to the judging?' Cal asked the others.

Mrs Whitcomb looked as though she was going to refuse, but Jack was too quick for her. 'Course us be coming,' he said positively. 'Idn't that what us've traipsed up to Exeter for? Let's be getting over there, shall us, else us won't get a good view.'

The exhibition tent was filling up quickly. Some of the interest was for the other exhibits such as honey and buttermaking, but the main crush of people was round the cider exhibits.

A buzz of excitement greeted the arrival of the judges. The noise died away abruptly as they clustered round the first exhibit, muttering together as the glasses of cider poured for them were first held to the light, considered carefully, then sampled.

'Lor', that be a job made in heaven,' murmured Jack, only to be prodded into silence by the combined elbows of Joan and Mrs Whitcomb.

The judges' progress was agonisingly show. When they reached the Oakwood exhibit, Maddy found herself feeling almost too tense to breathe. She tried to interpret their gestures and expressions. Was that nod one of approval? The inordinate amount of scribbling in their notebooks, was that a good or a bad sign?

There was no official announcement of the results, just a discreet placing of awards against the winners. In the surge forward to see, Maddy's view was blocked. Cal, being taller, had an excellent view. 'A gold medal for the Superior, a silver for the Regular, and a highly commended for the Rough.' At first he spoke in a matter-of-fact tone, then the realisation of it sank in. 'We got an award of some sort for everything!' he exclaimed, suddenly excited. 'One gold medal and one silver and a highly commended! It's better than I dared to hope.' He hugged Maddy tightly to him, while folks patted him on the back and tried to shake his hand. There was no restraint about him now, he looked absolutely delighted.

Maddy, pressed against him by both his encircling arm and the force of the crush, was too moved to speak. This was how she had wanted it to be - a bright future ahead for him, to compensate for any upset at the end of his betrothal. The accolades for his cider marked a new phase in his business, and an end to their relationship.

'This is all due to you, Maddy.' Cal disentangled himself from his congratulators and gazed down at her. 'I couldn't have done it without you.'

'Yes, you could,' Maddy found her voice to respond. The last thing she wanted was for him to think her indispensable. 'I just brought the oak leaves.'

'Just brought the oak leaves indeed,' he chuckled. 'From this moment on they'll be my talisman, as well as a trade mark. They'll be almost as much my good luck charm as you.'

Maddy heard him with a sinking heart. He seemed determined to make her a vital part in his success, and she feared that if he persisted she would find her resolve weakening. She had made the right decision, she knew that. At least, her head did; it was only her heart that turned traitor, suggesting to her that anything was better than a life without him. Sometimes she could almost believe her heart, until she was in his company for a while, with her need to betray her love stabbing at her like a physical pain, and then the knowledge that he did not return her feelings would be pure anguish. She knew that her unhappiness – for unhappy she would assuredly be – would poison their marriage and make Cal unhappy too, which was something she knew she could not bear.

The return journey from Exeter was a jubilant if weary affair. Even Maddy threw off her melancholy to smile and exchange reminiscences of the day with the others. It was Joan who was loudest in her admiration, not of the kilted band of the Black Watch, whom she described as 'proper handsome', but of the latest sewing machines.

'The shirts and petticoats I could make for my lot with that machine,' she breathed in awe. 'And in no time at all. There were one for only six pounds ten shillings. That idn't much, considering.'

'Not if you says it quick,' replied Jack. 'Lor', I despaired of getting these two away from they contraptions. They must've seen every sheet in Exeter turned sides to middle by my reckoning.'

'He's just scoffing because he's a man,' said Mrs Whitcomb. 'If he had to strain his eyes night after night sewing with needle and thread, he'd sing a *very* different song, wouldn't he, Cousin Joan?' As she appealed to Joan for support, she sounded surprisingly affable. Unexpectedly, after the first frosty hour or two, she had clearly enjoyed the day as much as anyone. Listening to her chattering away, Maddy realised that Mary Whitcomb's ill temper probably stemmed from loneliness and boredom. The poor soul needs some distraction to take her out of herself, decided Maddy. Perhaps when Cal and I are wed— She cut off her thoughts abruptly. For a brief, foolish moment she had forgotten that she was not going to wed Cal and that his mother would not be her responsibility.

'Are you all right?' asked Cal, noting her small wince of pain.

'Yes, thank you,' Maddy said untruthfully. Then to divert the conversation away from herself, she asked, 'Will you come back to Exeter for the second day of the Meeting?'

'I think so. There were many things I did not have a chance to see today.'

'I know where he'll be going,' said his mother, sounding almost flippant. 'To look at those smelly, noisy steam things.'

'I'd certainly like to see the latest in farm machinery,' smiled Cal. 'But I want to have a look at the cattle, too. I caught a glimpse of some very fine South Devons in the pens. Would anyone care to join me?' His invitation was general, but he was looking at Maddy.

'No, thank you,' she said. 'You go on your own and climb about your steam engines to your heart's content.'

'But wear stout boots,' advised Jack. 'The ground were churning up bad enough today, by tomorrow 'twill be a proper quagmire. And thanks for the invite, boy, but I reckons the missus and me have seen enough wonders to last us for quite a spell, eh, maid?'

'Us have,' agreed Joan. ''Twas like another world.'

'I shall be glad to spend the day resting my feet, I think,' said Mrs Whitcomb. 'As Maddy says, you go and enjoy yourself.' It was the first time she had referred to Maddy by name, the first hint of approval that she had ever given. Maddy was forced to bite her lip at the irony of it. She was thankful that she would have one whole day free of Cal. It would give her time to bolster her resolution and to think what she was going to say to him.

–

The next time Maddy saw Cal was in church on Sunday morning, where they had no chance for a serious conversation. Knowing she could put it off no longer, Maddy set off for Oakwood Farm that afternoon.

'You staying to tea?' asked Ellen in surprise when she saw her.

'No, thank you. I'd just like a word with Mr Calland, please.'

'Come in then. He'm in the front parlour, and making a right mess of un, too.'

As soon as she entered the room, Maddy saw what Ellen meant: booklets, brochures, and farming magazines – trophies from two days at the Devon meeting – were strewn all over the floor. Cal's face lit up at the sight of her.

'This is a grand surprise,' he said. 'Ellen, make some tea for Miss Shillabeer, if you please.'

'Her don't want none,' said Ellen bluntly, and left the room. Cal pulled a face. 'She doesn't get any better,' he said. 'I'll try again in a while, when Mother wakes up. She's taking a nap at the moment.'

'Please, I really don't want tea,' said Maddy, beginning to feel panic rising inside her. She longed to say what she had come to say and then leave immediately. Taking a deep breath, she spoke up. 'I have something to say that will upset you, I fear, Cal. I cannot marry you.'

He stood very still. 'What did you say?'

'I cannot marry you. You did me a great honour in asking me, and for a while I thought it would work, but it won't. The more I think of it, the more convinced I am that marriage between us would be a disaster.'

The colour had gone from Cal's face. 'I don't understand,' he said. 'What have I done?'

'You haven't done anything. Please don't think that.'

'But I must have done something. Everything was fine on Friday when we were at the meeting.'

'No, it wasn't,' said Maddy. 'I've been having doubts for some time, but I wanted you to go to the meeting and win your medals before I said anything.'

'Blast the medals!' Cal exploded. 'If you were unhappy, you should have said so. We could have talked things over. We still can. What is troubling you? Is it the thought of sharing a house with my mother?'

'No, it's not that.'

'Then it must be me. Look, I know I'm a clumsy fellow and often I'm more blunt than I mean to be. If I've said something to upset you then it was unintentional, I promise you. I would never distress you for the world.'

'It isn't you. I keep saying that,' cried Maddy.

'Then perhaps it's nerves. With the wedding not far off—'

'No, it's not that, either.'

'Then for pity's sake tell me what's wrong! And how I can put it right?'

Maddy took another deep breath to calm herself. 'There is nothing for you to put right because you are not in the wrong. When you proposed marriage to me, you set out the matter fairly and squarely. We worked well together, and saw eye to eye. Together we were making Oakwood more and more prosperous. We were an excellent partnership in business that would surely work just as well in marriage. Well, we were wrong. Business and marriage are two very different things. The union we were proposing was a very cold, matter-of-fact affair that could have produced nothing but a cold, matter-of-fact life ahead for the pair of us. You deserve much more than that, and I fear I am not the one to give it to you. What I can offer you is a mixture of balance sheets and misery, business matters and unhappiness. That is a terrible prospect for the future. I cannot condemn you to that.

Therefore I am releasing you from all promises, and I return this to you.' She slipped the gold and diamond ring from her finger and dropped it into his palm as she had done once before. This time, however, she would not be accepting it back.

'But everything was going to be fine, the two of us working together,' he said, looking down at the ring. 'Things were going to be so grand in the future.'

'No, they weren't,' said Maddy in a quiet voice. 'We only fooled ourselves into believing they were because it was convenient. We overlooked major considerations such as human nature, and just how long the future might be, tied together and growing increasingly unhappy with each passing year because we had both discovered that life should be more than a business partnership.'

'This is what you feel? And you have thought this way for some time? Then why did you not speak out before? Don't you realise the wedding is less than three weeks away?' He looked so grim that, amidst her other painful emotions, Maddy felt her conscience strike at her. Perhaps he was right, she should have spoken earlier. He was going to be humiliated by being jilted almost at the church door.

'I am sorry,' she said. 'I made what I thought was the right decision in waiting. My one motive was to save you as much distress as possible.'

'Then you are going a funny way about it,' he cried. 'Calling off the wedding at the last moment, and giving no sensible reason that I can understand.'

'We would make each other unhappy. Surely you can understand that!'

'But ours would not be the first marriage of convenience by any means. How do other folk manage?'

'They might manage, but are they happy? I know I could not bear to be the cause of misery to you, no matter how advantageous our marriage might be in other ways.'

'You are convinced of it. That we have no chance of being happy together?' He spoke more quietly, in a voice full of sadness.

'Yes. I am convinced.' Gently Maddy folded his fingers over the ring. 'It is not your fault, never think that. The flaws are all in me, and you can never know how much I regret upsetting you like this.'

'If you are so certain, then there is no more to be said.' His tone was abrupt, almost as if he wanted the conversation over and done with speedily. He opened his hand and held it out. 'Please keep this,' he said, offering her the ring. 'I will never give it to anyone else.'

Maddy shook her head. 'You will,' she said with certainty. 'Somewhere there is someone who will be right for you, and who will give you the happiness that I never could.'

As she spoke, her heart felt a sharp pain at the thought. But she knew she had spoken truthfully. More than anything else she wanted Cal to be happy. Turning on her heel, she went swiftly from the room and from Oakwood, hoping that Cal had not seen the tears begin to stream down her face.

—

'What did you do a mazed thing like that for?' was Jack's blunt reaction when she told her family what she had done.

Maddy opened her mouth to give some sort of an explanation, but the words never came. She buried her face in her hands and gave herself up to a storm of weeping. When at last she had no more tears to shed, it was to find that Joan was brewing up the inevitable tea.

'Why don't you go and have a lie down, maid,' her stepmother said kindly. 'I'll bring a cup up to you.'

'I think I will.' Not for the first time, Maddy was finding out how exhausting desperate misery could be. One alarming thought struck her. 'You won't go up to Oakwood, will you, Father?'

'No, course not.' Joan spoke for her husband. 'He'm got more sense, and if he habn't, I have.'

Much relieved, Maddy went upstairs to her tiny room. She expected to lie awake, going over her last meeting with Cal. Surprisingly she must have fallen asleep instantly, for she was not even aware of Joan bringing her the tea.

Sleep took away the tiredness, but not much else. Her unhappiness remained, along with an awful feeling of finality. It was over. Her relationship with Cal had ended, and she would have to rethink her future. She would have to find other employment, for one thing. It would be impossible for her to work for Cal now, but that was something which could wait. For the moment, knowing that he was no longer a part of her life was enough to occupy her entire heart and mind.

She could not have been asleep long, no more than half an hour, judging by the soft light of evening. Looking through her window she saw the swallows wheeling and screaming high in the deepening blue sky. Such beauty seemed to have nothing to do with her any more, and she felt a desperate sense of loneliness. But, she knew she could not hide in her room for much longer. Washing her face in cold water removed some of the heaviness she felt, and after she had changed her crumpled dress and brushed her hair she felt almost fit to face her family with the explanations they were awaiting.

'You'm feeling better, maid?' asked Jack solicitously as she entered.

'Your tea'm stone cold, I'll make a fresh pot,' said Joan, reaching for her panacea for all ills.

Before Maddy could reply, an urgent hammering sounded on the door. Opening it, she was dismayed to see Cal standing there. The last thing she wanted was to be drawn into another long discussion about their chances of making a success of marriage. She could not bear that.

Despite her misgivings, innate politeness made her stand aside for him to enter, but he ignored her silent invitation. He stood on the doorstep, Cal Whitcomb at his most immaculate, in his well-brushed brown broadcloth jacket, carefully pressed breeches and spotless shirt, his hair gleaming like burnished copper, the sheen on his boots glinting in the evening sun. He had the air of a man who had dressed with the greatest care, and the tense expression on his face betrayed that he had come on a mission of great importance.

'Maddy,' he said, 'I have thought a deal about what you said to me this afternoon and, upon consideration, one thing has struck me. You talked the whole time about my happiness and my welfare. You even seemed to put the blame for the ending of our betrothal upon something lacking in yourself. Oh, there were occasions when you talked about *our* future, but you were still really referring to me, I could tell. What I want to know is, what about you and your future happiness? Don't they count?'

'I'll manage,' replied Maddy.

'But is that sufficient? That's what you said to me, isn't it? That to manage wasn't good enough? It occurred to me that being so concerned for me meant you could not be totally indifferent to me, and it gave me hope. I have handled things badly, I can see. I wonder at myself for my blind stupidity, but maybe it isn't too late.'

This was the very thing Maddy had dreaded. He knew now that she loved him, it could not have been very hard to guess, and he was about to swear that he would do his best to love her in return. That was the sort of man he was, kind and considerate, but could he not see that to have him making an effort to love her would be the worst sort of torture?

'I have behaved like an unthinkable, unfeeling clodpole,' he went on with unusual diffidence. 'But I know where I've gone wrong. There have been no sweet words or tender moments during our betrothal, and there should have been. It is my fault. I have been a coward and I admit it. I feared you might be offended if I spoke such fancy trifles and that things would be spoiled between us. The truth is that when I truly care I behave like an idiot. Oh, I can flirt and dally with the best of them, as you know, but when it is important... Maddy, I've come a-courting, if you'll let me.'

'A-courting?' said Maddy, her eyes wide.

'Yes. I hope you'll agree. You see,' he went on hurriedly, 'I can think of nothing more empty and wasted than my life without you. When you rescued Victoria I nearly went mad, thinking how close I had come to losing you. It had nothing to do with business or how splendid you have been for Oakwood. It had everything to do with how happy I am whenever I'm with you. You don't feel the same, I appreciate that, but I fancy you have some affection for me, otherwise you would not have been so anxious for my welfare. Perhaps with gentle encouragement your love for me might grow, and you might come to care for me the way I care for you. That is why I have come a-courting like any green boy, to give us both a chance...' His voice, which had been growing increasingly unsteady, faded to nothing. 'Maddy,' he said, regaining his composure with an effort, 'please will you walk out with me?'

Maddy could not reply at first, she was too happy considering what Cal had just said.

'I will,' she said at last, her voice tremulous too. 'There is no need, for I could not love you more if we walked round the world together, but I will come with you, and gladly.'

'You love me? You say you love me?'

'I do, and have done for an age. That was why I wanted to break our engagement. I knew I could not bear to be your wife loving you so desperately yet fearing you did not love me.'

'Oh Maddy, can there be two such fools in this world?'

He reached out to her, but as she went to take his hands she exclaimed, 'You're bleeding! Your poor palms, they're scratched to pieces! What happened?'

Cal gazed bemusedly at his hands, as if momentarily he, too, had no idea what had happened. 'The roses!' he exclaimed in dismay. 'I picked roses in order that I might come to you as a proper suitor should. I must have lost them on the way! Oh, what an idiot I am!'

Her self-assured, confident Cal sounded so bewildered and distressed that Maddy, laughing and crying with love for him, flew into his arms.

'If the roses be bothering you, we'm plenty down the garden as you'm welcome to,' said Jack, gently reminding them that they had an audience. 'And if you wants a good place to do your courting, you knows where to go?'

Cal rested his cheek on the top of Maddy's head. 'On a May night such as this, with the moon rising and a nightingale singing in Duncannon Copse, where else but along the river?'

'You'm learning, boy, you'm learning,' Jack said approvingly.

With arms entwined, the pair of them set off down the garden and along the foreshore, to where the river ran sweet and slow.

'They forgot the roses,' observed Jack, watching them go past the bush unheeding.

'They'm true sweethearts, boy, anyone can see that. What need have they with roses?' said Joan. Then drawing her husband indoors, she discreetly closed the door on the departing lovers.